BURT HIRSCHFELD'S FIRE ISLAND

"This book is today, here, now, explicit in its language, with totally credible situations and pulsating entanglements between people who live and breathe . . . crisp, racy, sensual, often brutal, but always excitingly understandable . . . FIRE ISLAND is a power-packed motion picture in print!"

Jack Hoffenberg, author of SOW NOT IN ANGER and REAP IN TEARS

"A whale of a book—a lusty, sprawling smorgasbord of sex, cynicism and social comment, peppered with a bittersweet sense of humor."

Edwin Corley, author of SIEGE and THE JESUS FACTOR

Avon Books by
Burt Hirschfeld

CINDY ON FIRE	22657	$1.75
FIRE IN THE EMBERS	23242	$1.75
FIRE ISLAND	22624	$1.75
MOMENT OF POWER	10116	$1.25

BURT
HIRSCHFELD

AVON
PUBLISHERS OF BARD, CAMELOT, DISCUS, EQUINOX AND FLARE BOOKS

AVON BOOKS
A division of
The Hearst Corporation
959 Eighth Avenue
New York, New York 10019

Published by arrangement with the author.

First Avon Printing, August, 1970
Nineteenth Printing

Printed in the U.S.A.

It was the saying of Bion, that though the boys throw stones at frogs in sport, yet the frogs do not die in sport but in earnest.

—*Plutarch*

ONE

THE SEVENTEENTH SUMMER

Fire Island.

A narrow strand of beach, the world's best, to hear its inhabitants boast. A sandy rise in the Atlantic forty-five miles east of New York City, a buffer for Long Island and separated from it by the waters of Great South Bay.

Fire Island.

A green-and-white playground. From Democrat Point to Moriches Inlet, no more than forty feet above sea level, a thirty-three mile arrow aimed at Paris. Less than two hundred yards wide at one point, it swells to half-a-mile at another, is studded with communities as diverse in personality as in size—Ocean Beach, Seaview, Fair Harbor, Cherry Grove, Point o' Woods, Lonelyville, Ocean Bay Park, Davis Park, The Pines, Water Island, Dunewood, Kismet . . .

Fire Island.

White men came to it early, studied the Indians, learned their ways, and drove them off. Whaling stations were erected from which boats were launched into the rough surf at the cry of "Whale off!" And some men made a profitable way of life salvaging ships wrecked on the submerged reef. Others ran slaves into the island and out, a pause between the Gold Coast and the plantations of the South. And there were pirates and their treasure. Buried and found years later.

To sailing parties, the island, remote, beautiful, and wild, became a vacation site. And to the first Roosevelt President. To the bohemians of the Twenties. To the rum-runners of Prohibition. To jazz musicians, artists, luminaries of Broadway and the Silver Screen.

Fire Island.

Hurricanes and picnickers. Erosion and the danger of German saboteurs. Flappers and mothers' helpers. Homosexuals and the growing middle class. Hippies and students, businessmen and office girls, doctors and housewives, whores, firemen, policemen, boat people. Laws and regulations and federal bureaucrats. The island has stood against them all.

Fire Island.

It prohibits automobiles and sometimes bicycles. But not the child's express wagon, the main form of delivery. Here shoes are infrequently worn. Here certain men pluck their bodies and certain women expose theirs. Here sex and love are confused and talk takes precedence over both. Here tanning lotions are personal experiments and sunbathing becomes an art form. Here a party is a Sixish and commences at seven. Here seasonal renters are scorned but the residents own houses to let. Here garbage is filed and separated according to variety and it is illegal to do otherwise.

Fire Island.

Once, for writers and painters, a place to work and play during the hot months, and escape frenetic New York. A place for a fortunate few.

Change was inevitable. Columnists publicized the island, hinted at wild parties, at collectives of dedicated voluptuaries, wrote of sensual dramas played out in the sunlight. A spreading affluence, the extension of speedy highways onto Long Island, the promise of forbidden pleasures, these drew people in increasing numbers to the island. By automobile they came, and by the Long Island Railroad, by power boat through the inland waterway and the bay, by ferry and by water taxi, by Piper Cub and by helicopter.

Officially the action begins on Memorial Day and ends Labor Day. Most come just for weekends. But some stay the summer, those able to play freely, those with great wealth, those living off unemployment insurance, those without concern for the future, those able to drift from one day to another. And there are the young and pretty mothers, left alone by husbands grimly determined to succeed at important jobs in the city, clever young mothers, bored, curious, thirsty for a larger taste of life. And those anxious to satisfy that thirst. All of them assemble on the island. To look. To seek. To find . . .

Fire Island.

Chapter I

Neil

He woke, rigid and solitary, afraid. The lobes of his brain swelled and diminished as he strained to identify and locate himself. It came in fragments, who he was, where he was, a spreading awareness of his place in the order of things. There was the soft whir of the Fedders cooling the spacious room and the brief, rasping exhalations of the woman on the far edge of the bed.

He turned his head. In the gray morning light she looked young—younger than she was. The neatly arranged features did it, and the carefully tended skin. So many of them were that way, maintaining an appearance more youthful than their years. Add five years to what they claimed, was his rule of thumb. And sometimes more. Her eyes skittered about under blued lids and a small protesting sound came out of her. A bad dream. Now what the hell was her name?

Luellyn King, he remembered finally, all of it seeping back. Luellyn King, who did reasonably well performing in television commercials. Housewives mostly. Detergents. Deodorants. And she'd had a full thirteen weeks on that new filter tip, which meant a healthy fee.

He'd found her at M.C.J. & O., in that cinema-palace reception room of theirs. She was up for an interview on the Carter-Scott account—diapers and baby foods—and he to see Oscar Morrison, big man in charge of production for the agency.

Oscar had kept him waiting—cooling his heels as if they were strangers, as if Neil Morgan was some hustler off the street rather than a top guy with one fine track record. A typical Oscar Morrison ploy.

The seating was arranged in small groupings at M.C.J. & O.; Barcelona chairs in black or tan leather around glass-topped coffee tables. Very intimate, friendly. Neil sat in a black chair, placing his attaché case at his feet. His eyes focused on her legs, shapely, firm, lean. Nice.

Luellyn King had spoken first. She recognized him. And why not? His photograph was published frequently in the trade papers, and he often appeared on the tube for interviews or panel discussions. Neil Morgan owned a well-known face, one that photographed well, the kind of face women looked at.

She did most of the talking, the usual chatter about the difficulties of being an actress, of finding work, of the weary state of the American theater. And she let him know that she was twice-divorced and very much available.

When the receptionist said that Oscar was free, Neil stood up and so did Luellyn, offering her hand. He took it and looked into her eyes in the way he knew was so effective and said why didn't they have drinks at P.J.'s, say at four that afternoon. She had hesitated, feigning consideration. He had helped her make up her mind, saying that he was producing a new series. She had said yes. Actresses . . .

Oscar Morrison wasn't that easy. Never had been. How long since he had seen old Oscar? Three, four months, and almost a year since they had really talked. Not that Oscar had changed. There was the same round softness to him and the same glitter to the small eyes, the same forced smile. He was combing his hair to one side these days in a futile effort to cover his scalp. Still there was the same hearty manliness to his greeting, as if to contradict the impression made by all that roundness.

"Neil, baby." He took Neil's hand in both of his. "Great, kid. Simply great. The way you look. Younger than ever. Not a gray hair and that complexion. A baby's ass, baby."

"You look terrific yourself, Oscar."

"Ahh," Oscar said modestly. "You work out, right? Jogging, right? Calisthenics."

Neil maintained a bland smile. You could never be sure about Oscar Morrison; did he have the needle out or was he sincere? Neil decided to take no chances.

"Tennis, Oscar. Got started a few years back, you know. Beautiful game, Oscar, good for all the moving parts."

"How's it going, kid?" Oscar Morrison said. Less than a year older than Neil, he often assumed a patronizing seniority. "Fill me in. On Susan. And old BB. How's old BB?"

"They're both swinging, Oscar."

"That Susan, beautiful as ever, right?"

"Do I have to tell you about *that* face?"

"With that face, she should be doing commercials. You ought to peddle her. You know what the market wants, and she's got it."

Neil raised his hands in mock surrender. "Oscar, do I need a wife in the family or a model?"

Oscar grew sober. "You're right, right, right. A good, beautiful woman in the home. That matters." He brightened. "And BB, how old is that great son of yours?"

"Nineteen, almost twenty."

"Good God, tempus fugits all over the place."

"Too quick."

"Great boy, that BB, I bet."

"Do I have to say it, Oscar? A leading-man type. Tall, straight, hair as black as his mother's, and those baby blues. . . ."

"Got 'em from you, baby," Oscar laughed. "Nice to hear about a solid youngster, the way kids are nowadays."

"Oh, BB's a real boy. Now don't misunderstand, he's no Mr. Clean. There was a little problem last January, a car accident."

Oscar winked. "A couple of drinks, a girl, right?"

"He's a boy, Oscar."

"But you made it all right? A phone call or two, a couple of tenners strategically placed—right?"

"What's a father for?"

"Terrific. You're my kind of guy, Neil. BB's at Cornell, isn't he?"

"Well, no. The accident, you see. I figured he'd better transfer over, start fresh. He's up at John Bradford College, upstate. Beautiful place, great campus. Some real ballplayers have come out of there. Jimmy Little who was with the Redskins and Link McAdams."

"BB a jockstrap, Neil?"

"Well, no. Concentrates on the books. Books and broads, Oscar." He laughed.

Oscar laughed. "Way to go, baby. Brains is what matters." He rubbed his small hands together and leaned back in his chair. He looked at his watch. "I gotta tell you, I was surprised when you called. Long time no see."

"I always felt a certain . . . harmony, Oscar, between us."

"Glad you said that."

"So I told myself, it's only right and fair that Oscar Morrison should have first rejection."

"You've got something for me! That's great, kid. Really great."

"And it's a great something, Oscar."

"Baby, lay it on me."

Neil crossed his legs and placed his hands on his thighs. He spoke in a crisp, confident voice. "Oscar, you read. Not like so many decision-makers in the industry, you're literate. Guys get big they sometimes turn away from the things that count, from books, ideas, the basic stuff our business is made of. But not you, Oscar."

"I'm right with you."

Neil leaned forward. "I give you Capote's *In Cold Blood.* And *The Boston Strangler*. Louis Nizer's book. Are people interested in crime? You tell me."

"They're fascinated."

"On target. All right, what am I saying? I'm saying I want to package a series of specials, one a month, ninety minutes each. *True Crime Theater*. How's that grab you? It's all there in the title. Each show, a different crime, dramatized, naturally, with an epilogue by the cop who broke the case, or the lawyer involved. Whatever gives off the old authenticity." He snapped open the locks of the forty-dollar leather attaché case. "This may be the best presentation I've ever put together, Oscar. Outlines for nine programs, all researched and based on fact. Treatments for the first three shows. Here's a can't-miss offering. First of all—"

Oscar stood up and produced his benevolent smile. He trundled out from behind the big mahogany desk.

"Neat. I got to say it's neat. You've done your homework, and I dig that. But, baby, is it that different? I mean, true crime. After all, it has been done."

Neil rose, talking faster, urgently. "Not this way, Oscar. You see, what I have in mind——"

"Would I snow you, pal? Not in a million. Oscar Morrison. A square guy, right? That's my image and I stand in back of it. I got to be one hundred per cent straight arrow with you, kid, this package ain't for any of M.C.J. & O.'s clients."

"This is a hot package, Oscar. The timing is right. With star names, promotion . . ."

"Put yourself in my chair, Neil. Would you get excited about this idea? Would you say you must do this show?" He shook his head sadly. "You wouldn't."

Neil closed the attaché case. "I'll leave the presentation with you, Oscar. Show it around. This is close to me."

"Sure, baby." Oscar took Neil by the elbow and steered him to the door. "If this were a sensational gimmick . . . oh, hell, face it, it's you, Neil. You got a lot to overcome, your image. That *Make Your Bet* mess. That was dumb, to let yourself get squeezed in that way. It left you outside the door."

"Dammit, Oscar, every game show was set up. You know that. You were at the network in those days, you were in on it all. You—"

Oscar raised his brows and Neil fell silent. "I'm clean. Out before the stink bomb went off. But you, you're not clean. 'Producer admits fix,' the headlines said. Oh, Neilie-baby, never admit a thing. Very bad tactics."

"How do I get back in, Oscar?"

"You must have plenty of shekels tucked in the sock, Neil. Relax. Enjoy life."

"It isn't just the dough. I'm still a young man, Oscar, and there are things I want to do. Have to do. Aspirations . . ."

"Beautiful. You got to admire that in a man, ambition, drive. You're highly motivated, Neil. I always said that about you. But this show is not for us. Come up with something that gives me a hard-on and I'll go to the well for you. But don't ask me to lay my head on the block for a piece of zero. Zoom in close, give me an edge, some real fire-power."

Neil ached to drive his fist into Oscar Morrison's smug little face. Instead he smiled graciously. "You have to visit us out at the island for a weekend, Oscar. Susan would like that."

"And wouldn't I love to see that beauty of yours again? Make a call, baby. Don't be a stranger. And when you come up with the grand slam, remember old Oscar."

The little bastard.

Mike

For Mike Birns, Fire Island was a good place to write. He maintained a strict schedule during the week, four work hours every day before lunch. That done he felt free to sun himself, to swim, to roam the beach in search of girls. And there were so many girls—young and not so young, tanned and tight-bodied, receptive, agreeable—a seemingly infinite supply of near-naked flesh waiting for him to put it to use.

This was a bad morning. A bad morning in a bad week. The new book was not going well. He read the last paragraph he had written with disgust. A piece of crap. He pulled the paper out of the portable typewriter, balled it up, and heaved it in a soft arc back over his head. It landed on the floor. He glanced over his shoulder; more than a dozen paper balls dotted the floor.

"No shooting touch," Mike muttered. "Nothing drops for me. Take me out, Coach." He rose and placed a clam shell on top of the thin pile of white copy-paper. "Who said you were a writer?" he asked the portable.

He retrieved the paper balls, deposited them in a wicker trash basket, and went into the kitchen. There was a cup of apricot yogurt left and he made a mental note to buy a new supply. He began to eat. He suspected there were more calories in yogurt than he admitted. Still, probably less than two ham and cheese sandwiches, plus milk and cookies, which he preferred.

He ran his hand over his stomach. Flat. Solid. *Fairly* solid, he amended. He tightened his middle and pounded the ridged muscles with approval. Not bad for forty-four. And he weighed in at one-ninety, only five pounds over his football-playing weight. And that without special exercise, except walking.

A restlessness took hold of him, an undefinable craving, and with it came an uneasy twinge inside the supporter of his bathing trunks, a movement. He wanted a woman.

There was always the mother. She would be in her house now, making lunch for her three children. To be called upon on short notice usually didn't displease her. She would make sure the children were cared for, then lead him into the bedroom, jam a chair under the knob, and strip off her clothes. He visualized her, incredibly buxom, too wide of hip and thigh. She was an alarmingly aggressive partner, heaving her bulk around with determination, the sweet-sweat smell of her strangely stimulating. But afterward Mike was invariably left faintly dissatisfied; her lovemaking had the same clinical efficiency as a good bowel movement.

Perhaps there would be someone new on the beach. Trade picked up toward the end of the week with the coming of the long-weekenders. When did it taper off, he wondered, this almost obsessive desire for pussy? Or did it ever? He marked himself as having lived too many years, layed too many girls, to still play the game. And a game it was, obviously, played according to certain well-known rules. The same repartee, the same physical movements, all choreographed in detail, the ending always the same. What would it be like to have a girl say no? And mean it.

Some months before he had tried to list all the women he had had sex with. He soon gave it up as a bad job. There were too many unnamed faces, too many rainy afternoons with discontented married ladies, too many lost nights of switching partners, too many drunken evenings climaxed with unremembered women. In the twelve months after his divorce, he had managed a count; one hundred and three different girls of diverse size, age, shape, and color. All soft and willing, all reeking of that acrid pussy scent, all gaping mouths, moans and grunts, demanding thighs and clutching arms, hot breath and exploding declamations of sentiment. Memory ran together, distasteful, gray, without distinction.

He went out to the beach. The ocean was calm, the waves advancing in long, white-capped rolls, expiring on the hardpacked sand, a hissing foam. He spread his blanket and lay on his back and let the sun warm him. After thirty minutes, he turned over. The bulge of his supporter grew hard against the sand.

He wondered if there was a name for that, making it with the beach. How many people had copulated on this island? On the beach itself? So many girls had passed this way. So many men. He assumed the faggots up at the Grove and the Pines had their passing fancies on the sand at night. Passing fancies, he thought with professional approval. Not a bad phrase. The beach must be rich in protein, he decided. The millions of vital spermatozoa spewed out on the sand. —*"Oh, no, please, you'll make me pregnant."*— Had anyone ever literally fucked the beach? An interesting image. *There was this cute little orifice in the sand, all by itself.* . . . Jesus! he thought. I've become an old reprobate.

He sat up and forced himself to think about the new book, which wasn't coming together for him the way it should. Eventually the bulge subsided and he was able to stand up. He ran into the ocean and swam out about a hundred yards, floated for a while, then came out of the water. He walked along the surfline, searching the beach. He spied two girls in identical polka-dot bikinis. They were playing chess.

He walked over to them. Small girls, with long straight blonde hair, steel-rimmed glasses perched halfway down their tiny noses. Add neat little breasts, smooth skins, ready smiles. Identical twins.

Lilly and Leila. Leila older by five minutes. Lilly more outspoken.

"Are you a chess player?" she asked.

"Not since my teens."

"We're not much more than teenagers," Lelia offered.

"Twenty," Lilly said.

"Put together you don't quite make one of me," Mike said.

Lilly appraised him. "You're in very good shape for a man your age, don't you think, Leila?"

"Oh, yes."

"Would you like to sit with us?" Lilly said. He sat. "Do you enjoy good music?" she went on. "I think that's very important. Tchaikowsky, Bach, Mozart. The real greats."

Mike wondered how to separate them. "I'm not very musical," he said.

"Philistine," Leila murmured cheerfully.

"How can you not like music?" Lilly asked.

"Do you like baseball?" Mike said.

The twins made a face. "How can you like baseball?" Lilly said.

"Do you like the theatre?"

"Yes."

"Miller? Albee?"

"Shakespeare. Chekhov. Ibsen."

"Do you read Faulkner? Hemingway?"

"Tolstoy. Henry James."

Lilly laughed.

Leila laughed.

Mike laughed.

"It's lunch time," Leila announced, standing.

"Do you enjoy good food?" Lilly said. "We're going to make lunch. You must eat."

"I've eaten."

"Badly," Lilly said. "You're too thin."

"What?" Leila said. "What did you eat?"

"Yogurt."

"Ugh. We're having broiled striped bass in wine sauce. Asparagus prepared in a way that——"

"I couldn't eat," Mike said.

Lilly rose and so did Mike. Each girl was five feet tall, perfectly formed, very pretty. "What a great-looking pair you are." He kept his voice gay and light. "I can't make up my mind which one I want."

They laughed, an airy brittle sound. "Think about it," Leila said. "During lunch."

"Come on," Lilly said. "We're famished."

Mike held back. "Go without me. I'll see you later on."

He watched them leave, round tight bottoms swinging in unison. They were adorable, but a waste of his time. There was nothing here; he would never be able to separate them; each was the other's security blanket. He wondered what they would be like, the two of them at the same time. The familiar twinge came into his crotch and he thrust the idea out of his mind, setting out down the beach at a good pace.

BB

BB went up in the air, reaching, aware of the other hand coming over the net, the pressure sudden and strong. He got his shoulder into it and slammed down hard on the white ball. It ricocheted off the other hand, bouncing into the sand. Point and game.

"Pretty kill!" someone shouted.

Without acknowledging the compliment, BB headed for the ocean. He made a flat racing dive into the low surf. His chest scraped bottom but he ignored the pain, held his face in the water, and began stroking steadily. When he was beyond the shelf, he lifted his head, sucked air, and dived deep, crabbing along the bottom until it seemed his lungs would burst. He shot upward, breaking water to his waist, falling back, floating. Taking sea water into his mouth, he sent a stream of it toward the high sky. Clouds were forming in the west, scudding toward the island, toward Ocean Beach, toward him. It was going to rain again. There had been a lot of rain that summer, not that BB cared one way or another. He rolled over and swam back to shore.

He went over to where the other kids were gathered and heaved himself onto the sand, rolling in it until his skin was coated. Nice. Warm. Different.

"Hey, man! You're a veal cutlet—breaded."

BB made no response. He lay on his belly, chin on his forearm and studied individual grains of sand. The beach was white, yet a large number of grains were either black or brown. There was movement to his right and he knew without looking that it was Cindy.

"You played a marvelous game," she said.

"Do you know how long it takes before a clam shell or a mussel turns into sand?"

"No."

"Who would know that? An archeologist? A geologist? An oceanographer?"

"Who?"

"God, you're dumb."

Her finely etched mouth flexed in private amusement. She enjoyed BB, enjoyed his straight-faced wit, enjoyed his frequent sullenness, enjoyed the way he made love to her, the way he used her. Carelessly, almost disdainfully.

"Do you know?" she said.

"See. You are dumb. If I knew, would I ask? Go away."

"I won't. Unless you come with me. We could go over to my house. Maggie's out on the beach with your mother. No one is there to bother us."

"You're a sex maniac."

"A nympho?"

"Right."

"Because I like you?"

"You like everybody."

"You know that's not true."

"I don't know anything."

She chewed her lower lip, a delicately featured girl with hazel eyes and soft brown hair. "I do like a lot of different people."

"Men."

"Yes, men. Boys, mostly. I never really did it with a man."

"Are you kidding?"

"Well, I don't count that. I mean, when I *wanted* to do it."

"You got a peculiar way of seeing things, Cindy."

She sat up and hugged her knees, staring at him with fierce concentration. "Sometimes, BB, I don't understand you."

"You're not smart enough to understand me."

"I do whatever you want me to do."

He shoved himself erect and strode down to the ocean.

She trailed after him, walking east along the beach toward Ocean Bay Park. He glanced over his shoulder and motioned for her to join him and she did.

"Where are we going?" she said finally.

"Nowhere. And I'm almost there."

She laughed happily.

"What's funny?"

"You."

"Beat it, you think I'm a joke."

"It's the sand."

"I like sand."

"I'd hate for you to rub against me with all that sand on you. Rough, like sandpaper."

"I won't rub against you."

She frowned. "Come on, BB. You can rub against me any way you like. You know that."

He took her hand. "Don't talk, please. Okay?" He smiled pleasantly when he said it.

Roy

He was a tense man with a puffiness in his bloodless face. A crew cut, spotted with gray, made him look younger than his forty-five years. There was a suggestion of slack in his neck and his waist was thicker than he would have liked. He was a man of quick gestures and changes of expression. His small hazel eyes were never still. His frequent laughter was too loud, a rising peal. He spoke in explosive bursts, anxious to say the words before exhausting his supply of breath.

Now, standing at the bar in Goldie's New York, a gin and tonic in his fist, Roy Ashe felt expansive. Strong. A few more days like this one and he'd be in A-number-one shape. He'd knocked off work early, driven out to Aqueduct, come up with five lovely winners, including a pair of longshots. Beautiful. His pockets were stuffed with loot and the whole night stretched out clear and lovely. He glanced down at Shelia's breasts, large pale mounds under a delicate white blouse. Ten minutes after coming into

Goldie's he'd connected with her. A live one. Young, pretty, and stacked, patiently agreeable.

"Say when you've had it with this place," he said to her, "I'll spring for an expensive dinner."

She shifted around on the high bar stool, making no effort to adjust the miniskirt. Her legs, Roy decided, were first rate, full at the thighs, exactly the way he liked them.

"I dig good food."

"I dig you," he said insinuatingly.

She showed her teeth in what passed for a smile. "I know."

"What do you do?" he said suddenly.

She gazed at him blankly. "Just an ordinary working girl, a receptionist for some lawyers." She paused. "You thought I was a hooker."

"Come on. Why would I think that?" He patted her knee.

She addressed her drink. "I heard that some men prefer to pay. It relieves them of any responsibility, makes the girl just a thing, an object that they own."

"Not me, sweetie."

"Well, I hope not. I mean, if I put out it's because I like a guy. If he wants to give me a little present, that's his affair, you follow."

"I follow," he said dryly.

A sudden movement drew his attention and his head swung around. A surging weakness washed across his middle as he recognized Eddie Stander. There was no mistaking him, with his shaved bullet-head. The same wary, almost angry features, the same darting black eyes, the same plunging brows. For a moment they stared at each other. Then Roy went into that boyish grin and head-bobbing of his.

"Hey, Eddie! Eddie Stander. How'sa boy!"

For a beat or two, Eddie didn't move. "Hello, Roy," he said at last, speaking with a kind of light-footed caution.

"Say hello to my friend," Roy said. "Sheila meet Eddie Stander."

"Hi, Eddie."

"Hello, Sheila." Eddie took a step nearer. "How have you been, Roy?"

"Terrific. What about you? You look the same, all that

hair," he said, making a Roy Ashe joke. He pointed to Eddie's belt. "What's that lump? A cancer?" The quick rising laugh, abrupt̆ly gone. "Got one of those myself, pal. Too much booze, too much good living."

"How are things?" Eddie felt lost, without words, his brain ponderous, useless.

Roy dropped his hand on Sheila's thigh. "Things are fantastic. Get a look at this Sheila-girl. That face, that body. Those things, Eddie, those *things*."

Sheila giggled and finished her drink.

Roy snapped his fingers at the barman and pointed to the empty glass. "Another. How about a drink, pal?" he said to Eddie.

"I'm not alone."

Roy looked past Eddie to a table against the wall. The dim light failed to conceal the settled middle-aged look of the woman sitting there, the prim set of her mouth, the fleshy fingers folded at the table's edge.

"My wife," Eddie said.

Sheila said, "We can have a party."

"I heard somewhere you were married," Roy said.

"Seven years, almost. And two boys."

"Two boys. Where you living?"

"In Queens," Eddie said, almost apologetically. "We had to have a large place and you know what rents are in Manhattan."

"Sure. Still in TV, Eddie?"

"Not exactly. Advertising. I do copy for an agency. Select clientele. It's really quite a good——"

"I dig, Eddie. Well, you don't want to keep your wife waiting. Good to see you. Give us a blast on the horn sometime. We'll kick it around."

Eddie started away, paused. "You still go out to Fire Island, Roy?"

"Sometimes. I'm single-o, man, so I follow the action. Play it cool in Queens, pal."

When Eddie was gone, Roy turned back to the bar, brow rutted and bulging.

"Who was that?" Sheila asked.

Roy arranged a cheerful expression on his face. "A guy I used to run with a century or two ago. Now nobody. Nobody at all." He dug into his pocket and came up with a clutch of ten-dollar bills, brandished them under Sheila's chin. "Come on, let's live it up! There must be some way to get rid of all this bread."

Her smile was genuine this time. "Give me a sec, I'll think of some way. . . ."

Susan

She built herself another gin over ice, then returned to the broad deck behind the house. She stretched out on the wooden lounge and swallowed some of the gin. She put the glass down and reached for the *Bain de Soleil*, smoothed a thin layer of grease across her forehead and under her eyes, where the skin had begun to striate.

She lay back and lifted her face to the sun. Another hour, from the look of the clouds, and it would be gone. Another rainy weekend seemed likely. A lousy summer. The weather, anyway. There had been compensations. At least until August had come round and brought BB out to the island. She wished summer school had continued through until September, wished Rick were with her now. Rick in those tight red lifeguard shorts, showing his flat little ass, that fat crotch of his. Oh, Jesus. That sweet young flesh, that hardness reaching far up into her belly, that powerful sperm washing her insides. A thick lump formed up in her throat and a small tortured sound trickled out of her. She reached for the drink.

There had been so many Ricks, so many anxious, intense young men, their hard bodies providing the pleasure she required, the pleasure that settled over her like a memory-erasing mist.

All the dissatisfactions were forgotten with them. All the terrors. All the failures of her life. Dimly she remembered Arthur Rand. So tall, with those high shoulders and the silly way he had worn his glasses, halfway down his nose. It had begun with him. Arthur had been the first man to exploit her discontent. That first summer . . . No, she corrected distantly. That *winter*. He had wooed her, made her feel comfortable and safe. Until she liked him. Wanted him. Needed him. And one morning, after a particularly bad night with Neil—another lecture, this time on the need for a balanced diet, on her failure to care for the health of her husband and her child—she had telephoned Arthur, gone to his apartment, given herself to him.

Afterward, so soon afterward, there had been others. In the beginning it hadn't been the sex, she assured herself. That was almost bearable between herself and Neil and might even have grown better. Something else drove her, something vague, undefinable. A growing uneasiness, a sense of the impermanence of things, an awareness of time wasted, of life drifting away unmarked, unused almost. She had long ago labeled herself a failure. To herself. To her husband. To her child.

A regretful sigh passed across her lips. Hell, she told herself wryly. It hadn't been such a bad life. Not bad at all. Not once she discovered the young men. The sex machines. And when one would tire of her, as he inevitably did, there was always a replacement close at hand, ready and able to step into the breach.

She lay back, her eyes determinedly shut, holding herself very still, willing the sun to do its work, tan her, provide at least the illusion of youthful smoothness to her skin. The front door opened and slammed shut and approaching footsteps made the house tremble. BB, she supposed, and Cindy. There was something disturbing about Cindy, that almost naked expression on her face, as if she required protection from everything around her, protection only a man could provide. And something more, deeper and more subtle, something Susan had been unable to identify.

"Mother!"

Excitement charged BB's voice. Susan Morgan was in no mood for excitement, at least not *his* excitement. She kept her eyes closed and sought to will away the intrusion.

"Mother, look who I've found!"

Ah, well. He was her son and some maternal interest was his due. She allowed her eyes to open. There was BB, animated, covered with sand—Neil was insistent about using the outdoor shower after the beach—Cindy at his side. She looked past them. First she saw the long legs, with that fine shape and muscular definition that only men seemed to get. Then the narrow swim shorts, the same kind that Rick wore. Blue instead of red. And a faded blue workshirt. She sat up. She knew the face; it was the same yet dramatically modified. Leaner, the cheek hollows deeper, the set of the lips easier, the faded gray eyes steadier, with a faintly amused cast to them. The brown hair was sun-bleached and gray along the sides, long over his ears.

"Hello, Susan," he said, in a voice familiarly resonant.

She said his name and went to him swiftly, arms going around his neck, holding tight, aware of the size of him, the warmth of his flesh against her own. She kissed him on the mouth, remembering that they had never been as friendly as *that*. But she had always liked him, enjoyed him, bought his books. And she had often thought about him, wondered what he was doing. Then she remembered BB and Cindy and stepped back.

"It's so good to see you," she said, meaning it.

"I knew you'd want to see him," BB exulted. "I told him you would, the minute I saw him. I insisted he come back here."

Susan smiled at Mike. "You're better looking than ever, and bigger, too."

Mike grinned with pleasure. "Look at you, with this monster of a son. He must be someone else's. You're too young and beautiful. Mothers are short, overweight ladies who stand at stoves and tell you to get married. You can't be a mother."

BB cackled happily. "I recognized Mike right away, Mother. We were walking along and there he was. I know that guy, I told Cindy, right? And it was Mike."

"You've got a good memory," Mike said.

"How long since we've seen you, Mike?" Susan said, going after the drink.

"Six, maybe seven years."

"More than that," BB insisted.

"No, I was still married. It's six years since my divorce."

"I was sorry about that," Susan said. "I liked her," she ended, trying to remember the name of Mike's wife and failing. She stopped trying. She lowered herself to the lounge and invited Mike to join her.

"Get Mike a drink, BB. Gin and tonic?"

"Perfect."

BB disappeared into the house.

"Now," Susan said. "Tell me about yourself. Why aren't

you remarried? I don't understand the girls, letting a man like you roam around free."

"I'm a bachelor still."

"You wouldn't be for long, if I were single. Don't you agree, Cindy?"

Cindy turned that vulnerable young face in Mike's direction. "I'd marry him in a minute."

"It's a deal," Mike said, and she blushed. "Of course, I am a little old for you, Cindy. You know, your mother and I are contemporaries."

"Mike was in our first Fire Island house, Cindy. Mike and . . . oh, God, that was a long time ago." Susan shook her head. "Are you out for the summer, a vacation?"

"I'm up at Ocean Bay Park. Groupers. Picked over types like myself, men and women. Eight people each weekend but no one else is out during the week. That gives me a chance to get some work done."

"He's writing a new book," BB announced, returning with Mike's drink.

"I've read your books, Mike," Susan said. "I'm no authority on mysteries, but I did like them."

"You may be the only one," he laughed. "I'm not exactly getting rich from my books."

"How many books have you written?" Susan asked.

"Six. There'll be a new one this fall. I'm working on another now but it's coming slowly. I'm suffering from a constipated imagination."

They all laughed.

"I think it's great, Mike," Cindy said, "that you can write and not have to live like ordinary people."

Mike turned away. Those young breasts, tan, sleek, perfect. He didn't want to think about that, didn't want to carry away an image of how she looked.

"You've got guts," BB said very quietly.

"I had to do it," Mike said. "After my divorce I knew I had to start doing something else. Courage probably had little or nothing to do with it. I couldn't go on being a press agent. Not with what that kind of life was doing to me. I had to get out. Maybe for me writing was the easiest way out. One thing was clear, I didn't belong where I was."

"You did it," BB insisted. "You wanted out and you got out. You didn't just talk about it, the way people do."

Mike looked at his drink, swallowed.

"BB," Susan said. "You and Cindy go somewhere. Mike and I have a lot of years to catch up with. Some private talk, okay."

"Oh, mother," BB began.

"I'll come around another time," Mike said.

BB stood up. He gave Mike his hand. "Come back soon, Mike. I'd like to talk to you some more."

"Good-bye, Mike," Cindy said. "I'm very pleased to have met you again." There was an almost mocking glint in her eyes.

"Again?" Mike said. Then he remembered. "You mean when you were an infant. Okay. Nice seeing you again, Cindy."

They left and Mike returned to his seat next to Susan. She dropped her hand on his thigh and made small quick circles.

"It's so good to see you again," she said. "A big handsome man is always welcome around here." She removed her hand. "What happened?" she said. "I thought you and Jean were going to make it. At least, I hoped you would. Did you walk in on her with someone else? Or vice versa?" She took a long pull on the gin.

"Nothing like that, no dramatic confrontations, no big knockdown dragout fights. Just stopped talking to each other, literally, I mean. There wasn't much point to going on and so we didn't."

"Damn. Doesn't anybody's marriage work?"

"Yours did. You and Neil have been married for a long time."

"Twenty-two years." She grimaced. "Don't put that down as a triumph of love and understanding."

"Oh."

She finished her drink and stood up. "I'm going to have another. You?"

"No, thanks. You do better at it than I can."

She glanced at him. "You sound like Neil." She went inside the house.

She was still slender and firm, looking ten years less than her age. Still beautiful. That incredibly black hair, sleek and thick, cut short, evidence of some Tartar ancestor. The prominent cheekbones, the glowing eyes, the voluptuous mouth. In another time she would have been a tribal princess. Even now there was a regal suggestion about the way she moved. He watched her return to her place on the lounge.

"What did Neil say when you cut your hair?" he began. "He liked it long."

"But it's my hair," she said evenly.

"I was sorry to hear about that TV scandal."

"Neil knew what he was doing."

"What's he doing now?"

"Trying to get some kind of a series produced. I don't know, there's always something." She shifted around and lay back. "It doesn't matter, you see. We have money. Neil was always very good at making money. I used to think that that's what he was after, money. But Neil still hasn't got what he wants."

"What does he want?"

"Everything. The whole damned world."

"Power?" he asked, smiling.

"Under other circumstances, he'd become a politician. A dictator, probably, if he could swing it. Neil loves to control his environment, to make speeches, to tell people how they should feel, live. He's very good at that." She chewed on the edge of her glass, looked up at Mike. "You know what Neil's doing now? With one hand, he sells the production facilities of some local TV outfit to ad agencies for their commercials."

"And with the other hand?"

She sniggered. "He makes dirty movies. The big-time TV producer, the very moral husband and father, the great supporter of so many progressive political causes, who's been on every panel show espousing the *right* way of life, he's making stag reels."

"I can't believe it."

"Believe it. A cut above stag pictures, okay. For those jerk-off houses on Forty-second Street. He's made three of them and he's planning another."

"But why, if he doesn't need the money?"

She considered that. "I lied about the money. It's Neil's lie and I swear to it. That's part of the image, our image, his. To make people thing he's got it made, not hungry. Oh, there is money, a great deal of it, I guess, but not enough to keep us going forever. Not the way we live and Neil doesn't intend to back off one step from our standard, as he calls it. Those dirty movies, they keep us in luxury on East Seventy-eighth Street. They pay the mortgage on this house. They buy very impressive foreign automobiles. All of that."

"You don't seem concerned."

"I'm not. Neil has a knack for making money. He's properly constructed for the world he lives in. If he were a honeybee, he'd find a flower bed in a concrete desert. Once he had three shows on the air simultaneously, plus that late-night talk show he conducted. Neil Morgan will rise again. He wants to be king of the hill and the only question is which hill does he mount." She shook her head as if to clear it and smiled at him. "Enough of Neil. What about you?"

"You know about me. The books get published. They sell modestly, but with reprint rights and foreign sales I have no complaints. My reputation is building and though I'll never be king of any hill, never be rich, I'm out of that day-to-day rat race."

Suddenly she'd had enough. She wanted to be alone, to bake in the sun with her eyes closed, to allow the gin to do its work. She swung her feet to the floor, sat up.

"Don't be a stranger, Mike," she said, dismissing him. "Come and visit. There are lots of lonesome ladies around here between weekends. A big lover like you could make some of them happy."

"You, for example?"

She linked her arm in his, guided him through the house. "You're the only man I've ever known who never made a pass at me. Everyone, copping a cheap feel, propositioning me. You know, that's something, unique. What would it be like with you, I wonder. Too incestuous, I think. You're one of the family, almost. Come back another time. I'll introduce you around." They touched lips at the front door. "Maggie's out here," she said. "She's married again. I know she'd like to see you."

Watching him stride down the walk toward the beach, the muscles in his buttocks flexing at each step, she was reminded of Rick. The flood of emptiness returned to her gut and she made up her mind. It was a risk she would have to take. One more time before the weekend, the inevitable rainy weekend, and Neil. She went back in the house, slowly finished her drink. Then she headed down to the beach and Rick . . .

Chapter II

Eddie

Edith Stander opened the door of the Chevrolet and motioned for her two sons to climb into the back.

"I want to sit up front," the oldest boy complained in a whining voice.

"In," she said, glaring at him.

He obeyed, grumbling, and his brother crawled in beside him. They began to argue.

"Now, listen!" Edith shrilled. "There is going to be no fighting. This is the beginning of a vacation, *my* vacation, and I intend to enjoy myself. Forget that and you'll really get it."

The boys quieted. Edith went around to the back of the car. Eddie was loading the last of their luggage into the trunk.

"Almost finished?"

"We sure have a lot of junk."

"I need it all. We're going away for a month."

"It's not a wilderness, Edith. There are stores. You can buy things." He slammed the lid of the trunk down."

"Take it easy! My cosmetics. If those jars break . . ."

"Okay, that's it. Let's get going. I want to make the ten o'clock ferry."

On the Cross Island Expressway she lit a cigarette and crossed her legs. Her thighs rubbed together uncomfortably, moist, sticky. She should have kept to that diet. It was so easy to put on weight, so hard to get it off. Well, *hell*. Two kids did that to a woman. It ruined muscle tone, broke down the tissue structure, altered the entire metabolic condition. She glanced at Eddie, who was concentrating, glowering at the road ahead as if to attack it. The nutty bastard was kid crazy. If she'd been agreeable, they'd have had two more. Christ! He put it to her only once or twice a month and then hoped to knock her up. *Boy*.

"What's it like?" she said.

"Fire Island?"

"No," she snapped in that curt manner of hers, "Disneyland."

"A sandbar, really. Not very wide. You won't have to worry about the kids. No cars on the island so they can roam around freely."

She studied her fingernails, reached into her purse for the polish remover. "Slow down, will you. This is risky work."

He kept the speed of the Chevrolet constant, imagining it was a Maserati and he was driving at Le Mans. He and Andretti, neck and neck. The roadway was slick. There'd been a twenty-four hour downpour and oil patches glistened threateningly. It had no effect on his driving. He held to the race plan—140, 145, 150. Up ahead, that S-turn he'd been warned about. His brain turned over with cool efficiency, sorting facts, remembering details, sensing the condition of the car. On this day, on this course, in this car; the S-turn had to be cornered at 131 precisely, not an rpm more or less. His hands tightened on the wheel, elbows locked, jaw set. He eased into the first bend . . .

"Go slower, I *said*. I'm spilling this stuff!"

He obeyed. A month of isolation, he told himself. A month of quiet. A month without that squealing voice, without the boys fighting. A month to read, to clear his mind, to reflect. A month alone. Except for the weekends, of course.

He checked his watch. At this rate they would just make the ten o'clock ferry. He slowed the car even more. Missing the ferry would teach her a lesson. Let her wait out there on the pier, he thought with silent satisfaction. It would serve her right. Not that he would say anything. Oh, no. Not a word of blame. He would remain pleasant and equable. But she would know whose fault it was. She'd know.

The caution flags were up, a portion of his trained brain noted. An accident. Some poor bugger had spun out, racked up another car, gone into the wall, over it into the crowd. A bloody bad one. He went past, holding his place in the race. Tough go, old man. Some make it and others don't. Eddie Stander, he was still very much in the race, still up with the contenders, with a great chance to take down the big purse, to win . . .

Neil

A growing sense of danger embraced Neil Morgan. He frowned and made an effort to clear his mind. He had learned to trust his instincts and because of that trust had often managed to avoid pitfalls that might have entrapped lesser men.

Why now? There had been something in her voice, a strange new note, full of excitement, anticipation. What did it mean?

She was a mistake and he berated himself for making it. A mistake, right from the start. He should have resisted, he knew. But, oh, *God,* what a beauty! Special, that vitality and hunger for every experience, giving and taking more fully than anyone he'd ever known. *Living.* No one had ever been like her, not even Susan. And so young.

That was part of it. A big part. So incredibly young and new. The way her mind worked. That full-throated laugh, natural and free, genuine, never caring what anyone might think of her. The way she dressed, like one of those hippies at times. And other times the most chic of women. Not a woman, he reminded himself. Only a girl, a very young girl.

At times she triggered some vague, hot resentment in him, anger at what she said or did. Yet afterward there was no anger. Only a kind of pervading uncertainty. A fear. She was a threat and a promise. And both were frightening.

She had unloosed an alien craving in him, a desire for unnamed profits on the time of his life. To contemplate not gaining these returns shook him deeply.

The cab sped down Second Avenue toward her apartment. Apartment indeed. One small, very small, room. A mattress and box-spring on the floor. A wicker stool and a small ancient chest of drawers. A transistor radio constantly blaring out a rock beat.

He lived in an apartment, a real apartment. They had first met there, on a Thursday afternoon, almost six months before. He'd been alone, working on the True Crime presentation when the bell rang. Susan was off somewhere, a lunch date or shopping, BB was at school, and the maid had the day off. Irritated by the interruption, he went to the door.

Seeing her standing there had rocked him. She was more than just pretty, beautiful beyond any of her parts. Her face defied ethnic classification, features delicate and amused, *interesting,* with a mouth unable to close completely, the lips ripe; her eyes were round and large, neither green nor blue but somewhere between, looking into him in a disconcerting way. And her body. But he didn't discover that until later.

"Hi!" she had cried cheerfully. "I'm Marybeth Gibson. I'm with the I.S.F. The International Scholarship Fund. You've heard about us. I'm in the city for only a short time trying to collect points for my scholarship and I'm here so you can help—"

The irritation was gone. He listened with only a small part of himself, allowing the torrent of words to spread over him, at once soothing and stimulating. He let her go on until she ran out of breath.

"You're selling magazines?" he said.

She avoided saying so directly, referring again to the International Scholarship Fund. He admired the carefully constructed sales pitch, admired even more the vigorous enthusiasm that she generated.

"May I come inside," she said, "and tell you about it."

They went into the living room. He sat on the couch and she perched on the edge of a straight-backed chair opposite him. As she talked he listened, watching her with growing pleasure.

She rose once to hand him a sales folder, returning at once to her seat. "You can see that it's simply a question of points. Competitive, of course, in the good old American way. The first grouping nets me forty points toward my scholarship. The second means thirty points per magazine and so on and so on. Of course, I would like you to make your selections from the first group since it will enable me to win my scholarship so much quicker."

It was a cold day and she had dressed for it. She had on a heavy tweed coat and a long scarf wrapped around her neck; long leather boots ended midway up her thighs.

He said, "Would you like to take off your coat?"

Her smile was dazzling in its innocence. "Oh, thank you. I'll think about it."

"You do that."

She returned to the reason for her visit. She quoted subscription prices to *Esquire* and *Holiday*. *Cue,* she pointed out, was only for New Yorkers. She was sure he would find *Cue* quite valuable. He wondered what she looked like with the coat off.

"You're too much," he said finally, aware that he was trying to provoke a personal response.

Her teeth were large and even and might have been capped. But they weren't.

"Not too much," she said brightly. "Just enough."

"You're either terribly sophisticated or very naive."

Her laugh was brief and gay. "Oh, I wish I were sophisticated, very sure of myself, knowing. I guess I am naive."

"I'm trying to decide," he said.

"About the magazines?"

"About you." He wet his mouth, the familiar tightness coming on, the tension he always felt around a woman, a new woman, the fear of not making it, the desire to *succeed*. "How old are you?"

She never hesitated. "Twenty. Almost twenty, actually. Nineteen, really."

"About what I figured," he said.

That pleased her. That a mature man would accept her as nineteen, almost twenty. She wasn't, of course. She was not much past sixteen—something else he didn't discover until later. Too late.

"I think you are trying to hustle me," he said, making sure to smile, to let her know that he didn't mind at all.

"I think that if I give you money, I might not ever receive those magazines."

"Oh, you *would.*"

Her face grew serious and she shifted around to face him. Now he was able to see that the boots were held up by wide lace garters and he wondered what she would do if he went over to her, went down on his knees in front of her, spread her legs, just spread them as wide as they would go and. . . . His hands trembled and he folded them together to keep them still.

"Oh, you'll get the magazines." Again that cheerful laugh. "Maybe I am a bit of a hustler but I know what I want and I go after it. Shouldn't I?"

"What do you want?"

"To get you to buy some subscriptions."

"I pity the man you marry."

"Oh, I am married," she said quickly, running on. "For five months. His name is Jean-Paul Gibson. French, you see."

"Gibson? French?"

"Oh, *he's* Irish. That is, his father was. But he was born and raised in France, and he has the most fabulous accent. Jean-Paul is trying to earn scholarship points too. You see," she said confidentially, "he lost an arm, in Viet Nam. Oh, it was very bad for a while. The Army gave him a new arm, all cogs and wires and connecting rods. Very ugly and heavy. Jean-Paul wants one of the new arms. You've heard about them, I'm sure. They're quite beautiful and very practical. Why they even have *hair*. . . ."

He was laughing and she went on, pleased that she was amusing him, enjoying the way his narrow eyes crinkled up, thinking that he was very attractive for an older man. He seemed to be in fairly good condition, tall and flat, which was important. Round men disturbed her, the way they bulged against her at all the wrong times, in all the wrong places. It made it difficult for her to concentrate. Despite this preference for flat men, there had been an exceptional number of round ones in her life recently. She made a mental note to try, one day soon, to understand what that meant.

He made her talk for a long time, but in the end it was worth it. He gave her a check for subscriptions to three magazines. That done, she was on her feet, thanking him, moving toward the door.

"Listen," he said as she stepped into the foyer.

She turned, a deep patience shining out of the large eyes. "I'm listening," she murmured.

"I don't think I believe any of it, about the scholarship or the French-Irish husband with one arm."

"None of it?"

"You're going to have to find a better story, if you want people to believe you. Something less flamboyant."

"But it's such a nice story. It would make a wonderful movie, I think."

"Will you let me see you again?" he said.

Her eyes flickered, and she lowered them. "Old men keep buying magazines from me. I mean, *really* old men. Sixty-five some of them. Older. Some of them are mad, you know. They want more than just magazines." She jerked her head from side to side before he could speak. "Oh, I don't mean you. There's something very nice about you. If you were to put your hands on me it wouldn't be such a bad thing. This one old man, he was absolutely *insane*. He had to be. He insisted my hair was too long and he was going to cut it off. He had a scissors. And he said my legs were too long and too fat. That he was going to cut them off too. . . ."

Neil was laughing again. Her imagination was drifting off into unexplored territory again and he told her so.

"Oh, but it's true, about the old man with the scissors."

"Will you let me see you?"

She looked away vaguely. "If you want to."

"I do. I'll take you to dinner."

"You will! How nice. I would like that. I like to eat. You want to write down my address?"

He did. "And the phone number."

"I don't have a telephone."

"How will I get in touch with you?"

"Just come around."

"Suppose you're busy or not there?"

"Then I'll be busy or not there." She looked up at him from under blued eyelids. "You have to take some chances." At once the freshness returned, that naked look. "I must go now. Got to make my scholarship points. Enjoy the magazines, Mr. Morgan. . . ."

That was how it began.

The cab pulled up to the curb in front of the old tenement in which she lived. He went upstairs and found her painting an oversized marigold on the wall opposite the windows. She greeted him cheerfully.

"I feel so wonderful," she bubbled. "So *alive,* love. Won't it be nice to wake up every morning and see a marigold? Sit, be comfortable, I'll stop in a minute."

He watched her. She stretched to color the top of the marigold and the short shift she wore hiked over her thighs. It was exciting to see her flesh revealed. Even now, after all this time, all the hours and days spent in bed, her body was a continuously unraveling mystery to him, a marvel of sensual rewards. Her breasts were impossibly round, the nipples large and bright pink. Really pink. And her belly-thrust, her bottom—all gentle curvature and firmness. The feathering between her legs, so impossibly sparse, making her nowhere younger than in that precious place.

There was more. The feelings she engendered in him, a gladness that he was alive and with her, his being galvanized by her presence, her enthusiasms. Always there was another adventure, a new delight, an exploration to be made. They talked for long hours, walked through the streets of the East Village, ransacked many of the odd little shops with their varied stocks. Sometimes they went over to the river and watched the gulls as they circled, and the tugs, and once they tried to imagine what it would be like to drown. He said it would be a green descent into nothing; she was sure it would be more like a very good trip on acid.

That distressed him, that she used drugs. And once he lectured her, but she tuned him out and he never did it again for fear of losing her.

A change had taken place, these last few weeks, an unsettling ambivalence. Craving her more intensely than ever, he also began wishing her out of his life. He realized he had only to stop seeing her and that would be the end of it. He could say one word and she would make no complaint, no protest. Yet he was unable to say the word.

She stood back and assessed the marigold. Satisfied, she put down the brush and faced him. "You were surprised when I called." She stated it, allowing no room for contradiction. It was true, he had been surprised. She had never phoned before. She lowered herself onto the floor in front of him, the shift riding all the way up so that he was able to see that auburn triangle. He looked into her eyes.

"I was surprised."

"I knew you would be. But I was sure you'd want to know as soon as I was sure, love."

The sense of danger, of trepidation, returned. He wanted to be somewhere else, somewhere familiar, where the rules of behavior were clear and more to his liking. Fire Island. Playing a hard game of tennis, slamming at the ball, gliding in toward the net, smashing one at his opponent's feet, proving his superiority.

"What do I want to know?"

"That I'm going to have a baby."

"Oh, no."

"Isn't that neat?"

Careless. Stupid. Not neat at all.

"You said you were on the pill."

There was nothing but joy in the sound of her laughter. "I forgot. One night, I forgot. I remembered the next afternoon and I took an extra one. It didn't work, I guess. Isn't it lovely, I don't have to take them anymore. I'm already knocked up, I mean, so you don't have to worry about that anymore."

It was true, he thought. He didn't have to worry about that anymore.

Mike

Mike Birns hunched over the portable typewriter on the redwood picnic table and forced himself to concentrate. Nothing worked. All his usual techniques for unloosing the creative juices failed; nothing came. He tilted back in the canvas chair and stared up at the cloudless blue sky and tried to find some island of order in the chaos of his mind.

His plot was predicated on Walker having committed the murder. He had killed Carolyn's little girl out of jealous revenge. But not in heat. It had been a cold, calculating crime, designed to punish his former mistress—not once but twice. The second time would come when he testified at her trial for the murder, testified that she had admitted the murder to him. But it wasn't working, Mike confessed to himself. Some element was missing or overlooked. Perhaps the pathology was all wrong and Walker, as presently constituted, would not have been able to carry it off.

He decided. He would have to rethink Walker completely, from beginning to end, the whole picture. How had Walker lived before he met Carolyn? Had there been other married women with children? Had he ever killed before? Had he ever killed a child before? If so, why? And what part did guilt play in all this? Conscience? Would Walker be able to continue the duplicity *after* Carolyn's trial and conviction?

The questions continued to come and he listed them on paper. Perhaps he had taken on more than he could handle. This was a much more complicated idea than any of his previous books. No simple mystery here but a psychological thriller with undertones that were already taxing him. Was it beyond him? Maybe. . . .

The deck under him vibrated. Someone was coming up the front ramp, calling through the screen door, entering the house. He swore and stood up, tying the frayed belt of the old blue terrycloth robe more tightly.

"Who is it?" He spoke with annoyance. He didn't appreciate interruptions during his work time. He was too susceptible to temptation, to putting the work aside. The rear door swung open and Lilly and Leila stepped onto the back deck. They were wearing red and blue candy-striped bikinis and Lilly carried a kite with a fearsome Oriental visage painted on it.

"Good morning," Mike said, "and go away. I'm working."

"It's almost noon," Leila said.

"And too nice a day to waste working," Lilly added. She shook the kite and the paper rattled threateningly. "Come and play."

"I need an hour or so more by myself. There's a problem I'm trying to——"

"It's a fighting kite," Leila said. "You need a new bathrobe."

"Yes," he agreed. "I suppose I do. Now will you two——"

"We've got another kite with our things," Lilly explained. "On the beach. We'll have a combat, you against us."

"I'm trying to kill someone off in a most diabolical fashion. Fight each other."

"Mysteries," Lilly snorted.

"What trash!" Leila said.

"Why do you write junk?"

"Wouldn't you like to create something great?"

"Absolutely," he said. *"Crime and Punishment."*

"Then do."

"I will," he agreed solemnly. "I shall begin at once."

"Tomorrow," Lilly said, tugging her bikini, exposing the smooth pale skin underneath. "Aren't I getting a lovely tan, Mike?"

A hint of shadowed hair was revealed along the edge of the puckered fabric. "Sensational," he muttered.

"And me?" Leila lifted her panty.

Mike looked. The two sisters moved closer together, legs touching.

"A tie," Mike said.

"Some tans are unattractive," Leila said.

"A girl must be cautious," Lilly said. "Too much sun ages the skin. The right amount makes a girl look younger, more beautiful, sexier."

"Sex is the language of the beach," her sister said.

"Very profound," Mike said.

"You know what William Cartwright said about sex?" Lilly said.

"Who?"

"He was a poet," Leila explained gravely. "Sixteen eleven to sixteen forty-three."

"Oh, *that* William Cartwright."

Lilly began to recite:

I was that silly thing that once was wrought
To practice this thin love;
I climbed from sex to soul, from soul to thought;
But thinking there to move,
Headlong I rolled from thought to soul, and then,
From soul I lighted at the sex again.

"Beautiful," Leila said.

"That's from 'No Platonic Love'," Lilly said.

"Mysteries," Leila added disapprovingly. "That's what you should write—poetry. Love poems. Something of merit."

"I'm going to try, after *Crime and Punishment.*"

"You aren't a serious man," Lilly accused.

Mike tried to suppress a yawn, failed. They were beginning to bore him.

"Do you know what that means, to yawn when you're talking to members of the opposite sex?" Lilly asked.

"What does it mean?"

Leila supplied the answer with no change of expression on her precisely constructed little face. "It means you want to fuck or fight."

Mike refused to show any surprise. "I don't want to fight," he said.

In tandem, the two girls stepped closer to him. "Are you wearing anything under that ratty bathrobe?" Lilly said conversationally.

"Nothing. Now leave."

"We decided," Leila said, "didn't we, Lilly?"

"Yes. We decided."

"What?"

"That you must be a very sexy man. It has to do with the way you look at a girl, the way you hold yourself, with a sort of forward pitch to your pelvic area."

"Oh."

"We were wondering . . ."

"We discussed it."

"Of course we couldn't be sure."

"And this is a fine time to find out," Lilly pointed out.

"What?" he said. A mist of confusion settled over him and he felt crowded, pressured, on the far edge of panic. He took a backward step. "What are you talking about?"

"About whether or not you've got a big machine or a small one," Leila said with great patience.

Thoughts darted across the dividing chasm of his brain. Amusement changed to dismay to distress to resentment to anger to fear. "Beat it," he said, with no conviction at all.

"Let's go inside," Leila said.

"No," Lilly said. "The hedges are all around the deck," she pointed out reasonably. "No one can see."

"Open the robe."

Mike felt almost helpless, immobile. He watched Lilly approach. Her hands were sure and steady. She untied the belt. The robe hung loose. She opened it.

"But he isn't hard," Leila complained.

"Half," Lilly amended.

"Do you think there's something wrong with him? That he's one of those impotent types?"

"I don't think so. We took him by surprise, I think. He is very self-involved, especially his work. He'll respond, I'm sure."

"I hope so. Malnutrition would affect his sexual powers, you know, a vitamin deficiency. He doesn't eat properly at all."

"Well, we'll simply have to find out one way or another."

"We can feed him afterward with that simply superb lunch you made for us," Leila went on. "Cold deviled shrimp and chicken in the pot."

"With a lovely white wine. Something very dry, very light."

"Darling," Leila said to her sister. "How shall we begin? I do so want him to be big and hard. I love it big and hard."

"Let me see what I can do." Lilly slid to her knees in front of Mike.

Mike heard it all, perceived it all, as if through a thick filter, all sound and movement slowed and blurred. He felt the soft hands riding up onto his belly, the delicate fingers dancing back down again.

"Oh," he heard one of them say. "That's much better."

"But not all the way. . . ."

"What marvelous little balls he has. So cute, pretty."

"Now look, darling. So big."

"And smooth. All of it, fantastically smooth, soft . . ."

"Let me touch."

"I'm so glad he's circumcized."

"I prefer men who are."

"Prettier."

"And cleaner."

"I want to taste . . ."

"Go ahead, darling. And while you do, I'll undress you. And me. And . . ." Her sister was unable to answer, unable to speak. "Oh, dear, please. Make room, darling. Make room for me. . . ."

Roy

"You got to be kidding!"

Harry Nevin's mouth was the only part of his face that displayed any kind of animation. The thick lips rose and fell, pulled back, pursed, flattened, revealing the gamut of his emotion. And when he spoke again, the words exploded from between gritted teeth.

"Give you dough, am I crazy!"

He was a large man but shapeless, flabby. Layer upon layer of flesh rolled up out of his soiled collar, shimmering and gleaming with sweat. His small features were almost lost in the round fleshy face and his dark, tiny eyes were fine points of hard light. His voice was serrated and had a harsh nasal edge.

"Come on, Harry," Roy Ashe said, adjusting a smile on his mouth, keeping his eyes carefully focused in middle-space. "You know me. I'm good for it."

"Hah. I know you and you're good for nothing. Nothing. You are in to me for twenty-five of the big ones. Twenty-five. And you ain't here to pay off."

They were seated opposite each other at Harry's usual corner table in a dimly lighted saloon on Second Avenue in the Forties, one of his favorite places of business. There were two pay phones on the other side of the narrow room, at the front end of the bar, installed at Harry's expense for his exclusive use, his link with his clients. Now one of them rang and he trundled over to it, maneuvered his damp bulk into the booth.

"Yeh," he began professionally. "Yanks and Pirates, a parlay. Six-five on each. A yard-and-a-half. Yeh, you got it." He hung up and returned to the table.

"This is a big deal," Roy offered.

"Hah."

"I mean it, a big deal."

"Twenty-five thousand is a big deal."

You know I'm good for it," Roy repeated a little desperately.

Harry Nevin stared at the tabletop.

"A film library," Roy said, leaning forward. "An entire library, Harry. I can buy the whole thing. At bargain rates. Believe me. I know what I'm doing. There's real money in this and I can make it pay off to the last cent. You can understand, Harry. You see what it means."

"Nothing to me, that's what it means." The phone rang again and Harry made the journey across the room, breathing loudly. "Yeh." He listened. "No," he said at last. "Not my kind of action. Right. That I can handle. Lollipop, third at Belmont. Five-oh. You got it." He came back to the table.

"A hundred and thirty features, Harry. Full-length movies, Harry. Some of them with outstanding star value. Big names. I can peddle them all over the country, station by station. Rentals, Harry, and I'd still own the film. There's a fortune in it, Harry. This is my line. I know the market. I used to be in the business."

"Used to be. Used to be is worth nothing. Now you hawk hardware door to door. A been-no-place, going-no-place hustler."

"Harry, you know that's not fair." Roy straightened up in his seat, focused on the bridge of the bookie's nose. "I represent the Lenton Company. You know them. Top housewares firm in the trade. I am a manufacturer's rep. Strictly wholesale."

"You don't intend to place a bet, then go away. You're bad for business, hanging around this way."

"Tell you what, Harry. I'll cut you in for a piece of the action. Five per cent. No, ten. In addition to the interest on the loan. Could anything be fairer?"

"You got no action."

Roy came to his feet, hands resting on the table, the bleached face flushed and agitated. "Dammit! Can't you see what this means! Television is big dough. There are millions to be made. A chance like this, once in a lifetime. Don't pass it up, Harry. Don't make me lose it."

Harry lifted his eyes. Don't holler. It makes the drinkers nervous."

There was a growing unsteadiness in Roy's knees, a need

to convince Harry to let him have the money. To sell *him*. It was as if Roy had come to some crucial point in his existence, had to make a vital choice, as if everything had festered, swelled, was ready to burst open. He sat back down, fighting for control. He produced a confident laugh, that baritone laugh, showing the bookie that he was no longer excited, not as anxious as he had appeared. Back in command. The old Roy Ashe.

"Harry," he said conversationally. "We are not communicating. And it's my fault." Harry grunted. "I mean it, Harry. I accept the blame for not making you understand. If you understood the potential, the great profits that this deal could produce for us both and——"

"I understand a snow job. And something else. That you are a loser."

Roy manufactured his best grin. "Losers like me keep you in business."

"Right. For the first time."

Roy put his elbows on the table. "Tell you what. Advance me dough enough for the down payment on the library, Harry. Not the whole price."

Harry snickered. "I know who don't understand. *You* don't understand. Not a thing, that's what you understand. And nothing is what you get. Nothing. No dough. No credit. Not from me."

"I'll pay you back," Roy said quickly, aware of the liquid churning in his gut. "Within a year. With interest."

Harry gazed at him balefully out of colorless eyes. The lips moved. "Your credit's closed off. No more bets till you pay off and no loan. Even the sharks wouldn't let you have any dough. You're a bad risk, Ashe."

"Harry, please . . ."

"No. And one more thing. I want my twenty-five grand. Very soon."

Roy leaped to his feet. "Don't threaten me!"

Harry's mouth twitched and turned upward at the corners. "*Schmuck*. You're going to get yourself a broken head out of plain dumbness. Okay, now I am threatening you. And you know I mean it. I want payment. Because I'm a nice guy, you got ninety days."

"You stupid bastard!" Roy bit off. "I'll pay when I feel

like it, not before. You don't scare me, a cheap-ass bookie."

The fleshy face shimmered slightly in comprehension. "Ninety days is all. And don't come around again without the cash. People like you are bad for business. Makes people think about their luck."

Outside, in the thick August sunlight, Roy fought to breathe, nostrils clogged with pollutants and swelled with fear and uncertainty. He plumbed his brain. Somehow he had to find the money to buy the film library. Had to, had to. The library was his last chance.

There had to be somebody he could touch. Someone who had it; someone he hadn't already hit up; someone he hadn't burned. He ran down the list of people he knew. Neil Morgan. Of course! All those years in TV would have netted him a fortune. A brief triumphant laugh broke out of him. Oh, yes, Neil. He'd have a little tin box somewhere with a large amount of tax-free cash in it, a private nest egg. Neil would come through for his old fucking buddy. Good old Neil. He went looking for a telephone.

Cindy

The boat was a beauty, a forty-one foot Chris-Craft, set up for everything. The two men sat in blue canvas deck chairs watching the late movie on the Sony, smoking cigars and drinking rye highballs. They were a pair, brown-haired with fat lips and fleshy hands. Each of them wore a diamond pinky ring and a gold wristwatch.

"Hi," BB said from the pier.

The two men stood up and turned around. "Oh, hello there, young fellow," one of them said. "I'd about given you up."

"I said I'd come back."

"You said it and you meant it," the other one said. A nervous laugh expired on his lips and he shut off the television set.

BB helped Cindy into the boat. The two men looked at her admiringly.

"Well, young fellow," the first one said, "you told us she was pretty and she is pretty. Very pretty."

"Her name is Cindy," BB said.

"Hello, Cindy. I'm Jack and this is Louis."

Cindy said nothing.

"You approve, gentlemen?" BB said.

"Well, sure," Jack said nervously. "Why don't we all have a drink together? Get acquainted."

"I can't stay," BB said. "But Cindy will, if everything's satisfactory."

"Everything's satisfactory for me," Jack said. "How about you, Louis? Is everything satisfactory?"

"Oh, sure. Everything."

BB smiled shortly. "That's one-hundred dollars, please. Fifty for each of you."

Jack handed over the money and BB counted it before tucking it into his pocket.

"One hour," BB said. "You'll get your money's worth, but no rough stuff. Okay?"

"Oh, we're not like that. Just a few laughs."

BB climbed back on the pier. "See you later, Cindy."

She watched him disappear in the darkness, then looked at the two men. "Well," she said flatly. "Who's going to be first?"

Susan

BB went into MacCurdy's and had a beer. He finished it and ordered another, took it down to the other end of the bar and began to play the bowling machine. He matched his left hand against his right hand. Left won three straight lines. He wanted another beer. He started back to the bar, then paused in the wide entrance to the large back room to watch the dancers. He picked out his mother, dancing the Funky Broadway with that lifeguard Rick. She didn't do it very well, and he told himself that older people made themselves look bad when they did kids' dances.

The record ended and another came on. A slow number

this time. Rick and his mother danced again, very close this time. He watched Susan drop her hand onto Rick's ass, saw her wiggle against him, say something. They kissed. BB went after his beer.

Chapter III

Eddie

The Standers settled into the tiny weathered house with the yellow shutters on Cottage Walk, close to Midway. Edith spent the first two days cleaning, though the house had been prepared for their arrival by the owner.

"You can't be too careful," she said to Eddie. "I *know* how clean I am. I don't know about other people."

The cleaning was done and neat curtains had been draped over all the windows; the children had collected clam shells to be used as ashtrays. Eddie felt she was being overly meticulous, obsessively clean, but he was careful not to reveal his annoyance. Instead, he did whatever chores she assigned him without objection, anxious to get these preliminaries out of the way.

Finally it was done and he was free to do what he wanted, which was to locate a section of beach removed from other people, go there, complete with blanket and an aluminum backrest, and read the Ernest Jones biography of Sigmund Freud.

Two days in the sun and the pebbled skin began to turn brown, and the pimples that marched down his spine like an angry army almost disappeared. He would read for a while, then lay back, eyes closed, the heat of the sun humming against his naked pate, penetrating, dazzling flashes bouncing off his retina. Images faded on to the screen of his mind, a continuity of graceful action. He recalled a volleyball game, a body rising high off the sand, slamming a point home. It was Eddie Stander, younger, lacking the softness that now girdled his middle—an Eddie Stander with hair.

The picture changed. He was walking along the sandy strand with Mike Birns. They were arguing—ferocious but friendly. Just how good was *The Cocktail Party*, how meaningful? And how much did Hemingway owe to Dashiell Hammett? Mike had been a devotee of Hammett's, and of James S. Cain, the early Cain.

That was the time of the young Willie Mays, the young Mickey Mantle. Oh, God, Willie was beautiful to see in center field, circling under a fly ball, tapping the glove, all naturalness and ease.

They had been Giants fans, both of them, and hungry for any victory, no matter how small. And that season, their second summer on the island, the Little Miracle of Coogan's Bluff, the Giants coming from thirteen-and-a-half games back to win it. Willie and Maglie, Al Dark and Stanky, Westrum, Monte Irvin, Dusty Rhodes. Jim Hearn. Whitey Lockman. Bobby Thomson and the homerun heard round the world. The first Giants pennant in fourteen years.

He knuckled one hand into a tight fist. Oh, God, 1951. A moist anguish gathered in his eyes. So long ago, so young, all of them. Innocent. And now Willie Mays was thirty-six and having a terrible season, playing out the string. He wasn't finished. Mustn't be. Not yet. Not Willie.

And Eddie Stander. Older and marking time, he gritted, almost crying out. He slammed the fist into his other hand, desire for a cigarette strong in his mouth. He should never have given up the habit, never allowed Edith to talk him into quitting.

Hell, he had enjoyed smoking.

Mike

Mike Birns found a place against the protective dunes where he could be alone. Mike didn't want to talk to anybody he knew. Mostly he didn't want to meet Lilly and Leila. He wanted to wipe away all recollection of that afternoon, of the desperate cravings they had brought out in him, the frightening intensity of his lust, and the remoteness of theirs. When it was over, when they had finished with him, and each other, they had gone off to fight their kites, and he had tried to sleep. But it was impossible.

He had showered. Very hot, then very cold. Repeated the process. It did no good. There was no way to wash away the sense of wrongdoing, the waste. He went out on the beach.

He tried to read *The Autobiography of Malcolm X*, found it difficult to concentrate, listened to some show tunes on the transistor radio, dozed fitfully. The sun burned into his forehead. He stood up and squinted along the beach. Shimmering heat waves distorted his vision. He imagined he saw the twins coming toward him. He ran for the ocean.

The surf was up, the rollers high, capped, crashing impressively. He dived through the waves, stroking against the currents. He surfaced and kept going, riding the swells, until he was finally beyond the last of the breakers. He jackknifed to the bottom, searched until he found something, shot back up. He examined his find. An unimpressive rock. He dropped it and floated. After a while, he stroked with exaggerated slowness parallel to the shore.

This time he was sure he saw the twins. Avoiding them was marked down as a victory. His eyes worked around. Two boys sat astride surfboards, waiting for a ride; children played among the breakers, their shrieks carried on the soft breeze; some couples had formed a circle in the shallows; a lone woman did a strong breaststroke that carried her away from the beach.

Mike watched her. No strain showed on her face and it was clear she was in control of the situation. Then suddenly without warning, an expression of anguish distorted her features. She appeared to gasp. She had stopped swimming and her body was contorted. A sudden cramp, Mike decided, and he began kicking out toward her. He was ten feet away when she saw him. Her eyes went wide and one hand came up, a silent plea for help.

"Take it easy," he cried.

"No!" she shrieked.

He kept coming.

"Go away. Oh, damn you, go away."

Mike pulled up, treading water, puzzled.

"Please. Go away. My top came off. I lost it."

He grinned at her. "What are you going to do? How will you get out of the water?"

"I'm going to dive for it. I'll find it."

"And if you don't?"

"I'll find it. Go away."

"I'll help you look."

She laughed, a brief, exasperated burst, without humor. "Dammit, are you so hard up to see a pair of tits! All right, look!" She thrust herself out of the water, breasts white and wet, gleaming in the sunlight, the nipples dormant. She fell back. "There. Is that what you wanted?"

"I'm sorry. I only wanted to help." He made his way to shore. On the beach, he turned and saw that she was coming in. He watched her come out of the water, a slender shapely girl with dark hair and an easy stride. She was wearing both halves of her bikini. She saw him and turned in his direction, a smile lifting the corners of her mouth.

"I was a bitch out there," she began directly. "My only fault."

"You're lucky to have only *one* fault."

Her smile widened and he decided that with some makeup she would be pretty. Her face was narrow and small-boned, with no tension in her expression. "There are a few other things wrong with me," she said.

"I didn't notice."

"Don't be crude."

He searched her face. Her eyes were clear, pure green, and unblinking. A splay of pale freckles dotted the bridge of her nose. She *was* pretty.

"I thought you were drowning out there. I was going to save you. You ruined my chance to be a hero."

"Perhaps I can make it up to you."

"How?"

She made a thoughtful face. "We could lie, tell people that you did save me. Not only from the sea but from a vicious shark, a *school* of sharks."

"Let's not overdo it."

She laughed, a light, cheerful sound.

"My blanket's up near the dunes," he said. "Come and join me."

"Oh, I've had enough of the beach and there are some things I have to do."

"I see," he said stiffly.

"Now, don't get uptight," she said. "It's the way I said, I have some things to do. I like you well enough."

"Listen, I didn't feel rejected," he said quickly. "Don't make a case out of it."

"Okay," she answered, laughing. "Okay." She started to walk away, then looked back over her shoulder. "Would you like to walk back with me?"

He said he would and she gathered up her belongings. They didn't speak again until they were on the walk. He glanced sidelong at her. In profile, she looked very young, the pale skin smooth and without lines. At once a sense of irritation slithered along under his skin. He was tired of young girls and their compelling needs, their unsettled flirtations, their desperate cravings to take, to make a lasting connection. He wasn't looking for that kind of trouble.

"You're a baby, aren't you?" he said.

"I'm twenty-five, if that's what you wanted to know."

"Don't be a wise guy." He felt silly, on the defensive, younger than she, immature. "I'm almost twenty years older than you."

"Ah, that explains it."

"Explains what?"

"Why you're so nervous."

"Nervous!"

"Like I said, uptight. I thought it was me, that you didn't dig me. But you dig me, all right. It's because you think you're too old for me."

"Go to hell," he said, careful not to make it too strong. "You may be too old for *me*."

That made her laugh. "Maybe you're right. There are times I think I'm a hundred and eight."

"You're unbelievable," he said.

"How?"

"Unreal. Something from another planet."

"You think there are people on other planets, other galaxies, that they're trying to contact us?"

"Little green men?"

"I don't know. I've been reading—Arthur Clarke, Asimov. You know Asimov? He's great."

"I've read him."

"Have you? How nice it would be if there really were a superior race of beings, wiser, gentler, more loving and understanding. More *human* than we are. That way—" She broke off and lowered her eyes. "You think I'm a crazy lady. . . ."

"I think you're a marvelous-looking girl, and I'd like to take you to dinner, get you drunk, and—"

She shook her head. "No, please. Don't crowd me, please. You mustn't." She stopped and turned. "This is where I'm staying." She gestured toward the house behind them. "This is my holiday. I'm going to be here for the next few weeks. If you want to try me again . . ."

The irritation returned. She *was* far-out. Different, too different. She would present problems. That talk of life in outer space; she would probably be hooked on metaphysics, too, some form of religion, or be a devotee of Merce Cunningham or John Cage; she would drag him to Andy Warhol movies and esoteric Off-Off-Broadway plays.

And obviously she would present a sexual problem; it wouldn't have surprised him if she had declared her virginity, as well as a dedication to a continuation of that condition—despite her defiant display in the ocean. She would be trouble, the kind of trouble he didn't relish.

"Sure," he said. "We'll probably see each other on the beach again."

"Yes." She went into the house.

He went back to the beach, settled down to read. It was then that he remembered that he had forgotten to ask her name.

BB

Tight Man was wiry, with high shoulders that lent a locked appearance to his body as if none of the joints functioned. His face was hard and rocky, the eyes narrow and wary, the nose long and searching. Veins rippled along the backs of his hands and his wrists were thick, the arms under the green shirt he wore heavily muscled. He perched on the narrow wooden bench behind the community house that served Ocean Beach as a movie theater, behind the children's play area, looking across the marina at Great South Bay. A tanker, flanks crusted, headed for the sea. He watched with no curiosity as to its destination.

He was a man who looked at things without thinking about them, unable to connect a present incident with a subsequent result in another time and place. He was a man who spent a great deal of his time waiting, certain that eventually someone would come along and invite him to perform his function.

"Hey, man."

Tight Man would have smiled, if he ever smiled. Someone had come. He looked up. BB and Cindy stood there. Tight Man let his eyes linger on Cindy's breasts.

"You got taste in broads, kid," he said to BB. "You a good-looking broad," he said to Cindy.

She took a step backward.

"I came to make a buy."

"You got bread?"

"I'm loaded."

Tight Man looked at Cindy again. "I get the word, you cats went into trade. True? True, true. Maybe one day I make a buy from you, kid. A shot of smack for the broad?"

"No," Cindy said, unable to mask her distaste. She moved behind BB. "No."

"I want two hundred dollars worth."

Tight Man raised his brows. "Horse?"

"Yes."

"Wait here. I be back soon."

BB said, "Hurry."

Chapter IV

Mike

Mike slept for two hours. When he woke, all processes slowed, all passages clogged, he thought about the girl. He shaved and showered and that helped considerably. It was the first time he had shaved since the previous weekend.

Scrambled eggs, toasted English muffins, instant coffee and half a Sara Lee swirl cake made him a dinner. He tried reading Malcolm X, but was unable to concentrate. When he finished eating he got out the typewriter and tried to work. Increasingly restless, he gave it up as a waste of time.

He walked down to the beach and stood on the dunes. A soft breeze ruffled the beach grass and crickets chirped incessantly. The ocean surged aggressively in round-backed waves that thumped loudly on the shore, spuming white under a purpling sky.

He thought about her and smiled at himself. She had turned him on in some complicated way that annoyed and distressed him, a witch who had cooked up some strange hypnotic elixir or murmured some ancient incantation to bring him to her. He turned away. He knew how to exorcise her, to reduce her spell to manageable proportions. He would prove her to be just another female, not better, not much different from all the others.

He located her house without difficulty and knocked.

She appeared wide-eyed and uncertain in discreet white Bermudas and a green sleeveless blouse. Her hair was pulled straight back and knotted behind her neck. For the first time, he noticed that her green eyes displayed a slightly Oriental cast. Wearing no makeup, she looked almost girlish.

"Oh," she said absently, through the screen door. "It's you."

Well, hell. That was a piss-poor greeting. She wasn't all *that* desirable. Just another unclaimed girl on a beach of unclaimed girls, there for the choosing. Especially by a Mike Birns. Oh, come *on,* he told himself. Come off it. He grinned at her. "I just happened to remember," he said, "that I never told you my name. I'm here to correct the oversight."

"That's a reasonable thing to do."

"I'm Mike Birns."

"It's very nice to know you, Michael."

He grimaced. "I must be honest. It's Myron, not Michael."

She made no effort to conceal her amusement. "And you prefer Mike?"

"Wouldn't you?"

She appraised him. "You have the look of a modified Mike."

"What is that supposed to mean?"

"Mike is a name for a truck-driver or a football player. But I once knew a Mike who taught Art Appreciation in a girl's school. He was more of a Michael, I must admit. You must have been a Myron when you were very young. A sweet boy, properly behaved and round-faced. Later you became Mike. Muscular Mike, very athletic, I suppose. There are fragments of both remaining."

"Is that bad?"

"I like it."

"In that case, you might open the damned screen door."

"Oh. Yes. Would you like to come in? There's some coffee."

"No, thank you."

"I'd offer you a drink but there's nothing here. Everyone in the house has his or her own liquor, you see. Private stock. And I'm not drinking now."

"How would you like to see a movie?"

The green eyes glittered. "Oh, yes. That would be fun. I'd like a movie very much."

"It's over in Ocean Beach. A mile or so from here. Are you up to walking?"

"I walk very well. I like to walk. When? Right now?"

Her enthusiasm made him smile. "Right now. Bring a coat. It's liable to rain."

She allowed the door to slam shut, leaving him standing outside. "I'll be only a——"

"Hey!" he called.

She turned back.

"Do you have a name?"

She chewed her lower lip. "Elizabeth. Elizabeth Jordan."

"Okay. Get your coat, *Lizzie*."

She wrinkled her nose in distaste but made no objection.

The movie, a World War II film, was loud, bloated with blood and action and killing. During one extremely violent sequence, he looked at her. Her mouth was tight and her hands clenched in her lap.

"We can leave, if you like," he said.

She shook her head and continued to stare at the screen.

Afterward, he asked her about it. "You were unhappy back there. We could have left."

"But you wanted to see the picture," she said. She pulled the rain jacket tighter around herself.

"You're cold," he said. "How about some coffee or a drink?"

Before she could reply, he heard his name called. He turned to see BB and Cindy coming forward. Both of them carried ice-cream cones.

Mike made the introductions.

"See the picture?" BB asked.

"Ugh," Cindy said.

"I agree," Elizabeth said.

"You write better than that, Mike," BB said. "How come they don't make a picture out of your books?"

"Exactly what I ask my agent. Say hello to your mother for me, BB. You too, Cindy."

"Nice-looking kids," Elizabeth said when they were alone again.

"I shared a house with their parents when I first came out to Fire Island. Seventeen years ago. I could be their father. Your father," he added casually.

She looked up at him soberly. "You're not anything like my father." Then she added brightly, "Will you buy me an ice-cream cone?"

"I think I can manage that."

"With chocolate sprinkles?"

"You'll break me yet."

They strolled back through the quiet walks of Seaview, talking easily, licking the cones. He told her about his writing and his yearly escape from the city to Fire Island during the hot months, so he could work.

She told him about her job as an editorial assistant for a professor at NYU who was doing a historical study of the growth of the managerial class in the United States.

"Sounds interesting," he said automatically.

"It's dull," she corrected. "And my part, especially. I dig up musty old facts and do reports which Professor DeFabio incorporates into his manuscript." She made a face. "I have a very difficult time writing well."

"Maybe I can help."

Ice cream dripped down the outside of her cone and she licked at it feverishly. "That wouldn't be fair. You're a professional and I'm only playing at it."

"Well," he said, "it would give me an excuse to spend time with you, to put you in my debt."

"You feel you have to do that?" she said gravely.

"It might make things easier."

"Oh," she said, turning back to her cone.

In Ocean Bay Park, the walks were darker, even quieter. Only on weekends did the community come alive with movement and noise, the Groupers out in full force, anxious to take advantage of every moment, to have fun, to make contacts, to score.

"What are you doing here?" Mike asked. "Somehow you don't fit."

"Oh," she said, "I think I do." She was no different than other girls, she insisted. They all wanted the same things, she imagined. Like so many of them, she had responded to an advertisement in the Village Voice offering shares in a summer house. She had attended a meeting, had been questioned, examined, judged by the organizers of the house.

"Obviously you passed the test," he put in.

She hesitated. "Sometimes I think I may be different, a little strange."

"Oh, you are very strange."

She didn't respond to the jibe. "Most of the girls seem to know precisely *who* they are, what they want."

"And you don't?"

"Not really. Right now I find myself in a sort of limbo—I've changed a lot but I'm not yet what I hope to become."

"It sounds terribly alluring. Exotically mysterious."

"I'm not trying to be mysterious or different. I think I would like to be ordinary. Simple."

"You aren't simple and you are different. There's a remoteness about you, a distance between you and the rest of the world."

"You're saying I'm a cold person."

"I'm not sure."

"I like people."

"Men?"

"Men are people."

There was that obliqueness, a tangential quality to her answers, as if she failed to understand even direct questions. Another girl would have picked up on his remarks, declaimed on her warmth, her fondness for men; another girl would have recognized and responded to the sexual connotation. Not Elizabeth. She *was* different and the differences were disturbing. What was the phrase she had used? *Crazy lady?* Anything was possible with this girl, nothing too far-out.

"You're from another world," he heard himself saying. "Or maybe some kind of a mutant, a superior creature come to alter and reform us ordinary mortals."

"That's a terrible thing to say. You see me as some kind of square, all proper and pure. I admit to a Catholic background and education, but I'm not a nun, you know."

"You're Catholic," he said, as if that explained everything.

"I *was*. I don't practice anymore. I mean, going to mass and confession. At least, not on a regular basis."

"I'm sure you have nothing to confess," he said, alert to her response.

She smiled in the darkness. "I try to be good."

The answer left him dissatisfied. "I think you're still hooked on the Church," he said accusingly.

"Not the Church. Though I still take pleasure in some of the forms, the rituals. The Church is too crowded with priests, and they don't leave much room for God."

"You actually believe in God?" he said, after an interval.

"Yes."

He felt antagonistic. He spoke slowly. "I don't. I'm an atheist. I used to say that I was an agnostic, that I didn't know. Now I *know*—at least for myself."

"That's nice," she said lightly. "For yourself. I'm glad you're not a missionary."

They made the rest of the walk in silence. He sensed a gap between them, wider now, the differences more apparent, the reasons for not being together clear and dramatic.

"Here we are," she said, when they reached her house. "Thank you for the movie and the ice cream."

"I enjoyed it," he said automatically.

"I enjoyed our talk," she said. "Good night." She went inside. It wasn't until he was in bed and unable to sleep that he realized how angry he was. Goddamned angry.

Chapter V

Roy and Neil

Roy Ashe sat in the soft leather bucket seat of the Mercedes next to Neil Morgan.

"Nice of you to ask me for the weekend," Roy said, pleased with the manner in which he had forced the invitation from the other man.

"How you doing, Roy?"

"Beautiful, baby. There's a big operation on the fire and it's cooking away."

"That's great," Neil said cautiously.

How long had it been since he had seen Roy? Two years, three? And then by accident, one of those industry affairs, a testimonial dinner. Hell, they weren't friends. Yet Roy had been so terribly anxious to come out to the island and Neil was curious. Also, Roy was a hustler who got around. There might be a sliver of valuable information to be extracted from him.

They were halfway across Great South Bay when Roy mentioned his meeting with Eddie Stander. "You ought to see him," he said mockingly. "Not a hair on his head, shaved clean. The poor man's Yul Brynner. With a paunch and a surburban-type wife."

Neil nodded soberly. "He used to be so damned smart, critical of everyone."

"I taught him how to dress, you know."

"I didn't know."

"Sure. What did they know in the Bronx or Brooklyn or wherever about clothes? I took him to Chipps and J. Press myself. Ha! He looked lousy, I thought."

"Man ought to keep himself in shape," Neil said. "The body is a kind of a cathedral and it has to be sanctified."

"That's good, very good, Neilie. And you're doing it. You look like a million. Got all your hair still and a flat belly. And I know your track record. Great. Just great."

"Let me tell you, Roy. Discipline. Hard work. Full application of one's gifts. That's what it's all about."

"I couldn't agree more."

When they arrived at the house on Midway, Roy greeted Susan effusively, kissing her, telling her that she hadn't aged a bit, was as beautiful as ever, saying how much he liked her hair cut short.

"I prefer it long," Neil commented.

Susan ignored the remark. "I'm sure you'll be comfortable in the guestroom, Roy. The bed is fairly new and big enough to accommodate a friendly lady, if you get lucky."

"Roy's here for a couple of days of rest," Neil said coldly. "Besides, BB's here."

"He and Cindy see a lot of each other," Susan said. "Wouldn't it be funny if they got married."

"Great," Roy said.

"BB's just a boy," Neil said.

"I haven't seen Cindy in nearly two years," Roy offered.

"Your own daughter!" Neil said, making no attempt to conceal his disapproval.

Roy produced that sheepish, boyish grin of his. "Man, the single life, you don't know how it is. Busy, busy, busy. Cindy's a good kid. She understands. Maybe BB'll bring her around. Maggie won't want me around her house, not with a new husband."

"Bob's not exactly new. They've been married for ten years."

"That long?" Roy said. "Jesus!"

Roy and Cindy

There were about ten of them, none older than twenty, tanned, bright-eyed, sprawling over the sand and each other, dozing, talking, reading, laughing. A long-haired youth strummed a guitar and softly sang of a corrupted love. There was the sound of a palm slapping against soft flesh and a small friendly cry of protest.

Cindy kneeled over BB and said his name. He allowed his eyes to flutter open. Her heavy breasts hovered enticingly.

"Very nice things," he said. "A weekend like this, I could make a fortune with you."

"You promised," she said. "You've got plenty of stuff and——"

"And I'll run out soon and need more. It costs to feed my habit. One of these days I'm going to turn you on, when I get my hands on some real bread."

She made no reply. She would never allow that. Grass had done nothing for her and the two acid trips had been bad, frightening. She had sworn off acid and she was terrified of speed or any of the hard stuff. Besides, she needed no help to get her kicks. She knew exactly what she liked. And how she liked it.

She looked down at BB. His eyes were closed again, his breathing easy. He was becoming a bore, animated only when he needed a shot and then obsessed with getting it. Otherwise he existed in a kind of dead air space, euphoric, useless. It occurred to her that they were coming to the end, that he used her and gave little in return. Whoring had been a new kick for a while. But the gloss had worn off and she decided that she preferred to choose her own bed partners. BB always came up with fat men with plenty of money and weird tastes. She wanted something else, something more rewarding, something different. And she was pretty sure she knew where to find it. All she needed was a plan. . . .

"Oh, damn," she said.

"What?" BB said, not opening his eyes.

"Look who's coming."

"Who?"

"My father."

BB lifted himself onto his elbows. There was Roy advancing along the beach in Tartan swim trunks, thick-bodied, strutting that bantam strut of his, head bobbing, grinning thinly.

"I don't want to talk to him."

"He's your father."

"Big deal."

BB waved at Roy who waved back and veered toward them.

"Bastard," Cindy said.

BB fell back and closed his eyes. "Be a dutiful daughter."

"Cindy! Is that you Cindy?"

Cindy stood up. "Hello—" She couldn't call him father. She *couldn't*. "Hello, Roy."

"Boy," Roy said. "You look fantastic. If you weren't my own kid . . ." His laughter was coarse, grating.

She stared at him patiently.

"Is that good old BB stretched out there like a Greek god. How's it going, BB?"

BB lifted a hand.

"Hey, BB," Roy laughed. "You're a regular giant. You look seven feet tall, at least, which makes you a giant because I'm six feet and you're at least a foot bigger." Roy waited for his old joke to get a laugh. No one laughed. He grinned at Cindy. "Well, you don't win 'em all, right? Right. How about we take us a little walk, have us a little talk."

"Well," she said.

"That's a good idea," BB said. "Go with your daddy, Lucinda, like the good little girl you are."

Cindy started to reply, thought better of it. She picked her way out of the circle of young flesh. Roy caught up to her. He glanced sidelong at her. She had a fantastic profile, the brow straight, the nose short and upturned, the mouth full, inviting. And she did to a bikini what other girls only hoped to do. A juicy piece. He supposed every stud on the beach was trying to put the blocks to her. He wondered what it would be . . . Oh, Jesus! He pushed the thought out of his mind.

"How's the summer, kiddo?" he said.

They stopped at the edge of the water. "Okay, I guess."

"It's been a long time since I've seen you."

"You're busy."

"Sure," he said. "Still, I'm not much of a father. It's the kind of guy I am."

"I understand."

Did she, he wondered, and wondering he knew that he hoped she didn't, wanted kinder thoughts of her than the truth about himself. He chuckled.

"I want to buy you something, Cindy. Something you'd like and don't have. Something your mother or her new husband wouldn't buy for you."

"I don't need anything."

"Right. Still, you must want something."

"Nothing. Really."

He fell silent. The silence lay on him heavily. "You're a fine-looking girl."

"Thank you."

"What are you going to do with yourself, kiddo? I mean, you'll be going to college soon and all that."

She shrugged. "I don't know." She looked up at him from under her brows. "What do you think about the Peace Corps?"

"You, in the Peace Corps! Hey, I like it. I mean, if you're sure it's for you. If I was younger, that's what I'd do. There has to be more than just making a buck, right? Right. That's first-rate, my kid in the Peace Corps."

"I'm not sure. I'm thinking about it."

"Well, who's sure about anything?"

"BB was going to go down to Mississippi last year. To register voters, you know."

"Well, that's great."

"But Neil talked him out of it. Said what was the point and bought him an Austin-Healey, said he should take a trip across the country instead. BB ended up in San Francisco and lived in Haight-Ashbury for a couple of weeks. That's where—. Anyway, I'm not sure about the Peace Corps."

"Up to you, kiddo. After all, you're free to do whatever you want to do."

She raised her eyes to his. "I think it's not so good for kids like me to be free, no matter what we say."

"I dig it."

Again the silence. A nervous little laugh trickled out of him. "I don't know what to say to you."

"Whatever you want."

"I'm your father and I ought to be able to talk to you."

She looked out to sea. Fishing boats studded the horizon.

"Well," he said, with forced brightness. "I just wanted to let you know I was alive. Right. To let you take a look at your old man. Maybe from time to time I'll give you a jingle."

"All right."

"Or you can phone me, if there's anything—. Whatever you want, kiddo, is okay with me."

"Yes."

"Take care of yourself and say hello to your mother for me."

"I will."

"And if you need anything . . ."

"I understand."

He left her standing there and went off in search of Neil. He found Susan instead, seated with a group of women on the beach. She said Neil was playing tennis on the bayside court and Roy went there.

The game was still in progress and Roy watched with interest. Neil failed to look at home on the court despite his proper tennis whites from Abercrombie's and a racket that had cost a great deal of money. He was awkward, as if his joints were locked, unable to gain the ultimate loosening of his limbs. He was, Roy decided, out of his environment, a two-button man in a three-button suit.

After the game Neil put on a white cardigan trimmed with deep red and navy and joined Roy. He was scowling.

"Kills me," he began without preliminary, "to lose to a guy like that. He's built like an egg, in terrible condition. An alcoholic almost. He can't walk without complaining but he beats me every time."

"Bad luck."

Neil squinted suspiciously at the pallid man, decided Roy was sincere, muttered an unintelligible assent. They walked over to the boat basin and found an empty bench.

"I saw Cindy. That's some kid I've got."

"A daughter needs a father, Roy. Her real father. You have a responsibility."

"Right. And I'm going to start coming through for the kid."

"A man's got to fulfill his obligations."

"You know, baby, I've always felt an obligation toward you."

Neil looked at him. "How do you mean?"

"We've been friends for a long time. Like you inviting me out for the weekend. Damned white of you. Friendship evokes its own obligations."

"I suppose that's true."

"Bet on it. Always had the idea back in my brain that if one day I was able to help out Neil Morgan, I would do it post haste. Right down the line."

"I never knew you felt that way."

"I do. I really do. Now you didn't have to have me out for the weekend. I mean, well, after all, we haven't seen so much of each other these last few years, Neil. You've come a long way since you first opened your own agency. How long ago was that? Fifteen years, I think. I remember, Norman Wallace was your first client. And that Roberta Davis. What a piece of gash that was!" He leaned forward confidentially. "I still get a charge out of that, Neilie. Roberta Davis, big as she is in pictures and married to that society guy. A whore making it that way. Your work, Neilie, and I think that's just great, most terrific promotion job anybody ever pulled off."

"The bitch never appreciated what I did for her."

"Do they ever, baby? They do not. I tell you, you were smart, the way you kept rolling, moving into production. A man's got to keep his eye on the ball. That's what I should've done, made it into producing while the field was open. The times were right and you took advantage."

"A man would be a fool not to take advantage of any chances he gets. From agenting to production was a natural step, Roy. I saw it and I took it. I was doing all right until that trouble broke. That really wasn't my fault, you know."

"Of course I know. Everybody was in the same bag. Every one of those shows was rigged. Hell, that was show business. You couldn't take chances on doing a bad show. Or having one of the contestants look like a dummy."

"But I was the one that got burned. You won't believe

this, but there are still people in this business who hold it against me, try to hurt me because of that. You remember Oscar Morrison?"

"He was always a sonofabitch."

"And there are others. Not that they can do any real damage. But it slows me up. I've got a hell of an idea for a series that I haven't been able to close because of that kind of nonsense."

"The bastards."

Neil stood up. "Let's get back to the house. I want to take a hot shower before the old muscles stiffen up." He glanced at Roy, striding alongside. "You ought to do something about that fat middle of yours, Roy. During the winter I go up to the Y regularly, play basketball with some of the kids. Of course, I can't go for as long as I used to. But I play a pretty sound game while I'm in there. I've developed a very nice hook shot."

"Now that's great, great!" Neither of them spoke for a while. Roy cleared his throat. "You remember what I said about obligations? I wasn't going to say anything, but I was thinking about it, just now, about responsibility, what friendship means. Really means. I'm on to something, Neilie, something monumental. With very large bills involved."

"Sounds interesting," Neil said carefully.

"I am talking about rich-making money, baby."

"Good luck."

"I was going to keep it to myself, but—" Roy shrugged. "Hell, what are friends for but to share with? You want in, Neil, you *are* in."

"That's very nice," Neil said slowly.

"I don't have to tell you how TV devours material, eats up series and specials, film. All of it. You *know*. Well, I am on to a film library, more than one hundred full-length features this time. Good pictures, all of them, with top-flight star names. And a whole bunch of secondary stuff. Shorts, travelogues, the like. I have a breakdown of the entire list, of the profit potential over the short haul and the long haul both."

"Sounds good. What's the cost?"

"Not cost, baby. Investment. A sure thing. Nobody can lose."

"I worry about can't-lose propositions."

"Worry about what! There's nothing here to worry about. I give it to you straight. No risk involved. Just a small investment, only twenty-five grand, and you're set." Roy laughed shortly. "The kind of money you have tucked away in the old tin box, eh, baby! Here's a big play fixed for a winner. You and me, Neilie, and nobody else. A great parlay. We'll draw up papers, incorporate. You won't have to do a thing. Stay with your own outfit, push your own thing. I'll handle all the shit and send you a check each month."

"I don't think so, Roy."

"You don't understand. The potential is unlimited."

"I'd rather not."

"A million in two years. More to come. The profits are——"

"You better give someone else a crack at it."

"Listen, Neilie. Twenty-five grand is nothing to you. You carry that kind of bread around in your wallet. You rode high for a long time. All those shows, all that big money coming in. Neilie, this may be my last chance. Advance me the dough, for old time's sake. You know I'm good for it. Not a thing can go wrong with this deal. The film's always there and the idiot box has to have it. I can make it big on this deal and if it gets away I may never again get——"

"Try somebody else, Roy."

"Why, dammit?" The words tore out of him, rasping, thin, a bleat of despair and terror.

Neil said something about problems of his own, private difficulties. Money was tight and he was beset with financial obligations of his own. The market hadn't been good to him, and since the scandal his income had been uncertain, depressed.

To Roy, it added up to one thing. No. Something essential seeped out of him, something irreplaceable. His throat went dry and he choked on the dust of shattered dreams.

"Neil," he muttered. "I'm hanging by my fingertips and there's no safety net. . . ."

"What's that?"

"Not a thing, baby," Roy said quickly, showing his teeth in a Halloween grin. "It's all uphill and smooth for Roy Ashe. The loss is yours. There's a million bucks and a million laughs along the way . . . a million of each. . . ."

Chapter VI

Mike

For Mike Birns, time dragged. People were everywhere and only once over the weekend was he able to be alone with Elizabeth Jordan. On Saturday they took a slow walk to the Sunken Forest, a primeval woodland that provided a sharp contrast to the open beaches of the rest of the island. They picked their way along narrow trails under centuries-old trees, avoiding clumps of poison ivy and cat briar, passing through dank, dark patches never warmed by sunlight. Red-winged black birds challenged their presence, and they saw cardinals, brown hares, a darting fox, and a small deer.

Once they stepped back into the sunlight again she said, "I have to get back now." It was the birthday of one of her housemates and there was to be a party. "I'd ask you," she explained, "but it's for house members only."

A pang of disappointment came and went. He arranged a bland expression on his face, not wanting her to know that it mattered in any way.

"We can get together later, for dinner, if you like," he said, trying to sound casual.

She chewed her lip in what was a characteristic reaction. "Oh, but I promised to cook tonight."

He stared at her. Another girl would have displayed disappointment, indicated a preference for his company, talked at least of another time. Not Elizabeth Jordan. She gave nothing—cool, distant, controlled.

"Maybe some other time," he said.

Sunday night, he vowed. Sunday night the others, the weekenders, those intruding strangers in his house, and those in hers, would leave. Back to their frenetic lives, to the thick concrete heat, to the blare of traffic and early-morning garbage collections, to the foul air; they would leave Fire Island to him. The incessant weekend babbling, the oppressive tensions, the overweening cravings of people desperate to ease their loneliness; it would all end. Sunday night, a peaceful time, still, richly isolated and rewarding. Sunday night he'd take her to bed.

Sunday night, after the last ferry had left, he went to her house. She wasn't there. He went away and returned an hour later. He tried the door. It was unlocked and he went inside and called her name. No answer. To think of her being with another man infuriated him. He wanted to berate her for not being with him, instead berated himself for moving too cautiously with her.

Hell, she was just another female.

In the morning, he woke seeing her face on the inside of his eyelids. He opened his eyes and went to work. Nothing of value came. Seven times he wrote openings for Chapter Nine and seven times the words lay on the page flat, lifeless, doing nothing. Worse, it took him almost two hours before he was able to order his thoughts so that he remembered "the ritual".

He had developed the ritual for himself, a series of questions designed to indicate direction, isolate the salient ideas, clarify his thinking. He rolled a piece of fresh paper into the portable and commenced the silent interrogation.

What is this chapter supposed to do?

Answers came and he rejected them. Finally, it surfaced, highly visible, striking a visceral chord: bring Walker to a point that forces him to recognize the true threat to his life.

At what point in time must the action begin?

He reviewed the story so far, began to carve away huge chunks of extraneous material. Of course; at the moment he enters Carolyn's apartment, finds it ransacked.

What must the first sentence do?

Evoke Walker's abrupt awareness of the impending threat.

He wrote: *Walker wore fear like a hairshirt.*

It began to fall into place after that, better or worse, but being put down in readable fashion. The sentences were coming crisp and to the point. The verbs were strong, colorful; each word chosen to advance the story. Later, some cursory editing, then he would make a few marginal notes to indicate revisions to be made when he did a complete rewrite.

He worked through to two o'clock, ate a prune yogurt and an apple for lunch, then went to the beach. He spread his blanket and looked around while he applied Sea and Ski to his shoulders.

There she was—fifty feet away, trim and desirable in a black bikini that contrasted with her smooth tan skin. She was peering into the handsome face of a black-haired young man with that concentrated attention women give only to those men in whom they are singularly interested.

This accounted for the previous night, Mike told himself bitterly. She had been locked in combat, arms and legs hooked around that hard, youthful body, rolling around his bed, accepting his passion.

Mike dropped onto his blanket, tried to close off his brain. He turned onto his back, forced himself to visualize an imaginary shaft extending out of the bridge of his nose. The shaft shimmered and began to melt. A dull ache lodged behind his eyes and he gave up the game. He sat up and looked over at Elizabeth. She was laughing, head thrown back, face animated, gay. Too damned gay.

He couldn't blame her. The young man was her peer. They would have much in common, would understand the same things. He recalled his one and only visit to a discothèque, the flashing lights, the high level of electronic sound, the shifting bodies and shadows. It had disturbed him, tipped him emotionally to where he felt disoriented, out of place. But the young girl he had brought had accepted it all, enjoyed it, been a natural part of the scene.

The generation gap. He had always put it down as sociological jargon, but seeing Elizabeth now made him understand its true meaning. She had never been interested in him. He was an older man, a writer, and therefore mildly amusing to be with for a little while. But not what she required. Not what she desired. He heaved himself erect and dashed into the ocean.

He swam straight out until his arms were useless weights and his legs dragged heavily. Rolling over, he floated, the sun reassuring and warm on his face. He concentrated, made an effort to feel the tiredness in each muscle distinctly. The calf, the great flat thigh muscles, his shoulders and upper arms. He was out of shape and made a silent vow to do something about it—perhaps run along the beach each day and swim more, at least an hour a day.

This new commitment pleased him, and he headed back to shore at a comfortable stroke, renewed by this distraction. The tide was running stronger now and he gave himself to it, drifted east.

The weariness was pleasantly euphoric and when his feet touched bottom his knees gave way momentarily. He allowed himself to hang face down in the water. Out of breath, he stood up, pushed up the slope. A breaker hit him across the small of the back and he stumbled, went down, spitting sea water. He made it out of the surf and dropped on the smooth hardpack.

Cheek resting on the sand, he studied the beach and the sky, fused together from his low-angle perspective. And then a figure appeared, running in his direction. He heard a faint voice, growing louder. All reminiscent of an Antonioni movie, he told himself. The figure came closer, arms and legs flapping in that disjointed style that women have when they run. He heard his name and sat up. Elizabeth.

She stood six feet away, gasping for breath. The green eyes were grave, the brow furrowed with concern.

"You swam out so far and then I couldn't see you anymore. John said I shouldn't worry, that you knew what you were doing. But I was worried."

"John was right," he said flatly.

She nodded solemnly. "John was on the last Olympic team."

"Good for John," he bit off. He pushed himself to his feet and started back toward his blanket. She fell into step beside him.

"You're not all right," she said, after a moment. "There is something wrong."

He didn't trust himself to look at her.

"What is it?" she pressed.

"I came by your house last night. I called your name. But you weren't there."

"No."

"I suppose you were with John." He wanted to stop, to cut it off, but he was unable to. "Was he any good? He looks like a bull. I'm sure he gave you quite a night."

"You bastard," she said, very quietly.

"He's younger than I am and stronger. I imagine he's got a pretty good-sized tool and knows what to do with it."

"I hate you for this."

He swung back to face her. She was pale, the freckles more prominent, the pink lower lip tremulous.

"How do you think I feel!" he ripped out. "To see you—" He fell silent. What was he doing? They barely knew each other, had never even kissed or touched. They were strangers and she owed him nothing. "I'm sorry," he said, starting to walk again.

She followed a few feet behind. At his blanket, he threw himself down. She stood looking at him.

"Do you want me to go away?" she said.

He lifted himself onto his elbows. "I thought you wanted to go back to John."

She lowered herself to her knees. "I just met John. He came over to me a little while before you got to the beach. Please. I don't want you to be angry with me."

There was an almost pleading note in her voice, in her eyes. A kind of innocence. What a fool he was! This was no easy lay, putting out for every stud that came along. Mike trusted his instincts about sex; he'd had enough experience to know. She was a nice kid and a little out of her element with someone like him.

"I kept imagining you making love to someone," he said softly. "It made me a little crazy."

She looked away. "Nothing," she murmured.

"I know that. I'm sorry."

"One of the girls in my house stayed overnight. We decided to go to the movie and afterwards we had a drink at MacCurdy's. Two drinks actually. We talked and then we came back. Just the two of us. She left on the early ferry this morning. They call it the Death Boat. Did you know that?"

They spent the remainder of the afternoon sunning themselves, lying close enough to feel the heat of each other's body but seldom touching and then moving quickly apart. He was anxious not to crowd her, not to put too much sexual pressure on her. It occurred to him that she might even be a virgin. He meant to give her time enough to make up her own mind, to become thoroughly accustomed to him, to trust him and want him. Anything less would be a mistake.

A cloud masked off the sun and a breeze sprang up and Mike gave her his sweatshirt. It draped over her like a tent.

"You look very young."

Tiny frown lines appeared between her eys. "I wish I were older for you. . . ."

"Forget it."

"Inside I'm very old, ancient."

"Yes," he muttered dryly. "I can tell. Cleopatra reincarnated."

"Mike! Mike Birns!"

The voice calling his name was gravelly and masculine, immediately recognizable. He turned to see Eddie Stander advancing on them in that familiar muscular swagger. Mike felt a momentary sense of uncertainty, of resentment. He put it aside and extended his hand.

Eddie said how glad he was to see Mike, that he looked great, didn't show the years, and wasn't it lucky meeting this way on the beach at Fire Island. A remarkable coincidence.

Mike introduced Eddie to Elizabeth, invited him to share the blanket.

"We've got a house in Ocean Beach for the month," Eddie explained. "Edith and the boys. You've got to come visit. Both of you."

"Sure," Mike said.

Eddie ran a hand over his naked scalp. It gleamed brown. "Figured I might as well shave it all off, once it started to go," he explained. His eyes rose to Mike's head. "You've kept yours." An uncertain laugh seeped out of him. "Get yourself a trim, old buddy. You're beginning to look like a hippie."

"Maybe you're right."

Eddie smiled briefly at Elizabeth, turned back to Mike.

"Why don't we see more of you, Mike? How long's it been? Last winter, at the Knick's game in the old Garden."

"That was three years ago," Mike offered without emphasis.

"Three years! Boy! Where does it all go, time, I mean?" He gave that rasping, nervous laugh of his. "How's the writing, Mike? I read your books, some of them. I won't tell you what I thought." Again the nervous laugh. "Mysteries aren't exactly immortal literature."

"Not unless you consider *Crime and Punishment* a mystery," Elizabeth put in quietly.

"Say, you got quite a girl here," Eddie said quickly. "Got anything new coming out, Mike?"

"In the fall."

The laugh came and went. "I ought to rate a gratis copy, old buddy, autographed." His eyes swiveled over to Elizabeth. "You'd think an old friend would rate a free book once in a while."

"My business is to sell books," Mike said easily.

"Sure," Eddie said. "Sure, Mike."

Elizabeth shivered. "Oh, it's getting too cold for me. I better go back."

"I'll go with you," Mike said.

They stood up and Mike gathered up the blanket, draped it across her shoulders.

"Listen," Eddie said anxiously. "I've got a great idea. Come to dinner tonight. Both of you. There's so much to talk about, Mike. Things to catch up with. I'd like you to see the kids and Edith would love to see you again."

"I don't want to impose," Mike said.

"Your wife wouldn't be prepared," Elizabeth said pleasantly.

"Oh, she's very good about unexpected guests. Eight o'clock. Let's say eight o'clock. We'll have some drinks and some laughs." He overrode their objections. "See you later."

When they reached her house, Elizabeth folded Mike's blanket and gave it to him.

"Are you still cold?"

"I said that to help you get away. You seemed uncomfortable with that man."

"Eddie and I go back a long time, to my first summer

on Fire Island. We roomed together. We used to be friends."

"But not now."

He shrugged. "Relationships change. When he got married, everything was different. We seldom saw each other and then mostly by accident. Once or twice at parties, at a football game, once at the theater."

"We don't have to go to dinner, if you'd rather not."

"Funny thing is, part of me wants to. A kind of morbid curiosity, I suppose."

"The writer in you," she said brightly.

"Maybe so."

"I'll try to make myself pretty so you won't be ashamed of me."

He wanted very much to kiss her, to bury his face in the secret place of her, to drench himself in the sweet scent and taste of her. He suppressed the urge to tell her how he felt, certain she would be shocked and disturbed by the farce of his desire. It was going to take time to rouse her, time to bring her to that point of ease and freedom where she could accept and enjoy his passion.

"Seven-thirty," he said.

"I'll be ready."

And she was.

Eddie

"You must have another slice of the cheesecake," Edith insisted, overriding Mike's protest.

"Fantastic cook, isn't she?" Eddie said. "Makes the cheesecake herself. Really great."

"Very good," Elizabeth said. "A lovely dinner."

Edith began clearing the table. A plump woman bulging under pink slacks, pudge swelling at the backs of her elbows. Her brass-blonde hair swirled high off her head, lacquered and glittering.

"May I help?" Elizabeth offered.

"Don't trouble yourself," Edith said, without conviction. Elizabeth began to stack the dessert plates.

Eddie and Mike went into the tiny living room. It was decorated with rattan furniture and flowered curtains. Eddie brought out the Courvoisier and poured two snifters. "To friendship," he toasted.

Mike stared off into space. Dinner had been good, if somewhat overcooked, with Eddie monopolizing the conversation, holding forth on the moral inequities of the fighting in Viet Nam, insisting that any act designed to halt the war and allow the Vietnamese to settle their own political destiny was ethical and proper. Mike said he agreed. Eddie recalled what he termed the historical imperialism of the United States, mentioning the war with Mexico, the Spanish-American War, the rape of the Indians, slavery, the dispatch of troops to the Dominican Republic.

Mike pointed out that the record was not entirely negative. Eddie broke in to declaim about historical imperatives, insisting that the tide of Marxism had an irrevocable hold on the future, that violent revolution was the only answer to the ills of society. Mike considered Eddie's heroes and saw interesting contradictions in them: Marx and Frank Lloyd Wright, Freud and Jackson Pollack, Ché Guevara. Eddie perceived no warts on any of them.

"Tell me about your work," Mike said, deliberately changing the subject. "Still in advertising?" He wondered how Eddie reconciled his revolutionary fervor, his ardent Marxism, with the fact that he worked in that capitalistic stronghold, Madison Avenue.

"Yes," Eddie said, "and it's very interesting," he added smugly. "I do a lot of mail-order work these days and that requires an immense understanding of human nature."

"I throw away most junk mail."

"Most," Eddie gloated. "But not all, old buddy. I can reach you, Mike. No offense meant, but I read you like a book. That's my business. I can get you to open the envelope and read my sales pitch. To *buy*. You're skeptical. And that's part of my skill, recognizing your skepticism, using it against you, for my own ends. It's simply a matter of exercising the correct psychology."

"Manipulation, you mean."

"I'll accept the word. Let's face it, we all use each other."

Mike wondered how Eddie squared that with his social

conscience, with his passionate devotion to the cause of freedom and human dignity. He supposed Eddie had prepared a rather complicated rationale.

"Suppose you're wrong about me?" Mike said.

"What do you mean, wrong?" Eddie leaned forward, jabbed a finger in Mike's direction. "I get paid, paid damned well, not to be wrong."

"Is it possible that I don't fit into your sales-psychology textbooks, that I don't belong to a category?"

"Mike, you flatter yourself. You're a product of conditioning. Your home, schools, the papers you read, the books. Television, the films, the theater, all have shaped you, limited your experience."

"And enlarged it."

"True. But always within certain orbits. I *know* the orbits. I know how to make you function within yours."

"You make me out to be one of Pavlov's dogs."

Eddie leaned back and smiled expansively. "Precisely. Categories, you see."

"What if I belong to some remote category that you know nothing about? Or perhaps I'm starting a new category, with a membership of one? What then?"

"That's your ego talking."

"I should hope so."

A tight triumphant laugh sounded back in Eddie's throat. "Let's concede for the moment that you are something beyond my immediate experience. Something new even. Would you be new to Freud, to Jung, to Adler? I've studied all of them, all the contemporary behaviorists. There isn't anything I haven't read on the subject. I've immersed myself in it. And don't forget, I put in nine tough years on the couch."

"A long time."

"Worth it. Every minute, every penny. I discovered who I was and how to make the most of myself, at the same time do some good for my fellow human beings. Remember how I used to be? Hung on working in television, the glamor and all of that. On becoming a writer. What crap! Advertising, direct mail, that's where a man can really show his worth. He must come through, must move the product, see the results of his efforts. Sell. There are no tie games, no open ends. Always a decision, always a winner and a loser. And you better believe that Edward

Arthur Stander is a winner." Again the jabbing finger. "And there's big money to be made, important money. I'd be willing to say that I make more than you do, for all your books, all the superficial glory of being an author."

Mike allowed himself a wry smile. "You're probably right about that. Nobody gets rich doing mysteries these days, except the big names—Chandler, Spillane, John MacDonald."

Eddie massaged his slick skull. A sheepish expression crept into his face and he spoke in a quiet voice. "By the way, don't say anything about my going to a shrink in front of Edith. She doesn't understand psychiatry, calls it witchcraft."

Mike agreed not to say anything.

"Tell me, Mike," Eddie began again. "Do you ever hear from Jean?"

Mike formed the word precisely, anxious to give it no special emphasis. "No."

"I never understood that, you marrying her, I mean. Not at all the type I'd go for."

"I think we should talk about something else," Mike said softly.

"Sure, old buddy. Whatever you say."

A few minutes later, the women joined them. "I hate dishes," Edith announced, dropping heavily onto the rattan sofa. She indicated that Elizabeth was to sit alongside her. "It's good to see you again, Mike. You look great. A lot more gray and a couple of lines around the eyes. Why don't we see more of you? I know Eddie would like to. We enjoy your company. Now that you're a famous writer . . ." Her laugh was harsh, short. "When I mentioned that I knew you to some of the women in the neighborhood they were very impressed."

"Queens' housewives make everything into a big deal," Eddie announced. "It's simply a question of doing it, like everything else. I used to write myself, back in the pioneer days of television. Dramatic material, among other things. I did some work on a play which is when I decided it wasn't my cup of tea. Oh, I was good enough, talented. Maybe I didn't have the spark of genius of a Thomas Wolfe or a Faulkner. And if you haven't got that, what's the point? Just to make a dollar? Not enough for Eddie

Stander. Excuse me for being so frank, Mike. I don't want to put you down, but you know what I mean."

"I know."

"When the summer's over," Edith put in, "I want you to come to dinner, Mike. Bring Elizabeth. She's a dear sweet child. Some night."

"Yes," Mike said.

Edith manufactured a neat smile on her round face. "You are always welcome at Chez Stander, Mike. Anytime at all."

"Yes, old buddy," Eddie added. "Seventeen years of friendship. I mean, that is a lot of mileage."

Elizabeth

They walked barefoot along the beach. The tide was out and the rollers were topped with phosphorescence.

"We shouldn't have gone," Elizabeth said finally. "It was my fault."

"I wanted to go."

"It upset you."

"There's a history to it, to Eddie and me." He reached down for an empty clam shell, scaled it out to sea. It splashed three times before sinking. "Eddie was something when I first met him. Angry, but with a store of private energy and a refusal to compromise."

"I find that hard to believe," she said distantly.

"You couldn't know how he was."

"Oh, Mike, can't you see, he's struggling to justify his existence. All the contradictions, the hypocrisies. All the talk of social obligation and reform, of revolution. He's buried himself in facts and information, in quotable authors. But he has no understanding of how it really is. There's an ordinariness about him, his life, and he wants desperately to find meaning, to make himself seem important."

"I feel sorry for him."

"Don't. He tried so desperately to hurt you, to make you less."

"I know." They continued to walk. "That invitation to visit them. They've been married seven years and when they lived in Manhattan, only a ten minute walk from where I live, I seldom saw them. Twice in seven years, they had me to their home. Once on a Saturday afternoon —Edith had gone to the beauty parlor, I think, and Eddie wanted company. And one night at a party. We used to be friends. . . ."

She took his hand and squeezed. "You're so vulnerable. At first, I thought you were all muscle and balls and efficient defenses. But you're not very tough."

Muscle and balls. The phrase jarred him; it seemed so out of character, so impossible to reconcile with his concept of her.

"We went through a lot, Eddie and I. Maybe it's not good to know too much about another human being."

"He hurt you."

"I guess I was naive about friendship, expected too much. I don't do that with many people."

When they reached her house, she turned to face him. "I'll see you tomorrow," she said. "On the beach."

It was an effort to bring his mind back. "Yes, tomorrow."

She raised up on her toes and kissed him on the mouth, lips warm and lingering, a suggestion of movement. Then she went inside.

It was a long time before he was able to fall asleep that night. He lay in the dark reaching back through the years, brain flooded with images and events, memories from another era. And soon moisture formed in his eyes and he teetered on the edge of some momentous breakthrough. On the verge of a singular and evasive solution, the answer to the mystery of his life. It never came and in time he slept. But not well.

Chapter VII

Marybeth

"The Board of Trustees."

Neil Morgan spoke with pride. He measured Mike Birns for a reaction. "My second term," he added. "I believe in a man taking on responsibilities, doing what he can to create a significant and constructive community in which to live. Ocean Beach is my second home. We live here four to five months out of the year. Someone must assume the burdens of political office."

Mike had come to Ocean Beach to buy some paperback books at Kline's and to pick up a copy of *The Times*. He had been reading it on the curb of the village green when Neil appeared out of the Community House.

"Responsibility is a peculiar thing," Neil was saying. "There are times when it seems almost ludicrous, yet is no less necessary. One must dispatch small duties along with the more important ones. For example, last season I spotted this character speeding down Bungalow Walk on a bicycle. That may appear to you to be unimportant and in itself I suppose it is. But the ordinance states clearly that no one, *no one*, is to ride bicycles in the village. If the law is a bad law it should be changed but as long as it exists everyone must obey it. You see what I mean?"

"What about the man with the bicycle?"

"I arrested him. My authority as a trustee permits me

to do that. He tried to resist but was no match for me. I applied a simple judo hold to his arm and he came along, docile as a lamb. He was subsequently tried and punished."

"Punished?"

"A ten dollar fine. As I said, that may seem unimportant to you. But we live in a nation of laws."

"I suppose we do."

"Of course we do. But there are more dramatic concerns. Some of the parents are worried. Rumor has it that some of the teenagers use drugs. Pot, I imagine. Not that I believe it for a minute. The kids out here all come from good families, families who are established, set good examples. They get first-rate educations and they don't need to look for illicit thrills. Also there is always going to be some nervous parent raising the specter of juvenile sex. But it won't wash, not with these kids. Take a boy like BB. His future is clear in front of him, everything he could possibly want. A boy like that won't jeopardize it all by using narcotics or by making some trampy girl pregnant. You can see that."

"I see what you mean."

"It's not the same for a boy like BB as it was for me, Mike. I mean, I had to work for things. Oh, my father was successful, quite successful, always provided a target for me to shoot at, to surpass. Still, I had to get out there and hustle. The kids today have it all. They aren't about to risk it all for some kicks. Some of those worriers on the Board. They see only the dark side of the moon, if you know what I mean." He lifted the corners of his mouth in a humorless smile, eyes narrowed, veiled. "How goes it with you, Mike? Still writing?"

Still writing? It was as if Neil anticipated his failure, a forced return to press agentry, wished such a failure. Mike cleared his head, decided he was mildly paranoid.

"Still writing," he said mildly.

"I haven't read your books," Neil said, a prideful note in his voice. "But you can't be bad, if you're selling. Adventure stories, aren't they?"

"Mysteries."

"Ah. I'm putting together a package for TV. An important series. True crime. You do that sort of thing?"

"I write fiction."

"Too bad. Maybe when the project is launched I can throw something your way anyway. Come up with a great idea and I'll see what I can do for you. The big money's in TV." He started away, stopped. "Come on down to the house. Susan's preparing breakfast. She'll be glad to see you, and BB too. He admires people who don't conform. It's a stage, I guess, and he'll outgrow it."

"Another time."

"Right. Any time at all."

Neil drove back to the city that afternoon. Usually he remained overnight, catching one of the early ferries on Monday mornings. He told Susan he wanted to spend the evening preparing his syndication presentation for Harvey Singleton, an explanation that she accepted without question.

It was not yet six o'clock when he parked the Mercedes in the building garage. The appointment was for seven. A walk would do him good, stretch the legs, exercise the heart, the lungs. He set a brisk pace—120 steps per minute, the old Army tempo—finally cutting across Eighth Street through St. Marks Place.

All those hippies! The boys filthy and scraggly, all hair and beards. The girls, though hardly clean, managed to look pretty and desirable, with a bold way of staring at a man. And in their tight jeans. A clot of yearning lodged in his throat. He walked faster.

Marybeth was naked when he arrived at her apartment. She greeted him happily, bouncing around the room, laughing gleefully.

"Oh, Neil. Look at *me*. I'm swollen already, don't you think? My belly is bigger." She placed her hands flat on the soft white expanse. "Oh, *God,* Neil. A life is in there, a life that's part of me, part of you, darling Neil, and growing this very second. A baby. My baby." She squealed and did a pirouette. Her breasts shimmered and swung from side-to-side.

"Put something on," he commanded.

Planting her legs firmly apart, she flung her arms wide. "Look!" she cried dramatically. "My titties are bigger. They *are*. Filling up with milk for the baby. Oh, Neil, I am going to breast feed my baby, let it suck and suck until I'm dry. Then while he sleeps I'll manufacture more milk for him, like some great cow. Oh, God, I can't wait."

"What are you prattling about?"

"The baby, our baby, Neil. The baby in my belly. Your seed and mine, Neil. You put that thing of yours in me here and now I'm going to give birth."

"No you're not."

She frowned, quickly brightened. "Of course I am. It will be perfectly fine. I'm strong, Neil, and quite healthy. I have already begun eating the right things. No more pizzas and beer. I drink milk now and I bought some vitamins. You take one a day and it makes the baby strong, gives them strong bone marrow and all. Thick blood, too. I stole a copy of Dr. Spock from Brentano's on University Place and I'm reading it, underlining things. . . ."

"Listen to *me*. You're sixteen years old. *You're* the baby. That's too damn young to have a baby."

She laughed. "If I'm big enough, I'm old enough."

"Marybeth, you mustn't have this child."

"Oh, yes, I must. I really must. I love it, you see."

"For God's sake! Listen. There is no baby yet. Only an embryo. You're only a week along. Your belly hasn't gotten bigger and neither have your breasts."

She cupped her breasts, lifted them. "I can feel the milk squishing around, the heaviness. Here. See for yourself."

He turned away. "Will you listen to me?"

She crossed her ankles and folded into the lotus position on the floor. "I'm listening."

He swung around, eyes coming to rest on the dark wedge between her spread thighs. A hot flush rode down his spine. "For chrissakes, Marybeth, cover yourself."

She rose and padded over to the bed, shrugged into a flannel nightshirt. "Is this all right, Neil?"

"Sit down somewhere. *Listen.*" He fought to control the seething emotion that throbbed through his veins. How could this have happened? He and Susan had gone through hell trying to have another child. The doctors, the tests, the drugs, all to no good end. Now *this*. "I've been thinking about you, about this."

She perched on the edge of the mattress, hands folded primly in her lap. "Yes, Neil."

"You can't have the baby. . . ."

The tip of her tongue appeared between her pale lips. "I can," she said very quietly. "I will."

"You're only a child yourself. A baby is entitled to certain things."

"Love."

"More. A home, a family, a father. I'm a married man."

"You needn't worry. I would never do anything to embarrass you, Neil."

"Who will take care of the child?"

"Me."

"You can't take care of yourself. Look at the mess you've gotten yourself into."

Her brow ridged up in puzzlement. "What mess?"

"You're pregnant!" he almost shouted.

That amused her and she laughed. "That's beautiful."

"Try to understand. I have a son older than you. We live in a nice neighborhood. There's money set aside for his education, to put him through graduate school. He's always had the best, I've seen to that. Clothes, medical attention, schools, everything. He can have anything he wants. If something should happen to me, there's insurance to protect my son and his mother. You see!"

She nodded sagely.

"They're safe because they have a husband and father to look after them."

"Are they happy?"

"What kind of a question is that? Of course, they are. Who wouldn't be?"

"I'm happy."

"Nonsense. How could you be? This place is a hovel. The building should be condemned."

"I like it. It's cozy and the neighbors are friendly. People talk to each other and there are stores open at all hours and I have friends. I don't want insurance, Neil. I just want my baby."

His head jerked from one side to the other. "Be practical! To become a mother at your age is absurd. You should be able to live freely, learn what life is about, find yourself a good man."

"You're a good man, Neil. Better than you allow yourself to be."

"What the hell are you talking about! I'm exactly the

man I want to be. I've constructed my life on a proven set of values, a sound foundation, on knowing what is right, what will work and what won't."

"Yes, Neil."

"Pay attention to what I'm going to say to you."

"Yes, Neil."

"I am going to take care of everything. Everything. There is no need for you to worry. I made some discreet inquiries and I located a good man. I made the contact."

"Do you intend to marry me off?" She smiled doubtfully.

"I'm talking about a doctor," he said tightly. "And he really is a doctor, a surgeon. He does this kind of thing because he is sincerely convinced that someone competent must, you see."

"I don't see at all."

"You're not going to have the baby. This won't take long. We'll drive over one afternoon during the week, the two of us. To Newark. A few minutes, and it will all be finished. He uses anesthetics and has a full surgical setup. Nothing can go wrong. Afterward, I've arranged for you to be under the care of a good doctor here in the city. When your strength returns, I thought you might go off somewhere on a trip. A holiday. Naturally, I'll take care of all the expenses."

She stared up at him, eyes wide, unblinking, lips parted. "What are you telling me, Neil?"

"That I've arranged for an abortion."

Her hand came halfway up to her mouth. "No," she muttered. "No, no, no. You can't kill my baby. You can't."

I can, he answered silently, the words skittering around the arc of his skull. I can, he repeated, tensing his muscles against the sickness in his bowels. I must.

Chapter VIII

Roy

Roy Ashe took a taxi out to Brooklyn Heights. The idea of traveling by subway depressed him; he had managed to avoid riding in the hole during the last twelve years and he had no intention of resuming now. Even during the strike he'd stayed out, renting a chauffeured limousine. Expensive, but worth it to see the faces of the guys at the shop. First ticket, that was the way a man got a feeling for himself, his own worth.

The building was one of those sad tenements, perhaps forty years old, with black painted fire escapes climbing the beige brick front like latticework. A spacious courtyard led to an inner lobby. On the left wall, there was a bank of mailboxes, on the right, a directory of apartments. No different in Washington Heights where he had been raised, Roy recalled wryly. No different anywhere in the city, tenements similar to this one, occupied by families with middle-class aspirations and values attached to lower-class incomes: Jews, Italians, Irish, some Poles.

"In a country like this one," Roy's father would say, "a man can do whatever he wants to do. All he needs is to use his brains and work. It's all there for the taking."

Roy grinned at the memory. The old man had been all talk, no action. Take, my ass. The Depression was the best thing that ever happened to the dumb bastard. It made everybody poor so that you couldn't tell a good man from a failure. Max Asherman, man of deeds and courage. Hah! He had worked for the WPA, later gone on to become a records clerk for the Veterans Administration. Some career. Raise a family on eighty-four-fifty a week, retire at sixty-five with no money and few good memories. Two years later, a chintzy neighborhood funeral. Some life.

No thanks. Not for Roy Ashe. Brains had gotten him out of the Heights, won him a scholarship to an Ivy League college, put him next to the kind of people who mattered, who could do him some good. Brains even won a fashionable wife. Maggie. Very chic. First ticket.

Roy located the name he wanted and punched the call button. An answering buzz unlocked the glass-paneled door and he went inside. The stairs were to the left and he trudged up three flights. A faint odor of sweat filled Roy's nostrils and he grimaced. It reminded him of his black, high-topped basketball shoes, stiff with sweat and too old, shredded. Everything he had owned had been that way, in use long beyond its time. There had never been money enough to discard anything that might still be wearable. But no more. The very Mod six-button double-breasted suit Roy wore had been tailored especially for him, as was the fine English broadcloth shirt. And the antiqued leather ankle boots.

The door was at the far corner of the landing. Painted a bilious green, it was secured with two Segal locks. Roy knocked. Someone shuffled to answer. A muffled voice sounded questioningly.

"It's Roy Ashe."

The locks clicked and the door opened, a safety chain in place. Half a face and a wary eye peered out. The half-face wrinkled in distaste.

"You. Who wants you?"

"You make a fellow feel right at home, Harry."

The door eased shut and the chain rattled off. The panel swung wide and Harry Nevin, in a faded blue robe, blocked the entrance. "How'd you find this place?"

"I asked."

"Who knows? The bartender at Corio's? No, I never tell that big mouth a thing. The hooker at Delaney's? She knows better. She's on my payroll."

"The cop on the beat," Roy suggested.

The bookie shook his head. "Carter and O'Hare both know better. Those guys look out for my interests." He peered narrowly at Roy. "You trail me?"

"Invite me inside, Harry, so we can talk."

"You got the dough you owe?"

"Harry, this is important. I didn't come all the way out here to stand in the hallway."

Harry scowled, glanced over his shoulder. "I'm busy." He sighed. "Okay. Come in. But make it quick."

Harry led the way down a narrow corridor, past the kitchen, through the living room, into a small chamber indifferently furnished. An old mahogany desk stood against one wall. Harry went behind the desk and sat down. "Okay. What's on your mind?"

There was a battered attaché case lying on the desk. Roy placed a hand on it. "Money is on my mind, Harry. I must get some."

The bookie's fleshy features gathered together in disapproval and his tiny eyes grew smaller. "You need money to pay your debts, Ashe. To me."

"I came to talk about a loan, Harry."

"You already got your answer to that one." The tension drained out of Nevin's face and he laughed. "You are some kind of a case. You think I'm gonna let you snow me into advancing you twenty-five more? Cross it off. You are scratched with me. Better get those big-shot friends you're always talking about to come across for you. Not Harry Nevin."

Roy hefted the attaché case. He produced that crescent grin of his. "I'll bet a hundred there's enough collection money in this case to cover me."

Harry held himself very still. "Put the satchel down, Ashe," he said carefully.

Roy still grinned. "What if I didn't, Harry? What if I walked out of here with it now?"

Harry flexed one fleshy hand. "I was four years in the Marines, Ashe. Four island landings. The Canal, Tarawa, Saipan, Okinawa. I never played golf or tennis, Ashe, or any other games. But I had five hundred fights and there was never any referee. I was wounded twice, once by a Jap officer with a sword. I took the sword away from him and cut his throat with it."

"You surprise me, Harry."

"Put the satchel down." Roy hesitated, then did so. "You're right. There's enough cash in there to cover your losings and twenty-five more a few times over. But you get none of it. If you were clean with me, maybe I'd let you have the twenty-five, at ten per cent, maybe. But you're not clean. What's more, I don't think you can raise what you owe."

"That's not fair, Harry."

"I don't get it. Why'd you come here? You really didn't think I'd let you off the hook, that I'd give you the dough. Why'd you come? Your time's running out."

"Harry, I'm offering you a legitimate deal. A chance to make a lot of money and with no risk."

"Bullcrap. There's always risk. A smart guy cuts down on risk. He lays off bets when the action is too thick. He knows the house never gambles, always has the edge. Find your own edge, Ashe. Stop bugging me."

"You'll get paid."

"And on time. Otherwise it stops being friendly. In this business, reputation is very important. One sucker doesn't pay and right away other people get ideas. . . ."

Roy left the apartment. In the tiled hallway he listened to the chain being replaced, the two Segal locks clicking into place behind him. A sense of isolation took hold and Roy was vaguely frightened—a long way from home. Outside, it had started to rain and he was unable to find a taxi. After a little while he gave up and took the subway back to Manhattan.

Chapter IX

Mike

Mike Birns nursed the tension, the widening irritability, finding a secure warmth in the discontent. Tomorrow night would bring her back to the island, and he was anxious to see her, to be with her. At the same time, he was annoyed, resentful, angry.

Elizabeth Jordan. Just another girl. Pretty, sure. But not that pretty. And too damned young. What the hell was he doing with her, with anyone so young, so *childish?* Day after hot day, night after romantic night. Those endless, rambling philosophical-spiritual exchanges on the beach, the talk about poetry and nature, the sanctity of life, the love of knowledge, the essential goodness of people. What sophomoric crap!

He'd been there before. It recalled his college days, the bull sessions on the porch of Mrs. Halsey's boarding house, those cool evenings drinking beer and smoking, deciding that the world was a mess and what was needed to repair the damage. How *they* would improve on the job done by their parents. The kids were saying the same things today, the hippies with their talk of love, the revolutionaries, even the black nationalists. In one form or another, he had heard it all before.

Elizabeth. Goodness rose out of her like a sweet-smelling cloud and he was almost overwhelmed by it. It inhibited his normal behavior, his reactions. How long since they had met? A month? Five weeks and some days, to be exact. Oh, God, *that* long, and nothing had happened. *Noth*ing. A painful desire seeped through his gut, and he could almost taste her mouth under his own. So much time together, her two-week vacation, the weekends since. And through all of it, just occasional kisses, and even those, for the most part, brief. And after each kiss, that vulnerable, abiding expression, all faith and trust.

"I don't understand you," he said one night, when they were alone. "You seem to care for me. You *say* you do and yet you hold me off."

"What do you want me to say?" she said in a small voice.

The tension ballooned swiftly, the irritation. "Don't you understand? When two people like each other—" He broke off. "Are you so afraid of sex?"

"Maybe . . ." The voice grew even smaller.

He sat up and lit a cigarette. "You haven't learned. There isn't that much in life. Some people are always on the go. Action, action. But they don't seem to accomplish much, to get much satisfaction out of transient pleasures."

"Isn't casual sex just that?"

"Who in hell said anything about casual sex?" he snapped. "I've been very patient with you."

"And I appreciate it."

"I don't want appreciation." He took a deep breath, began again. "One thing I know, there isn't much that matters in this world. A man's work, being with friends, making love . . ."

"Being in love," she murmured.

"You want me to tell you I love you?"

She shook her head. "No."

An almost overwhelming urge to strike out took hold of him. He jerked around and kissed her hard, tongue probing deep into her mouth. Her breath was warm and sweet and her hands were light against his chest. He reached for her breast, found his way under her blouse, under her brassiere. It was incredibly exciting, as if he had never before touched a girl. Her breast was cool and firm, the nipple tumescent under his palm.

She began to quiver and make small sounds back in her throat. A protesting whimper, he decided with regret, the anger retreating swiftly. He stopped and they sat embracing for a long time, not speaking. When he finally left her and got back to his bedroom he ached. He couldn't sleep. And for the first time in years he masturbated, and hated himself for doing it.

The next day they had an argument. Earlier, they had spotted a school of porpoises and that had eventually led to a discussion of whales. She said a whale could live out of water, being a mammal, and he insisted she was wrong. He scorned her logic and she said he was opinionated, that he lectured her. He told her she didn't know what she was talking about and that if he lectured her it was in order to impart some precious amount of information into her fine but generally unused brain.

After twenty minutes of that, she began to choke on her words, began to weep. She left him sitting there, running back to her room. Furious and lacking a target on which to expend his fury, he strode down the beach, cursing himself for becoming involved with a damned kid. A stupid kid. A *virgin*. And for what? So she could play little girl with an older man.

"Oh, God," he muttered to the ocean. He must be out of his mind to tolerate her. Why was he doing it? Love? Hell, no. No love since Jean, since before the divorce, centuries ago. There had been laughs, good times, a hundred girls. A thousand. All soft and moist and anxious to please.

A slender blonde in a tiny bikini came strutting past, reminding him of the time he had wasted with Elizabeth Jordan, of the girls he hadn't met because of her, hadn't made love to, of the telephone numbers he had failed to collect. The summer was almost ended and nothing to show for it.

He went into Ocean Beach and bought *Time* magazine and a copy of the weekend *Post*. He started back. To hell with it. There was nothing back there for him. Not now. He spun around and headed for the Morgan house.

Susan

A driving rock beat reached out to him. Through the glass door he saw the blur of dancing figures. He went inside. Eight or nine people were there, in a variety of beach attire, but only two of them were men, and both were unknown to Mike. But all the women were familiar, friends of Susan and Maggie whom he had met at different times during the summer. Susan spied him from across the room and shrilled out a greeting, coming forward.

"There he is! Big Mike! Just what we need, another handsome man." She slid her arms around his waist and raised her face to be kissed. He obliged her. Her lips were wet and her tongue pushed unexpectedly between his teeth. She smelled of Scotch.

He pulled away and she grinned up at him mockingly. "You're much too sober, darling. Have a drink, a double. You know everybody, of course. Everybody! This is Mike. He's single and very sexy—or so I hear. . . ."

She poured some vodka into a glass with some ice cubes and handed it to him. He added tonic. "Where's Neil?"

She wrinkled her nose. "He went back to the city, some business or other. Besides, who cares. . . ?"

A sharp-featured woman in a peasant blouse and a miniskirt came over. "You know Elaine," Susan said. "Watch out for her, she eats men like you alive."

"With pleasure," Elaine agreed cheerfully. "Where shall I begin?"

"What's the occasion for the party?" Mike asked.

"Desperation," Elaine laughed. "And the absence of husbands. Except Stephen over there. He's married to that skinny brunette with the flat ass. They'll split soon. Very square."

Elaine shuffled off in time to the music, her movements becoming freer and fuller, hips jerking in a desperate tempo. Her head swiveled loosely and her long brown hair screened her face.

"Wild," Susan muttered. She moved closer to Mike and he felt her hand on his back, caressing absently, moving in circles, lower.

Elaine raised her face to the sky and a long wail issued

from her throat. She lifted the miniskirt so that her full fine thighs were exposed. She was wearing bright colorful panties.

"Pucci," Susan said informatively.

"Let's live it up!" Elaine cried.

Across the room, masked off by the writhing forms of the dancers, Stephen and his skinny wife were making their exit.

Susan's hand traced the waistline of Mike's swim shorts; the nail of her forefinger felt thin and light against his skin. He shivered and she giggled.

Elaine unhooked the skirt, allowed it to shimmer down the length of her legs as she moved. She stepped out of it.

"Terrific body," Susan said.

Mike agreed.

Elaine unbuttoned her blouse, tossed it aside. A narrow, brightly colored, matching brassiere barely contained her bobbing breasts.

"Fantastic glands," Susan said.

The others had ceased dancing, had formed a circle around Elaine, urging her on. She responded with broader movements, her body thumping and shaking, each part of her seemingly unrelated to the others.

Susan leaned against Mike and he could feel her small hard breasts digging into his arm. Her fingers reached under his swim shorts, played against the rise of his buttocks. "I've always wondered about you," she murmured. "Most of my friends have. Maggie and I have discussed it, what it would be like with you. You must be something special, the way you get women."

"Cut it out, Susan."

Her hand went under his trunks, and her fingers traced the line between his firm cheeks.

He shifted his position and her hand came away. She laughed. "Afraid, Mike?"

"I'm almost one of the family."

She made a disparaging sound. "There's a new lock on the bedroom door. Let's find out, Mike, what it's like, you and me. In my bed. In Neil's bed. We'll do it on his side, where he sleeps. That'll be a kick, won't it?" Her laughter was shrill and painful to his ears.

At once Elaine was there, breasts heaving, the soft

brown skin gleaming with perspiration. "Hey, beauty, dance with me."

"I don't dance."

She came closer and the thick animal scent of her drifted into the cavities of his skull. He felt his manhood shift and stir.

The old familiar craving spread out to his nerve endings.

"I could teach you to dance," Elaine husked, dropping a hand on his belly. "Lying down," she added.

"You're cutting in," Susan said.

"Oh, I was afraid of that. Well, let's both teach him. Together."

Susan gazed up at him challengingly. "Mike. Are you up to both of us?"

A vision of the twins, Lilly and Leila, faded onto the screen of his mind. He sucked air into his lungs. "Not today, thanks." He headed for the door.

"Saving yourself, darling?" Elaine taunted.

"For your wife?" Susan added.

Their laughter, coarse and derisive, trailed after him. He went directly to Elizabeth's house but she was gone, She had left Fire Island.

He knew that he would never see her again.

Chapter X

BB

"Nonsense!"

"Not to me. I mean it."

"You will go back," Neil declared. "And that is the last word on the subject."

"Why?" BB said challengingly. "I'm not learning anything at school. There's nothing there for me. Why must I waste my time?"

Neil was ready to return to the city. He had told Susan something about an early appointment on Monday morning. It was true. But he had neglected to tell her that it was with Marybeth Gibson.

"Now you listen to me good, BB," he said in that deliberate manner, projecting as if anxious to be heard in the last rows of a large auditorium. "You will go back to college. You will get your degree. And you will go on to graduate school. That's all been decided."

"By you, not me."

Neil narrowed his eyes. "I want you to think. Consider the situation. There is the war in Viet Nam, for example. You have a student deferment. Not all young men are as fortunate, you know. Poor boys, Negroes. Leave school and you'll be drafted, go into the Army, go to Viet Nam."

BB shook his head. "I won't go. I won't be drafted. I won't step forward."

Neil scowled. "I refuse to listen to that sort of stupidity. My son's no draft-dodger, no coward. Not my son. I was in service, almost four years. And when your turn comes, you'll do your duty too." His manner softened and a reasonable expression spread across his face. "But you needn't go. Not as long as you remain in school. Use your brains, BB. All you have to do is to get passing grades and you're out of the draft."

BB chewed on his tongue. A confusion of emotion and thought swirled under his skin, made him uncertain and anxious. "I don't understand you," he said plaintively. "You tell me to stay in school in order to keep my deferment, but then you get uptight when I say I don't want to go into the service."

"No conflict there, son," Neil said easily. "You know me, I am a patriot. I believe in doing the right thing, right down the line. A man has to live by a set of worthwhile ethical standards. I believe we're right in Viet Nam, morally right. We have to oppose the Communist menace, extend the battle for freedom and democracy. I served in my time, BB, and I expect you will in your time. That time is when you're called. But you haven't been called—and you won't be if you play it smart—stay in school. Keep your options, BB. Wise up."

BB hesitated. He wanted to oppose his father, stand powerfully against him. His resolution wavered. "I'm wasting the time of my life," he protested, without force.

"Tell you what," Neil said, reaching into his pocket, counting off some money. "Here's a couple of hundred. Go out and get yourself some new threads. A couple of jazzy jackets and turtlenecks. Live. And stop this silliness about quitting school. You're going to make your mother very unhappy. You listen to your dad, he knows what's best for you, for us all. Now come on down to the ferry and wave me off."

Neil

She was gone.

The plan had been simple, effective. They were to meet at her apartment and he would drive her out to Newark, to the doctor's office. Afterward, he would bring her home. So easy, so practical.

But she wasn't at the apartment. He waited, thinking she might have gone for a walk. Or shopping. Or visiting. There was no telling with a girl like Marybeth. A half hour passed and she didn't return. He went back downstairs and wondered what to do. Two young men in old clothes lounged on the stoop smoking and talking. He turned to them.

"Do you know Marybeth Gibson? On the third floor."

The two youths appraised him. A slow smile curled the moustached mouth of the one nearest to him.

"Marybeth. That's a beautiful child."

"I was supposed to meet her. Perhaps you know where she's gone."

The other man spoke in a light, high voice. "Sure, he knows. I know."

Neil felt relief. "Oh, good. I was worried. I have to find her."

"You must be Neil," the first man said.

Neil groaned silently. Everyone knew. That's why it had to be done, why he had to finish this affair, get Marybeth out of his life. She had no sense of responsibility. It wasn't that he *wanted* her to have the abortion; it was *necessary.*

"Can you tell me where she is?" he asked, keeping his voice conversational.

The second youth sucked on his cigarette, swallowed the inhalation, and looked up at the sky.

"Man, you are really strung out."

"What?" Neil said. "What do you mean?"

"Marybeth has split, man, cut you off, had you."

"Marybeth has flown far away. The bird has made a new nest, a friendly coop where all is love and niceness."

"I want to help her," Neil said desperately.

"Oh, man. Trouble's your bag. Pain's your bag. And hating and killing. Scoot. There's nothing for you here."

Neil jerked around, strode stiffly away. He was confused and afraid. Very afraid.

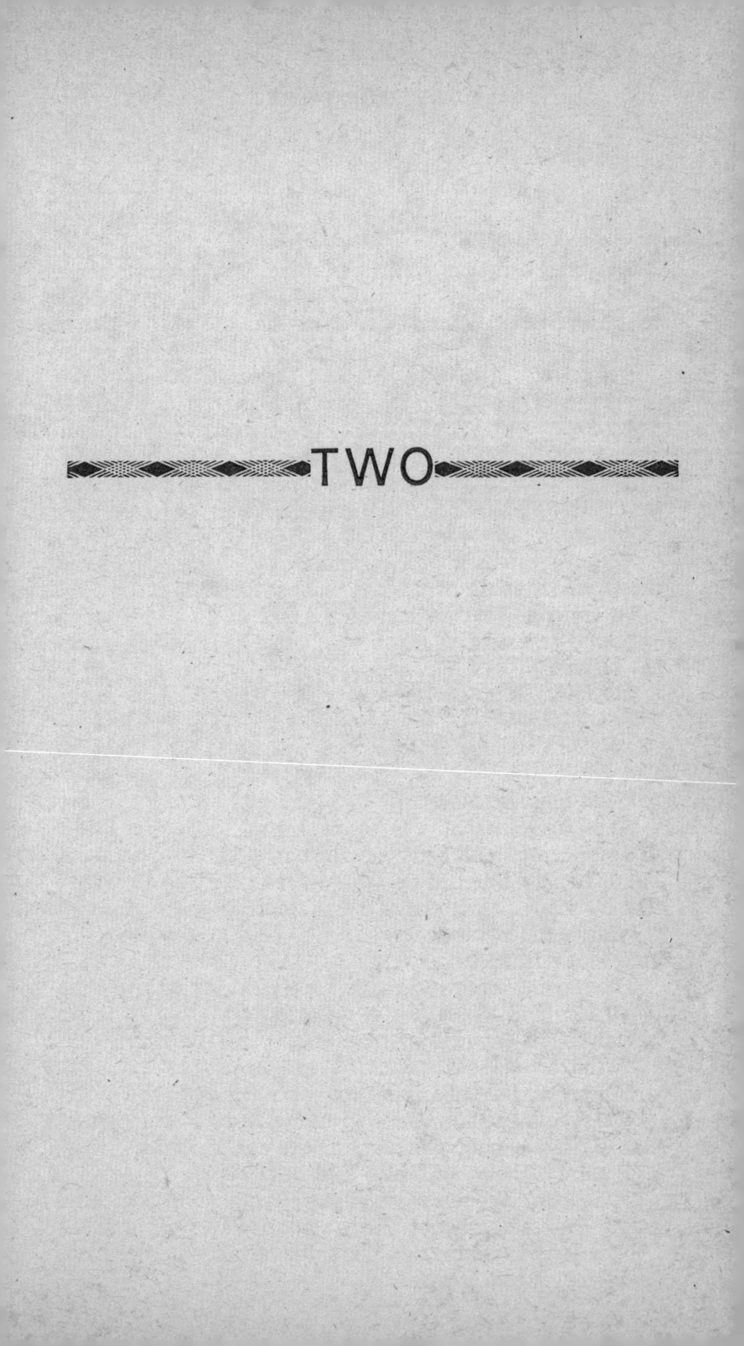

TWO

THE FIRST SUMMER

Beautiful.

The people that summer. Selected almost. Cast for their roles.

The women—girls mostly, all round and curving in neat proportions. Limbs extended, artistically articulated. Sweet and symmetrical bottoms, clenched and youthful. Breasts stylishly lifted and shaped, the contours carefully nurtured. Fashionable. "The best are champagne glass style, y'know. . . ." Faces finely constructed, delicate. Mouths level that summer. Teeth square and brilliantly white. Noses narrow, but never pinched, short. Eyes so bright, searching, blue mainly. Hair so casually coiffed. All deposited with calculated disregard into one-piece tank suits that enhanced each curve, revealed each depression and cleft, or into khaki shorts and a man's blue cotton shirt. Faded and frayed, of course.

The men—suspended in time, eternal youths. Bound to remain so. Bodies lean and muscular, proportioned. Swinging strides, easy, trained, certain. Aggressive. Purposeful. Faces firm and closely shaved, except on weekends. Voices rich, deep, vibrant, masculine. The determined expression of success. Men who tanned evenly without blotch or peel. Without burn or blister. Men in control. Their world, man.

That summer, that first summer for so many of them.

A new generation almost. The hope of the future, the New Team, the makers of a better world, the victors over Hitler and Tojo, the bright and brave ones.

They kicked it all around. In the know. Hemingway and the Yankees. Rocky Marciano and Harry Truman. The United Nations. The world that was going to be. The brief bathing suits the girls on the French Riviera were wearing.

That summer Earl Caterson, cousin to an English Duke, acting in a Broadway hit, was arrested for indecent exposure on the second Sunday in June. And Hardy Minton got drunk and tumbled into the Bay one night and drowned. And each Saturday before cocktails, there was a softball game on the beach for a case of beer.

That summer, Steve Plaine, a Closet Queen, star of his own late night television show, married Toni Laurence, his secretary; she was a lesbian. And that summer, too, a clutch of furious mothers descended upon the boat basin at The Pines insisting that the yachts were polluting the water with the issue of their heads. That summer a sated art director went to sleep on the beach and was run over and killed by a beach taxi. And Lulu Napoleon's middle son won the clamming contest—302 clams in three hours. And Jake Jacobsen went fishing every morning of every day during the season and caught nothing; his wife hooked a record-breaking striper her first time out. And Ted Bessman met the girl who would become his third wife and they lived happily ever after. And Sam Poole put in eight hours a day on his fourteenth play, sold it to Hollywood, bought a villa on Majorca and never came back to Fire Island.

That first summer . . .

Chapter I

Mike and Neil

Six Sioux brought them together, behind third base at Yankee Stadium during the Cleveland Indians' first Eastern swing around the league. Casey Stengel had won his first pennant and World Series as manager of the Yankees the year before but the Clevelanders figured to change all that this season. They had a fine pitching staff and good power in Al Rosen and Larry Doby.

Mike Birns herded the six Sioux into the dank passageway behind the Cleveland dugout, trying to remain out of the way until it was time for the ceremonies to begin. He adjusted the knot of his tie and ran his fingers through his thick auburn hair. A trio of baseball players passed, eyed the Indians. One of them raised his right hand in Mike's direction. "How!" he said, with mock solemnity. His teammates laughed.

Mike lifted the corners of his full mouth in what he hoped was an encouraging smile. He looked over at War Pony. The chief of the Sioux was a man of almost ninety years, erect and alert. Nothing showed on his bronze face. In his buckskin, beads and feathers, War Pony managed to look as if he belonged wherever he happened to be. Mike Birns, in a pin-dotted gray suit from Bond's, felt out of place.

"We'll be starting in a few minutes, Chief," he said.

War Pony gave a slow nod but said nothing.

Oh, Jesus, Mike moaned silently. How did I ever get mixed up in this!

"You Birns?"

He swung around. The man who had spoken wore a serious expression. He blinked once or twice as they shook hands. "I'm Morgan," he declared. "Neil Morgan."

Both men were in their late twenties and about the same height, but different in all other respects. Mike had fair hair and light eyes; Neil Morgan was dark, glowering. Mike had wide sloping shoulders, Neil Morgan was angular, pigeon-chested. He appeared very sure of himself in word and gesture.

"You Birns of Civic Theaters?" he demanded, eyes raking over the Sioux.

"Yes," Mike said. "And you're from. . . ?"

"B & C," Neil interrupted. "Bonten and Crenshaw, public relations. Terrific costuming, Birns. Nice work. Brooks, I suppose. Terrific outfit, Brooks."

"The real thing. They brought them along from the reservation. I'll introduce you to the chief."

"Never mind. Let's get onto the field."

Neil climbed the steps leading to the dugout; Mike and the Sioux followed dutifully. Some of the players looked at them and a thick-necked man came over, spikes scraping on the slatted floor.

"What's happening?"

Mike recognized the third baseman for the Indians—one of the stars of the league—and felt dwarfed by him, though they were the same height. "A promotion for a movie," he said sheepishly. *"Battle of Sioux River."*

The player grinned and made a friendly gesture toward the Sioux. "They look almost real."

"They are," Mike said. But the ballplayer didn't hear him. He had already run onto the playing field.

"You'd think the ballclub would have one of its press people down here," Neil complained.

"He's on his way," Mike said. "I checked earlier."

"You should have told me. These hokey gigs are a pain. Ordinarily I don't get involved in this kind of thing. But the producer of the picture is one of our clients. What's the pitch? What are these jokers going to do?"

Mike hoped that War Pony and the others hadn't heard.

He spoke softly, trying to set an example for the other man. "War Pony and his people are going to do a little victory dance on the field, with some of the Cleveland players. The news photographers——"

Neil Morgan cut him off. "I know all about photographers. You handle them. See that we get a credit for the picture. That's my client's interest."

"I prepared some material—" Mike broke off. "Here's the press guy from the ballclub."

"Leave him to me."

Neil turned smoothly, a pleasant grin on his face, his hand outstretched. "I'm Neil Morgan, B & C public relations. Welcome to the tepee. I've been looking forward . . ."

They rode back downtown in the hired limousines and deposited the Sioux at their hotel. Neil said it was too late to go back to his office and why didn't they have some coffee. Mike suggested a drink instead. Neil, though he didn't drink, said that would be fine.

In the Delmonico bar, Mike ordered a rye and ginger ale and Neil had orange juice. "What's it like at Metro?" he asked.

"All right, I guess. I've done pretty well so far and I think it's the kind of place I can get ahead in."

Neil considered that. He appeared to weigh every sentence, every word, altering the expression on his face deliberately to match what he said. Now he gathered his brow together in a thoughtful frown.

"Publicity's all right. But not over the long haul. I'm after much more. The real money lies in other areas."

"You think so? I'm making eighty-seven-fifty, and that's not bad considering—"

"Is that all?" Neil sipped some orange juice. "Come over to B & C, you'd double it in no time. Plus liberal expenses."

Mike felt a need to explain, to regain ground he had somehow lost. "Well, it isn't what I really want. I had hoped to become a reporter."

"Why didn't you?"

"When I got out of the service, all the papers were overstaffed, guys coming back from the Army plus all the people who filled in during the war. You couldn't get a copyboy's job without a degree from Harvard."

"Where did you go to school?" Neil asked with mild interest.

"I put in a couple of years on the G.I. Bill at a place called Nebraska Tech. I hoped to——"

"I was graduated from Dartmouth," Neil said. He waited for a reaction. Mike didn't disappoint him.

"That's a fine school. They had some good football teams, too. I remember..."

Neil stood up. "I should be going. I've got a beautiful wife and a fantastic son waiting for me at home."

"I'm still single," Mike said, with an apologetic grin. "I'm beginning to think I'll never get married."

"Try it. Greatest thing in the world." He hesitated. "I suppose you've got your own apartment around here someplace. . . ?"

"Well, no. I live at home with my folks."

Neil made a face of disapproval. "A guy your age, you should have your own place."

"I've never really thought about it."

"What do you do with broads? Go to a hotel, I guess."

Mike wanted to appear worldly and sophisticated, but wasn't certain what was expected of him. "I sort of ad lib it. A lot of them live alone."

Neil accepted that. "I'm looking around for a convenient place to use once or twice a week, when I get something on the side. I thought I might be able to borrow your place. Well, I better go. Susan—that's my wife—Susan and I have to start planning for the summer. It's only three weeks until we begin going out to the island."

"The island?"

"Fire Island. Don't tell me you never heard of it!" Neil sat back down. "Well, it's not a place everybody goes. A lot of artists, writers, show people. People like that. We rented a house there for the summer."

"It sounds very nice."

"Terrific. I plan on leaving early on Fridays, making a good weekend out of it. And I'll take my vacation there, too. Susan will stay out all summer. Be great for her and BB."

"BB?"

"My son."

"Oh."

"I'm sharing, of course. Another couple, the Ashes, and a friend of theirs. The house is right on the beach. Big, lots of rooms, a great old fireplace. This is going to be a very important summer to me, a chance to make the right contacts. People who matter go to Fire Island."

"It sounds very nice," Mike said again.

Neil cocked his head. "Where are you going this summer?"

Mike hesitated. For the last three summers he had spent his two-week vacation at an adult camp in the Berkshires. Not an exciting place, but he felt comfortable there, safe, knew the kind of people he'd meet, what was expected of him.

"I haven't decided yet," he said. He took a long swallow of his drink. It tasted almost sickeningly sweet.

"Come in with us," Neil said. "We've been trying to find another single man—to room with the Ashes' friend. That'll finish off the house. You seem like a reasonable man. Bright enough. Clean. I guess you'd be all right. What do you say?"

"I don't know—"

"I get it. You're worried about the cost. Don't. The entire summer, a half-share in the room, only one hundred and fifty dollars. That's a real bargain. You see it's prorated. A child, the Ashes have a little girl, rates as a half-share. The girls are going to do the cooking and we'll work out the food and booze costs the same way. It'll all work out just fine. Figure it out, every weekend beginning the week before Memorial Day and running past Labor Day. You won't get a better deal."

A ripple of excitement stirred Mike's bowels. The idea appealed to him. A weekend place, getting away from the city, from his parents. And new people. Girls. A twinge of visceral fear passed through him, then faded into a shadowy place. He turned it out of his mind.

"Yes," he said. "I think I'd like that. Count me in. What do I have to do?"

"That's it," Neil said. "You're in. The decision is mine to make and I've made it. I'll call you in a couple of days and you can send me your check. I'll fill you in on details later on. You should meet the Ashes. You'll like them. Beautiful people. An ideal couple. Perfect marriage. And that friend of theirs." Neil thrust himself erect. They shook hands briefly. "I'll be in touch. Take care."

Mike watched him leave, striding aggressively into the outside world, arms pumping, head jutting forward as if searching for the enemy.

Mike paid for the drinks and walked slowly to the subway. On the way up to the Bronx he reflected on what he had done, was frightened by it. An unsettling thought surfaced: he would have to open a checking account, something he'd never needed before, never done before. There was so much he hadn't done before.

Chapter II

Maggie

Eddie Stander arrived at the Murray Hill apartment fifteen minutes early. In tennis shoes and an old sweatshirt under a worn brown tweed jacket, he gave the impression of fashionable muscularity. His pebbled face glowered, under thinning brown hair, and his long nose was bent, bumped, as if by too many sharp blows. The scowl seemed permanent.

Maggie Ashe, wearing a floor-length housecoat, admitted him. She offered her cheek and he kissed it. He put down his scuffed leather suitcase and followed her into the kitchen.

She was a slender woman who looked younger than her twenty-five years with small features and a thoughtful expression in her soft eyes. She began breaking eggs into a mixing bowl, whipping them. "Would you prefer something else?" she asked. Her voice was whispery and her lips barely moved when she spoke. It was difficult to hear her in a crowd, but then she never talked much when many people were around.

"Eggs are fine."

She continued to work.

"Roy up yet?" he asked.

"He's shaving."

"How's Cindy?"

"Very well."

"May I go into her room?"

Without turning, she nodded.

He went into the nursery, lifted the infant out of the crib. Cindy Ashe, six months old, was a plump and pretty child, and as Eddie held her she reached for his mouth. Her fingers dug into his lower lip, and she began tugging. He laughed and hugged her and she emitted a silent laugh in return. A warm sensation washed through his middle as Cindy squirmed in his arms. Oh, God, he wanted a child of his own. A wife of his own. A home. He kissed Cindy and put her back into the crib.

Roy was in the kitchen, already sitting at the table, when Eddie got there. He looked up out of streaked eyes and spoke in a sleep-deepened voice.

"Tomato juice?"

"No, thanks. That's some kid you've got there."

"Take her, she's yours."

"Funny man," Maggie said, serving Eddie.

"I mean it," Roy said. His young-old face jerked up and down in confirmation. He ran his hand over his crew cut. "I mean it. Kids are a drag."

"Be quiet and eat," Maggie said tonelessly.

"It's the flesh," Eddie said. "Just the joy of holding that warm, living flesh."

"You're sick," Roy said, laughing loudly.

"My husband is an animal," Maggie said.

Eddie swallowed some eggs. "You're a terrific cook, Maggie. I'm going to gorge myself this summer."

"You met Neil's friend?" Roy asked.

"Mike Birns. Not yet. We talked on the phone but I was too busy when he called. So we never got together."

"Too busy screwing," Roy cackled. "That's your trouble, old buddy."

"Get your mind above your belt, Roy," Maggie said. She looked over at Eddie. "In my husband's world, everybody screws, as he so delicately puts it. Nobody makes love."

Eddie concentrated on the eggs. "I'll spend enough time with Birns this summer."

Roy issued a gravelly laugh. "He lives in the Bronx with his parents. I don't have to meet him, I know all about him."

"Well—"

"I'm sure he's a nice fellow," Maggie said vaguely. She took a sip of coffee and stood up. "I'm going to dress Cindy. If we're going to take that ten o'clock ferry . . ."

"We'll make it," Roy said curtly.

Eddie watched her leave. "You're lucky to have a wife like Maggie."

"Right," Roy said. He patted his mouth with his napkin. "She's okay. The most stylish girl at college."

"She does look . . . *right.*"

"Too bad her boobs aren't bigger. But then she wouldn't be so right, would she?"

Eddie made no reply.

Chapter III

Mike

He went with the Morgans—in that dark green Chevrolet sedan that Neil was so proud of. Mike sat in front with Neil, Susan in the back with BB. The mother and son were carved from the same stone; both black-haired and intense. Both with that penetrating look that seemed to see beyond the horizon.

Mike agreed with Neil: Susan Morgan was one of the most beautiful women he had ever seen, her skin drawn tight over finely sculpted bones, her mouth lush, her chin delicate and proud. Her hair was pulled straight back off a high forehead, then dropped down her back in a thick formidable splay.

"BB," Neil was saying. "For Boyd Benjamin. Not bad, Boyd Morgan. Has a ring to it, the sound of America." He went on. "Too bad you didn't come out to the island with us last weekend. We could've used your help. We carried out most of our things, the crib—"

"The company sent me to New Orleans. We opened a picture and—"

"That sounds like fun," Susan said, in a small voice.

Before Mike could reply, Neil spoke out. "Press agenting is okay for a while, but no way to spend a life. A small-change line. There's an awful lot of gold lying around in show business. I mean to mine some of it."

"Neil wants to produce," Susan said, with pride in her voice.

"I used to do some acting," Mike said.

"So did I," Neil put in enthusiastically. "If I didn't have a family—" He broke off.

Mike glanced at him. Neil was attractive enough to be an actor, the face all angles and shadows, set in a tense mold, animated by some dark emotion.

"You like musical comedy?" Neil asked. "There's no one like Berlin."

"Irving Berlin?"

"Right. A man of his time—his songs, I mean. His message gets home to me."

"What message?" Mike said lightly.

Neil frowned. "Come on. You must be kidding." He began to sing.

"The girl that I marry has got to be
As fresh and as clean as a nursery . . ."

"That's Neil's favorite song," Susan said.

"Why not?" Neil responded. "Look at *her,* Mike. Look at that face. Fantastic. Perfect." A harsh laugh trickled out of him. "I sang that song to Susan the night we met."

"It was the most romantic thing that ever happened to me," she said.

"We met at a USO dance. I was a public information officer, Army, and one night I went to this dance. There was Susan. They had bussed a bunch of girls in for the evening. One look was all I needed, one glimpse of that face. I made up my mind. She was for me. She would become my wife."

"And she did," Mike offered.

"Right. I wasn't about to let that face get away."

They swung onto the Southern State Parkway. The traffic was still comparatively light and Neil sped past most of the other cars. Mike looked at the speedometer. The needle moved past seventy and that made him nervous. But he said nothing.

"We're going to make it to Bayshore in less than an hour and fifteen minutes," Neil announced. He patted the dashboard. "Old Greeny is all heart." He laughed with pleasure. "I've made the trip twice now. Made it faster each time. I'll do better . . ."

He began to sing, his voice serrated but not unpleasant, passing easily from song to song. Soon they were on the outskirts of Bayshore, and Neil crossed the Long Island railroad tracks without slowing.

"The train isn't in the station," Neil said. "The train from the city."

"So?"

"It means we're going to make the ferry I planned to catch. They wait for the taxis from the station, you see."

Mike stored that away as a valuable piece of information.

They tooled past old frame houses, past an oil storage tank, across the main street, and through a parking lot behind a supermarket, turned right. Moments later they were out on the pier.

"We'll unload the things," Neil announced, "get everything on the ferry. Then I'll park Greeny."

There was a boat moored at the pier. "Is that the ferry?" Mike asked.

"One of them," Neil said.

"The *Fire Island Queen,*" Susan said.

The *Queen* was a substantial two-deck vessel almost sixty feet long. It reminded Mike of the sightseeing boats that circled Manhattan.

Once aboard, they climbed up to the open-top deck. A sense of excitement, of anticipation, gripped Mike. Freedom. As if he had entered a different world, a world clean and fresh. The day was bright, clear, the breeze off Great South Bay salted with spray. Gulls circled overhead cawing to each other and occasionally one would dive, coming up with a fish in his beak. A small boat went past, headed for the bay, two boys with fishing rods seated in it, their smooth faces solemn, intent on the adventure ahead.

They took seats along the rail and Mike looked around. He liked what he saw. Here everyone was beautiful. Even those who were not pretty came off well. The men were trim, stylishly turned out, in three-button sack suits or tweed jackets. They wore sweat socks and tennis shoes or brown loafers. A few wore leather flight jackets that announced their service during the war. A man strode past in a gray shetland sweater, gray flannel trousers and brown bluchers. It occurred to Mike that he would never have dared to wear brown shoes with gray pants.

And their luggage. Scuffed leather and soiled canvas bags in every imaginable design and shape. And children. Bright-eyed, with thick hair and a boldness of expression that Mike had never seen before. And dogs. Poodles and Beagles and Schnauzers and Great Danes. A man in an Army field jacket fired a watergun at a man in a gray flannel suit; he produced a gun of his own and squirted his assailant. Blue stain ran down the field jacket; ink. The battle drew loud cheers.

And the women. Girls, mostly. In their early twenties, vivacious, with an easy, swinging confidence, seemingly unaware of their beauty, of their bodies. There was a carelessness about the way they dressed and sat and Mike was able to see under flaring skirts to where smooth thighs disappeared into pristinely provocative white panties. A thickness came into his throat and he knew he would have a bad time with such girls. He was not used to them, hadn't truly known they existed, would not be able to cope with them.

He had never felt easy around women, any woman. He had never been sure of his own attractiveness, his ability to court them and win them—even to please them. He did not consider himself a good-looking man and knew that he had won the favors only of those girls whom nature had not favored, those who could do no better. He had never had a really pretty girl. One like Susan Morgan.

The *Fire Island Queen* began to quiver under them, its engines rumbling below. Suddenly Mike was afraid of the long summer ahead, of his ability to deal with it.

"Where are the others?" he heard himself ask.

"I imagine they caught an earlier boat," Neil said, obviously unconcerned. "We'll see them at the house."

That had a nice ring to it. *The house*. Their house, *his* house. And at once Mike was anxious to get to it, to unpack, arrange his belongings, put down roots.

The *Queen* began to move away from the pier. Mike turned his face upward and let the sun and wind play across his skin. It would be a good summer, he told himself. New and different, crowded with adventures. Rewarding. Something special would happen to alter radically the course of his life. For the better. And he was ready, he insisted silently. Ready, ready, ready, ready . . .

Chapter IV

Mike and Eddie

People were standing.
"There it is!"
Fire Island. A low lay of land, hazy blue, looming up out of the water off to the right. The *Queen* plowed a course that brought her closer inland. A cluster of houses was identified by someone as Fair Harbor. Another community. Farther on, a water tower.
"There," Neil Morgan said. "That's Ocean Beach."
Mike followed Neil's hand. Ahead, a village with houses that were old, for the most part, shingled and weathered gray. Many more of them than Mike had expected. There was also a hotel, restaurants. He had had visions of primitive living, of isolation, of long empty stretches of flat sand and dunes studded with thickets of bayberry and beach plum.
The engines of the *Queen* quieted and the ancient craft eased slowly along the channel toward the ferry slip.
"Well?" Neil asked.
"I thought it would be more sparsely settled."
"This is a wild place," Neil said cheerfully. "On a holiday weekend more than five thousand people show up. "You'll have a ball. I envy you, being single."
Mike glanced sidelong at Susan who gazed with tolerant

approval at her husband. "Perhaps Mike doesn't want that kind of summer, Neil."

He snorted disparagingly. "Sure he does. That's why he's here. To meet broads, to make it with them. Did you see the beauties coming over? From what Roy Ashe tells me, you'll have to fight them off."

Mike grinned. "I'm not sure I'd know how to fight them off."

Susan laughed and lifted BB onto her shoulder so that he was able to see ashore.

The *Queen* had maneuvered into the narrow neck of the boat basin. Ropes were heaved and tied. On the pier, people waved and called out to those aboard the ferry.

"Wave, BB," Neil ordered.

BB laughed and did as he was told.

"There's Roy," Neil said. "And Eddie."

A number of men and women stood on the dock and Mike was unable to pick out his new housemates. Children chased each other, screeching. Others, clutching possessively to the handles of toy express wagons, called out to the passengers across the narrowing span of water as the ferry completed the docking procedure.

"Wagon! Wagon!"

"What's that about?" Mike asked.

"No cars are allowed on the island," Neil said. "And no bicycles in the town of Ocean Beach itself. So wagons are used to transport luggage, to carry food, and so on. Wagon-rustling is frowned upon though," Neil added solemnly. His mouth flexed and Mike understood that Neil had intended that last as a mild joke. He smiled.

"Which ones are Eddie and Roy?"

"There! Near the ticket booth."

Mike looked. Eddie Stander in soiled tennis whites cut an athletic figure. He was close to six feet tall and husky, and Mike was immediately impressed with his hard, muscular looking body.

Roy Ashe was almost as tall, well-proportioned, with the soft set of a man who seldom extended himself. He was even-featured and his dune-white face wore a happy grin. He waved and called something lost in the cacophony of sound.

The *Queen* docked.

Fifteen minutes passed before they were able to disembark, locate all their belongings, and get them loaded aboard the two red wagons Roy and Eddie had brought. Devaney II was painted in white on the bed of each wagon.

"Devaney owns the house," Roy explained. "He owns five houses, in fact, plus one that he lives in himself. Rents them out during the summer and does very well for himself."

"More and more people are doing that," Neil put in. "Buying or building to rent out to summer people, groupers like us. I may do the same thing, once I get some extra cash together. Property values must go up."

Eddie's wary eyes darted quickly at Mike and away again. "Where'd you get the jacket?" he muttered. "Howard's?"

At once Mike felt out of place, obvious, cheap, the same sensations he had experienced on the *Queen* earlier returned. In his tennis shorts, Eddie seemed at ease. *Right.* Mike lacked that confidence, knew that he looked wrong.

"Bond's," he answered shortly.

"Same thing." Eddie turned away.

Roy was talking to Susan. "Maggie's back at the house, cleaning up, I suppose. She's a little compulsive that way. Eddie and I are going to do the shopping. Maggie says she'll cook tonight."

"I'll help," Susan said. "Once we get settled."

"Maggie makes a first-rate Strogonoff," Eddie boomed.

They had left the pier, moved past a rooming house, past the telephone office, turning into Baywalk, the main street. They stopped in front of the market.

"Let's keep things simple," Neil said.

"Neil doesn't care much for fancy foods," Susan offered.

"And salad with every meal," Neil added. "No dressing on mine. Just fresh squeezed lemon."

"Why don't I shop with you," Susan said.

Roy laughed too loudly. "I'll remember. Salad-makings and lemons. I think I've got it."

A man in tight, faded blue jeans came toward them with a harlequin Great Dane. BB disengaged his hand from Susan and went staggering happily toward the huge beast. "Doggie," he sputtered.

Neil hurried after the child, snatched him up.

The dog's owner smiled confidently. "It's all right. Prince Albert's not vicious."

Neil ignored the comment. He brought BB back to the others, set him down, and crouched, features gathered in sober concentration. "Now, BB, I want you to listen to me and understand what I have to tell you."

"Doggie," BB cried, starting off again.

Neil restrained him. "BB, you have to learn. Dogs can be dangerous."

"Doggie!"

"It's a question of judgment, son. Animals are not human beings and their reactions are not always predictable. I want you to remember that. A small boy doesn't stand much of a chance with a large dog. And I don't want you to be hurt. So you will remain away from dogs while we're here. Is that clear?"

"Doggie," BB said, trying to break free.

Neil shook him. "Do you understand what I'm telling you?"

BB began to cry.

Neil straightened up. "Take him," he said to Susan. "I hate it when a child bawls that way."

"He's only a baby," Mike said tentatively.

"He must learn," Neil shot back, "what is expected of him."

Roy laughed and rubbed his hand across his thick sable hair. "Why not throw him back, Neil? Get another model that suits you better?"

"Let's do the shopping," Eddie said abruptly.

"Right," Roy said. "You hit the market and I'll go after the booze."

"What booze?" Neil said. "I don't drink, you know."

"We've got to have booze in the house," Roy said. "Right? Right," he answered himself.

Neil nodded grudgingly. "Well, I don't drink and neither does Susan. Still, if it's to be a communal matter I can go along, if it's reasonable."

"See you back at the house," Roy said.

Neil, with a wagon-load of luggage trailing behind him, led the way. Mike came next, pulling the second wagon. Susan and BB brought up the rear. They went past shops, a bar, a rooming house, past the village green and the Community House, which was used as a movie theater six nights each week, past Kline's, a general store, and the hardware store. They made a left turn, heading toward the ocean. Here small houses lined the narrow concrete walk. For the most part, they were old, shingled affairs, some painted white, some decorated with shells and driftwood. Many of them bore names: Joy Reigns, The Last Resort, Pieces of Eight, Good Times.

A sign had been nailed into place over the door of Devaney II. It read: Neurotics Anonymous.

"Roy's work," Neil commented, without enthusiasm.

Mike was fascinated by the house. The last on the street, it perched on the crest of the dunes, gazing down at the beach and the ocean. He first perceived it as a jerrybuilt construction of weathered planks and shingles, of jutting corners, of gables and haphazard levels. A closer look revealed that Devaney II was, in fact, soundly built, designed to accommodate a growing family. Mike later learned that Devaney, a painter of secondary importance, had once occupied it, raised his sons in it, and produced many of his paintings there.

Inside, he was immediately struck by a sense of calculated sprawl. Corners opened into short hallways which led to rooms or sundecks, to an enclosed porch, to a bright dining area, to a shower cubicle, to a rear door.

They entered through a foyer, coming into a high-ceilinged central room of massive proportions, dominated by a huge brick and stone fireplace. Bookcases lined the walls and here it was dim and cool, promising the same even for those hot days of August. To the right was the kitchen and off that two small bedrooms, to be used for the children and for guests.

Left of the entrance foyer was the bedroom to be occupied by Mike and Eddie Stander. "The beds are good," Neil declared, "and it's convenient to the front door so you two studs can sneak your women in and out." Later, when Mike considered it, he realized that this was the least desirable room in the house, the noisiest, the smallest. The warmest.

Beyond the fireplace was a staircase; upstairs, two bedrooms, one facing the Atlantic; the other, smaller, less attractive, had no view of the sea. The Ashes and the Morgans would use each room for half the summer.

As for his own room, Mike faced it without judgment.

It's limited dimensions failed to please him but he told himself that it was a place for sleeping and little else. There were some clothes and books scattered possessively on the bed nearest the window and he assumed Eddie Stander had staked his claim. It made no difference to Mike. He unpacked and arranged his belongings in a tiny wooden chest, then made his bed.

He glanced out the window. There were already people on the beach and in the water. Mike turned away from the window and began taking off his clothes.

He put on his bathing trunks. They were new, a deep blue gabardine with a narrow braid of white running down the side of each hip. His mother had gotten them for him. He viewed himself, with no special pleasure, in a dirty and distorted mirror that hung over the chest of drawers. What pleasure could he get? He had no muscle tone, he was too thin, and absurdly pale. He braced his shoulders, which were lean and wide, and made his stomach hard. He was a tall man with a full head of auburn hair, a generous brow, a lean face. His chest was broad and flat and there was a splay of orange freckles across his upper back. His mouth was held stiffly, as if to convey determination and there was a searching wariness in his pale gray eyes.

He sighed and wished he had been blessed with a thick chest and bulging biceps. More, he would have preferred an olive complexion and a square, resolute jaw. He shrugged into a new gray sweatshirt, took his beach towel and started out of the room. He went back and found the suntan lotion. He was going to have to be very careful. He burned easily.

Mike cradled his head in his arms and willed the sun to dry up the pimples on his back. They embarrassed him. At twenty-seven Mike was too old for pimples.

The sun was warm, penetrating, but an occasional ocean breeze cooled his skin. He tried to estimate the time; too much sun would mean blisters and pain, peeling. He had been tan only once; on Guadalcanal, during the war. The tropical sun had transformed his skin into a golden color.

"Mike."

He sat up. Eddie Stander stood above him.

"Want some company?"

"Be my guest."

Eddie spread an old blanket and heaved himself on top of it. He took off the blue button-down shirt he wore and began to oil his swarthy shoulders and heavily muscled arms. "I am going to get black," he declared. Eddie handed Mike a small bottle. "Do my back." He rolled onto his belly and Mike poured some of the liquid onto his skin, began to spread it evenly. An army of pimples marched along Eddie's spine, Mike noted, with some reassurance.

"Don't mind if I shut my eyes," Eddie said. "You can talk to me, I mean. Best tan on the beach by July Fourth."

"I have to be careful."

"Try some of that stuff. Iodine in baby oil. First rate."

Mike completed the oiling. He recapped the bottle and dropped it on Eddie's blanket. "Is this your first time on Fire Island?"

The question rang foolishly in his own ears. The same sense of foolishness that came over him at a dance or a party when he tried to speak to a girl he didn't know. Talking to strangers was always a strain, a forced effort, and he envied men who were always at ease, smooth, never at a loss for the right thing to say.

"First time," Eddie said. He had a deep, heavy voice, and there was an almost angry sound to it. "I intend to have a first-rate summer. That Maggie, she's really a terrific cook."

"You know the Ashes well?"

"Roy's my best friend."

Mike regretted that there was nobody to say that about him. He knew only a few men and none of them well. Casual acquaintances to double-date with, or go to a ballgame with. But not *best* friends.

"Roy and Maggie," Eddie went on. "They're something. Great people. Fine marriage. I envy them. And that kid of theirs, Cindy. Beautiful little girl. That's what I want, a first-rate marriage and children."

Mike considered that. He felt no compulsion to marry, never considered it seriously or for long. And he surely entertained no compelling paternal instinct. He closed his eyes and leaned back, watched the sunspots swirling on the underside of his eyelids.

"I'm in television," Eddie said. "How do you earn your living?"

Mike told him.

The words growled out of the other man. "That's shit, flacking. Why do you do it? You must feel like a whore."

Mike sat back up, emotions churning. There was a reasonable amount of pleasure to be found in his job and he was proud of the progress he had made. Oh, yes, there were things he'd rather be doing—working in theater or on a newspaper or writing, perhaps—but he knew those were only dreams to be casually entertained in dull moments. He never believed he'd get to do any of them. Not really.

"I taught for a while," he said. "A couple of years. High-school English."

"You should've stayed with it."

"I never felt right. I heard about an opening at Civic Theaters, way down the line. It cost me money, but I took it."

"That was a mistake. Never take a cut in pay. No steps backward. Keep upgrading yourself all the time. That's the way I do it."

"I've done okay," Mike said uncertainly. "A couple of promotions, raises . . ." He wet his lips. "What do you do in television?"

Eddie turned onto his back, began to oil his chest. "I write," he said. "TV's the thing. There were more than three million TV receivers in the country at the start of the year. There'll be more. Ten million by December, I'd say."

Mike was impressed and said so.

Eddie lay back down, closed his eyes. "A few weeks ago, in Baltimore, more people watched the tube than listened to radio. First time it ever happened in a major city. You ought to get into the industry."

"How did you get started."

Eddie had graduated from Columbia with a degree in English. But even before graduation he'd made up his mind. Television was an infant affair, experimental, with room for ambitious young men. Warm and willing bodies, was the way he said it. He found a job at one of the networks as a production assistant, doing odd jobs, learning the business.

"I learned fast," he amended. "You know *The Leona Tate Show?*"

"I've heard of it."

"Leona's on her way to becoming the biggest item in daytime programming. Interviews, features, some comedy. I write for her. Joined her staff last year. I'm on my way to the top."

"I thought she ad libbed the entire show."

Eddie laughed without mirth. "Don't be dumb. Nothing is ad lib. Everybody in the industry has writers."

"How many people write for Leona Tate?"

"Four of us. A couple are real stiffs. I'm sure Leona's going to dump them soon."

Mike made himself laugh lightly. "Well, if there's room for another warm body, think of me."

"Sure," Eddie said. "You a baseball fan?" he asked, changing the subject.

"The Giants are my team."

"How do they look to you?"

"I keep hoping," Mike said, putting on his sweat shirt, certain he'd had enough sun.

"This year," Eddie said. "This year the Giants go all the way."

"I don't know. . . ."

"I *do*. Use your head. They've got the power. Mize, Cooper, Sid Gordon, Marshall . . ."

"I'd like to think so. But Brooklyn looks good. Robinson, Reese. And the Phillies. Del Ennis is a fine hitter and Jim Konstanty . . ."

"The Giants are going to win," Eddie said with certainty.

Mike nodded. "Well," he said, after an interval. "I've had enough sun. I'm going back to the house."

Eddie grunted but his eyes remained shut.

Mike picked his way up the beach. Everywhere girls, each better-looking than the others. A big-busted girl in a black tank suit rested on her elbows and watched him with lidded curiosity as he moved past.

"Hi," she murmured.

"Hi," he said automatically.

She smiled but he moved on. Damn, he swore silently. Why hadn't he stopped, joined her. His heart thumped in his chest and there was a faint trembling in his knees.

Somehow he was going to have to conquer his terror of women, learn to deal with them. Yet he had never felt sure enough. He glanced back at the girl in the tank suit. A man had joined her, said something that made her laugh, sat down next to her. Mike cursed his cowardice.

Neurotics Anonymous was pleasantly shadowed and cool. Roy and Maggie were in the central room drinking martinis. Neil and Susan were seated on the couch, holding hands. Neither of them was drinking. All of them were clean cut, handsome, looking as if they belonged, had been designed specifically for this time and this place. Mike felt vaguely discomforted.

"Hey, there he is!" Roy cried, lifting his glass. "The big stud himself."

"Oh, shut up, Roy," Maggie said good-naturedly.

Mike grinned and eased himself into one of the deep chairs. He found Roy slightly unnerving. The cocky manner, the barbed and taunting speech, the sudden mocking laughter. All intimidated him.

"What time is dinnner?" Neil said.

"After the party," Maggie said.

Mike straightened up in the chair. "What party?"

"I don't want to eat too late," Neil said. "I don't like to eat late."

"The entire house is invited," Maggie said, smiling at Mike. She was a lovely girl with a neatly structured triangular face and small features. Though slender, she had round hips and tapering, graceful legs.

"At home," Susan said, "we always eat at the same time each night."

"The body functions better if fed regularly," Neil added.

"Maybe we should work out a schedule," Roy said thinly. "We could post it," he laughed.

"Do the right thing by your body," Neil answered, "and it will do right by you."

"A rolling stone gathers no moss," Roy said into his glass.

"What does that mean?" Neil asked.

Roy shoved himself erect. "I'm after another drink. Mike?"

"That sounds good."

"Name it."

"Rye and ginger ale."

Roy made a face. He disappeared into the kitchen, to return with the drinks minutes later. "Last one and then I shower and shave. Next, party time."

Roy

They waited for Eddie to finish dressing. He appeared, wearing muted plaid Bermudas and a blue button-down shirt with water-buffalo sandals. An old challis tie served him for a belt.

"I'm ready," he announced.

Roy grinned and jabbed a forefinger in Eddie's direction. "Very slick, buddy-boy. Very Brooks Brothers."

"J. Press," Eddie corrected.

"That's the way to dress," Roy said to Mike. "Take lessons." His eyes wandered down to Mike's feet. "Those shoes have got to go."

Mike was wearing crepe-soled black bluchers. "What's wrong with them?"

Roy shook his head in despair. "You're going to embarrass the house," he declared. An abrupt laugh seeped out of him. "Get some loafers," he went on. "Brown. Try Lloyd and Haig."

"Or tennis shoes. Go to Abercrombie."

"Those khakis are okay," Roy said, "but not that way. Roll up the legs to the ankle. Thank God you're wearing sweat socks and not argyles." Again that quick laugh.

Maggie stood up. "Stop picking on Mike. He dresses fine."

Mike smiled in her direction. "I don't mind, Maggie. I may learn something."

"Not from that pair of clowns."

"Are we going to the party?" Neil asked.

"What's the rush?" Roy said. "Don't want to seem anxious. Or obvious . . ."

"Oh, Roy, be quiet," Maggie said. "My dear husband,

the free soul of all time. Except that he exists by a most rigid catalogue of regulations."

"Most of us do, I suppose," Susan said tentatively.

"Party time," Roy said. "Let's go."

They went.

Chapter V

Mike

The Woodwards were a beautiful couple by any measure. He was tall, swarthy, and handsome. She was finely boned, with creamy skin and features perfectly ordered and proportioned. He had made a large fortune in retailing; she had been a successful model when they met. He had graduated from Harvard and taken an advanced degree at the University of Chicago. She painted, studied jazz ballet, and read poetry. They had three handsome children, owned a cooperative apartment on East Eighty-first Street, a house in Palm Beach and this house on Fire Island. They spent no evenings together, if they could possibly avoid it, and they slept in separate bedrooms. Two years before, a society columnist had nominated them for the "happy couple of the year."

The Woodwards' house was new and very modern. All redwood and glass, it loomed up over the dunes like an angular crane, its great glass eyes peering this way and that. Inside, the contemporary mood continued to prevail. Paneled walls were hung with abstract paintings and all the furniture was built-in, without frills.

The living room, extending up through the two levels of the house, was crowded with people and alive with sound. Men and women of all ages and shapes, looking remarkably similar despite variations of costuming, posed with glasses and cigarettes, talking brightly, faces animated, gestures broad and quick, eyes darting.

"Nobody looks at anyone," Mike observed. He and Eddie Stander had taken up positions against one wall, strategic locations which protected their rears and provided a clear view to the front.

"What do you mean?" Eddie asked.

"When they talk. Watch. People seem to be hunting for something, someone. Never the person to whom they're speaking. They look past people, as if hoping to find something better."

It troubled Eddie to hear that, yet he suspected Mike was right. There was a general kind of dissatisfaction that prevented these people from enjoying the present conditions of their lives, and they always sought after some temporary nirvana in another drink, another funny story, another person. It had taken him a long time to perceive it, the time of his friendship with the Ashes, and the exposure to their friends.

These people. They were also the ones Eddie admired. And envied. Wanted to emulate. The men were sleek, clever, successful. They existed in the ad agencies and television studios, or the lushly quiet law offices on Madison Avenue. They were copy writers or artists or photographers or account executives and they gave off the so desirable scent of achievement. Of money.

Eddie took a swallow of his drink. He wanted to rebut Mike's remark, wipe away the sudden uneasiness that ebbed and flowed in his veins, return matters to normal. He plumbed his brain for something that would do it.

"Have you ever seen so many beautiful girls in one room before?"

Mike nodded an enthusiastic assent. "Have you noticed, they run to a type," he said easily.

"What's that supposed to mean?"

Mike ignored the hostility in the heavy voice. "Look at them. Slender mostly, on the flat-chested side, all of them. And they dress alike. Bermuda shorts and men's shirts."

Eddie growled out the words. "I like that kind of girl."

"Give me Susan. She's not only beautiful, but the most unusual girl I've ever seen. Those angular features and that long black hair, like some Indian princess."

"I'll take Maggie. The pick of the lot. Roy is a lucky bastard."

"So is Neil."

Eddie looked at Mike from under his plunging brows. "An idiot. First-class . . ."

"Oh, he's a little stiffnecked sometimes but——"

"A jerk," Eddie insisted.

Mike chose not to reply. He sipped his drink. Rye and ginger ale; there was something wrong with it. Too sweet, he decided. Gin and tonic, that was the popular drink. He made a mental note to try one soon.

Neil

Neil and Roy went out on the broad deck facing the ocean with Oscar Morrison. In his middle thirties, Morrison had the well-fed roundness of a man who already had tasted many of the more rewarding things in life. There was a comfortable set to his pudgy mouth and his ample girth gave him the look of substance, of authority. Roy had told Neil that Oscar was in line for a vice-presidency at CBS-TV, and he had promised to introduce them.

They leaned on the redwood railing and gazed out at the ocean, which was smooth and inviting. They stood silently for a moment, watching the sandpipers scurry up and down the beach in their frenetic search for sand crabs.

"Pretty shot," Oscar Morrison said finally. "Make a dramatic backdrop for a romantic scene."

"Let's get a camera crew out here," Roy said, "make a half-hour film about Fire Island. Bet it would go over. And provide some good stock footage for your film library, Oscar."

Oscar allowed the corners of his mouth to lift, but said nothing.

Neil glanced at Morrison. It was difficult for him to believe that this unimpressive little round man was as successful as everyone claimed. He looked weak, indecisive, not at all the sort you'd want to depend upon under pressure. And Oscar was beginning to lose his hair, an indication to Neil of some dark inadequacy. He was certain he would always retain his own.

"I'm not interested in film," Neil said, framing his thoughts carefully, determined to impress himself on Oscar Morrison. "I see live television as the answer for the industry, at least for the immediate future. What do you say, Oscar?"

Roy broke in before Morrison could respond. "Film is cheaper and more efficient. You can store it and that means repeat shows."

"But live productions have a sense of immediacy to them, excitement, a dramatic force that film can't possibly provide." Neil glanced sidelong at Oscar Morrison.

"Crap on that!" Roy said. His mocking laugh seemed to linger in the closing night air. "TV is a business, right, Oscar? You can edit film, cut or add to it, shoot on your own terms, make things come out exactly the way you want them to. Anyway, the public isn't concerned with good drama or quality in any form. Right, Oscar?"

Morrison turned toward them. His movements were awkward, those of a man used to remaining in one position. "Well," he began, "there's something to be said for both arguments. At the network, the sentiment is that we should proceed with all deliberation. Take a long, close look at which way the trees are bending. A great deal of thought must be given to where one's essential interests lie. . . ."

"Let me tell you where my interests lie, Oscar."

It was a strange voice. Neil swung around to see a slender man approaching. There was an anticipatory thrust to his deathhead's face, and a mirthless smile angled his flat mouth.

"Tell us about it, Sy," Morrison said easily.

"Where the money is. That's the crux of the situation. All situations. Find the gold. All that talk of art and talent. Birdshit, say I."

"Ah, Sy," Oscar breathed. "You are a perfumed and perfected example of the race, man at his loftiest, his most cultivated, gracious——"

"Shit me easy, Oscar, especially in front of strangers."

"My manners are abominable," Morrison said. "This is Sy Melman. An agent, a talent agent. Meet Roy Ashe, Sy, and Neil Morgan."

"You guys out for the summer?" Melman said.

"Watch it, boys," Morrison said happily, "or he'll claim ten per cent every time you put the blocks to your wives."

Neil produced a gracious smile and addressed himself to the agent. "We were just arguing the relative merits of film versus live television. What do you say, Sy? Where does the future lie?"

"Who cares! As long as I get my cut. I place an artist, collect my fee, and move on."

"Peddler," Morrison drawled.

"Aren't we all, Oscar? It's a great big market place and everybody's hustling something."

"There's a certain amount of truth in that," Neil said carefully. He wanted to cultivate both men, to offend neither. That meant he was going to have to walk a very narrow line. "Most talent—actors and writers, directors—they aren't capable of handling their own business affairs. Isn't that the case, Oscar?"

"I suppose, though I wouldn't put them all in that same situation. Some actors——"

"Actors are morons," Melman put in harshly.

"Performers should be able to concentrate on their art," Neil went on. "They require bright and responsible representation. Good agents."

"You said it," Melman said. "You I like. Neil Morgan. I got a rental on Bungalow Walk. Fourth one off the bay on the right-hand side. Come and visit," he said. He turned away abruptly. "See you boys around. . . ."

Morrison looked into his empty glass. "I'll say this for Melman, he's one of the hottest agents around. He's going places, and so am I. After another drink."

Neil followed him inside the house.

Susan

"Do you happen to know how Fire Island came to be called Fire Island?"

The man was exceptionally tall, with square, high shoulders and a face that at first glance was remote, bland.

Horn-rimmed glasses perched a third of the way down his long nose giving him the appearance of someone lost in the stacks of the Public Library. He gazed down at Susan Morgan and spoke in a voice both gentle and plaintive.

She had found a place for herself in a quiet corner. From there, she was able to observe without attracting attention, to give herself time to adjust to the tone of the party, to the easy aggressiveness of the people. She viewed them as incredibly sophisticated and attractive and she felt slightly overwhelmed. She was, she had been thinking wryly, a long, long way from home. She lifted her eyes to the tall man and cleared her throat.

"I don't know."

His smile was slow, reassuring. "In that case, I do know."

Her nervousness drained away. There was something about him, a suggestion of shyness along with his quiet confidence. She allowed herself to smile.

"Then tell me."

"Well," he began. "A long, long time ago, before the Mayflower, before Peter Stuyvesant, before cocktail parties and martinis had been invented, there lived on Long Island a very middle-class tribe of Indians." Susan began to laugh silently. "Well, on Sunday afternoons after listening to a lengthy sermon in the shaman's lodge, they would all get into the family canoe and paddle across the bay to this place and have a little barbecue. Those barbecue fires . . ."

Susan shook her head. "I don't believe that story."

"I see," he murmured thoughtfully. "Try this one. Prior to the American Revolution, little old men used to live out here, their only responsibility to keep great bonfires going so as to keep ships from running aground."

"That's better."

"But not totally convincing?"

She shook her head again.

"How about this one? Whalers used to burn blubber on the island and——"

"How many stories do you have?" she broke in, laughing.

"Twenty or thirty. And if those won't do, I'll make up some more." He leaned forward and spoke very softly, very intensely into her face. "You are the most devastatingly beautiful woman I have ever seen."

She flushed and drew back. "You mustn't say things like that to me."

"Indeed I must."

"I'm a married lady."

"An annoying triviality."

Her eyes flickered and the nervousness returned. "I love my husband very much."

"Why?"

The question startled her. "Neil is the best man I ever met."

"Until now."

She decided he was teasing her. "You are a very egotistical man."

"In my business, it's a prerequisite."

Now the footing was more secure. "What business are you in?"

"I'm a lawyer, a criminal lawyer. My name is Arthur Rand."

"I'm Susan Morgan."

"My name means nothing to you?" he said with controlled disbelief.

"I'm sorry. Should it?"

He laughed briefly. "You really don't know! Marvelous. I must tell you then. I am really very successful, a very famous lawyer. My name and photograph are in the newspapers regularly. You see, I get very large fees for defending very disreputable people."

"And you set them free? I'm not sure I approve of that."

"Don't be too moralistic with me. I can't afford it. I have another reputation, as well."

"Oh."

"I'm said to be devastatingly successful with the ladies."

"I'm sure you are. You're a very attractive man."

He moved closer. "That's better. There's hope for us."

"I meant what I said about my husband."

"You're too young to know what you're saying," he said lightly.

"I'm twenty-two."

"You look much younger. In any case, a woman like you deserves the best. I'm the best."

She was sure he meant it as a joke and she laughed.

She enjoyed laughing, enjoyed the way it made her feel, enjoyed the pleased glitter that came into his eyes. It occurred to her that Neil seldom made her laugh. She sobered immediately.

"You mustn't talk to me that way," she said.

"Women marry for biological reasons very often," he said, as if conducting a seminar. "Their bodies are frequently more advanced than their minds or their emotions. But now, you're older, turning the corner, so to speak, ready to gain more out of your experiences, your life. Ready for me."

"I think I'd better find my husband."

"Don't leave. Without you I'll be forced to seek another woman and that will make us both miserable."

"You're mad," she told him.

"I'm sane in a mad world," he corrected. "Admittedly my intentions are dishonorable by ordinary standards. But I stipulate that my actions will provide you with more than ordinary pleasure and satisfaction. That makes all the difference in the world."

"Are you saying the end justifies the means?"

He grinned. "I'm saying the means is the end."

She pursed her lips in disagreement.

"You have a marvelous mouth," he said. "I would like to taste it and all your other parts. . . ."

"You mustn't talk to me that way. Never again." She backed away hurriedly, leaving.

"Arthur Rand," he called after her. "Remember the name. We're going to see each other again. And again . . ."

She knew that he meant it and the idea pleased her, though she had every intention of avoiding him. Arthur Rand confused and frightened her.

Mike

A sense of solitariness encased Mike Birns. Surrounded by people and movement and sound, he felt isolated, abandoned. He went off in search of the bathroom, had to wait on line, and when he finally made it back to the living room found Eddie Stander gone. He looked around for a familiar face. Across the room, Roy Ashe stood among a group of people.

Mike joined them, and as soon as he approached a taunting snigger broke out of Roy.

"Meet Mike Birns, people. One of our bachelors. As you can see, he has to be educated, taught how to dress, how to live, how to drink. He's on rye and ginger ale."

"That would be unforgivable," a lithe blonde with impeccable features murmured, "if he wasn't such a big, good-looking sonofabitch."

Mike looked uncertainly from face to face. He wasn't used to the edged repartee that seemed so much a part of these people. Nor was he used to being mocked by a beautiful woman. He wondered what it would be like to make love to a woman like her.

"Meet Lil Blacker," Roy said. "Her face was on the cover of Cosmo last month. She's got a very tough, very jealous husband."

She took Mike's hand. "Don't say things like that to him. You'll frighten him away." She took a step closer and gazed up into Mike's face. "How tall are you, darling?"

"Six-one."

"Just right. A perfect fit. Before the summer is over, I may be unable to resist your determined advances, especially if that dumb-ass husband of mine doesn't wise up." She released his hand.

"How is Jack?" Roy said.

"Fuck Jack," she said, face clouding over. She handed her glass to Mike. "Be a dear, dear, and get me something to drink. Gin and tonic. Mostly gin."

Mike pushed his way to the bar, immersed in flesh and sound. At once he longed to get away from this party, away from Fire Island, certain that he would never feel at ease in this strangely disturbing world. Somehow everything was slightly out of focus, off-register. He would go back to Neurotics Anonymous—what an apt name—and wait for the others to return, for dinner.

But first Lil Blacker's gin and tonic. The drink made, he went back to where he had left her. She was gone and so was Roy. Nor was she out on the deck. He gazed helplessly at the cold glass in his hand.

"Go ahead," a female voice said. "Drink it. It's the slowest kind of poison."

He turned. She was short and thin, and freckles splashed across her pert, animated face. Her hair was wiry, the color of copper.

"It's gin and tonic," he said, as if that explained everything.

"Of course. That's what everyone drinks out here."

"I guess I'm a social failure. A rye and ginger man."

She wrinkled her nose in distaste. "That's too bad. Still, it isn't fatal. Try the gin."

"You think so?"

"A small sip."

He nodded and lifted the glass to his mouth. A faint aroma of flowers drifted into his nostrils as he drank. The liquid was cool and tangy. He lifted his brows. "Not bad."

"You have to develop a taste. Will you share your drink with me?"

He handed it over and she drank. "Nice party."

"I guess."

"I'm sure. Nobody warned me there would be so many lovely men in one place."

He exhaled softly. "I suppose you're right."

She placed a graceful hand lightly on his chest. "I am talking about you."

Again, he thought. First Lil Blacker and now this girl. He wanted to believe them.

"You could tell me that I'm lovely too," she was saying.

"Oh. You are."

She chewed on the rim of the glass. "Hetty Molinos is my name. Who're you?" He told her his name and there was an extended silent interval.

"I should be getting back," he said finally. "The women have prepared dinner and——"

"What would happen if you didn't go back? What would happen if you remained with me, took me to dinner instead? Would they ostracize you, banish you from the island? Strip off your merit badges?"

She was teasing him, he knew. Yet he felt compelled to explain himself. "It isn't like that. It's just that——"

"Then you will buy me dinner and some more drinks. I would like that very much, Mike. And while we're eating, you can tell me the story of your life. . . ."

Neil

Eddie Stander settled into the window seat of the entrance foyer of Neurotics Anonymous with a book, *Today's Architects: Tradition and Modernity.* Architecture was Eddie's summer project; he intended to provide himself with a thorough grounding in the subject. He wanted to commit to memory the names of the men who counted in the field, past and present, to understand the pragmatic considerations as well as the aesthetics, to be able to talk about a building and make sense. He had devoted the previous summer to reading the Elizabethan playwrights. Next summer: classical music. Eddie believed that a man should know about such things, should understand them, be able to offer informed opinions.

He made notes as he went along, jotting down the names of the giants in the field for future reading: Sullivan, Wright, Johnson, Corbusier. The return of Neil and Susan broke into his concentration.

"Is Maggie back yet?" Neil said without preliminary.

"No."

"Damn," Neil muttered. "That's what I mean, Susan. It's nine o'clock, long past a decent hour for dinner. I think you'd better make something for me. Some eggs and toast, a little salad. I'll get my protein that way. . . ."

"They should be back soon," Susan said.

"If you won't cook for me," Neil declared, "I'll do it myself."

"I'll do it. Would you like me to make something for you too, Eddie?"

"I'll wait for Maggie and Roy. I want some of that Strogonoff. Maggie's a first-rate cook, you know."

Mike

The guest cottage was separated from the house in front, shielded from the walk. It consisted of a single room and a tiny bathroom. There was a hot plate on a table in the corner. Mike Birns sat in the only chair in the room and looked at Hetty Molinos. She was sprawled out on the double bed, had been since they arrived. She finished her drink and sat up, measuring her guest with infinite patience.

"You are a difficult case," she said.

"Why is that?"

"I've never known a shy man before."

Mike didn't respond.

"It has a certain appeal, but it can be quite annoying over the long haul."

"I don't understand."

"I know you don't understand," she said with exaggerated regret. "Perhaps there's something wrong with me."

Mike wondered what was wrong with himself. To be alone with a girl this way—with a girl who clearly liked him and was obviously provocative—and still to do nothing. He sought to bestir himself, to get out of the chair, cross over to the bed, throw himself upon her. Instead, he manufactured a wan smile.

"You're very nice," he managed.

"But not attractive?"

"Very attractive," he heard himself say, as if from a great distance.

"Men have told me that I am pretty."

"Yes. Yes, you are."

"Then explain something, why haven't you made a pass at me?"

"I'm a fool," he said.

"There seems no other word for it."

Move, he ordered silently. Spring into positive motion. Act like a man. She had put it directly, making clear her reason for bringing him here. Move, he commanded.

A great, intimidating space stretched out between them, an unbridgeable gulf. He patted his lap.

"Come here," he muttered.

"You are a fool!" she snapped tightly. Then, with an almost pleading softness: "If you don't want me . . ."

"Oh, it isn't that."

She slid off the bed. "Maybe it would be better if you went away now."

He heaved himself erect, hands spread helplessly. "I'm

sorry. It isn't like that. Don't be sore at me. I want to stay. Really."

"I'm not sure I want you to. Now."

"I told you I was shy."

"You are a fool, a damned fool."

He grabbed her by the shoulders and pulled her close, his mouth coming down on hers. She struggled, managed to turn her face away.

"Easy, lover. Don't break my teeth. They're capped. Here," she said, barely audible. "Make your lips soft. Like this, baby. Ah, yes. And move them. Just a little. Ah, ah." She pressed against him, belly rotating to a private beat. "Ah, yes, so big, so strong. Here, on the bed. Let Hetty do it for you." Her hands reached for his belt, dragged at his trousers. "Ah, beautiful, just beautiful." She bent over him, eyes lidded and veiled, tongue darting at the corners of her mouth. "Hetty's going to do for you, for you. And for Hetty . . ."

He watched, fascinated. Nobody had ever done that to him before.

Neil and Susan

Neil leaned back in the chair and studied Susan at the sink. The slacks she wore were a little snug around the hips and her fine round bottom was in bold outline. Her ass had always excited him, gleaming unblemished rounds, the skin tinged with a suggestion of color. A flicker of annoyance passed through him.

"Those pants are pretty tight," he said.

"You think so?"

"Either let them out or don't wear them anymore."

She turned. "I like them. I thought they fit rather well."

"I don't want other men seeing my wife's ass."

"Oh, Neil . . ." She wondered if other men *did* look at her that way. Arthur Rand, she thought. A blush came into her cheeks.

"Do what I say, Susan." Neil pushed himself up from the table. "You almost finished with the dishes?"

"A few minutes more."

He looked at his watch. "Ten o'clock and the Ashes aren't back yet. We're going to have to resolve this eating schedule at once."

She reached for a dish towel. "Would you like to take a walk along the beach? It's lovely out and——"

"Not tonight. I'm tired, Susan. Besides, I want to give you something before we go to sleep." A thin laugh issued from his mouth.

"Oh," she said, disappointed. It *was* lovely out there, the ocean calm and tranquil, the night air pleasantly cool. A walk *would* have been nice. "All right." She finished drying her hands.

"You take a shower," he said. "I'll go upstairs."

"Yes, dear."

He went up to their room and undressed, lay down on the bed, head cradled in his hands, waiting. Five minutes later, she appeared wearing a floor-length black lace nightgown. He raised himself onto his elbows. In the soft glow of the lamp on the night table he could barely make out the pink tips of her small breasts, a suggestion of that black patch between her legs.

"Jesus!" he said, voice thick and rough. "You look fantastic."

She held herself very still and let him study her, the way he liked to.

"There's something about you," he muttered harshly. "Something whorish . . ."

Her response was automatic. "Is that what I am, your whore?"

"Do you think you could? Do it for money, I mean. A lot of money."

She hesitated. "No one ever offered me money."

"Were you really a virgin when we met?"

"You know the answer."

"Have you ever wondered what it would be like with another man? Would you like to make it with someone else?"

"I'm your wife."

"Would you like to?" he insisted.

"Just with you," she managed, thinking of Arthur Rand, of what he would look like naked, of how it would feel to have him inside of her. "Just with you."

"Take off your nightgown."

She lifted it slowly, tantalizingly slow, pausing as it reached her full thighs, then going on, exposing the dark and feathery wedge.

"Beautiful," he breathed, gazing along the length of his naked body, past his erect manhood. "It's perfect, so neat, every hair in place."

"I'm glad you like me."

"Now come here," he said gruffly.

She dropped the gown to the floor and took her place beside him. He kissed her hard.

"Spread your legs," he commanded. He rolled on top of her, middle thumping anxiously. "Help me. Help . . ."

"Wait, Neil. You're hurting me. Wait a minute. Let me get something."

"Put it in. Now, now. Oh, yes. Here. Here, here's what you want, a good stiff cock into your belly, all . . . the . . . waaaay. . . ." And in that split moment of time it came and went, was ended. A series of short sobs sounded back in his throat and he felt himself blinking reflexively in the darkness. But it made no difference since there was nobody to see. He rolled onto his belly and went to sleep.

Chapter VI

Susan

Mike woke startled and afraid. Seconds elapsed before he was able to locate himself. His sleep-crusted eyes worked around the small, still unfamiliar room. The other bed was empty. It had been late when he got back and Eddie had been asleep. Now he was gone. Sunlight filtered around the edges of the curtains. Mike peered out. The beach was dotted with people.

He wrapped a towel around his middle and headed for the bathroom. Finished, he donned swim shorts and the sweatshirt, went into the kitchen. Susan was seated alone at the table, drinking coffee and smoking a cigarette.

They greeted each other.

"What would you like for breakfast?" she asked, rising.

"Just some coffee."

"You should eat something."

"You sound like my mother."

She brought the coffee and sat down again.

"Have the others eaten yet?" Mike asked.

"Eddie's on the beach, working on his suntan. And my husband is out somewhere with BB."

"And Roy and Maggie?"

"Still asleep, I imagine." She dragged on the cigarette and he watched with interest. She held it awkwardly between thumb and forefinger.

"I thought you didn't smoke," he offered.

"I don't very much. At least not when Neil's around. He doesn't care for it."

He studied her while sipping the hot coffee. Her thick black hair was tied back in a bun, accentuating the exotic look of her. She seemed very young and startingly beautiful.

"Do you always do what Neil wants?" he said absently.

"I try."

"You really love him very much?"

"He's the best man I ever met."

He looked into his cup. That was the second time she had said that. And in precisely the same words. Could Neil Morgan be that exceptional a man? He viewed Neil as being aggressive, if not courageous, shrewd but not particularly profound, a man who did many right things for the wrong reasons. He supposed it was too soon to make such judgments, that he barely knew Neil. Or his wife.

"Who's taking care of Cindy?" he said.

Susan brightened. "I gave her breakfast. That child is the most independent creature I've ever come across. And the happiest. Right now, she's in her crib and not a sound of complaint from her. BB is different. Leave him alone and he screams and throws a tantrum."

"Cindy's a beautiful child. So is BB." He searched for something more to say. "Do you intend to have more children?"

"Oh, yes. At least two more."

"Well, you've got lots of time. You haven't been married very long."

"Two years, ten months, three days."

That amused him. "You keep a very exact record."

She blushed. "I figure it from BB's age, you see. He was conceived on our wedding night."

He raised his brows skeptically. "How can you be that certain?"

She giggled and averted her eyes. "Nothing happened before that night."

His disbelief showed.

She lowered her voice. "It wasn't my fault. Neil wouldn't. I wanted to, but he said it wasn't right, that I had to be pure on our wedding night."

"I see."

"I wish he hadn't been so determined about that. It wasn't very nice and I hurt for a week afterward." Again the smooth cheeks grew red and she looked away. "I'm sorry," she muttered. "I never talk about such things."

Looking at her, listening, getting to know her, he found it easy to believe that she had been a virgin before her marriage. There was an innocent, almost helpless quality about her. She had been raised in a small town in Minnesota, had never been farther than fifty miles from her birthplace until Neil brought her to New York. That was a dramatic change, Mike reasoned. And she probably still hadn't gotten used to it.

He swallowed the last of his coffee and carried the cup to the sink.

"I'll wash it," Susan said.

"Guess I'll hit the beach for a while."

She watched him leave, his bottom tight, flat, muscular. She wished Neil had a bottom like that.

Neil and Mike and Eddie

BB trailed a receding wave down the sandy slope. Then, shrieking happily, he scampered back as a new wave came rolling in. He repeated the ritual with wave after wave, giving voice to an exaggerated joyful terror.

"He seems to be enjoying himself," Mike said, coming up alongside Neil. They stood watching BB.

"I don't like the boy running away from things," Neil declared firmly.

"Give him time. BB's just a baby."

"He's old enough to stand his ground."

He moved across the sand, calling to his son. BB turned and Neil crouched down, took him by the shoulders, gazed soberly into the boy's face. "Look here, BB. There is no reason for you to be afraid of the waves."

The boy laughed. "Not afraid."

"Then don't run away from them."

"Want to."

"Now, you listen to me, BB. In this world, a man has to

face things head-on and learn how to deal with them. Do you understand me? Running away just won't do." He reached for BB's hand. "Come, we'll go into the ocean together.

BB pulled back. "No!"

Neil scowled. "Don't raise your voice to me, BB. I said we're going into the water and we will go in. Let's go, Son."

BB began to cry. Neil lifted the boy and walked into the water until he was waist deep. Holding BB under the arms, he dipped the boy into the swelling sea. BB kicked and howled out his despair. It did no good. Gradually, Neil lowered him until his feet touched the ground, the water covering his shoulders. BB screamed and struggled frantically. For a brief moment Neil lost his hold on the child and he went under. Neil retrieved him, but he came up coughing seawater and sputtering. Neil held him up.

"Now BB, you are making a fuss about nothing," he said in a reasonable voice. "The water doesn't even reach to your chin. And you aren't at all hurt. A little salt water went down the wrong way, that's all. Now stop acting like a baby. Isn't it time you grew up a little?"

He carried the boy out of the water and put him down. BB, his face pale and tear-streaked, staggered a few steps up the beach. He spun around, shouted an unintelligible and defiant something at his father, then ran for the house.

Neil went back to where Mike was standing. Sure of himself, he cheerfully told Mike, "Next time it won't be so difficult for the boy."

"You think that's the best way to handle the situation?"

"A boy must learn to stand up on his own two feet. It's something that can't happen too soon in life. I intend to make sure BB learns that lesson. It's my duty as his father."

Before Mike could reply, they were joined by Eddie Stander. He was wearing a baseball cap. "I just bought it in the village," he explained. "The sun's a little too strong for my scalp." He gave a small, deprecating laugh. "My hair's a little thin, I guess."

"You're already brown," Mike said enviously. "I'll never get that color if I stay out in the sun all summer."

"It's a good walk into the village," Eddie went on.

"About half-a-mile," Mike said.

"Nonsense," Neil said. "It can't be that much. No more than half that. I bet I could run it in under a minute."

Eddie and Mike exchanged a skeptical glance. "For how much?" Eddie gritted out.

Neil hesitated. "Well, maybe it is farther than I thought. But two minutes, for sure. Not a second more than that."

"Tell you what," Eddie said. "You do it in two minutes, I'll buy you and Susan all you can drink at Mom Stones."

"I don't drink," Neil said. "But I'm going to do it. This afternoon. You can time me."

"I'll take your word for it," Mike said, wanting to change the subject. "You left the party early," he said, turning to Eddie.

"I wanted to do some reading," Eddie said.

"Those parties are good for only one thing, to make contacts. Otherwise, all empty talk and cigarette smoke and people getting drunk."

"What are you reading?" Mike said to Eddie.

Eddie told him.

"I just finished a terrific novel," Neil said. *"The Cardinal.* It's by a man named Henry Morton Robinson, and it really impressed me. He really has something to say in this book."

"What does he say?" Eddie said thinly.

Mike sensed in Eddie a growing antagonism toward Neil. If Neil was aware of it, he gave no sign.

"It reveals how a man of purpose and belief can make it, no matter what sphere he functions in in this world."

"Anybody can do anything, if he wants to badly enough. Is that what you're saying?"

"That's it. I'll bring the book out next weekend so you fellows can read it."

"Don't bother," Eddie said.

"I'm into an interesting book myself," Mike said, hoping to ease the tension. *"The God That Failed."*

"One of those self-help books?" Neil asked.

Mike fought to suppress the laughter that came into his throat. "Perhaps, in a way. Six writers recount their experiences with communism and their withdrawal——"

"Don't waste your time with that crap," Eddie snapped.

"Koestler, Richard Wright, Gide, Silone . . ." Mike said mildly, refusing to argue. "Interesting men. Why crap?"

Eddie jabbed his forefinger at Mike's chest. "The only salvation for this screwed up world is socialism. Face it, those men, they lacked the moral strength, the guts, to see it through. All quitters and quitting makes me sick."

"I go along with you about quitters," Neil said. "Determination, staying power. These are the qualities that count."

Mike frowned thoughtfully. "I think capitalism may be on the decline as an economic system. But pure socialism doesn't appear to be the answer either. Some combination . . ."

"I'm a one hundred per cent capitalist," Neil said. "Sure, if this was a socialistic system then I'd be a socialist. Don't think I don't know a man has to be adaptable to get on. But if I had the choice . . ."

"We were talking about quitting," Mike went on. "Men see things differently. They change their minds, evolve, grow."

Eddie stared out to sea. "Better drop it." His heavy voice was larded with anger and implicit threat.

"All right with me," Neil said. "I don't read that much anymore, except an occasional novel. I prefer to watch television or go to the theater."

"Did you enjoy *Caesar and Cleopatra?*" Mike said. "The performances were superb."

"I prefer musicals," Neil said. *"Gentlemen Prefer Blondes.* That was magnificent. Carol Channing's performance was outstanding. That's what I call show business."

Eddie snorted contemptuously. "Show business. Especially musicals. They're all brassy and corny."

"Not the better ones," Neil said aggressively.

"They're all the same," Eddie said caustically.

Neil responded with unexpected fervor. "What about *Annie Get Your Gun* and—?"

Mike looked down the beach and saw Hetty Molinos. For a moment he was surprised, even startled, as if she belonged to the past and should have remained there. He felt a mild reminiscent desire. In a green bathing suit, her slender figure was invitingly curved, and desirable. He moved toward her.

Mike

They sat next to each other on the sand and talked about the weather, the temperature of the ocean, the danger of over-exposure to the sun. She leaned forward, hugging her knees, and he was able to count the verterbrae marching down her back. She *was* too thin for his taste and not as attractive as she might have been. Her features were good enough and she had a pleasant smile, but somehow the combination fell short of true prettiness.

Still . . . The memory of the previous night came flooding back and there was a shifting response in his crotch. He lifted his knees and leaned forward. He glanced over at her and she smiled briefly.

"I love the beach," she said. "Don't you?"

"Not really. I'm not much for ocean swimming and the sand feels peculiar against my skin."

She faced him, eyes wide with curiosity. "Then why are you here?"

"It seemed like a good idea. I never did anything like it before."

She settled back. "You'll have a marvelous summer, I'm sure."

"What makes you so sure?"

"Look around. All these beautiful girls. You'll have a different one each weekend. You'll make out like mad."

He filled his lungs with air. "About last night . . ." he began.

"Yes?"

"I don't want you to think that that's all I'm interested in."

She laughed happily. "You don't have to say a word. I did what I wanted to do and I enjoyed it."

"So did I. Very much."

"I've never had any complaints."

"Why don't we get together tonight, have a drink or two . . ."

She avoided his eyes. "I don't like to make plans." She swung around, the freckled face grave. "I'm only here for the weekend, you see. I have to spread myself around, meet some new men, I mean, it isn't that I don't like you.

I do. You're very sweet. But I can't depend on one man for dates, can I? If we shouldn't get together again, why don't you give me a call back in town. I'm in the book."

"Oh," he said, startled, disappointed, caught off-balance. "Yes, I'll call you." He stood up.

"Where are you going now?"

"I thought you wanted to be alone, to meet other people."

"There's time enough to do that this afternoon," she said, gazing up at him. Her face was guileless, her voice wispy and girlish. "Wouldn't you like to show me the house you're staying in? And your room. You could offer me a drink, too." Her soft thin mouth lifted at the corners. "Wouldn't you enjoy some more of last night? I know I would."

He found it impossible to speak, his throat glutted with desire. He extended his hands and drew her to her feet.

Neil

After lunch, the lifeguards erected the volleyball net. Neil promptly recruited a team: Eddie, Mike, and three other men. Roy refused to play.

"A game for goons," he declared cheerfully. "Look at all of you, big and ungainly. I'm at least six feet tall myself and you all tower over me. I won't have anything to do with you freaks."

They took it as a name—Neil's Freaks. They won their first game handily which permitted them to remain on the court to face a challenging team. Neil went up to each of the players, offering congratulations, urging an even greater effort.

"You'd think this was the World Series," Mike said quietly to Eddie, while they waited for the new team to warm up.

Eddie grimaced. "And he's such a lousy player."

It was true. Neil played with tremendous intensity, but he lacked grace and coordination. He knew what to do, how to do it, but his execution left much to be desired.

From the back court, his returns were either too deep or too shallow. And at the net, his timing was invariably bad.

Thanks to a number of flashy kills by Eddie, and Mike's steady play, Neil's Freaks won their second match. They lost the third game by eight points.

Mike, gleaming with perspiration, headed for the ocean. Eddie followed right behind him. They swam out side-by-side, then floated for a while. When they returned Neil was waiting for them on the beach.

"We should've won that last game," he said, by way of greeting. "Mike, next time you play in closer to the net. Use your height to advantage. Hit down on the ball, kill it more. You've got to take the game more seriously."

"Why?" Mike said.

Neil stared at him without comprehension. "To win, of course." To Eddie, he said, "You did fine up front but when you're playing back you have to——"

"Knock it off," Eddie growled.

"It's just a game," Mike said.

Neil blinked. "Winning takes practice. Even in games. It prepares a man for the real battles. After all, winning is all that really matters. Now you two boys have the athletic ability, but you aren't using it properly. You fool around too much."

"Crap," Eddie said, running back into the ocean.

"It's for fun," Mike said.

"Winning is the most fun," Neil replied. "Winning . . ."

Roy

Mike lay on his stomach. A beach towel drawn up to his shoulders protected him from the late afternoon sun. He dozed, the thrum of beach-sounds a dull, comforting shield. It was a warm, soft world, pleasant and secure. Suddenly, a brassy blast startled him into a sitting position. It was repeated, familiar this time. A bugle.

First call.

"What the hell is going on?"

Eddie, spread-eagled alongside, facing the descending

sun, grinned with malicious joy, not even opening his eyes. "That's Roy. Cocktail time."

Mike looked up at the top deck of Neurotics Anonymous. Roy stood there in his brown leather flight jacket. In his left hand, a martini glass. In his right, the bugle. He delivered another blast.

"Is that what we're in for all summer?" Mike said.

"According to Maggie, yes."

"Somebody is going to murder him."

"That's Roy. Everybody likes him. Always laughing. A first-rate guy."

Mike stood up and gathered his belongings. "A drink would go good now. And a hot shower. You interested, Eddie?"

"Why not?"

Neil

They ate the day old Strogonoff with noodles and salad. Except Neil. Susan broiled a steak for him and prepared some salad without dressing.

"This dinner problem has to be settled," Neil announced over coffee.

"What problem?" Roy said absently, pouring beer into a glass.

"The beer, for example," Neil said. "I don't want to appear to be picayune . . ."

"He means cheap," Roy put in.

". . . but Susan and I don't drink beer."

"Relax, buddy-boy. I'm paying for the beer." He grinned mockingly at Neil. "Have a brew. On me." He lifted the glass and drank. "Every man a tiger!"

"There's also the question of what time we're going to eat."

"When we're hungry!"

"Stop it, Roy," Maggie said softly.

"That's all right," Neil said evenly. "I've got as much sense of humor as the next one. But take last night, for example. It was ten o'clock when I finally finished eating.

And no one else was here. Now if we are to have a community kitchen then it seems to me all of us must be responsible to it."

"What have you got in mind?"

"We should establish a dinner hour and hold to it. Lunch and breakfast are another matter. A certain amount of flexibility is in order there."

"Sorry about last night," Maggie offered. "Roy and I went to the Joyners for drinks and lost track of time."

"Which reminds me," Roy said. "There's a piece of fluff over at the Joyners, a real prize. One of you studs ought to knock her off. It's prime stock."

"The boys can find their own girls," Maggie said.

Roy spread his hands expansively. "Just doing a good deed. Her name's Lucille and she's there for the taking. I imagine we'll bump into her later when we make the rounds."

"Rounds?" Mike asked.

"Of the bars in town. Big doings on Saturday night, a social routine."

"If we can get back to the food for a minute," Neil said.

"What about the food?" Maggie said, with quiet concern. She wanted to put an end to Roy's constant barbs, his refusal to deal seriously with the ordinary events of their lives. She wanted them all to work at making ther summer existence unfold without friction. She had warned him to temper his mockery, to make allowances for the peculiarities of others. It had done no good.

"I think we should work out some sort of an accord regarding the purchase of food," Neil said. "Decisions have to be made as to who does the shopping and what gets bought. There has to be some kind of a balance."

"Agreed," Roy said thinly. "Work it out with the girls, Neil. Anything is okay with me."

"All right, I will."

"I just want to know one thing. How you can eat salad without dressing?"

"My health is a matter of some importance to me."

"A little French dressing can't hurt you."

"You're wrong. Oil, vinegar, spices, that combination of ingredients results in a high degree of stomach acidity which . . ."

Roy stood up and wiped his mouth with his napkin. "I arranged for a sitter to come in," he said to Neil. "To watch the kids while we're out tonight. Will you split the fee?"

"Well, of course. That's the way to handle it. The first one back can dismiss her. No sense running up costs."

Roy

Mom Stone's faced the bay, not far from the ferry slip, a few steps above street level. A long room, it widened considerably toward the rear. Tables were scattered about to form a dining area, and beyond them was the long bar, now crowded and noisy. Up front, along the right wall of the narrow entrance area, a big-bellied man played rinky-tink piano. A cluster of people had gathered around him.

A slender youth with yellow hair stood alongside the piano and began to sing, doing an imitation of Johnny Ray. It was a very good imitation, Mike conceded. He stood along the opposite wall with Eddie, working on his second drink, watching people flow from group to group, looking at the women, trying to pick out those who were unmarried, trying to work up nerve enough to approach one of them.

"That boy's not bad," he said to Eddie.

"I can't stand faggots."

"You mean he's queer? How can you tell?"

"I can smell them a mile away."

Roy appeared with two girls, a broad grin angling across the sunburned face. "I been hunting for you studs. Look what I've brought. A present for each of you. Can't have you standing around with empty hands." Then indicating a short, slender girl with a lively expression on her face, he said, "This is Mildred." He put his hand on her backside and pushed her forward. "Pick a man, Millie."

She giggled and pointed to Eddie. "This one. Okay?" she added uncertainly, looking at the man she had chosen.

"Sure," he answered. "Why not?"

"Can't you do better than that?" she responded, disappointed.

"Sure he can," Roy said, laughing too loudly. He indicated the second girl. "You're all that's left, Mike. She's stuck with you."

She was a round girl who would fight against encroaching fat for the rest of her life. In her early twenties, and at the apex of her beauty, she had full hips and breasts, but her flesh was still tight and smooth. She opened her mouth in a silent laugh and looked up at Mike.

"Being stuck with you is going to be a pleasure. Can you say the same?"

"Of course," he said quickly.

She looped her arm through his. "Good. Then you can buy me a drink." She led him toward the bar.

Neil and Susan

Roy pushed his way into the center of the group, a glass in each hand. He gave one to Susan. "Gin and tonic, lady."

"Thank you, sir."

"Is that all I get?" He manufactured a leer. "A drink should be worth more."

"Watch out, Susan," Maggie said. "A playful Roy is a Roy who's all hands."

"All mouth," he corrected. He kissed Susan on the lips, a lingering caress. His tongue brushed against her teeth and she shivered. He withdrew.

"Not bad," he said. "You ought to have it copyrighted, Neil."

The tall man scowled at his wife. "That's your second drink, Susan. I think you've had enough." He took her face between his hands. "Such perfect beauty, I don't want it ever to spoil." He released her and she sipped her drink.

"What a lovely sentiment," Peggy Woodward gushed. The violet eyes fluttered and her moist lips lifted in a wide smile. "The only time my husband says anything nice to me is when he wants to ball it up."

Bette Miller, a tall woman with close-cropped hair, spoke. "My husband doesn't say much about anything. Half the time I don't even know when he's shot his load, except that he rolls off and goes to sleep."

"Don't they all," Lil Blacker said. "The bastards!"

"I think your husband is cute," Bette Miller said to Peggy.

Peggy grinned thinly. "Be my guest."

"I think you're cute," Roy told Peggy. "Especially between those great big boobs of yours." He placed his glass into the shadowed cleavage.

She squealed happily. "I can't tolerate cold, you horny little man. Next time try something hot."

"You'll have to get down on your knees for that."

"Oh, Roy," Maggie burst out. "For God's sake!"

A tall man joined them. It was Arthur Rand. Peggy looped her arm through his and pressed her huge bosom against him. Susan experienced a pang of jealousy.

"Does everyone know Arthur Rand?" Peggy was saying. "The world's best lawyer and he's good at other things too. Not that I'd know from first-hand experience."

He disengaged himself and greeted Susan by name.

"I didn't know you two had met," Peggy said, her voice dropping insinuatingly.

"At your party," he said quietly.

"Well," Peggy said, "then you should meet Susan's husband. This is Neil Morgan."

Arthur Rand offered his hand and Neil shook it perfunctorily.

"I want to congratulate you, Mr. Morgan," Rand said. "You have a most charming and lovely wife."

"Everybody thinks so. I thought she was the most beautiful woman in the world, first time I saw her."

"Where was that, Mr. Morgan?"

"Oh, Christ!" Peggy Woodward exclaimed. "Call him Neil."

"At a dance," Neil said. "An Army dance."

"How romantic!" Bette Miller drawled.

"Go on," Lil Blacker said. "I can use a little romance, even second-hand."

"The minute I saw Susan I knew I was going to marry her."

"Marry!" Rand said. "Not dance with her or make love to her? Marry."

Susan drained the last of her drink and Roy took her glass, withdrawing in the direction of the bar.

"Marry," Neil repeated. "One look at that face convinced me. I spoke to her and danced with her and later I took her home. I had to hire a taxi and it cost me twenty-three dollars round trip, but it was worth it."

"I bet it was," Peggy sniggered. "Tell us all the gory details."

"Well, the first thing I had to let her know about was that I was Jewish. Susan had never seen a Jew before I came along. Her father was an itinerate Methodist preacher, a ridge-runner."

"How quaint!" Lil Blacker muttered. "Get on to the good parts."

"I think every woman should make it with a Jew," Peggy said brightly. "There's something special about a stripped dick."

Bette Miller's features gathered in a disturbed frown. "Aren't all men the same?"

"Not by a long shot," Peggy said. "And I do mean long. Are you suggesting that Clark's the only man you've had? Oh, sweet Jesus, we've got to do something about *that*."

"All right," Bette said.

Roy returned, handed a full glass to Susan.

"Number three," Neil said, without emphasis. Susan drank, looking off into space. "You know I don't believe in alcohol and tobacco."

"You make it sound like some sort of tribal ceremony, having a drink," Roy offered.

"You were telling us about your first night with Susan," Lil Blacker urged.

"Yes," Neil said, picking up his place easily. "I explained about being Jewish, that not all Jews were bearded, synagogue types. I have my own private, personal arrangement with God. I told Susan about my plans for the future, for advancing myself, that I intended to have a family. I outlined my philosophy of life."

"Better believe it," Roy said.

"Be still," Maggie said.

"Go on," Peggy said.

"We reached Susan's home."

"And you went inside?" Lil Blacker prodded.

"Oh, no," Susan replied. "My father wouldn't have approved. He was very strict, you see."

"You went out into the wheat fields," Peggy said hopefully.

"You found a haystack," Roy added. "I made it once in a haystack. Terrific. Very fine odor, fresh-cut hay."

"Roy," Maggie said. "Shut up."

Neil spoke in a controlled, well-modulated voice. "The cab was waiting and there was no point in running up an exorbitant tab. Still, I was determined to impress Susan, to make sure she'd remember me. . . ."

"So?"

"So I kissed her. I mean, I *really* kissed her, a kiss she couldn't possibly forget. No one had ever kissed her that way before."

"Was it as good as all that?" Bette Miller asked Susan.

Susan chewed on the edge of her glass. "No one had ever kissed me that way before," she said softly.

"Or since," Roy added, giving his dirty old man cackle.

Even Susan laughed at that.

But not Neil.

Eddie

Adjoining Ocean Beach to the east was Seaview. This was a family community, which meant fewer groupers, fewer single people. In fact, Seaview, in appearance and attitudes, was a sand-laced wedge of suburbia. Beyond Seaview was Ocean Bay Park. Less developed than the neighboring communities, the Park drew mainly singles, but a different breed than Ocean Beach.

"Cops and firemen," was the way Roy Ashe described them, with fair accuracy. "Civil-service types who consider beer an upper-class beverage and a college education evidence of a Communist plot. . . ."

Eddie Stander and Mildred walked along the beach to the far end of the Park, to the fence that proclaimed the beginnings of Point o' Woods, a private community.

"Let's go back," Eddie said. They were the first words he had spoken since they had left Mom Stone's.

The moon was high now and almost full, dropping a silver shaft across the night sea. Waves broke with gentle lapping sounds, depositing bits of phosphorescent animal life on the sand.

They strolled without haste, an arm's length apart, never touching. Mildred glanced at Eddie once or twice. He puzzled her. Not like most of the men she met. He was silent, and that pleased her. Most men talked too much, as if selling something. Always trying to convince her of their cleverness, their wittiness, their sexiness. This one was different. Back at Mom Stone's, when he had spoken, it had been with an almost electric urgency, all hot concern, passion. She wondered what it would be like to have that passion inside of her.

He was, she decided an exceptionally attractive man. The hardness of him reminded her of those statues of warriors at the Metropolitan Museum. Roman warriors. A gladiator, she amended. There was a battered cast to his face, and a deep, forbidding quality about the thick brows, the twisted nose, and his down-turned mouth. And those almost black eyes. A shiver traveled down her spine.

"Tell me about your work," she said, not really caring. "About Leona Tate. I hear she's a very kind and generous woman."

"A tough broad. She knows exactly what she's after and how to get it. She's had three husbands and each marriage advanced her career. When they outlive their purpose, she dumps them."

"But her success on television. Surely her husbands didn't do that for her."

"People like me do that, writing for her, making her sound clever or funny or sympathetic."

"You must be a good writer."

"And getting better."

"What do you intend to write finally? Books? Plays?"

He stared at her. A furrow appeared between his brows. "I intend to produce. Television. That's where it all is. The money, the power, the rewards—personal and otherwise. With power in his hands, a man can accomplish all the good and decent things that should be done in the world."

She smiled encouragingly. "Give me an example."

He looked straight ahead. "I want to be able to change everything in this country. Uproot all the fat cats, shake them up. I want to educate people to the evils of a system that enslaves for profit and personal gain. A system that puts millions of human beings in social and economic bondage."

"I'm not sure I understand."

He glared at her. "That's the trouble, nobody understands. We've got a country that's rich and getting richer, powerful and becoming more powerful, yet there are people in the United States literally starving to death."

"I can't believe that."

He slammed a fist into his other hand and a taut urgency crept into his voice. "The Indians," he spit out. "They are dying and not a thing is being done for them. The Negroes. Who the hell cares?"

"But it's all changing and——"

"Nothing has changed. Nothing's going to change. Unless people like me change it. The system is rotten and must be radically altered. To do that means violence."

"You mean a revolution?" she asked, surprised by the passion in his voice.

"A revolution. A cleansing by fire and blood that will purify this corrupt nation and its people."

"Oh," she said, returning to her matter-of-fact voice. "I don't think there will ever be a revolution in the United States. Not the way things are. Things have to happen gradually. . . ."

"Why don't you shut up!" The words tumbled out of him hard and short. "You don't know what it's all about. I've made a complete and profound study of every revolution the world has ever known. Ours. China's. Russia's. France's. I've read everything Marx wrote. And Lenin. And you think you can tell me! Who the hell are you to dispute Karl Marx's theories?"

"You don't have to get angry," she said apologetically.

A spasm rode up his limbs and he jerked around toward her, stiffly, awkwardly. She retreated, afraid he was going to hit her. Waves broke across her feet.

"You're stupid," he snapped hoarsely. "Stupid. Go away! You're dumb and ugly and I can't stand the sight of you. . . ."

Roy and Maggie

Maggie lay on her side in bed, facing the wall. Even in the darkness he was able to make out the deep cleavage between her firm buttocks. He lay next to her and cupped one cheek.

"I approve," he said thickly. "When they invented the phrase 'piece of ass' they must have been thinking about you."

"I'm very tired, Roy," she said.

"I'm not." His forefinger traced along the crack.

"Roy, please . . ."

He shoved his hand between her legs, fingers curling into the hairy Venus mound. She gasped and her thighs tightened automatically.

"Don't!" she murmured, keeping her voice down. "You always do that."

A smug chuckle sounded back in his throat, and he worked his hand, seeking her clitoris, and he found it. His fingers cleared the silky hairs, separated the lips of the vagina. After a minute, the muscles of her thighs grew slack and she rolled onto her back, legs spreading.

"There," he husked. "I do it this way, because it gets to you, makes you hot."

"Be gentle, Roy . . ."

"Sit up."

"Oh, not yet, Roy."

"Now."

She kneeled between his legs, facing him, and her fingers performed a skillful dance down his belly, along the inside of his thighs, to his testicles, his penis.

"You look great," he said. "You've got a great body, your ass, your legs, that hairy box of yours."

"I'm glad," she said flatly.

He was all hard and quivering now and she stroked him with practiced indolence.

"You approve?" he asked.

"You know I do. Very much. I approve. I love it."

"Remember the first time we did it? In that old Buick, in the back. You had one leg out the window and the other over the front seat. I surprised you, didn't I?"

"You surprised me, yes."

"Say why."

"You were so big. I didn't expect a man your size to have such a big tool."

"Not many guys have a rod like that going for them. Do they? *Do they?*"

"No," she managed.

"Tell me."

"Please, Roy . . ."

"Tell me. About the others."

"There's never been another tool like yours. Never. It's the biggest, the most beautiful, the best."

"How is it with other men? Touching them, I mean, getting fucked by them?"

"I don't want to talk now. I want you inside me."

"Tell me."

"Please, Roy. You promised you would—"

"I bet Peggy Woodward doesn't argue with her husband."

"Oh, Roy."

"Can you imagine her stripped? That great ass of hers, those fantastic tits. One of hers would make six of yours."

"I'm sorry I'm not bigger."

"What would you say if I told you I made it with her? If I told you how it was?"

"Don't, Roy! Please."

He laughed coarsely. "I didn't, Maggie. Not yet, anyway. What about you, Maggie? Have you been unfaithful to me yet?" Abruptly he pulled her down, kissed her mouth roughly. "I'm just talk, you know that. I wouldn't make it with Peggy or anyone else. And I don't want you to screw for anyone else."

"I know."

He pushed her onto her back, mounted her. "Here," he husked. "Take it. The way you want it. I'm going to be good for you, very good. Very good . . ."

And he was.

Neil

They had arranged their blankets in a cluster. Maggie, Susan, Bette Miller, and Peggy Woodward were playing Monopoly in one corner of the woolen spread. Cindy's crib was set up under a beach umbrella nearby. Eddie was flattened out on his back, face lifted to the sun. Mike lay alongside, wearing a shirt, reading. Neil stood watching BB play his game of retreat and attack with the waves. No one knew where Roy was.

"It's getting cooler," Maggie said.

"It's nearly four o'clock," Bette said. "What time are you all leaving?"

"What ferry shall we take back, Eddie?" Maggie said.

"Whatever you say," he said, not moving.

"How about you, Mike?" Susan said.

"Same answer."

Neil joined them. "Keep an eye on BB, Susan. They're getting up a volleyball game. You guys want to play? The lifeguards against the groupers. Let's show those kids how it's done."

Mike closed the book and stood up. "Want a game, Eddie?"

"Go without me."

They played three games and lost them all. That night, driving back to the city, Neil kept replaying each game, recalling errors, their strategic mistakes, suggesting ways for them to improve. "Next time," he declared, with confidence, "we'll beat those kids easily."

Mike doubted it very much.

Chapter VII

Mike

Two weeks later, on a Thursday, Civic Theaters ordered Mike Birns to go to New Orleans to publicize the opening of a new movie. He spent ten days there, missed two weekends at Fire Island, and lost the beginnings of his tan. An hour before he was scheduled to return to New York, he received a call from the home office instructing him to do advance work in six cities in Georgia and Alabama for a personal appearance tour in connection with the release of another film. Not until the final weekend in June did he get back to Ocean Beach.

Changes had been made. Maggie and Susan had moved into Neurotics Anonymous on a full-time basis, with their children. By now the women were tanned and sleek, their attractiveness enhanced.

"You're getting better-looking all the time," Mike told Susan.

That drew a pleased smile and a mock curtsy from her. "How kind you are, sir, to say so."

This lighter side of her had never been revealed before and he was charmed by it. He resisted the impulse to embrace her.

The next morning Mike began working again on his tan. He went about it systematically, intelligently, but without the obsessiveness Eddie brought to the procedure. He lavished large amounts of lotion on his pale skin and timed his beach sessions to the minute. Two exposures each day, morning and afternoon; thirty minutes on each side at each session. By Sunday evening, his skin was perceptibly darker, more crimson than tan, and tingling hotly.

Determined to expedite matters, Mike bought a portable sunlamp at Bloomingdale's and spent a few minutes under it each evening during the week. By the following weekend he felt fairly secure about exposing himself to the sun for long periods of time. To add to his satisfaction, his back had cleared up.

Friday noon he telephoned Neil Morgan at his office. But Neil had already left for Fire Island. Next Mike dialed Roy Ashe.

"Hey, stud, how's it going!" Roy greeted him.

"Pretty good, Roy. I just called Neil. He's already taken off for the island."

That knowing chuckle sounded over the wire. "He's got a thing going."

"What *thing?*"

"He's been in training," Roy said. "Running."

Mike had an urge to laugh, to say something clever and full of mockery. Instead, when he spoke, his voice was tinged with disbelief and wonder.

"He's really working out?"

"Regularly. Not only is he running back and forth across the island, but he's been practicing in town. He joined a gym and——"

"But why?"

"Partly for the dinner Eddie promised to buy, if he did it."

"It's got to be more than that."

"It matters to Neil, winning. More than anyone I've ever known. You've seen him play volleyball. He said he'd make the run in less than two minutes and he'll break his hump trying."

"How's he doing?"

Again that caustic laughter. "Eddie's got nothing to worry about. Neil's got it down to three minutes. But he'll never make two."

Mike wasn't so sure. A man who could dedicate himself with such single-mindedness might very well accomplish his purpose. He experienced a grudging admiration for Neil. If only he weren't so damned pompous. . . .

"I suppose you're calling about a lift out," Roy was saying.

Mike brought himself back. "Yes."

"No can do, buddy-boy. I'm carrying a pair of pretty chicks with me. I told you about Lucille Quirk. She's with the Joyners. And a friend of hers."

A familiar sense of loneliness took hold of Mike. Fire Island seemed very far away and almost unapproachable. "Well," he made himself say, with appropriate lightness, "guess I'll take the train."

"Call the Long Island for information. At Bayshore, taxis meet the train. They'll take you to the ferry. Check with Eddie. Maybe you can ride out with him. See you on the sand, buddy-boy."

Mike dialed CBS, was put through to Eddie Stander. "I thought we might go out together on the train. . . ."

"I arranged for a ride," Eddie said brusquely. "You know Oscar Morrison. They just made him a V-P. Anyway, I bumped into him in the corridor this morning and he offered me a lift. I'd invite you along, but frankly, there's some business I have to talk to Oscar about."

"Oh, sure. No sweat. See you on the sand."

He hung up and called Long Island information. It took nearly three-quarters of an hour to get through. Only then did he remember that this was a big weekend, the Fourth of July.

The *Queen* eased away from the pier and began its slow run up the channel toward Great South Bay. On the upper deck Mike found a seat along the rail, watched the gulls perched on the pilings, the people fishing off the pier, the small cruisers plowing past. Out in the bay, the *Queen* picked up speed. The hot rays of the afternoon sun and the soft breeze raised a ballooning exultation in Mike. The pressures of the city, of work, fell away like extraneous baggage. A feeling of tranquility came over him, of easy strength, of belonging. Anticipation came alive behind his navel and he thought about the pleasures the island had to offer, pleasures he had not yet tasted. He remembered his times with Hetty Molinos and vowed to have other such times with other girls. He vowed to act more aggressively with women, to go after what he wanted, to miss nothing. He intended to store up some memories—happy oncs.

There was an extensive world beyond his experience, Mike reflected, and Fire Island was simply a part of it. A microcosm of what was and what could be for him. He thought of the people he had met, the sleek, beautiful people, so sure of themselves, so successful in everything they did. There was Eddie with his varied and extensive knowledge of so many things, reading constantly, committing so much to memory. There was Neil, dedicated, resolute, knowing who he was and where he was heading. There was Roy with his nimble brain and sharp tongue, his carefree mobility.

They were all of an age, yet Mike felt younger than each of them, less adequate. And with good reason. They had accomplished so much more than he. In their careers. In their personal lives. Their futures loomed bright and secure. Eddie had talked about his plans, a series of exciting projects that included writing for such network shows as *Studio One* and *Westinghouse Playhouse,* eventually producing programs himself. Neil would certainly accomplish big things, using publicity as a springboard to a stunning career in show business. And Roy, selling advertising space, was being rewarded richly. He was a natural salesman; he could sell anything, go anywhere.

Mike felt squeezed and helpless. Civic Theaters bought his services cheaply, and he feared he was worth no more. An ordinary press agent. Without much to look forward to. He was no hotshot flack; he didn't have the drive or the flamboyant skills required; he would never become a department head at Civic. Or anywhere else.

He supposed it was better than teaching English. At least there was the promise of greater income. A teacher knew his salary limitations.

A groan of frustration died behind his teeth. There was so much he wanted to do, to accomplish. To *be*. It went beyond the obvious rewards, beyond making money.

At college, he had done some acting and had often dreamed about a career in theater. If not acting, then directing. That appealed to him. Or writing . . . That was a bitter thought. Whatever he had done, or fantasized about doing, he had always yearned to write. Yet nothing had come of it. Three incomplete short stories. Some descriptive paragraphs that stood alone and proved nothing. A few character sketches. Oh, *God,* how he wanted . . .

"We're almost there."

A pleasant, faintly accented voice, drew him back. Ahead the island swam into focus, the clusters of houses, the outlying sandbars, the clamming boats.

"Are you out for the summer?"

He shifted around. The woman had a healthy, comfortable look that made her seem older than she was. Matronly, almost. Her pink cheeks were round and her blue eyes were clear and unblinking. Large-boned and heavy-bosomed, with a stunning white smile, she glowed with good health and friendliness.

"Yes," he said. "You too?"

"Yes. Schottland and I are in a house called 'Last Stop.' Perhaps you know it. A big shambling place near the beach on Evergreen. You must come by sometime. We have cocktails every Saturday at five. Some very nice people."

The sudden invitation was pleasant to hear, but he put it down to her particular graciousness. It meant nothing.

"Thank you for asking me," he said, pleased. She was a remarkably handsome woman and reminded him of Ingrid Bergman. The accented voice heightened the resemblance. She might also have been Swedish, he decided.

"I meant it," she said gravely. The big smile returned and she offered her hand. "I'm Eva." He took her hand and was surprised by the strength of her grip. He told her his name. "I've seen you on the beach," she said, the words coming out separately and distinctly, declaratively. "You did not notice me. Once you were walking by yourself, deep in thought. I imagine you are a man who thinks deep thoughts. And another time I was with Schottland. You were playing volleyball. You play very nicely."

"Thank you."

"Also, you have a very marvelous physique. I said so to Schottland. 'That man has the best body on the beach,' I said."

Mike flushed and drew his hand away. She sounded sincere but he was unable to accept the compliment as meaningful. There were too many young men around with hard, tight bodies, with layers of muscle on their shoulders and arms, with deep, sculpted chests. He was too slender. His shoulders and chest lacked bulk. She was teasing him, he decided, and he didn't enjoy that. He rose and looked out at the slowly closing span of water between the *Queen* and the ferry slip.

Wives and children were collected on the pier in great numbers, waving energetically and crying out. This was the "Daddy" boat, the Friday evening ferry that so many of the working fathers rode in order to spend the weekends with their summering families. The cries of the children were audible now.

"Daddy! Daddy!"

He waved at the wavers, though he saw no one he knew.

"You should wear tighter trousers," Eva said conversationally from her place at the railing behind him.

Annoyance slithered along his nerves. He looked down into her face. There was no maliciousness there, no veiled sarcasm. The annoyance dissolved quickly. He returned her smile.

"Everybody seems to be telling me how to dress these days."

"You have a fine body, a flat belly. You should display it, I think. Not too much, but a little. Schottland agrees that——"

"Who is Schottland?"

Her smile widened. "He is my husband, of course."

Eddie

The enclosed deck at MacCurdy's looked over the bay. Eddie Stander hunched over the small table in the far corner. Opposite him, Oscar Morrison sipped a Bloody Mary. Looking at the younger man, Morrison sought to describe the tense expression on that tense face. Like a clenched fist, he told himself. He repeated the phrase to himself. Very nice. A solid ring to it. Pleased, he allowed his gaze to drift out to the water.

"The *Queen* is coming in," he said.

"The people from my house will be on it, I suppose."

"You getting along all right?"

"Nobody bothers me much. If they did, I'd smash 'em in the mouth."

"I believe you would."

Seeing the carefully bland expression on the pudgy face across the table, Eddie realized he'd made a mistake. Morrison was not comfortable in the presence of violence. He gave a reassuring laugh. "A figure of speech, Oscar. I don't go around slugging people."

Morrison set down his glass and traced its rim with his middle finger, producing a tiny squeaking sound.

"Oscar," Eddie said. "I can do the job for you. I've got enough experience, and I've got the feel for it. The talent. I can put together the kind of program you want. The network can depend on me."

Morrison leaned back in his chair. "That damned tube is becoming a voracious monster, Eddie. It devours material and costs keep going up."

Eddie milked his fingers. "Oscar, I *understand* the problems. Haven't I been in the pool from the beginning, Oscar? Right out of college. I jumped in with both feet, got wet all over. I know what it's all about and——"

"Let's be frank, Eddie. You've been involved with daytime stuff. Quiz shows. Game shows. Some interviews for Leona. Eddie, boy, I like you, but be honest. Are you the most creative guy in the industry?"

Eddie swallowed the anger that rose into his mouth. It lined his throat. He forced the words out with deliberation.

"I've served my apprenticeship, Oscar. I'm smart, smarter than most people. I know what has to be done and how to do it."

Morrison exhaled lengthily. "Can you get other people to work for you?"

"Yes. Absolutely."

"I don't know. The risks get more immense each day, the money is so big. A guy like Godfrey, he earns about fifteen hundred dollars a minute. And you know what air time costs. And it's going up. Millions of people watch the box each day. Now, if you were to come up with some fantastic idea, like *Kukla, Fran, and Ollie* . . ."

Eddie brushed nervously at his thinning hair. "That won't last, Oscar."

"I don't know. Tillstrom is an authentic talent."

"All right, Oscar. But we've been talking about a game show. And that's my strength. You said so yourself."

"I said you've done it."

"And I can again. I'll put together a first-rate show for you. Just give me the chance. Let me try, Oscar." There was a gentling of tone and manner, almost a pleading.

"I'll tell you, Eddie," Morrison said, after a moment. "I like you. I told you what my idea was, what I want. It's up to you to come through. Make a presentation I can show to the sponsor, the agency people. It sells and you've got a good thing going. If not . . ." He drained his glass.

Eddie was relieved. For a moment back there, he was afraid he'd lost it. Getting to know Oscar Morrison socially was a break and he'd made every effort to nurture the relationship. Meeting him in the corridor this morning, getting a ride out to the island with him, both were contrived. He'd learned about "It's All Yours" only two days before and had recognized it as Opportunity.

"How much time have I got?" he asked.

A thin smile turned the fleshy mouth. "You're lucky, this is a holiday weekend. I can give you an extra day. Let me have your presentation on Monday."

"That's only three days!"

Morrison raised his crescent brows, looking like a surprised Buddha. "Guess you'll have to do a rush job, pal." The bland face was split by a satisfied grin. "I got to get out to my house now. The little lady is waiting and I wouldn't want her to think I'm playing around with some young pussy. Especially when I'm not. . . ."

Eddie and Mike

Mike came off the beach pleased with himself. He'd played three games of volleyball, sunned himself with no apparent ill-effects, gone for a long, cooling swim. Now showered and refreshed, he studied his reflection in the mirror. He was tan. The effort had been worth it; now he would be able to remain in the sun for hours without concern. He put on dry trunks and a new chambray shirt and headed for the kitchen, suddenly hungry. He found Eddie there, bent over a legal pad, pen in hand.

"Hi," Mike said.

Eddie grunted without looking up.

Mike found some cheese in the refrigerator. He made himself a sandwich and opened a Coke. He settled down at the far end of the table.

"No sun for you today?" he asked.

Eddie lifted his head, the lidded eyes glowering, the brows bunched. "I've got work to do."

"How's it coming?"

Eddie put down the pen. The muscles of his face eased off and he shook his head. "Not good. Too bad you're not a TV man. I could use some help, I suppose."

Mike detected a note of uncertainty in his voice, almost of fright, and was startled by it.

"Maybe I can help."

"I don't see how."

"Sometimes it helps to talk things out."

"I'm supposed to make a presentation for Oscar Morrison. If it sells, I have a chance to be the producer."

"That's great!"

"It's not happening for me. It's as if my brain just won't function properly. I know it's a good instrument. All the evidence proves that. My academic record, my reading habits, my retentiveness. The way I think, my interests, my taste. But there are times when I can't seem to put it all together."

"Maybe you're trying too hard."

"I've only got until Monday."

Mike finished the sandwich and poured the rest of the Coke down the drain. "I don't really like Coke," he said. "Want to take a walk?" he went on. "You can use me as a sounding board."

"Okay," Eddie said after a moment. "What can I lose?" He brought the pad and pen with him.

They walked toward the western end of the island, beyond the limits of Ocean Beach, past Lonelyville, toward Dunewood and Fair Harbor. Eddie outlined Morrison's concept of the program, then ticked off his own ideas, some of which he had already rejected.

"I like the question and answer format," Mike said at one point. "People are attracted to entertainment that is informative, too. Most of the great novelists knew that and——"

"Spare me the literary philosophy," Eddie bit off curtly.

Mike suppressed his resentment. Eddie was under pressure, he reminded himself, and he was there to help him, if possible. He turned his mind back to the show.

"It's All Yours," he murmured. "That's a rather inclusive title. It could mean anything. Something's been troubling me and I've finally decided what it is. The business of opposing panels. I don't like that. Two teams of celebrities competing. . . ."

"Try not to be stupid," Eddie muttered. "The celebrities are the gimmick, the bait for the fish who watch this kind of junk. Names draw."

"What if your people are unable to answer the questions? They'll look bad before——"

"They'll know the answers," Eddie said dryly. He stopped walking. "I knew you wouldn't be able to help. You're just out of it." He started back down the beach.

Mike caught up with him. "How can you be sure they'll know the answers?"

"I'll make certain they do."

"You'll give them the answers!"

"Now you're smartening up. This is show business. Nothing gets left to chance." He swore. "But I still want a gimmick, something to make it different. The way it is, Oscar doesn't need me."

Mike considered the problem. They were almost back to Ocean Beach before he spoke again. "Suppose instead of celebrities you were to have ordinary people. Truly ordinary people. Shopkeepers, salesmen, a shoeshine boy."

"Forget it."

"Eddie, listen. You've studied journalism. If a hundred people get killed in a landslide in the Swiss Alps it's a terrible calamity, but it's good for only a day or two of attention. But let a single man get trapped in a mine and the whole world focuses on him. People identify with individuals, not groups."

"So?"

"So this. Eliminate the panel idea. Use one contestant at a time. And a master-of-ceremonies to put questions to him. Or a questioning panel, if you prefer."

"No good."

"Why not?"

"I can give you a dozen reasons but here's one good one. The questions would have to be too easy. The man in the street, he doesn't know a damned thing. He's dumb as can be."

"Suppose he wasn't. Suppose you were able to find the man in the street, and the woman, who is an expert in some special area. Not professionals, mind you, but ordinary folks with hobbies and interests. . . ."

"Come *on*. People like that *are* experts, earn their livings by their specialties."

"Not necessarily. The man who owns the candy store in my neighborhood is an authority on horse breeding. He knows the blood lines of every racer who's ever run. Who the stud was, the mare, the jockeys, the trainers. Everything."

"So does every other loser who bets horses."

"That's the point. Frank doesn't gamble. Never made a bet in his life. Says it would spoil it for him to bet. Now you get Frank up there, put some really tough questions to him. Make the prizes big. Not radios and freezers, but money. Important money. I think the combination would work, win an impressive audience."

"Forget it. No show is going to spring for big dough when it's so easy to promote toasters, dishwashers, even automobiles—and for free." A wise smile spread across Eddie's fleshy mouth. "I'll just have to work it out for myself."

"Let's keep trying," Mike said. "We'll come up with something."

"Relax," Eddie bit off. "It's just not your area. Stick to press agenting. I'm going back to the house and whip this thing." He strode off, head down, shoulders bunched aggressively.

His enthusiasm deflated, disappointed by his inability to help Eddie, Mike continued along the beach until he came to Neil standing with the talent agent, Sy Melman. A few feet away, Roy was sprawled out on a blanket with Maggie and Susan.

"Hey, there's the stud!" he crowed. "How's the hunting?"

"Maybe he hasn't been hunting," Maggie offered mildly.

Mike sat down. "Been minding the beach for me, Roy?" he said lightly.

Roy hawked his throat clear and squeezed his wife's thigh. "Minding my part of it. Look at that leg. Juicy."

"Stop it, Roy."

Sy Melman and Neil had drifted closer. "I agree, Roy," Sy said. "A fine piece of leg. Are they as effective as they look?"

"Better."

"And there's nothing the matter with your wife's thighs," Sy Melman said to Neil. "Or any other part of her."

Neil's mouth flattened out. "I'd like to keep her in a vacuum cabinet to shield her from the impurities of the world."

Sy Melman laughed but without humor. "I would never do that to a woman. Besides, Susan seems too much alive to be incarcerated at this early age."

"Thank you," she said. "I'm beginning to think I may have been shielded from too much already."

"You see," Melman said to Neil, "a woman isn't a museum piece."

"That's for sure," Mike said.

Melman stared down at him. "Tell me, why isn't a nice boy like you married?"

"Too busy making it with every piece of gash on the beach," Roy put in.

Melman considered that and looked at Mike with new interest. "I hear what Roy says but how can I be sure it's true?"

"We could arrange a showing," Roy chortled. "A circus, with Mike as the star. We'll sell tickets and make a fortune. Continuous performances, if Mike is up to it."

"Very nice idea," Melman said. He lifted the corners of his mouth in Mike's direction. "Come over to my house for drinks this evening."

"He doesn't need your liquor," Roy said. "Besides, there are no chicks at your place. Not even a wife."

Maggie straightened up. "If Mike is going to have anything to do with wives, let him begin closer to home. Right, Susan?"

Before she could reply, Neil spoke. "Maybe it was a mistake to have two single men in the house, Roy."

"Oh, I don't know. Takes a load off us husbands."

"I can carry my load," Neil said evenly. "What would you do, Roy, if you found someone with Maggie?"

Roy grinned thinly. "Invite him to dinner."

When the laughter died away, Neil spoke again. "I know what I'd do."

"What?" Melman said curiously.

"I'd kill him."

All eyes turned to Neil. "You mean it?" Mike said.

"I mean it."

Roy gave that harsh laugh of his. "I never realized what a romantic you were, Neil. Killing lovers can be a problem."

"That's true," Melman added. "I suspect most guys who service married ladies would object strenuously to being killed. And usually they're the kind who own the equipment to prevent it from happening."

Melman looked down at Susan. "Anyway, in my house nobody gets killed. Unless they fuck themselves to death." He waved as he left.

Neil called his name, went after him. "There's something I want to ask you . . ."

Mike

"Party time!"

Roy shuffled toward the door of Mom Stone's doing an Indian war dance, emitting tiny cries behind his palm. A troupe of revelers trailed him. They were on their way to Leo's, at the far end of Baywalk. Intimate and dim, Leo's was more reminiscent of a Manhattan cocktail lounge than a swinging beach bar. Yet every night of every weekend, a certain group headed for Leo's just before midnight as if by silent signal, joining to exchange the latest jokes and gossip, to discover who was giving the late party, who was doing what to whom. In the crowded space between the tables and the bar, husbands lost wives and wives met brown young men they had never seen before, and single women had drinks thrust at them. Phone numbers were given, arrangements made.

Leo, pale and effete, was picking out show tunes on the piano when Roy's group arrived. He greeted them with a halfmoon smile, a quick nod. Seconds later Neil was at the piano singing "Mountain Greenery" in his pleasant baritone.

"He's not bad," Bette Miller said to Susan.

"He sang to me on our second date," she said, keeping her back to Neil, not wanting him to see that she was smoking again. "I was very impressed."

Maggie spoke confidentially. "Sy Melman is also impressed. With you, that is."

"I don't think so. He and Neil have been spending a great deal of time together. They seem to like each other. And anyway, I'm a married woman. And he's married, too."

"That never stopped anyone," Bette Miller said. "Not on the island, anyway."

Susan blushed. "Oh, I could never do that. Could you, Bette? Maggie?"

Bette grinned lasciviously. "Only when someone asks me."

"And no one's ever asked me," Maggie said.

Roy stood near the doorway to the back deck with Mike and Eddie, drinking. Roy was telling them of a stock purchase he had made and of his expectation of a large profit in a short time. He broke off when the Woodwards appeared, accompanied by a tall girl in white shorts and a sleeveless black shirt.

"Have you heard?" Peggy Woodward greeted them brightly. "They're fighting in Korea."

"What do you mean?" Eddie said sharply.

"It was on the newscast," Hal Woodward said, his manner diffident. He was a tall man, thick-necked and muscular; but his face was soft, the features plump. "The North Koreans crossed the thirty-eighth parallel into South Korea."

"I've had my war," Roy said, drinking.

Mike shivered. "Not again," he muttered. "Not so soon . . ."

"I don't believe it," Eddie said curtly.

"It's true," the tall girl said evenly. "I heard the broadcast too."

"Mike, Eddie," Peggy Woodward interrupted, "meet Lucille Quirk. She's staying with us for a while."

"The South Koreans must've begun it," Eddie growled. "That bastard Syngman Rhee. They must have." An oath broke out of him and he pivoted away, pushed his way through the crowd and disappeared.

"What's he so upset about?" Peggy asked lightly.

Roy gave that rasping laugh of his. "Eddie is a political worrier. Let's get to important things, Peggy. You and Hal making it regularly?"

She pursed her lips with exaggerated innocence. "Every night on schedule, darling. My afternoons, however, are relatively free. . . ."

Mike looked at Lucille Quirk, and she gazed back steadily. Her eyes, a soft brown, matched her thick hair. "Can I get you a drink?" he asked.

"That would be nice. A dry Rob Roy on the rocks, please."

It took almost ten minutes to reach the bar, to order the drink, and return. When he got back, she was gone. He located her across the room, listening intently to a tall, handsome man, who might have been a movie actor. She had a drink in her hand. The expression of intense concentration on her face told Mike he had lost his chance.

He glanced around, saw a startlingly beautiful blonde at the far end of the bar. How would she respond if he walked over to her, and handed her the Rob Roy? "I want you to have this," he would say in a soft, urgent voice. She would take it, studying him all the while, sipping provocatively. "I like it," she would say finally. "In fact, I like you." "Finish your drink," he would reply. "I'm taking you out of here." And she would put the glass aside at once and follow him to the door.

Mike turned away. He was not going to approach the blonde. He simply lacked the nerve. He tasted the Rob Roy. It was much too strong.

Roy

"I was right, godammit!"

The words ripped through the bright Sunday afternoon, through the lulling sound of the surf, through the cries of the playing children, the hum of conversation. Heads came up off blankets and rattan pillows, off cradling forearms, eyes blinking against the glare.

"Right about what?" Mike asked sleeplily. He had been dozing, his mind idling around Lucille Quirk, trying to understand what about him had turned her away. He had seen her earlier wearing one of those new brief two-piece bathing suits. She was a stunning sight, with shimmering breasts and full round bottom, her flesh tight. He had started after her but the handsome actor got there first. His scrotum crinkled in desire at the thought of her.

"I telephoned a friend in town," Eddie was saying, too loudly, too aggressively, voice tinged with triumph. "He's got contacts. He knows what goes on. No crap. The South attacked the North. . . ."

"The Confederacy shall rise again!" Roy bleated gaily.

"It's no laughing matter," Eddie shot back. "Korea, I mean. That Rhee, a fascist bastard. He invaded the North with American support. But it won't work. The soldiers of the People's Republic of Korea have thrown back his mercenaries. They'll get what they deserve. . . ."

"What are you talking about?" Roy said, falling back on his blanket.

"Seoul has come under attack by the People's Air Force. The Army is advancing on all fronts. Victory is just a matter of time."

"You sound like Lowell Thomas," Roy said.

"That's not funny."

"You really believe the North Koreans will win?" Mike asked.

"The tide of history is running for them. Socialism is the wave of the future."

"What does that mean?" Susan said.

"The radio said America has called for a meeting of the United Nations, the Security Council," Maggie said.

"Truman won't dare interfere," Eddie snarled. "That cheap little haberdasher . . ."

"Come off it, Eddie," Mike said.

"This country has a duty," Neil declared in his deepest baritone, "to uphold freedom around the world."

"Crap!"

"It's the responsibility of power," Neil added. "A nation must take care of its obligations."

"Christ, you're an ass!" Eddie plunged up the slope toward the house.

"That man is wrong," Neil announced solemnly. "Dead wrong."

"Eddie takes politics very seriously," Maggie said.

"War is serious," Mike added.

Roy laughed back in his throat. "Screw 'em all, I've had my war. . . ."

Chapter VIII

Eddie

The first party of the season at Neurotics Anonymous finally took place. All expenses, all the work, were shared. BB and Cindy were deprived of their afternoon nap so that that night, overtired, they would go to sleep when ordered.

Guests began arriving at nine and soon the house was jammed. People overflowed into the ground-floor bedrooms, onto the decks. Some sat on the steps and others drifted out onto the dunes, clutching paper cups sloshing with Purple Jesus.

Eddie was self-appointed keeper of the punch. Following Roy's recipe—gin, grape juice, and lemon, all in generous amounts—he was in the kitchen mixing a second batch.

A girl in a striped shirt and tight orange slacks appeared. Her hair was in disarray and her lipstick smeared. She smiled crookedly. "Well, hello! Are you the hired help?"

He kept his eyes on the mix, stirring. "That's it," he drawled. "I am the colored cook."

Her eyes worked over his bare forearms, muscular and very hard. "Well, I approve, whatever your color." She raised her eyes. "I am in dire need of the johnie."

He jerked his head. "That way."

She drained her glass and extended it for a refill. He obliged.

"Thanks."

"Better get on with your mission before you reach flood stage."

She laughed briefly. "I may be too tipsy to go alone. I think I need help. Would you like to help me?"

"I've got my work."

She teetered. "Have you ever watched a girl go?"

The face he turned toward her was tight and brooding, the eyes lidded. "Beat it. Take your sickness someplace else."

She drew back, mouth working. "Queer!"

He took an involuntary step forward. She retreated swiftly, left the kitchen. He ached to follow, to smash her face. To hurt her. Hurt someone.

Mike

No pain. Only a soft, drifting peacefulness. Three cups of Purple Jesus and a tingling numbness had settled into Mike Birns' extremities. He viewed the noisy, heaving collection of bodies in the house with blurred benevolence, and he circulated among them, without purpose, talking to strangers with an unaccustomed ease.

From somewhere distant, the pleasant sound of music mixed with muffled voices. One of those Hollywood orchestras, he decided, that play on cue, music appropriate to the action on the silver screen. All those violins. *Beautiful.* Soft arms embraced him and warm flesh pressed close. A heady scent drifted through the cavities of his skull and it came to him finally that he was dancing.

It was an effort to bring his unknown partner into focus. A vaguely familiar face smiled up through the mist.

"Do I know you?" he managed.

That drew a wistful smile. "You forget so soon. Hetty Molinos. We met a few weeks ago. . . ."

Concentration was difficult. His eyes wandered. He identified Peggy Woodward; she was dancing with Clark Miller. And Bette with Hal Woodward. How friendly! On his left was a buxom blonde in a loose-fitting blouse, whose partner hovered over her, peering at her great breasts. Roy, somewhere, laughed loudly. And there was Sy Melman with Susan, words coming out in that slow way he had, fingertips resting lightly on her shoulder. Neil would object to another man touching his wife. A smile curled Mike's mouth; this was not the killing offense.

"I'm wasting my time," a voice was saying, with some irritation.

"Yes?" he replied absently.

Hetty Molinos disengaged herself. "I guess I'll have to look elsewhere. You aren't at all up to my needs tonight, darling."

Mike made it into the kitchen. A wiry man labored over the punch bowl. "My cup in no way runneth over," Mike complained. "Fill 'er up, pal."

Eddie grinned. "You have no cup."

"I am destroyed. For want of a cup, a thirst was born. For want of a drink, a life was lost. For want of a life, a prince expired. For want of a prince, a throne went empty. For want of a king, an empire was lost."

"Very nice. I didn't realize that you were a prince."

Mike drew himself erect, swaying. "A Jewish prince, I'll have you know. A cup, varlet," he demanded.

"You *are* drunk," Eddie laughed.

"And you are sober."

"Someone must uphold the honor of the room, your highness." He filled a cup and gave it to Mike.

Mike accepted it with unsteady dignity, raised it over his head and bowed. "With thanks, I dub thee well-tanned knight, keeper of the wine, reader of the books, lover of the sun god Ra. Or is it goddess?" He went to the door, spoke without turning. "You're not a bad guy, Eddie. When I'm drunk, that is, and you're not pissed-off at the world."

He was gone before Eddie could respond.

BB

Neil stood alongside the crib and gazed down at BB. The boy smiled up at his father.
"You should be asleep, BB."
"Too much noise."
"It's a party."
"What's a party?"
"People having fun."
"Playing?"
"Yes, playing. Grown-up playing."
"I like to play."
"This party is for big people. When you get older, you'll have your own parties."
"I want to play all the time."
"Go to sleep, now. See, Cindy is sleeping like a good girl."
"Cindy's a baby."
"A very pretty baby. But you are a big boy, and you're going to do what your father tells you to do. Your father wants only what's best for you, only tells you right things. So you must obey your father. Now close your eyes and go to sleep."
BB shut his eyes. He opened them at once. "I can't sleep."
Neil spoke in a sober voice. "You can do whatever you want to do. You just have to try harder. I'm going back to the party and you're going to sleep."
"I try," BB said. But he didn't. Not really.

Maggie

"You must stop!" Maggie husked, anxious that no one overhear. She hated this role, the jealous wife, wanted to make sure he understood. "The way you've been clutching at that blonde . . ."

Roy laughed scornfully. "You got to be kidding. A little harmless fun. What the hell!"

"You were feeling her fanny."

"Is that what you're all worked up about? A little feel. Oh, come on, Maggie. I was just fooling around, kidding about her keister. Did you see the size of it? And those tits? I mean, it's kind of a joke."

"I'm not laughing, Roy."

He leered at her. "Not my fault you've got small boobs. I didn't do it to you. Besides, I like it that way. How many times do I have to tell you?"

Her gaze was steady. "If you feel compelled to maul other women, please do it where I won't have to see it."

"You know me, I like to horse around. It means nothing." He reached out and cupped her bottom. "Come on. We'll go up to the room. I'll give you what that blonde'll never get. Right now."

She tried to answer but no words came out. Only an angry exhalation. She spun away and pushed her way through the crowd, out of the house, fleeing toward the beach. He shrugged and went after the big blonde.

Neil

Neil located Sy Melman in the entrance foyer. The lanky agent with the bony face was standing very close to Susan, talking earnestly. She held a drink in one hand and a cigarette in the other. Neil suppressed a caustic comment. He arranged what he hoped was a pleasant smile on his thin mouth.

"Quite a party, isn't it?" he began.

Melman straightened up. "Very nice."

Susan took a long swallow of her drink. "I'm having a good time. I love parties."

Neil ignored his wife and looked Melman in the eye. "Well, Sy. Have you considered my proposition?"

"Have you told Susan what you want to do?"

"Nobody tells me anything," Susan complained.

"My wife will go along with whatever I do," Neil said

sternly. Then, with a toneless straightforwardness, "I meant what I said, Sy."

Melman had thought about it, had reached a decision. Why not? He had very little to lose. And he stood to gain handsomely. "I'd like to be sure you've considered it from every point of view," he said. "In the beginning, it's going to mean less money each week. And there's no promise that it will work out for you."

"That's a sacrifice I'll make, a chance I'll take."

"You're that sure?"

"I've got what it takes, Sy. You said so yourself, yesterday on the beach."

"Talking on the beach is nothing. Back in that snake pit, that's a whole different game. For keeps."

"I'll take the gamble."

Melman measured Neil. "You have a wife, a child."

"In the Morgan family, I make the decisions."

"Will somebody tell me what's going on?" Susan said, with no special interest. She took a final drag on her cigarette, looked around for an ashtray. Melman relieved her of the butt.

"You are persistent, Neil," he said, "and that's a necessary trait. Tell you what. Let me sleep on it. We'll talk again. Phone me, middle of the week. We'll have a drink and finalize matters. Oh, but you don't drink, do you? Lunch then." He looked at the smoking butt between his fingers. "I have to dispose of this. Come on, Susan, your glass is almost empty. Excuse us, Neil. We lushes have to latch on to some more of the grape." They went off together, Susan giggling at something Melman was saying.

Watching them, Neil assured himself that Melman represented an opportunity too good to be lost, one Neil had been searching for diligently. He was determined not to lose it. He made up his mind. He would fill Susan in before they went to sleep. She could begin working on the agent tomorrow on the beach. Melman enjoyed her company, was receptive to her influence. She would move him closer to a favorable decision. A beautiful wife was a valuable asset in so many ways.

Mike

The punch bowl was unattended, but Mike managed to refill his cup without help. When he turned to go, his path was blocked. A tall form with an abundance of auburn hair flaring to its shoulders stood in his way. He concentrated hard.

"You're a girl, aren't you?" he managed.

"Very good."

The voice was clearly female and he squinted, trying to clarify the blurred features. "At a guess, a pretty girl."

"There are those who say so."

"Have you a name?"

"Lucille Quirk."

"I know that name! Oh, yes, the Woodwards' friend. You are enamored of handsome actors."

She frowned thoughtfully. "He wasn't an actor at all. Just a stock clerk in the garment district."

"A very good-looking stock clerk. Better looking than I am."

She cocked her head and appraised him. "Different. Anyway, he kept making jokes about my name. You know—what are your quirks, Quirk? Ugh."

"You seemed to be enjoying his company."

"Oh," she said brightly, "you were watching me. How nice!"

He drained his cup and refilled it. "It is my intention to get very drunk," he announced.

"Apparently you've already succeeded."

"That is my decision to make."

"Are you up to changing plans?"

"What do you mean?"

"I would like a cup of coffee, someplace less noisy."

"Are you asking me to go downtown with you and——"

"Exactly."

"Well," he said. "Okay." He lifted the cup but she put a restraining hand on his wrist.

"Don't drink anymore."

Something in her voice caused him to put the Purple Jesus aside. She took his hand and led him out of the house. The night air was cool against his cheeks and without warning his brain tilted and turned.

"I think I do need some coffee," he muttered.

The coffee slowed the peregrinations of his brain and he had a second cup. She declined in favor of a cherry ice-cream cone with chocolate sprinkles.

"I haven't had sprinkles since I was a kid," she said, licking the drippings off the sides of the cone.

"You're not much more than a kid now."

"You're soberer."

"How can you tell?"

She shrugged. "Fellows ask certain questions all the time. But not when they've been drinking. Then they're different, amorous or philosophical or insulting. Sober they ask what a girl does for a living, how old she is, where she lives. In the city, I mean. That's very important to them, to make sure a girl isn't geographically unsuitable."

"How old are you?" he said deliberately.

"I'm not jailbait, if that's what you're worried about."

Her directness kept him off balance. He wanted to clear away the alcoholic mist that lingered around the arc of his skull. It inhibited his thought processes, made it difficult to know what to say, to summon up the right words in effective order. Mike had always found this kind of girl unsettling, and he felt defensive in her presence. Her dramatic physical appearance, her confident eyes, that stunning figure, all that hair, and her way of talking. So damned blunt, as if making less of everything he said.

To hell with her! He didn't need that crap. He was going to finish his coffee and head back to the party. There were plenty of girls on this island who would welcome his presence, his attention, who would treat him kindly and gently.

"Mike," she said without warning. "You do like me, don't you?"

"What?"

"Well, if you're not interested, there would be no point, would there?"

He peered at that still blurred, impenetrable face. She directed her attention to the remainder of the ice-cream cone.

"I don't get it," he said. "Up to now, you've been pretty cool."

She shrugged and bit into the cone. It cracked and ice cream dripped. He handed her a couple of paper napkins, and she made the necessary repairs. "Cool is what I am, mostly. It's my style, I suppose. But you didn't exactly break down doors to get to me."

"Maybe I'm shy," he temporized.

She measured him. "People talk about you. They say you make out like crazy." She allowed her mouth to curl upward briefly. "Is it true?"

"All lies." He felt his cheeks grow warm.

She laughed softly. "You blush. I like that. You seem pretty smooth, as if you know what you're doing. . . ."

His mind floated backward to his first date. He had been seventeen. She was a chubby girl with a mouth like a fish and a shrill laugh. He thought she was beautiful. They had gone out with two other couples. First a picture, at Lowe's Paradise, then sundaes, and then over to Poe Park. The other couples had begun necking immediately, but Mike had been unable to bring himself to try to kiss the chubby girl—or even to put his arm around her. He felt clumsy and stupid and was sure he bored her. He wanted desperately to say something amusing and clever. Nothing came. They sat side by side, neither of them speaking, for nearly two hours. When he took her home she went inside without saying good night.

That night, as he lay in bed cursing himself for being an inept and cowardly fool, he vowed never to spend such an evening again. He made a compact with himself: he was going to learn to talk, to teach himself to speak with surety and wit, to make girls pay attention, to amuse them. No longer would he sit there silent and ill-at-ease.

The next day, he launched a course in self-improvement. He began by reading the newspapers closely, clipping out those items which were unusual or contained information likely to be unknown to his friends.

—*There were only 8,000 motor vehicles registered in the United States in the year 1900.*

—*William Shakespeare's most productive decade began in 1600. During the next ten years he wrote:* Midsummer Night's Dream, Henry V, Twelfth Night, Merry Wives of Windsor, Hamlet, Macbeth, King Lear, Othello, The Tempest *and more.*

—When the American Revolution ended, there were only 5,000 men in uniform for the new nation.

More, he appropriated for his own use the routines and gags of comedians he heard on the radio, developing a patter for use at appropriate moments. He read more intently now—especially history and biography—committing a great deal of information to memory.

Words and information became his defense against most threats; they became his strength and his weakness, even though he neglected very often to consider what he was reading, concerning himself only with how the information could be used in social situations. More than once his verbal outpourings backfired—when more knowledgeable or more thoughtful people tore his pronouncements to shreds. But he learned quickly and began to temper his wordiness, to consider what he had absorbed, to reject or accept what he read in light of his own experience, reach his own conclusions. Though his confidence had grown, he was still a long way from being the man he wanted to become. He raised his eyes, wondering how his transformation would finally affect his encounter with Lucille Quirk.

"I'm not very smooth," he said quietly. "It's all an act. Most of the time I'm scared of girls."

"I've always been a little frightened of men."

They fell silent and he tortured his brain for something to say, to fill the uncomfortable void.

"Did you know that the worst mine disaster in the United States took place in Monongah, West Virginia, in nineteen-oh-seven?" he said. "Three hundred and sixty-one people were killed."

She stared at him shortly, then stood up. "I'm tired," she said quietly. "I would like to go back to my house now."

He cursed himself and wanted to ask her not to turn away from him, not to be tired, to give him another chance. Outside, he touched her arm.

"Why don't we go to MacCurdy's?" he said. "Have a nightcap."

"No, thank you."

Disappointment welled up in him. And confusion. For a moment back there, he had the feeling that she liked him. Obviously he was wrong; she was anxious to be rid of him. He made his voice detached and distant.

"Well, I guess I'll head on back to the party. Things should just be livening up about now."

"What about me?"

"What about you?" he said too quickly. "I mean, you said you were tired."

"You are not going to leave me here unescorted," she declared firmly. "You brought me and you will see that I get home safely."

He sighed. "Oh, sure. All right."

She began walking and he hurried to catch up. "I'm sorry it's such a strain," she said. "I'll try not to bore you."

"Oh, *God*. You don't bore me. Really. You *don't*. I just don't know what to *do* with you!"

She made no reply and they proceeded to the Woodward house without speaking. When she failed to dismiss him at the door, he trailed her inside. He felt miserable and couldn't wait to get away from her silent judgment, which lay over him oppressively. In the middle of the darkened living room, she faced him.

"I don't understand you," she said abruptly.

"What? What is it? I'll explain. If I can," he ended lamely.

"All that about being frightened of girls. . . ."

"I am."

"I don't believe it. I've seen you, the way you operate. Half the girls on the beach have eyes for you. You're supposed to be a big make-out man."

"It's not true. . . ."

"Roy Ashe says you're a stud and Peggy Woodward thinks you're the most successful man on the beach."

That he was a subject of conversation made him uncomfortable.

"So you see you may as well stop using that line on me."

"What line?"

"That you're shy, don't know your way around women. It's very good and successful, I imagine. But don't waste it with me. I've already decided. Unless, of course, you really find me unattractive."

"I think you're incredibly attractive. I'm overwhelmed by your attractiveness. It's startling, disturbing, and that's what the problem is, you see, I——"

"Oh, please," she said softly. "Don't talk."

He nodded glumly. He'd made still another error, increased the gap that separated them. "I'd better go."

Her hands found his in the darkness and guided them to her waist. "Please. Kiss me, Mike. . . ."

Her mouth was set under his. He put his tongue against her tight lips, felt them stir.

"Mike," she said, her voice a whisper. "What should I do? I mean, tell me what you like."

A thought flickered to life in some dark portion of his brain. "Lucille, don't you know how to kiss?"

She giggled nervously. "I don't think so."

"Oh, my God."

"Tell me, please, what I should do."

"Well, make your lips soft, don't clench your teeth."

"Yes."

"And let your imagination go. I'll kiss you and you'll get the idea. You can respond, do whatever you want. The same things I do. . . ."

"With my tongue, you mean?"

It embarrassed him to talk about it. "Yes."

"All right. Let's do it, please."

He obliged her.

"Was that all right?" she said, after a while.

"Much better. The lips," he offered. "Not so wide. And softer."

They kissed again. After a moment, her arms circled his waist and she pushed up against him. His crotch came alive, and he felt himself grow hard. A soft moan sounded back in her throat. He moved and moved again. His hand reached for her bottom and she bent backward to fit.

"Wait," she said finally, breathlessly. "Not here. Come with me."

Her room was in the rear of the house, small and very dark. "Do you want some light?" she said, matter-of-factly.

"I don't care."

"Oh," she said. Then, after a pause, "Shall I get undressed now?"

"Yes."

He stripped off his clothes quickly, turned to her. She was a shadow in the blackness, a faint pale form stepping out of her panties. He moved forward. They found the bed in a confusion of limbs, of anxious desire, of thick murmurings, awkward and without refinements, all clutching hands and spreading thighs, thumping bellies.

"Listen," he managed, after a while. "Do you use a diaphragm."

"I'm sorry."

"I better wear something."

"Oh. *Oh!* I never thought about that."

There were two Trojans in his trousers. He peeled the tinfoil off one. The darkness and his rising passion, the nervousness, made his fingers clumsy. He swore.

"What is it?" she said.

"I hate these things."

"Shall I turn on the light, so you can see?"

"No. It's all right now."

"You're sure?"

"Lay back."

He lowered himself on top of her.

"Is there anything I can do?" she asked.

"Help me."

"How?"

"Put it in."

"Ah, yes. I understand."

It was difficult.

"What's wrong with me?" she asked anxiously.

"There's nothing wrong with you."

"Then why won't you go in? Am I too small? Perhaps I'm not normal."

"You're fine. Just a little tight. Be patient."

"Of course. Yes."

He reached and his fingers found her, worked gently.

"Ah," she said. "Ah . . ."

"Put it in now."

It was better, the moist warmth encasing him. He thrust and she moaned.

"I'm sorry," he said.

"It's . . . all right. Please. Don't stop, Mike. I want . . . so much . . ."

He thrust hard and her head went to one side, but she made no protest, fingers digging into his shoulders. He made an effort to exercise control, to move in such a way as to gain maximum contact.

"You're so tight," he muttered. "So hot and wet."

"Mike . . ." It was a feeble plea.

He responded, middle beating against her in long, strong strokes. A rising shriek exploded out of her and he kissed her hard, absorbing the sound in his own mouth. Then with a dismaying swiftness there was that special gathering, that welling up to a point past tolerance that froze him inside her. Then, the flood, spasm after spasm. Her arms went around him and she murmured instinctive reassurances, encouragements. At last he lay still, gasping.

"Are you all right?" she said eventually.

They lay next to each other, touching at shoulder, hip and ankle. "That wasn't much for you," he said.

"Oh, lovely. I'm very pleased."

"You didn't have an orgasm."

"It was very nice, and I'm glad it's over. You see, I've been working up to it for about a year."

He lifted himself onto his elbow. "My God, you're a virgin!"

She laughed, a soft, knowing laugh. "Not anymore, thank you."

"No wonder you were so tight."

"Hush," she said.

"You brought me here to deflower you," he accused her in wonder.

"I hope you don't mind, I thought you were very nice, very attractive. And even more important, experienced."

He lay back down. "I'll try to be better for you next time."

She moved closer and her lips brushed his shoulder. "That would be so nice."

She was asleep when he left. He picked his way carefully through the dark house. Muted music drifted to his ears and he became aware of movement in the living room. He stopped. Shapes drifted across his line of sight. A couple dancing.

"Hi, there!" came Peggy Woodward's cheerful voice. "Coming or going?"

"On my way out," Mike heard himself say.

"Hope you had fun," Peggy laughed.

"Be careful," her partner said. It was Bette Miller's husband, Clark. "Don't step on Hal and Bette."

For the first time, Mike saw the others, sprawled out

on the floor very close to each other. As he watched, they kissed. A surge of distress gripped Mike, as if he were part of some community exercise, on public exhibition. He hurried away.

Chapter IX

Mike and Maggie

They lived for the weekends. The days between were offending time lapses, somehow to be gotten through. Most of the men stayed over on Sunday nights now, going directly to their offices on the "death boat" early Monday morning, returning early Friday afternoons. Twice Neil was able to get away on Thursdays and both Eddie and Roy were able to take extra days on the island.

For Mike, that chance never came. His position at Civic Theaters was not important or secure enough to risk stealing away before the end of the work week, so that when his two-week vacation came in the middle of August, he repaired to Neurotics Anonymous with relief and need. He spent the time playing volleyball, swimming, and working on his tan. His skin had taken on the warm color of Army summer issue and though he would never get as dark as Eddie Stander, he was quite pleased.

And there were the girls.

Platoons of them, appearing like a succession of waves breaking on the sand, all gay and spritely, with a surprising willingness to accommodate him. In time he came to accept this situation as his rightful due.

The beach was a changed place during the week. It was quieter and less frenetic, intrusions were less likely, the abundance of near-naked flesh thinned out. The nights were different, too. Leo's and Mom Stone's were quieter, the hours passed there more leisurely. There was a parallel lessening of urgency, of the need to get on with it, whatever one's "it" might be.

One evening, after dinner, Mike joined Susan and Maggie and the children on the upper deck. They watched the sun, a blinding orange ball, sink through a blue haze over the mainland. It was a stunning sight.

When the children were asleep, the adults made themselves comfortable in the living room, sipping brandy and talking easily. Susan went to bed first. Alone with Maggie for the first time, Mike again realized what a startlingly beautiful woman she was, her small features perfectly matched, her mouth deftly shaped, her eyes clear, patient. She was rereading *Lord Jim*, and they discussed Conrad for a while. He had recently discovered William Faulkner, whom she appreciated, and they talked about the Snopes and about the characteristics of the larger society which they represented. It grew late and they spoke only intermittently. During one pause he wondered what her response would be if he should cross over to where she was sitting and kiss her. He restrained the impulse.

"It's almost three o'clock," she said finally. "Time I went to bed."

He went into his own room and got into bed. Sleep wouldn't come so he switched on the light and reached for *Absalom, Absalom*, and began to read.

A distant, faint sound intruded on his concentration. He listened and recognized the cry of an infant. It was Cindy. He waited for Maggie to respond. When no footsteps came down the stairs, he slid out of bed, wrapped a towel around his middle and padded toward the rear of the house.

Cindy was standing in her crib, tears streaming down her round face. His appearance did nothing to stem the tide of unhappiness. He debated whether or not to pick her up. He stroked her cheek gently. She cried louder. Mike marvelled at BB's ability to sleep through the caterwauling. He patted Cindy's back and spoke her name. Children were pleasant to play with for a few minutes on the beach, but at such moments as this they terrified him.

"Please stop crying, baby," he murmured.

Cindy responded with a louder wail. He studied her with dismay.

"Are you dying little girl? If so, you are doomed. I can't help you. Why isn't your mother here? Tell me that."

He turned away and started toward Maggie's room. Midway up the stairs, he remembered something. A conversation some weeks before. Meaningless, idle, concerned with sleeping habits. Maggie had said that she often slept naked. A thick glob of desire formed in Mike's throat. He wanted very much to see her that way, asleep, vulnerable, exposed. And in that moment he knew that if he reached for her at such a time Maggie would accept him. Now, he thought. This night. And he realized that he wanted it to happen, had wanted it all along.

He had never made love to a married woman. Would it be different? The idea was frightening. There would be demands made, standards to measure up to, and he wasn't sure how well he could do.

Below, Cindy emitted a thin howl of distress. Mike hurried up the stairs. He hesitated outside Maggie's room, then knocked. He knocked again, louder this time. Still no answer. He opened the door and said her name. She stirred.

"Yes. . . ?" There was no alarm, only curiosity, mild, unemotional.

"It's Mike, Maggie."

She turned to face him. "What do you want, Mike?"

"It's Cindy," he said. "She's crying. I tried to comfort her but it did no good."

She came off the bed. She was wearing a pink nightgown that fell in generous folds to the floor. She smiled and moved past him, went downstairs. He trailed after her.

As soon as Maggie picked her up, Cindy's wailing ceased. Maggie laughed.

"Just a filled-up diaper."

Mike felt foolish. "I never thought of that."

"I'll take care of it."

Mike went back to his bed. He found his place in Faulkner but was unable to concentrate. After a while, he heard Maggie leave the children's room. He willed her to come to him and imagined he could hear her approaching. But the footsteps faded, the stairs creaked, and she returned to her own room, her own bed. He was disappointed and, at the same time, relieved.

Eddie

It was a bright day, the sky high and clear, the heat of the sun tempered by a soft breeze. The ocean was smooth and appealing. Mike walked along the surfline on the lookout for unusual beach stones or shells. He was almost into Ocean Bay Park when he heard his name called. A woman waved, gestured for him to join her.

As he came nearer, he recognized her. It was the woman he had met coming across on the *Queen*, Eva Schottland. In a bathing suit, she was something out of a Brueghel painting: large-boned, golden flesh turned in ample and dramatic proportions, cheeks glowing, her eyes bright, lively, and mischievious. Her short hair was sun-bleached and rumpled.

"Hello, again!" she cried, in a voice a little too loud. "I did not see you since that day on the ferry. I have thought, ah, he is hiding from me. Is that so?"

He laughed and issued a denial.

"Of course," she agreed. "The beach is full of pretty girls, so many of them, and they take up your time." She invited him to share her blanket, arranging herself cross-legged, leaning slightly so that her immense breasts appeared ready to tumble out of the bathing suit. She eyed him speculatively. "So, I was correct, I think. You do have a very superb physique. Good shoulders and chest. Strong but not bulging. And a flat belly. The legs are also nice. Very nice."

This time his laugh was uneasy. He was still unable to accept compliments gracefully. A residue of self-consciousness about his body remained and he still didn't feel totally at ease on the beach.

"You are the one with a fine body," he heard himself say.

"Ah, you think so! Good. But one day I shall be fat, I

think." She straightened up, pounded her stomach. "Right now the body is at it's peak, you see."

"I see."

"The belly is not too round and the boobs are still solid. Soon they will begin to sag."

"You're too young for that."

"They will, of their own weight." She gave a pleased laugh. "Also, I am older than you, I think. I am thirty."

"You don't look thirty."

Again that laugh. Her hand came to rest on his thigh and he held very still.

Schottland is younger than I. By four years. But he likes the way I am."

Her husband. He had forgotten. Schottland. Referring to him that way had a foreign ring to it and there was a suggestion of an accent in her speech.

"You weren't born here," he probed.

She leaned toward him, hand sliding higher on his thigh. He did not look at her breasts.

"I am German."

Germans. Nazis. Hitler. They were an evil people, the cause of so much suffering. She was the first German he had met.

"Ah, you do not like me. Because I am a German, no?"

"I judge people as individuals," he said, the words sounding pompous in his ears. And untrue. "I fought the Germans during the war. I helped liberate a concentration camp. I can't forget what I saw."

She nodded gravely. "We did not know about such things, myself and my family. Still, we were there, responsible in some way, is it not so? But I was never very political, you see. Not like Schottland. Naturally he felt as you do in the beginning. But after he knew me he understood that it was not my fault."

"You came here after the war," Mike said. "That's when you met your husband?"

"Oh, no. He was stationed in Belgium. There we met and began going together and so we became married." She looked out at the ocean. "So exciting it is, the sea. See that bird, like a single finger flitting over the waves. All of life moves past that way. And death also, I think." She glanced at Mike and spoke with no change of expression. "Shall we march into the sea, you and I? It will be like nothing, over in a second or two."

Mike couldn't be sure whether she was joking. He produced an uncertain smile.

"I do not like the sea," she continued. "The water is offensive to me. There is so much of it—all so powerful and rough. I always get hurt when I go bathing." She shifted around to face him, her movements heavy but strong. Both hands came to rest high on his thighs and her thumbs worked against the flesh. "We can be friends, Mike, yes?"

"Yes."

"Friendship with a bed?" She recognized the uncertain expression in his eyes and laughed at his discomfort. "That frightens you? I frighten you. Do not be afraid. I am not a frightening person."

He smiled, convinced she was only teasing.

"Ah," she said, removing her hands. "Do you want babies, Mike? Do you always want to make a baby in a lady's belly when you are in her?" She didn't wait for an answer. "But of course not. Men are not that way usually. But Kenneth is. He wants babies."

"Your husband, you mean?"

"Kenneth is my lover. He is hungry to place a seed in my belly and it makes me afraid. It is a physical thing with him, to make a baby. The craving for him is such that I think he aches with it. Worse than in any woman. It frightens me."

"Why do you see him then?"

"He comes to me and even when I refuse him and send him away he takes me. He is very strong and very sexual."

"You must want him that way."

"Perhaps. But not really. Can't one be both ways, wanting and not wanting? I am, you see. I would get rid of Kenneth, if I knew the way. He is so jealous. Even of Schottland. But Schottland is not jealous of him."

"Your husband knows about you and Kenneth?"

"Of course. I love Schottland very much. He is a beautiful man, and I would not deceive him in any way."

Tension settled into the muscles in Mike's legs. He wanted to spring up, to run away. Very carefully, he climbed to his feet.

"I must go now," he said deliberately. "The women in

my house expect me to help with the shopping and the heavy work."

She smiled up at him. "I will be here all afternoon. Come back and visit with me."

He said he would try.

She called after him. "Good-bye, pretty man. . . ."

When Mike got back to the house, he found Eddie Stander there. All Mike's conversational efforts were met with a grunting sullenness until he gave it up as a bad job. That night, after dinner, he invited his roommate to join him for a drink.

"Fuck off!"

He decided he'd had his fill of Eddie's dark moods, his rudeness, his seething angers. He went to Mom Stone's and had a gin and tonic before moving on to Leo's. There were two women at the bar alone, but neither appealed to him, and he left. MacCurdy's, too, was almost empty, but he ordered a drink anyway. A few minutes later someone slid onto the stool alongside. It was Eddie.

"Mind if I join you?" he began, in that heavy voice.

Mike looked away. "Suit yourself." Eddie called for a bourbon and water. It came and he drank half of it in a single gulp.

"What is it with you? Mike bit off. "For no reason, you bite my head off. You got some kind of a bug up your ass?"

"Lay off."

"Hell, no, I won't lay off. You're living with me, mister, but I'm not your mother. I don't have to baby you."

The battered face seemed to shrivel, the uncertain eyes to turn inward. "Okay. You said it, now let it go." Then he added in a swift flood of words, "I got trouble. At home. My kid sister. She's acting up, running around. Who knows what the hell the little cunt is doing? She ought to be tied down and whipped good." He shook his head as if to clear it. "Oh, dammit, I think she needs treatment. Analysis. I'm looking for a doctor now."

A vague helplessness came over Mike. He was out of his element, swimming in strange waters. Psychoanalysis was an alien activity to him, something to be joked about, something one read about occasionally, mentioned in passing. There was Freud and couches and crazy people. It was not something which touched people you knew. Or their relatives.

"Well," Eddie grumped out. "Why don't you say something?"

"I don't know what to say."

Eddie's strong blunt hand tightened around his glass as if he intended to shatter it. "You know what's wrong with you?" Eddie said through clenched teeth.

Mike made himself laugh. "Too much to say in one breath, I'm afraid."

"That's it, right there. You're afraid. No guts."

An ancient fear came alive in Mike's middle, the fear of trouble, of fighting, of hurting and being hurt. Of being named for what he was so afraid of being, a coward.

"Take it easy, Eddie," he said quietly.

"Shove it, fella." Eddie pivoted around, the hard face rocky, tight, the winged brows bunched over the twist of nose, the deep-set eyes opaque. He brushed reflexively at the thin, sunbleached hair. "Don't tell me what to do. Or what not to do. You're nothing, you know that, don't you? Nothing at all. A two-bit press agent. And dumb about everything. I've been stuck in that room with you for over two months now and you are a big drag. You don't know a thing. You haven't read one-tenth of what I've read. Just a nothing guy from the Bronx. No style. No flair. You don't even know how to dress. . . ."

"What brought this on?"

Eddie jabbed a stiffened forefinger in Mike's direction, glaring at some point past Mike's right ear. "The only thing you can do is get laid. The world is coming down around us and all you care about is that big prick of yours. Well, I make you out to be a fourth-rate lover, too. You just haven't got it."

Mike slid off the barstool. Anger salted his bewilderment and he tried to isolate the cause of the attack. Nothing came.

"You've been building to this all summer. You carry around a load of hostility and——"

Eddie sputtered. "Hostility! Where'd you find that word? Don't pull any of that cocktail party bullshit psychology on me, fella. I've read it all. Everything. Freud, Jung, Adler, Erich Fromm, the new behaviorists. I know it all. And I taught myself. Boy, you are something. Obvious. Transparent. I watched you. At parties. On the beach. The way you look at girls. You expect them to fall over when you talk to them. The way you operate. The way you look into their eyes when you talk to them. As if they matter to you. As if you care. An act, all of it. I'll give you this much, you talk a good game. But nothing worthwhile comes out of you. Not a word. People see you—on the beach, always with a girl—and they know what you're up to. You're too tall to hide. Your shoulders are too big. People are catching on to you. . . ."

A heaving silence followed and for a moment Mike thought Eddie was going to be sick. Gray patches appeared at the corners of his mouth and his lips trembled. His eyes grew glassy, darting anxiously. And he tugged in short quick jerks at his fingers.

Mike's anger dissolved, transformed into sympathy. Pity, almost. A vague emotional comprehension of the other man. The sister, that could be a shock. . . .

"I'll leave you alone, Eddie," he said mildly. "You can use some time to think."

"Don't patronize me, you sonofabitch."

Mike almost smiled. "All right, Eddie. You'd like to hit me. I don't know why, but *you* do. You want to go outside and fight? I imagine you can whip me. I'm not very good with my hands. But when it's over everything will be exactly the same. Whatever pisses you off about me will still be there. Okay, let's go, if that's what you want."

Eddie swayed slightly but made no attempt to get off the stool. After a long moment, Mike jerked around and left.

Chapter X

Neil and Roy

The four of them sat in the living room drinking. Except Neil Morgan, of course. They were celebrating. An exultant peal of triumph seeped out of Roy. He reached over to where Maggie sat, bare legs curled under, and squeezed her bottom.

"I am going to be rich!" he gloated.

"Both of us," Neil said.

Roy grinned thinly and swallowed the remainder of his drink. "You know what they say. It's not enough that you succeed, your friends must fail. In your case, I'll make an exception." That quick, loud laugh came and went. "Here it is, Labor Day weekend. By this time next year, I'll have it made. That's when we'll really celebrate."

"Easy, husband mine," Maggie said.

The icy hazel eyes glittered. "Thanks to your old man, Maggie. A prince, coming across with the dough. Boy, when things happen, and you know what you're doing, they happen fast. Three days and the deal was set."

"How many pictures did you buy?" Neil said in a flat, toneless voice, concealing the envy he felt.

"Fifty-five. All features, full-length."

"Are you going to sell them to television?" Susan asked.

"Not a chance. I'm renting to individual stations across the country. So much per film per play, depending upon the station and the potential market. That way I can still sell repeats and maintain ownership. Once I recoup the investment, pay back Maggie's father, I'll spring for some more. Build up a real library. Let's face it, kiddies, the future of the tube is in film. I'm sure of it."

Maggie smiled at Neil. "This has been a good summer for you too, dear," she offered encouragingly.

Roy, laughing that big laugh, leaned over and kissed Maggie's leg. When she protested, he bit her. She pushed his head away. Laughing still, he licked the inside of her thigh. She rose and crossed to a chair on the other side of the room.

"My husband should be working in one of those Havana whorehouses."

Roy went after another drink. "A wild town," he said over his shoulder. "Anything goes. We saw a show . . ."

"Be still, Roy."

"This black stud, hung like a horse, and two broads. They worked him over and he never stopped. . . ."

"Tell me about your new job, Neil," Maggie broke in.

Neil fought back the deflation which Roy had triggered in him. It appeared that the other man was on the verge of accomplishing everything that Neil wanted and still had not achieved. Yet Neil had known what he was doing all summer long. Week after week, on the beach and at the parties, all those boring nights in town with Sy Melman. Listening to the agent talk about himself, bluster and bellow, boasting about his business adventures, his sexual prowess.

Yet not all those nights had been wasted. Three or four times, Sy had arranged parties, parties to which wives were not invited. The girls present had always been spectacular, nubile, ready for anything. For Neil, there was an almost total excitement with a strange girl, as if it was the first time all over again. The anticipation and the fear, the anxiety to get on with it, to plunge in and fill her up with himself. To *perform*. Always that sense of performance, a segment of himself uninvolved, looking on without emotion.

"Well," he said to Maggie. "You know that I'm quitting B & C. I'm going over to Sy Melman Associates. Naturally it's going to involve a period of apprenticeship, until

I learn the agenting field. But that won't take me very long."

"You'll be class of the track, tiger," Roy said.

An image of his father drifted into Neil's mind. The elder Morgan, jowled, his face round and content under a fine white cap of hair, a man sure of himself and his accomplishments. There was always a thin, challenging smile on his mouth, mocking, full of disbelief. It was a smile Neil intended to wipe away for all time. He intended to prove clearly who was the best man.

"How's the dough?" Roy said.

Neil snapped back. The new job would pay him fifty dollars a week less. Melman was amenable to presenting him with a chance to switch careers; he wasn't prepared to support him while he learned. But Neil had been unable to allow the chance to slip by. He had overridden Susan's nervousness, had assured her that their savings would carry them through the apprenticeship—a period that would not last long, he was sure.

"Better money than I expected," he told Roy. "And it'll get even better. And quick."

Roy lifted his glass. "I'll drink to that. Okay, let's hit the bars. This is the biggest weekend of them all. No sense missing all the action. . . ."

The girl was all wrong. Eddie wanted a slender girl, with the controlled and cultivated look of Vassar or Barnard. He preferred girls who spoke softly in the accents of New England or the Middle West, girls able to discuss politics or literature with equal facility, girls who knew about Jackson Pollack and Dada, the kind of girl he would enjoy being seen with, a girl he could show off.

This one was too heavy by ten pounds with uncommonly large breasts that looked flabby under a brash red sweater. Her features were not unpleasant, though she wore too much makeup, and she spoke with a sputtering anxiousness in the harsh accents of the Lower East Side. He figured her to be a bookkeeper or typist in the garment district.

Yet when she first talked to Eddie at MacCurdy's, he did not send her away, did nothing to discourage her. She chattered about the movies she had seen. She was particulary fond of *Father of the Bride,* gushing over Elizabeth Taylor.

"I wouldn't waste my time on that kind of a picture," Eddie cut in. "Did you see *Sunset Boulevard?*"

She had. "I think William Holden is about the grandest looking man I ever saw, present company excluded," she simpered. "And I just adore Miss Swanson. She's so beautiful. But the picture was just too grim for me, too *sad,* if you know what I mean."

She went on until Eddie stood up and abruptly announced he was going for a walk.

"Oh," she said. Then, "Take me along."

"Suit yourself."

They walked for almost an hour and she chattered incessantly. Twice he urged her on with a thinly concealed maliciousness, taking pleasure in the way she mangled the language, her limited vocabulary. At last he'd had enough and turned back. She had to run to catch up to him.

"Hey!" she cried, "slow down. Wait for baby."

He stopped and waited.

Her laughter was shrill, abrasive. She leaned against him heavily and her breasts felt oppressive. The laughter died out and she took his hands and directed them to her hips, gazed up into his face.

"Boy, I really go for the way you look." She ran her hands along his arms. "You're so hard. That's good, for a man to be hard." She giggled and moved closer. "You wouldn't get no argument if you kissed me."

The kiss was perfunctory. He drew back, but she took his face between her hands and kissed him again. Her lips were very soft and wet, her tongue too large. She rotated her belly against him and acknowledged his response with a small, pleased moan.

"That's it," she said, after a while. "Start easy, finish strong." Her hand drifted onto his bottom and she squeezed. "I like the way you feel, so hard, even here."

"You like everything."

She giggled. "I think you're right. Let's be comfortable, sweetie." She sank to the sand and he allowed her to draw him down next to her. He lay back and gazed at the deep black sky, ignoring the fleshy hand working under his shirt, exploring his chest. He tried to imagine an infinite universe, solar system after solar system, galaxy after galaxy, going on beyond time, beyond thought. The effort created a pressure above his eyes.

Her fingers fumbled at the fastenings of his jeans and he held himself very still. Her mouth worked across his belly, her tongue exploring. He squeezed his eyes shut and fought not to think, not to anticipate. Not to be afraid. A thin film of perspiration broke on his skin and the night air was suddenly chilly.

"What we need," she husked, her voice harshly sibilant, "is a little help here, to make this beautiful thing of yours stand at attention." Again that quick giggle and under the lapping of the surf a voice moaned despairingly. *His* voice. And her wet demands responded.

"Now," she breathed, after a while. "Now."

She climbed onto him, adjusting herself with heavy-handed competence, coming down on him, tugging, directing, pushing. The sagging belly, the oppressive breasts; he felt pinned to the sand.

He kept his eyes shut and tried. No use. It began in his throat, a spasm, thick and resentful, jerking along the complex of nerves and muscles down the length of his torso, and his flesh leaped and shivered, all energy directed finally to that already softening place, expiring in a futile seepage.

"No," she cried helplessly, moving with frantic energy. "Not yet. Please, not yet. Please go inside. Inside . . ."

He was finished. He shoved her away and stood up, adjusted his clothes, and started back down the beach.

"Wait," she cried. "It's all right. The first time never is very good anyway." She was on her feet, trundling after him. "You were excited, that's all. I'm flattered. Rest a minute and we'll do it again. I'll work you up. There are tricks I know." She caught up to him, clutched at his arm. "Wait," she panted.

He pushed her away. "Get away!"

"You had your fun. What about me?"

She reached for him and he pulled his arm away. "Don't touch me!"

Her face was transformed, the lips turned back, the eyes narrow. "Bastard!" she shrilled. "There's something wrong with you. What kind of a man comes that quick? Fag! Dirty fag. Couldn't wait till you got in. You're no man."

His hand flashed out, caught her on the cheek with a

stunning impact. She went down, squealing, more in fright than pain. He took a step toward her, fist clenched.

"You disgust me," he bit off tightly. "A slab of rotten meat, maggots crawling all over you. You're filthy, corrupt. A man would have to be insane to put himself inside of you."

He swung away, muscles bunched and taut, lurching down the beach, fighting against a ballooning anger, lusting for a suitable target.

Mike

"We were traveling, Mother and I. Mother was a magnificent woman, handsome. More beautiful than I."

Eva Schottland smiled a modest smile in Mike's direction. Mike emptied his glass and Schottland rose from his chair across the room and refilled it. Schottland was a man of medium height with flowing yellow hair. He had the impeccable features of a male model, detached, balanced, his face perfect in every detail. Mike found him disconcerting, the steady way he stared while he spoke, his sentences neat and precise, the words coming out of a small red mouth that hardly moved.

He handed Mike the fresh drink and returned to his seat. He directed his attention to his wife. "You were right."

"Yes," she said.

Schottland gazed at Mike. "Eva said you were nice. You are nice."

Mike took a long swallow. He was drunk and getting drunker. Drunk even before he came. After leaving Eddie at MacCurdy's he had gone from bar to bar, having a drink in each, dissatisfied with his handling of the situation, resisting the impulse to go back, to confront Eddie again. He began to walk until he discovered he was on Evergreen. He recalled Eva's invitation and the name of the house. He had no trouble finding it. And was immediately made welcome.

Eva was talking, recalling how it had been in Germany

during the war. She had been a member of the Hitler Youth. But not *really* a Nazi, Schottland explained. All the young people belonged. They had to. It was expected. Demanded.

"It was like the Girl Scouts," Eva went on cheerfully. "There were parades, lot's of parades, and most everybody loves a parade, is it not so? Of course we girls were always trying to get away, to go our own ways. So you see, I was not a political."

Schottland had met her while on a walking tour in Europe after the end of the fighting, he explained. "I wooed her and won her. She had a very hard time during the war."

"We were traveling, Mother and I," Eva repeated, with the same inflection as before. "There was this train for the wounded. One was not permitted on board, of course. But there was this officer, a lieutenant, not more than twenty-five or so. I spoke with him. He asked if I was alone and I told him about my mother. He said though it was not permitted we could come on the train. He arranged a berth where mother could sleep and I stayed with him in his compartment. We were up all night, kissing. Only kissing.

"That night there was an air raid. At night it was the English and during the day the Americans. The train stopped and we all got off, except the wounded, of course. In a raid, you run from one side to the other side to avoid the explosions. When the planes come again from that side, you scramble underneath so that the train is between you and the bombers always. Then you go the other way. It is simple.

"We came to this village and Mother and I remained while the train went on. What an empty feeling. To make love to a handsome young man for three nights—even only kissing—you are bound to feel lonely afterward."

"You see how she is," Schottland offered quietly.

"We lived on the top floor of a building, which the village authorities said was a furniture factory but which really made Messerschmidt airplanes. From the window of our room we could see the funny little onion-shaped church, the kind they have in the East.

"One day the bombers came. They had learned about the factory, you see. There was this boy, very pretty, sweet, younger than me. He was playing the crossover game with the planes, using a truck in the factory yard. But he was doing it wrong, backwards. I ran to him. Yelled at him. But he would not listen. He argued that he was doing it properly. All at once he was dead. A plane came down spitting and there was nothing left of that sweet young face. He should have listened to me."

"Tell Mike about the MP," Schottland urged. "And the older American."

"You think so?"

"Yes."

She nodded. "My first real affair was with an American. He was twice my age but very kind to me. He taught me everything. About men. About myself. My own body."

"Imagine what she looked like then," Schottland suggested. "All that youthful beauty, innocent, able somehow to survive the killing and the degradation. Isn't she a marvelous-looking woman?"

She was seated at the other end of the sofa, a Maillol subject in tight white shorts that bit into abundant thighs. Her breasts were clearly outlined under the sleeveless blouse she wore.

"Marvelous," Mike agreed.

"He followed me home one night," Eva said, "this MP. A big man, very strong. I had seen him watching me before, but he had never spoken to me. Not even once. This night, he drove up alongside in his jeep and ordered me to get in."

"A German girl in occupied Germany," Schottland added. "She must have been terrified."

"He drove to a dark place and parked," she said. "Then he put his hands on my boobs and squeezed until it hurt. I said, 'You are hurting me. Stop it.' I told him I was a good girl."

"He laughed at her," Schottland put in.

"He opened his pants and took out his mister and it was all swollen and red. Very large, you understand. He told me what to do but I didn't understand."

Schottland cleared his throat. "The poor kid couldn't know what he was talking about."

"He made me," she said. "He took my head in his hands and put it close to him and forced me to do it. And when I did it wrong, he hit me across the back of my head and told me how I was supposed to do it so that it pleased him. I was afraid, you can see, so I tried to do it properly. . . ."

"War does terrible things to people," Schottland said. "In a way, I can't blame that MP. Think of what she must have looked like to him in those days. Blooming, unspoiled. This woman is the nearest thing to being alive you'll ever find, Mike. She's a stainless-steel rose. I'm sometimes afraid that if I touch her she'll disintegrate under my fingers. She's too beautiful and delicate to touch and spoil. I am always afraid to do anything to tie her down, to imprison her, to make her less free in any way."

Eva uncrossed her legs and came over to where Mike sat. She sank to the floor in front of him and placed her cheek against his thigh. "You are a very nice man," she sighed.

Schottland took Mike's empty glass and refilled it. "Every man Eva has ever liked I have liked."

"Except Kenneth."

"Except Kenneth. With that one exception, Eva has never introduced me to a man who wasn't a good man."

Mike took the fresh drink and downed half of it. He watched Eva as if through a shifting veil. There was an absent smile on the pink, open face, and her blunted fingers marched up his legs, toward his belt.

Schottland, back in his place, watched with detached interest. "Eva doesn't like people who aren't nice. This is a compliment to us both."

Mike looked down. His belt was open and she was manipulating his trousers downward. Mike watched with fascination as her gaping mouth came down on him, surrounded him, devoured him. And from across the room, Schottland's voice, less precise now, less detached. "Ah, beautiful, my darling. Beautiful. So exciting for me, so good, so very good."

Mike closed his eyes and waited for it to end, a tormented scream echoing somewhere behind his eyes.

Mike and Eddie

Fully clothed, Eddie plunged into the night surf. He swam straight out until the muscles of his arms and shoulders ached and his legs were helpless, trailing members. He turned on his back and floated, drifted without thought, a kind of tranquility found in the soft swells that lifted and transported him.

How much time expired before he started back to shore he never knew. He staggered out of the water, legs trembling, and sprawled out on the damp sand, cheek resting on his curled arm. Weariness gripped him. But not enough. He yearned to force his flesh to the edge of exhaustion. Past the edge. To collapse from fatigue, to lose consciousness, to be unable to think. Or feel.

He heaved himself erect and walked back into the water up to his waist. He moved parallel to the shore, taking satisfaction in the effort of working against the tide. He attacked the ocean, aware of each muscle in his thighs as they flexed and tugged, thrust him ahead. A tightness came into his groin and he almost hoped that he had hurt himself. Pulled a muscle or torn a ligament. He stumbled and went down, came up sputtering. He tried to go on but his legs refused to support him. Finally, he crawled back onto the beach, falling flat.

There was only the present. The soft night sounds. The harsh exhalations of his battered nose. The thumping of his heartbeat in his ears.

Gradually a change, an intrusion. His head came up. An unreal vision swam into focus. He blinked and looked again. Before him was a tableau that reminded him of "The Burghers of Calais," that fantastic lifelike sculpture. But unike Rodin's work, these were in motion, heaving back and forth across the sandy strand. A protesting cry drifted to him and he squinted in an effort to make out what was happening.

There were four figures; one girl and three men. They were tearing at her clothes, stripping her, even as she tried to escape.

A surge of joy came alive in Eddie's gut. Here it was. In front of him. A justifiable outlet for his fury, a target for his clenched anger. At once he went charging up the beach, the weariness gone, making no sound, giving no warning.

"Leave me alone!" the girl cried.

"You've been asking for this."

"Not like this. Not all of you. I'm not that way."

"Now you are!"

One of the men laughed and Eddie wanted to make him choke on it.

"Look out!"

The laughing man whirled in time to take Eddie's fist in the mouth. He went over backward, moaning, swallowing blood and chips of teeth.

His two friends leaped to his aid. A forearm across the shoulders sent Eddie rolling. He tried to avoid their kicking feet. Another blow toppled him onto his chest. He scrambled away.

The first man was back on his feet, spitting blood and cursing. "I'll kill the bastard. Let me kill him."

A hard boot caught Eddie in the ribs, sent him spinning. He struggled to his knees and something struck him behind the right ear. Down he went and a great weight descended on his back, swift pain materializing along his spine. And with the pain came the realization that he had acted rashly, stupidly, without thought.

As if to emphasize the point, his face was driven into the soft sand. His nostrils clogged, he couldn't breathe. He knew then they meant to kill him. Panic set in and he struggled vainly, desperate to survive, willing to do anything.

Suddenly the pressure on his head was gone. He forced himself up, fighting for air. One of his assailants lay on his back, unconscious. Another, on his hands and knees, his head hanging, was helpless and defenseless. The third fled down the beach.

Hands helped Eddie to his feet. "You okay?"

The voice was vaguely familiar. He made an effort to identify it. Mike Birns.

"I'm all right," Eddie said.

"What happened?"

"I wanted to be a hero."

"I don't believe in heroes anymore."

Eddie tried to laugh but the effort sent a sharp pain

stabbing under his ribs. He groaned and held himself. "Then what were you doing here?"

"Getting rid of something. Disgust with myself, I think."

Eddie looked around. The girl was gone. He supposed he couldn't blame her for that.

"What about these two?" Mike said.

"To hell with them. They've had enough and so have I." He took a long, slow breath. The pain was easing. "Let's have a drink."

"Sure," Mike grinned. "MacCurdy's? That's where all this began, I think."

"I don't think I can make it down town. How about our own booze in our own house?"

Arm-in-arm, they started up the beach. "Back at MacCurdy's," Eddie said, "I acted like a jerk."

"That's true. So let's forget it."

"Something happened and it scared me."

"Your sister?"

Eddie shook his head. "My job. It's over. The Tate show is going off the air and I've got nothing else. That bastard, Oscar Morrison, turned down my presentation. I don't seem to have what it takes."

"Come off it."

"I mean it. Sometimes I think there's something the matter with me."

"Knock it off," Mike said casually.

"Mike, can you forget about MacCurdy's? It's been a bitch to be with me this summer, I know. But I want us to be friends."

Mike grinned at him. "This has been one fine summer and we are friends. Okay?"

"Okay."

They climbed the steps that led over the dunes and walked off the beach together.

THREE

AFTER THE SEVENTEENTH SUMMER

This was the year that the permanent residents proposed a higher tax on all houses, certain the summer people wouldn't bother to trek out to the island during January to vote in the referendum. But come they did, in numbers great enough to defeat the tax rise.

This was the year that Charlie Sellers shot a white-tailed deer on the dunes beyond Sunken Forest. And black skimmers, common terns, and black-crowned night herons settled in the pitch pine trees along the length of the island. And migrating waterfowl dropped down out of the Atlantic Flyway to winter in the coves.

In October, Al Spitzer's house caught fire, burned down in twelve minutes. And that week, Lou Reilly floated a complete house across the Bay from Patchogue to Ocean Ridge, where there was still no electricity; it was the first house on the island to have a bathtub.

Great South Bay froze over after the New Year and when Herman Garner's pregnant wife went into premature labor, the Coast Guard sent a helicopter. The baby was born aloft, a perfect boy. Herman named him Chopper and got drunk and fell off the roof of a house he was shingling.

In February, with the wild cat population having reached threatening proportions, a hunt was organized. Terry McAdams killed twenty-two cats on the first day and fifty-

three in all. He had the largest of them stuffed and mounted as a weather vane atop his home which forever-more would be called "The Cat House."

That winter on Fire Island . . .

Chapter I

Mike

It was a bad week. The weather was gray, penetrating, uncomfortably humid. All processes were slowed, emotions depressed. But it was more than the weather.

Summer had ended officially for the inhabitants of Neurotics Anonymous after Labor Day. Their lease ran out, the house reverted to the owners. That had been almost two weeks ago and Mike still had not adjusted to life in the city, to the confines of his apartment. His tan had faded quickly and with it went the euphoria in which he had lived. On the island everything had been easy, simple. In Manhattan all the complications returned. There were the harsh, intruding sounds of life in the city, the crowds, the dirt, the difficulty in getting about.

That was only part of it for Mike. On the previous Monday he had completed the first draft on the new mystery. A period of exultation should have ensued, a few days of relaxation, satisfaction, contentment with his achievement. That was how it had been in the past. This time was different. He felt compelled to return to the work the following morning, to read what he had written. Halfway through the book, he knew it was wrong. *Bad*. But he forced himself to keep reading through to the end.

Panic set in. A slow steady descent into uncertainty and terror. He began to drink.

This was his eighth book. He was an accepted, recognized talent, a writer of mysteries that were solidly built, with characters of flesh and blood. Critics had termed his work superior, and his lack of popular acceptance was put to the flawed tastes of the reading public.

But this book was badly done. Less a mystery than a love story, it was too shallow to be meaningful. The plot was obvious, formless, as if all his skills had deserted him. More, his hero, the intrepid college professor-private eye, seemed suddenly stilted and sated, unable to rise to the occasion, a man more observer than participant.

Mike slumped down on his couch and swore at the ceiling. He was getting drunk and was glad of it. Drunk on Scotch and self-pity. And fear. Writers sometimes lost their ability to write. Blocked it all off emotionally. Made strangers from that mysterious and unidentifiable magic that allowed them to perform. Had it happened to him? Would it last for a long time? Forever? What could he do about it? If he were unable to write he would be in serious trouble. His savings were low and his royalties hardly enough to pay his rent. It would mean going back to a square job, to becoming a press agent again. A groan of despair trickled across his lips, the very thought making him ill.

The telephone rang. Let it ring. There was no one he wanted to talk to, no voice he wanted to hear. He would remain supine on the couch and continue to pour Haig & Haig Pinch down his throat in numbing swallows. Let the outside world take a flying fuck at the moon. Up yours, mystery fans. Up yours, movie executives, non-buyers of seven books. Up yours, world.

Curiosity drew him off the couch, into the bedroom. Sprawling across his bed, he reached for the receiver.

"Identify yourself," he muttered thickly.

"May I talk to Myron Birns, please."

All that youthful vibrancy, the voice gay and crackling with life. There was no mistaking it. He wished she hadn't called and was glad she had.

"Don't call me Myron," he said gruffly.

"Mike, it's Elizabeth Jordan."

"So."

"Mike," she said softly, after a moment. "Do you hate me?"

"Uhuh."

"You were so sure of yourself, so opinionated. So damned stubborn. But you were right."

"About what?"

"About whales. They can't live under water. They come up to get air."

"Christ. Is that why you ran away?"

He could hear her breathing. "No," she said, "that isn't why."

"Dumb," he ripped out. "To run off that way, without a word. A kid's trick . . ."

"Mike, please. Don't be angry with me. I kept hoping you could come and find me but you didn't. I cried when I realized you weren't coming after me, Mike." When he said nothing, she went on. "I had to call you. Mike, it wasn't the whales."

"What then?"

"You know."

"Tell me," he insisted.

"Mike. Are you alone? I'm not interrupting."

A rasping response tore out of him. There was the irony. All the evenings alone since the summer ended, with the thick urge looping knots in his bowels, the crotch bulge swelling and diminishing, making him more aware of his unfulfilled needs.

"I'm alone," he said.

She spoke after a short interval. "May I come and visit?"

The familiar stirring came and there was a perceptible shifting in his trousers. He couldn't remember a comparable period of celibacy since his divorce. He had been careful to arrange his existence so that a number of women were always available to him. On call. Now here was this virginal voice inviting herself back into his life, to frustrate him, to give him a hard time. It wouldn't do at all.

"What's the purpose?"

"Please, Mike." There was a lingering plea in her voice and he felt himself grow weak with wanting.

"All right. Dammit, all right."

He slammed down the phone. For a long moment, he lay very still, forbidding himself to think. Then he got up and went into the bathroom, shaved and brushed his teeth, took a shower, alternately hot and cold. He dressed quickly and sat down to wait.

Neil

He sat stiffly behind the massive desk in his private office and studied the contents of the folder on the desk in front of him. The True Crime presentation. That there was something wrong with it, he had long ago conceded to himself. But what was it? The answer continued to elude him. He resisted the confusion that kept clogging his brain. This was a time for clear thinking, for logic, for reason. A way had to be found to break the impasse. True Crime *was* a good idea. Right for its time. *This* time. There was the Capote book and the movie made from it; and *The Boston Strangler*. People were buying that kind of thing. They would buy *this*.

What was wrong? His connection with the game-show scandal? Oscar Morrison had offered it as an excuse but there had to be something else. Something that could be repaired. A weakness in the presentation, a flaw in his approach. Correct that error and success would inevitably result. It always did. To believe otherwise was too disturbing to consider.

The phone interrupted his thoughts.

"There's a Mr. John Vardis calling," his secretary said.

"Put him through." The connection was completed. "Vardis."

"Mr. Morgan."

"What have you found out?"

Vardis cleared his throat as if to begin a lengthy speech. Neil visualized him. Fleshy but powerful, with incredibly thick wrists and huge hands. His face would be flushed, cheeks splashed with tiny purple veins. His eyes were pale, cool, suspicious. Neil had been impressed with Vardis from the first; the big man looked like a detective.

"This was quite an assignment," Vardis intoned. "Very interesting. Complex."

Neil said nothing. He understood that Vardis wanted to impress him with the difficulty of the job, a tactic he had often used himself. He was better at it than Vardis. Much more subtle.

"To pick out one kid in hippieland is a very sticky

undertaking. The East Village is like a jungle of them hippies."

"Did you find her?"

"I wouldn't swear to it, but I think so. Without a photograph, positive identification isn't possible. Still, every profession has it's little techniques, you might say."

"You think it's Marybeth?"

"There is reason to believe that the young lady we've turned up is the subject of our interest, Mr. Morgan."

"Where is she now?"

"I have this address. One of those so-called 'crash pads'. On Eleventh Street, near First Avenue. We have cause to suspect it is she."

"Give me the address."

Vardis cleared his throat again. "I don't think you want to go alone, Mr. Morgan. Some of these young people are not what I or you would term rational, if you know what I mean. It would be smart if I escorted you."

That made sense to Neil. He wasn't looking for trouble. He simply wanted to get Marybeth out to New Jersey, to that doctor. Nearly two weeks had passed since her disappearance and that meant the foetus in her womb was developing, fast approaching the stage where an operation would be dangerous. Perhaps impossible. Neil was anxious to end this unpleasant duty before matters became even more distasteful. Marybeth was too immature to understand how he felt. That he wished her no harm. That he simply could take no chances, a man in his position.

To allow her to have the child was unthinkable. A bastard child with an unstable young mother. There was no telling when both would come back to cause trouble for him. He could afford neither the risk nor the luxury.

"Name a place where we can meet," he said to Vardis.

Vardis was in a phone booth on First Avenue. "There's a coffee shop on the corner."

"Give me thirty minutes."

Neil hung up and took out his address book, located the number in Newark, dialed. A female voice answered and he asked for the doctor by name, saying he was a personal friend. The doctor came on.

"Doctor, this is the gentleman who was forced to cancel his appointment almost two weeks ago. I said I'd call again."

"Yes," the doctor said, his voice guarded. "I recognize your voice."

"I'm ready to make another appointment."

"I see. Well, there are arrangements to be made. When an appointment is broken . . ."

"This one will be kept."

"How soon?"

"Today, if possible. I should be able to confirm within two hours."

"Very well. Let's make it for tonight at nine. The same place. You will confirm?"

"I will." Neil went out into the reception room. "Cancel my appointments for the rest of the day."

"You have a tennis game with Bill Douglass at the Vanderbilt courts."

Bill Douglass was a pro. It was he who had introduced Neil to tennis. And Neil hated to give up the game. Still . . .

"I won't be able to make it. Call and make some excuse. See if he's available for tomorrow. Too bad. I feel very strong today, ready to beat him."

"And Roy Ashe called. Wants to see you."

"Say I'll get back to him in a day or two. I know what he's after and the answer's going to be no. Call my wife and say I won't be home for dinner. Say I'm on my way to Baltimore to meet with a client. She'll understand."

Neil rode a cab downtown. He felt a mounting confidence. The girl Vardis had located, it *would* be Marybeth. Soon this matter would be over and again he would be able to direct his attention to business. This was a good lesson. Stay in your own league, for business or pleasure. Play only with people who play by the same rules.

Still, Marybeth had provided some sweet hours. He would miss them.

Neil found Vardis hunched over a cup of coffee at the counter of a dingy luncheonette. Neil took the stool alongside, dwarfed next to the detective.

"Finding the subject," Vardis began, lips barely moving, "was no easy business, Mr. Morgan. These hippies stick together, protect their own, so to speak."

"You said you were sure it was her."

Vardis lifted his great shoulders and lowered them.

"There's only one way to be absolutely sure. Take a look-see."

"Let's go."

They strode east along Eleventh Street, Vardis explaining that among the hippies, too, money could buy information, open doors otherwise firmly closed.

"Put it on your bill," Neil said curtly. In his British-tailored tan gabardine suit, custom-made shirt and hand-tooled cordovans, he felt out of place in these shabby surroundings. Neglect streaked the walls of the buildings and the people were in a state of equal disrepair.

The big detective nodded solemnly. He recognized the growing tension in Morgan. It was always that way with his clients, whenever there was the threat of personal danger. The people Vardis dealt with were seldom equipped to cope with the kind of trouble his work frequently turned up. That, he reckoned with grim satisfaction, was why they paid him so well.

They stopped in front of an ancient tenement. The once yellow brick was dark, stained, chipped. Rusted fire escapes marched up the ruined facade like some avant-garde sculpture.

"Pretty, ain't it?" Vardis said.

"These crumby joints," Neil said bitterly. "They should all be torn down. The neighborhood cleaned up. Decent buildings built that would house decent people."

"These are mostly poor people around here."

Neil snorted irritably. "To be poor in a country as rich and full of opportunity as America is almost criminal," he muttered. "No excuse for it. A man can do anything in this country, be anything he wants, get anything he wants. Unless he's too damned lazy to work," he ended.

Vardis began to reply, thought better of it. "Ready to go inside?"

"That's why I came."

Vardis was careful to show nothing of what he felt. "The subject is on the fourth floor. There are other people present." He hesitated. "There could be trouble."

Neil considered that. He had no wish to expose himself to physical danger but he seemed to have little choice. To ask for police help was out of the question, and it would take too much time to hire additional private operatives.

"I don't want a fuss," he said flatly. "This has to be done quietly."

"I understand."

They climbed three granite steps, went inside. The narrow hallway was dingy and reeked of fresh vomit and stale urine. Neil held his breath and tried not to consider the odor. The steps creaked under them as they climbed, the staircase unsteady, the bannister shaky.

"Catch a breather?" Vardis said on the third-floor landing.

Neil turned on that thin, confident grin. He wasn't even breathing hard. Vardis might be blessed with greater size and more muscle, but he wasn't in as good shape. No fat hung on Neil Morgan and his legs and lungs were first-rate. First-rate.

On the fourth floor, Vardis stopped in front of a door decorated with day-glo paints. Stripes and circles covered the lower half of the door and an oversized eye dominated the upper portion.

"Pretty, ain't it?" Vardis said sincerely.

"Knock," Neil ordered.

For the first time Vardis almost smiled. He turned the knob and opened the door. They went inside.

BB

Robert Bradford College. A liberal arts school devoted to tolerating those sons and daughters of the rich and near-rich unacceptable at other institutions of higher learning. Permissiveness guided the actions of the Bradford administration which layed down only one immutable regulation —*don't get caught*.

Bradford was situated in the rolling hills of upper New York State, some thirty miles from the state's fourth largest city. An easy run for its students, most of whom owned cars. The area had once been famous for farming and producing salt. No longer. The remaining farms were small affairs, doing little more than supporting the families who worked them; and salt was a thing of the past.

Industry had moved into the area, making more money available to more people. With it came an influx of immigrants seeking their share of the pie. As a result, the population of the area trippled during the last decade. Houses and stores were built, roads put down. Doctors came and lawyers and hi-rise luxury buildings were erected on the shore of the lake. People came to where the money was, and suddenly other things became available, too.

BB drove into town after dark and parked the car on a business street to save the cost of a parking lot. Every penny counted now. He sniffed and scratched his cheek and coughed as he shuffled through the quiet commercial streets beyond North Avenue, the main drag. He stopped in front of the big, brightly lit show windows of Sear's, studying the appliances. That washing machine. That would do fine, bring a good piece of change. Too large, he decided, and impossible to account for. Typewriters were good and portable televisions. Easy to carry, easy to peddle. He'd gotten thirty-five dollars for a Remington the previous week. But that had been a lucky break, an open door in the men's dorm. At that, he'd almost been caught on his way out. The risks were great but so was his habit, growing bigger all the time.

Bread was becoming more difficult to come by. His weekly allowance failed to cover his needs. Twice he'd phoned home to say there was trouble with the car and twice Neil had come through. But that one wouldn't work again.

He considered selling the car once again. And once again decided against it. Without wheels, he'd be married to that damn campus where no one pushed shit.

His desperation grew daily. He had to find some way of getting money. Earlier in the week he'd called Cindy, invited her up for the weekend. He figured that when the hot-rocks got a look at her they'd be panting to score. Twenty-five a throw would be about right. Two days of hustling with Cindy and he'd be set for a while.

No, she told him. She was finished with that bit. From now on, she said—and there was a crisp firmness in her voice that told him she meant it—from now on, she would do it only for love or for fun.

If you love me, he had pleaded. That drew a caustic laugh and the suggestion that love was a two-way street.

Get another girl, she advised him. As if he hadn't tried! The coeds, so willing to give it away, were too damned stupid to make it pay.

And now Carl was climbing his back.

He'd been in his room alone, aware of the increasing urgency, of the deeper craving that took root in the mucous membranes of his mouth and throat, the thicker craving.

His concentration had been so completely turned in that he didn't hear his name being called. The door opened and a curly-headed senior looked in.

"Hey, Morgan! You deaf? Telephone."

He shuffled out to the hall phone. "Yeah," he began.

The sharp, nasal voice was instantly recognizable. "BB, I been waitin' to hear from you."

BB stalled. "Who is this?"

The harsh nasal tones grew peevish. "This is your mother, man. Your *mother.*"

His mother. The source of life, sustenance, of all good things. His supplier. His pusher. His mother.

"Carl, I——"

"No names, man. You know that."

"I was on my way to call you," BB lied. "Coincidence, isn't it?"

"Shit me easy, man. The day has come. You have run out of time. Student, meet your debts. Don't they teach you that at that school? Unpaid bills got to be paid, you see, and collectin' day has arrived."

"A couple of days more . . ."

"Today. Man, you know what you are? A junkie, that's what you are. And junkies can't be trusted. That's important money you're into me for and I want it."

"How am I going to get it?" BB almost screamed. Then, more quietly, his breathing harsh: "How?"

"Junkie, find a way."

"If I had a shot, Mother. My nerves are gone. . . ."

The nasal laugh was ominous, brief. "Junkies find junkie ways. Use your brains. You are the student, not me."

"Let me have a fix then."

"You've run out of credit. The day ends at midnight, student. Pay off or somebody will come to see you."

That had been earlier. How long ago? BB looked at his watch. His wrist was bare. He had hocked the watch last week. Last *month.* Time was needed and he was running out of it. He willed it to cease, stand still, wait for his mind to clear, to function in the way he knew it could.

Once Carl was paid off, he vowed silently, that would be quitting day. Off the stuff for good. He refused to be a prisoner to it for the rest of his life. A man could do anything he wanted to do. How often Neil had said that to him. He wanted to believe it, had to believe it. Pay off Carl and quit. It was that simple. Oh, not cold turkey. No sense kidding himself about that. A gradual, sensible withdrawal scheme. He'd work it out carefully. Smaller doses each day. Fewer shots each week. Good planning. Control. Will power. These would do it.

Oh, *God.* A spasm took hold of his guts and squeezed, a cramping that flooded his viscera. Keep a tight asshole, man. Hold *on.* The pain eased and went away.

He raised his head. He was on a still empty street lined with darkened factory and loft buildings. Lost. And alone.

At once he was no longer alone. Coming out of one of the buildings across the street, hurrying his way, a single man. He moved with short quick steps, head down, hands deep in his pockets, as if shielding himself against the winter that would soon be upon them.

Winter was a bad time in Upper New York State, BB reflected idly. The man came nearer, passed into the cone of yellow light from a street lamp. He was balding, his remaining hair gray. A short man with shimmering jowls and a weary expression. A man who could have been BB's father. An old man and fat.

BB straightened up, flexed his fingers, sensuously aware of his young body, his hard muscles, the quickness in his limbs. His tongue was dry, swollen, and his breath came in short takes. A pulse beat irregularly in his throat.

The little man looked up and saw BB. A flash of fear came onto his face. He appraised the youth in front of him—tall and slender, with a kind of easy gracefulness in his expensive rainjacket and faded blue jeans. A student. A nice-looking boy. Obviously from a good family. A boy with proper values. No threat there. The fear washed away, to be replaced by a small, friendly smile.

"Nice night," the man said, as he came abreast of BB.

"Nice . . ."

The little man trundled past, head down again, deep in

his own concerns. BB sucked air and sprang after him, fists aiming at the vulnerable neck. The man tumbled forward, grunting, protesting. BB kept hitting out. A thin voice cursed and he knew the voice was his own. The man rolled, trying to escape. BB went after him, striking with all his strength. A man like this, so smug and square, carefully turned out. Such a man would have money on his person, a lot of money.

The round bland face turned up toward him, mouth working soundlessly. BB slugged away at that gray blob. The little man fell back, lay still.

BB kneeled, hands trembling, going through the man's pockets. He found the wallet, emptied it. Seven singles. There had to be more. He searched for a hidden compartment. There was none. He went through every pocket again. Nothing. An anguished groan seeped out of him. Seven dollars. Not nearly enough.

Another spasm gripped his middle. He heaved but gave up nothing. Finally it passed. He hurried away, shoving the money into his jacket pocket. He was going to have to find another victim, as many as were necessary. He had to have the money and there were only a few more hours to midnight.

Elizabeth

Waiting, Mike's desire abated, and he regretted her coming. As a sexual partner, she had suddenly become unappealing. Certain to be unsatisfactory. And a problem. Elizabeth Jordan. One of life's innocents, pure at twenty-five. She would be without passion, without experience, without skill. All this in the midst of the sexual revolution! Revolution, hell. If there'd been one, mark her down as a non-participant.

He tried to imagine sex with Elizabeth. He envisioned tears and recriminations, all designed to rouse his guilts. And she would talk of marriage. No, thanks. He was locked in his own groove, too far down the path, too damned old. Particularly for someone like her. That naïveté, that small-girl manner, that sweet innocent zest for life. All that had passed him by. Too many years chasing and catching women, bedding them. Enjoying them. His techniques were refined to the point of instinct, and he acted and reacted with a confidence that bred success, not frustration.

For some men it was a game, a need to prove. And some simply had a need for women, a sexual requirement they tried to fulfill. Like eating. Or sleeping. Another natural function. It was different for Mike. Women made every event, every experience, more vivid and rewarding, exciting. He cared for women, all of them. And for some in particular, those that turned him on, he felt an almost overwhelming desire. He wanted to please them and be pleased by them and was sure that his interest in women had increased over the years. God, how he loved the sweet-sour scent of their lust, the clogging muskiness.

Sex was the fuel of his existence. The single most rewarding factor of his life, its promise and its fulfillment. He could think of nothing about a woman he did not like, could remember no experience that had been less than good. And so many that were incredible. Fantastic. Great!

What did Elizabeth Jordan know of that? She would equate sex with love, sex with duty, sex with marriage. Always it came to that, to paying for what you got. She would want a house in the suburbs and two cars and twice as many children. Let others go that route, not Mike Birns.

He liked life the way it was. Had it made. He was his own man, free to come and go as he pleased. No one made demands on him. And he owed nothing to anyone.

Another person, a wife. That would mean a variety of obligations: bills to be met, things to do, to own. The price was too high.

Admittedly there were rewards. Jean had provided him with years of pleasure. *Mostly* pleasure. When it went sour, it went fast.

Thoughts of his marriage emerged from a shadowed memory bank. Slightly out of focus, the details put aside, the vision tinged with a nostalgic regret. She had toured New England that summer, a stock company production. He had been sent south to open a new film. Atlanta was first, then Houston, Dallas . . .

The letter reached him in Dallas. It wasn't much of a letter, studded with cliches, but to the point. Another man was the heart of the matter. A man who had moved into the void in their marriage. A void that had been deepening each day. Perhaps their separate career interests were at fault. The enforced separations. In any case, love had gone. And with it, the marriage. She wanted a divorce.

He had pictured her with another man, bodies entwined, fondling each other, saying the same words she had said to him. Pleasing a stranger in all the ways she had pleased him. His anger and hurt had been monumental. He stayed in his hotel room drinking for three days. And he cried.

Afterward, he would not permit himself to think about it at any length. He assured himself that he had handled it with maturity, with equanimity, that he needed no single person. Surely not Jean. Not *really*. But he knew that there was a place behind his navel scarred and twisted out of shape.

Elizabeth's arrival interrupted his thoughts. She was breathless, more beautiful than he had remembered, the slender cheeks flushed, the freckles across her nose more pronounced. Only the green eyes were cool, a protective veil drawn down over them. Her smile was unsteady. He wanted to embrace her but didn't. Kept his distance.

"Well," he said.

She took a step or two into the apartment, appraising him, and it, warily. Another step, head swiveling. He was reminded of the brown rabbits that hopped around Fire Island, pausing in the open, dumb and vulnerable.

"This is nice," she said in a small voice.

He reached for her and she retreated, one hand raised protectively. "Dammit," he said. "What do you think I'm going to do?"

"Are you angry with me?"

"Sore as a boil. But I won't hit you." Again he reached and this time she held still. He drew her close. Her cheek was warm against his and he could feel her heart beating crazily. She shifted her feet as if to move away and his arms tightened.

"Be still," he admonished her mildly. Her body remained rigid, arms at her side. He released her with regret and led her to the couch. "Sit," he said. She remained standing, staring at him. He filled his lungs with air. "What would you like to drink?" She frowned thoughtfully, as if considering the question. "Oh, come *on.* A drink. Will you relax, please? You aren't obliged to . . . Look, what kind of a monster do you think I am? Rape is not my bag."

"I know that."

He went over to the bar. "I'm going to have a Scotch. You? Very weak."

A faint grin lifted her mouth. "Too weak won't be much good at all."

He laughed and made the drinks. He gave her one glass. "You can sit down now."

She perched tentatively on the edge of the couch, chewing at the rim of the glass, watching him sidelong.

"The wolf and the lamb," he muttered sarcastically.

"What makes you think I'm a lamb?"

"What makes you think I'm a wolf?"

Her face brightened. "I don't think so. Wolves are monogamous, you see. When they mate, they stay together. You're——"

"I get the picture."

They looked at each other.

"This is nice," she said. "Out on the island, I never had a chance to look at you from a distance. We were always so close, intimate, talking or kissing. . . ."

"Kissing," he said, moving closer. "That's a good idea. . . ."

She waved him back and he obeyed. "Don't try so hard."

There was something reassuring about the way she said it.

"You're beautiful," he said, as if discovering it for the first time. The features, the figure, the coloring, all were good. Better than good. And she had fine legs and full pale thighs. A sensual mouth.

"You're angry with me," she said. "About the way I acted. On the island, I mean. You have the right, I suppose."

"It was a stupid argument, about whales."

"It wasn't about whales."

"You said that over the phone."

She wet her lips, took a sip of the Scotch, and put the glass aside. "It was because we hadn't slept together."

He appraised her quizzically. The words had come with surprising ease and she appeared perfectly relaxed.

"Isn't it?" she went on.

He spoke carefully. "You ran away because you were afraid to go to bed with me?"

"Yes and no," she said, almost inaudibly.

"What does that mean?"

She reached for his drink, put it next to her own on the coffee table, moved closer to him. "I think we talk too much sometimes. Will you kiss me, please?"

It was different. The cool lips were hot and hungry, her tongue a wet electric probe. Her hands clutched and grabbed, reached and stroked, squeezed and tugged. Sounds and squeaks and moans came out of her and she bore down on him, forcing him backward, legs spreading across him, her middle wiggling and squirming, thumping, pounding, rotating, in a succession of gyrations more wild than anything he had ever known.

She was everywhere, attacking with a fever and a ferocity that put him at her mercy. Her hands tore at his belt, buttons, zipper. Clothes were drawn down, pulled off, stripped away. Soon he was naked and she wore only a garter belt and stockings. Her lips worked over the outer curve of his shoulder, onto his bicep, underneath, into the armpit, tongue dancing to some ancient mating song. And all the while, her hands were busy. Her fingers made a fantastically evocative march up one side of his hard member and down the other, across his tender scrotum, along the inside of his thigh. *Too much.*

He tried to alter the balance of power, to regain the offensive, to assert his manly prerogatives. He went at her with renewed energy. He stabbed her, opened her. Skewered her. She loved it, fought back joyfully, urging him on, naming each act in hard, short terms, insisting he repeat this, duplicate that, give again. More, more, more . . .

She twisted and maneuvered until her head touched the floor, body riding up the side of the couch, legs forming the victory V. He adjusted himself to her and through the swirling crimson mist that enclosed him the sound of her triumphant laughter reached out.

They clung to each other and heaved apart. Smashed together in a cataclysmic joining, launched as if from a great distance, zeroing in. On target. Gymnasts in an orgy of physical improvisation, arranging themselves in combinations and shapes beyond repetition.

Now gentle, all murmurings and easy caresses, a poem of affection and concern; lips warm and urgings faint, full of unselfishness.

Now fierce, all nails and teeth, muscles hard and punishing, fingers digging painfully, bodies toughly demanding, insisting voraciously, all pelvic pounding to unimagined heights and mutual triumph.

He was a satyr.

She was a bitch.

He teased her.

She tormented him.

He commanded.

She demanded.

They gave.

They took.

And took.

They rolled onto the floor, snaked under the table, rested on the Oriental prayer rug, revived on the window seat, collapsed into the leather chair, crashed against the bookcase, leaned on the television, crawled into the bedroom. Surrendered on the bed.

They slept.

They woke.

And waking lunged again at each other, bodies drenched with sweat and passion, the sheets reeking of it. They slipped and slid, clutching for a handhold, finding it. They slept again.

"More," she said. "More, more, more."

"You're insane."

"You're wonderful."

"And I thought you were a virgin!"

"I was fighting for a hold on myself. I was like you, sexy, skipping from bed to bed, finding it here and there, as long as I got it. I recognized you at once, the minute we met that day in the ocean."

"Then why—?"

"Because I had enough of all the men in the world. I wanted to be my own woman, own my own flesh and emotions. And I did. I stayed away from men for six months. I don't *need* them all anymore."

"Only me," he boasted.

She sucked his middle finger. "Only you."

"You'll kill me," he said, after a while.

"Fuck you to death," she agreed, burying her face in the slack softness of his sexuality. Her tongue darted out, defied him, dared him, challenged him to respond. Her lips worked.

"I'm too old for you."

"You're a stripling, full of life, not yet used. A sexual giant. A marvel of human construction. A living wonder. Every girl should have her own sex maniac. At last I've got mine," she said, filling her mouth with him.

"I'm worn out. I must rest."

"Later," she managed.

"I can't," he protested. "Not again."

He was wrong. And was proved wrong—beautifully, sensually wrong. Afterward, he was allowed to rest. He deserved it.

Both of them did.

Susan and Maggie

The fountain in the plaza of the Lincoln Center complex sent its water shooting skyward. Susan watched with interest as the pattern changed. Fountains had an ambivalent effect on her, at the same time restful and stimulating. The stream held, glistening under the bright autumn sun. A few minutes later, Maggie arrived.

"Traffic gets worse all the time," she complained. "I had to take a bus crosstown."

"How chic! To mingle with the common people."

They both laughed, headed for the Vivian Beaumont Theater behind the reflecting pool. "When I was young," Maggie said. "When Roy and I were married, a few centuries ago, I used to ride buses all the time. To save money. To help him. He had gone into debt, borrowed money from my father, from some other people. Some film deal or other. It failed."

"Poor Roy. Everything seems to fail for him. You've done better this time."

"One's second husband should have money," Maggie said brightly, "if nothing else."

"I've always meant to ask, Maggie, is Bob any good in the hay?"

"Darling, I barely remember. I know we made it on our wedding night and a few times after. None of them recently."

"What a relief that must be."

They entered the lobby of the theater and went down the red-carpeted steps to the box office. *Tiger at the Gates* was the current play.

"The reviews were not very good," Maggie said.

"I know. But BB's coming in next weekend and Neil thinks he should see it. He claims it says something profound about the inevitability of war."

"For or against?"

Susan shrugged. "Ask Neil. It's his idea."

"I imagine he finds some parallel in it to Viet Nam."

"You know it."

"After all these years, I think I'm beginning to understand your husband."

"He's utterly predictable. I can finish every sentence out of his mouth before he speaks."

"Has Neil become a peacenik?"

"Hardly. He's all hawk. And he's disturbed because BB refuses to take ROTC training. Neil says a man has an obligation to his country."

"Is he trying to get your son shot?"

Susan made a face. "My husband has some contacts in Washington. He made a couple of training films for the Defense Department a few years ago. He's sure he can get BB stationed in Washington, if he goes on active duty."

"There's a certain contradiction there."

"I don't care, as long as BB doesn't get shot."

She moved up to the box-office window and purchased the tickets. "Now," she said, when they were back outside, "where shall we lunch?"

"The Opera Cafe?"

"Why not The Ginger Man? There are lots of pretty young men there to flirt with."

They had to wait for a table for nearly thirty minutes. They ordered martinis and then seconds. Neither of them was in a hurry and there was much to talk about.

Susan didn't notice the young man who was watching her until after they had given the waiter their lunch orders. There was a permanently mocking cast to his face, the eyes narrow, speculative, his mouth angled to match. His skin was smooth and too tight for the wide cheekbones, the jaw heavy. Thick brown hair hung almost to his shoulders. He stood at the bar, peering at her over the dividing panel. He was very sure of himself. When their eyes met, he inclined his head and flexed his mouth. She turned away first.

All during lunch, he continued to stare at her. Always that taunting half-smile, the squinting eyes. To hell with him, she thought, and forced herself to not look again.

The waiter brought coffee and Susan stood up. "It's the ladies for me. Be back in a sec, darling." She picked her way between the tables with no urgency. Let the arrogant bastard get a good look! She lengthened her stride, allowed her hips to follow naturally in an easy sway. She felt him studying her and she was pleased. She still had it, could still set the young ones on edge, trigger the juices. For all the good it would do him, let him enjoy himself.

He was waiting when she came out of the ladies room. Taller than she had supposed, he was lean, with high, bony shoulders, and an intense thrust to his head. His eyes narrowed when she appeared and he moved into her path. Confident. Smug. Like so many of the young men she had known.

"Hey, listen," he began. "You are something special and I haven't been able to take my eyes off you."

His skin was creamy, his mouth blood red, the eyes pale blue. Not more than twenty-five, she guessed, and used to succeeding with women. He would be difficult to resist. A man this tall, she wondered how big he was.

"I suppose you think I'm coming on pretty strong," he said.

She nodded, watching him carefully.

He ducked his head boyishly. An affectation, she was certain, but effective. Cute.

"Okay. So I'm not shy." He laughed, a soft baritone that found a responsive chord in her.

"You're anything but shy," she said. "Arrogant, I would say. Overly aggressive."

"You've found me out. Okay. Now ditch your friend and I'll buy you a drink."

There was no point in being coy, she assured herself. Or in prolonging the inevitable. He roused her as no one had in a very long time. He was also young enough to satisfy that desire, mature enough to need no coaching, not to be babied and coaxed. Not to be spoiled. She reconsidered . . .

"You're a child," she said, with no particular emphasis. A cautious smile let him know that she wasn't sending him away. "I could be your mother."

"You're nothing like my mother. I'm almost twenty-four and I've read Oedipus three times," he finished, with a bright grin.

"You're a dirty young man."

"Leave your friend. . . ."

"My friend and I are going to have our coffee, finish our lunch together and our conversation. In case you don't realize it, I *am* a married lady."

"I never doubted it for a moment."

"It doesn't matter to you?"

"You matter. You're fantastic. I want to be alone with you, talk to you, let you get to know me. . . ."

What about getting to know me, she asked silently, certain he had little interest in doing that.

"I know a place, very comfortable, very private, where we can be alone. I'll tell you all about myself."

"I'm certain of that." She took a step past him. "I must get back to Maggie."

"Dump Maggie."

"You can wait," she said. "Take your chances."

"Please."

"Well," she said, over her shoulder. *"That's* a step in the right direction."

Maggie understood and said she envied Susan her good luck. Perhaps he had a friend, for some other time, some afternoon in the future. They finished the coffee and Maggie left. Susan waited for him to come over to the table. When he didn't, she joined him at the bar.

"I was waiting for you," she began.

"I figured you'd come around when you were ready. Do you want a drink?"

"I don't think so."

"Let's go, then." He took her elbow, guided her out into the street. He steered her around the corner, up Columbus Avenue.

"Where are we going?" she said.

"My apartment."

She stopped and they faced each other. "You haven't even bothered to tell me your name. Just, here I am, let's screw. Well, to hell with you, sonny."

He protested. "It's you. You turn me on and I'm all whacked out. Sorry." Again the boyish grin. "Judd Martin is my name and let's be friends. Okay?" He raised his hands in mock surrender. "So I went too fast. The way you look, I can't be blamed, right? Right," he answered easily. "You don't trust me alone. I don't blame you. Sure, I want you. I intend to make a very large pass the minute we're alone. But I understand 'no', lady, if you say it. I can be handled and you're just the one to do it."

She heard him out. It was so patently a line, but he delivered it effectively, with exactly the right amount of youthful sincerity. And his animal attractiveness lent an added impact.

"So you see," he was saying, "I meant no harm. You don't want to come over to my apartment, you don't come. It's just a place where we can be alone and quiet, get to know each other. I've got some Scotch and a good brandy and—" He broke off. "No promises are necessary. No obligations."

They began to walk again. "I think I would prefer to have a drink and our little get-acquainted talk in a more public atmosphere, if you don't mind. A quiet saloon."

"Oh," he said. "Sure."

Without looking, she was aware of his disappointment. He was not used to being rejected, even temporarily. And not by married ladies who allowed themselves to be picked up in restaurants.

"Where shall we go?" she asked.

"Well," he temporized, keeping his face averted. "There

really aren't any places suitable around here. The unfashionable West Side."

"We could go to O'Neal's. Or Des Artistes."

"Oh, you know the neighborhood."

She laughed back in her throat. She had shaken him up and that really had been all she wanted to do. To tame that surging arrogance, to let him know she wasn't easy to manipulate.

They went to Des Artistes. He dropped a five-dollar bill on the bar and ordered Scotch sours for both of them. An idea came alive in her mind.

"Is that it?" she said, indicating the bill. "The extent of your fortune?"

He spoke too quickly. "My finances are my affair."

"Not to have money is nothing to be ashamed of." The words sounded meaningless in her ears.

His face was cold and expressionless. "That's something you don't have to worry about, not having dough." His voice was larded with resentment.

"My husband has been fortunate," she said. "He produces in television and films. Neil Morgan is his name."

The barman brought the drinks and left. Judd spoke in a more normal voice. "That means nothing to me. I'm a writer. A playwright."

"Have I seen anything of yours?" she said.

"You will. The bastards can't keep talent buried forever."

He'd been an actor, he told her, with two seasons of stock to his credit and one Off-Broadway play. He didn't tell her that his acting was dull and uninteresting and he lacked all stage presence. A year earlier, he had begun to write. He'd plunged right in, doing a full three-act play. It had made the rounds of producers' offices with no results. No encouragement. No interest. The neglect served only to rouse his fighting instincts. Cursing the stupidity of the theatrical establishment, he began submitting the play Off-Broadway. Still nothing. But he wasn't discouraged. He wrote a second play. An Off-Broadway director read it and offered some advice. Judd Martin had listened carefully, decided the director was right, and had started to re-write. He had to make it somehow, *had* to. One New York success would do it. Hollywood would be the result. The end to jazzing middle-aged ass for rent money. Hollywood, TV, the flicks. Tons of bread. And all those crazy young birds.

To Susan, he said, "I'm going to make it big because I've got something to say and I say it well. I might have made it acting, might still, but writing is my bag now and forever, strong and perfect."

"Like Hemingway," she said.

"You know it. Clean. Right. Pure."

She studied him over the rim of her glass. Those lean good looks, the narrow hips, flat belly. He perched on the barstool with athletic grace, legs forming a wide V, pants tight over a soft bulge. She raised her eyes and discovered that he had been watching her. The mocking smile returned.

"Finish your drink," he said deliberately. "We're going."

"To your apartment?"

He nodded.

She sighed briefly. There was no point in continuing this game. She wanted to go with him, had intended to all along. She put the glass down and stood up.

"All right."

His apartment was a single room with a pullman kitchen on the second floor of an old brownstone. Set in the back, it was small and dark. A stack of old newspapers were piled on the floor in one corner. There were some books, a few chairs, an old television set. A bed. A small desk.

He started toward her but she waved him away. Then pointing at the bed. "Your workroom, I presume?"

He moved up behind her and made a small sound that passed for amusement. "My actions speak for me."

"That will be a relief. Most men talk a better game than they play." She swung around. "Is that all you care about, getting laid?"

His mouth drew down and the eyes narrowed balefully. "You want to discuss love and meaningful relationships?"

"Is it profitable, making it with older women?"

The expression on his face never altered. "Usually. Women generally want to keep me happy."

"With money?" she challenged.

He shrugged. "Gifts of various kinds."

"Do I look like a woman who has to pay a man?"

The answer was evident. This was a woman men desired

and went after, were grateful to when she favored them with just a smile. He wanted her very much, more than he had wanted anybody since that fifteen-year-old dancer with the State Ballet. Ease off, he instructed himself. Don't crowd her into a corner. She was not yet sure. Give her breathing room, he warned silently. Don't lose her. With that tawny Tartar face, that cap of black hair and those dramatic eyes, she brought an unaccustomed craving into his middle. Even more, with a husband like Neil Morgan, she could do him some real good.

"I'm not quite as bad as I seem," he offered.

"How bad are you?"

The ducking head, the boyish grin. He kept himself from shuffling his feet. "Okay, you read me. I come on kind've strong with women. Right. I know. Maybe it's a cover."

"For what?"

"A man goes through stages in his life. He changes. His experiences are different. Sure, women like me. But I'm not all that sure of myself. Once——"

"You were awkward and shy," she urged.

He spied the trap and backed off. "I don't expect you to believe me."

She felt a grudging admiration. Maybe he *was* a writer of some skill, some talent. He had a quick brain, could change directions, think on his feet.

"I was almost nineteen when I had my first experience with a woman," he said, with a disarming ingenuousness.

"What's this I keep hearing about a sexual revolution then?" She spoke without disbelief, wanting to know about him.

He shrugged and went on. "A lot of conversation, I think. Girls do it younger but they still want to get involved, to get married. And you keep hearing all the old clichés."

She laughed. "What do you know about the old clichés?"

"The movies. I dig old pictures. I go to the Thalia or the New Yorker. Get the flavor of the past that way."

"Tell me about that first woman."

He started to refuse, thought better of it. "I come from Staten Island," he said. "My name is really Jerry Martino. Anyway, I went on the bum when I was eighteen. Boy, does that stink! Hustling for handouts. For a bunk. Nothing and nowhere. I spent a lot of time at Coney Island, on the beach. I thought about sex a lot in those days"—she grinned up at him and lowered herself to the edge of the bed—"But I never did anything."

"Nothing?" she prodded.

He sat on the floor in front of her. "Not even *that*. I would lie to other kids, say that I did it. One day I went into the basement of this building and pulled my pud and at the crucial moment the janitor came in. He was sore as hell and yelled at me and threatened to beat me up and call the cops, but I was a big kid and he was scared."

"Did you like it?" she asked, with clinical interest.

"The best thing was that I wasn't a liar anymore."

"And the woman?"

"Oh. I met her the next day. She was older and she talked to me on the beach. We made a date to meet after dark under the boardwalk. She told me that she wanted to do it and said I should go to a drugstore and buy some rubbers. It was very embarrassing. The clerk asked me what kind I wanted and did I want three for a dollar or three for a half. I didn't realize it could be done more than once and besides I only had a dollar on me so I bought the cheaper kind. I decided that since I'd never done it, I better practice. So I went into an alleyway and tried putting one of the rubbers on. Well, that meant I had to get excited and suddenly it was all very difficult to do. By then it was time to meet her.

"She was waiting when I got there and bawled me out for being late. Then she grabbed me and kissed me a couple of times and told me to do it. I had trouble with the damned rubber. I was nervous and it wouldn't go on and finally I pushed my thumbs through it, trying to roll it open. 'What's the matter?' she asked. I told her and she wanted to know how many I had left. I told her only one and she got sore, said she'd put it on for me. She was more experienced at it than I was. I got so interested in what she was doing that I lost my hard-on and she got mad again. Anyway, she knew how to fix that. Then she pulled me down on top of her and we did it."

Susan began to sputter. "I'm sorry," she managed. "But it is a ludicrous picture."

"The worst of it, I never really knew whether or not I was inside her."

They were both laughing now. "You're much nicer," she managed, "when you don't play the big swordsman."

"But I am, you see, the big swordsman."

She sobered quickly. "And all that was a long time ago?"

His hands slid to the outside of her legs, moved upward under her skirt. "A long time ago. Now I know exactly what I'm doing. And I'm never afraid."

"You are a bastard."

"You deserve me," he muttered, lowering his face to her knees.

Her legs were stiff with sudden tension and a faint trembling took hold. He forced her legs apart, moving his face from side to side, nibbling at the soft flesh. His hands were on her bare thighs, his touch delicate and knowing. It took all her will power not to scream in anticipation and excitement.

He shifted position. An early stubble made his cheeks coarse against her naked skin. He emitted a small sound of approval and his tongue moved lightly against her. She jerked reflexively.

"This," he was saying, "this is where I wanted to be, the minute I saw you. Between your legs with my face. Going into you. With everything. Everywhere."

His hands were inside her knees, separating them, his head coming forward. A weak protest trickled out of her and she fell back on the bed, body rising and falling to his touch, to his manipulations, and she knew he was going to get everything he wanted from her. Every damned thing.

Mike and Elizabeth

It was dark when they woke. They reached for each other, touching tentatively. Reassurance, recall, affectionate gratitude.

"I'm famished," she said.

"We'll go out. I'll buy you an expensive dinner."

"Let's stay here. I'll cook for you."

"There is no food. Only some eggs."

"You rest." She kissed his mouth. "I'll tell you when dinner is ready."

She made a delicate banana omelet with rye toast and small round potatoes fried in butter. And coffee. They ate off their knees on the couch where they had begun earlier, touching each other from time to time, grinning at each other. Talking occasionally.

"You're a marvelous actress," he told her. "You fooled me completely."

The green eyes were grave. "I wasn't trying to deceive you. It's what I *am* now. You must understand. I didn't like myself at all. I had to change. I have changed. The world's girl isn't Elizabeth Jordan. Before . . . well, that was for *you.*"

"And you."

"What a beautiful man you are!"

The words and her naked sincerity embarrassed him. "What have you been doing?" he said deliberately, "since Fire Island?"

"Working mostly." She drank some coffee. "A special report for Professor Salisbury on the creative function of the managers of the country's top one hundred companies."

"What creative function?"

"Professor Salisbury believes that because we live in a materialistic society based on profit many of the most intensely creative intelligences have entered the business world. . . ."

"Nonsense."

"You think so? Professor Salisbury insists that in other cultures many of these men would have become artists or poets. Today they're salesmen and heads of companies."

"Salisbury is a charlatan. Find an honest job for yourself."

She presented a dutiful smile, went on. "My research tends to support the thesis, Mike. I've been interviewing a man who owns an electronics firm. He's more than just a businessman concerned with dollar income. He's patented a number of inventions. A kind of gravity lock, for one, and he has developed more efficient techniques for assembling television and shortwave components and—"

Her enthusiasm was contagious, her logic persuasive. His arguments failed to stand up and he found himself beginning to agree with her. In the midst of it, she broke off.

"Oh, I'm chattering, I think. And I don't know what I'm talking about."

"I think you know a great deal."

She weighed his words. "Not really," she said thoughtfully. "My brain is good enough, but sometimes I don't think properly. In an orderly fashion, I mean. And I'm not at all creative. I never think anything or say anything that excites me or sounds new or different."

"Few of us do."

"You do, Mike. You're terribly inventive. I read your books."

"Oh."

"I hope you don't mind," she offered apologetically. "I borrowed them from the library."

"That's bad. Buying is better than borrowing."

"I don't have much money."

He touched her cheek lightly. "I was joking."

"I want to buy your books, for them to be mine."

The earlier depression began to fill the forward hemisphere of his brain. The coffee tasted bitter suddenly. She sensed the change.

"What is it, Mike?"

"Nothing," he said quickly. Then, seeing the vulnerable expression on that pale face, he added more softly, "The book I'm working on. Awful. Worse than awful. A piece of junk." He went to the bay windows and adjusted the shutters, gazed down at the street. A boy strolled past, listening to a transistor radio. A rock beat filled the still night. "It's unpublishable."

"You're a good writer. You'll work it out."

He jerked around, scowling. "I'm a fraud. Not really a writer at all. I began writing only to get out of that competitive jungle out there. I was scared. I even thought about returning to teaching, that so secure twelve-months-pay-for-nine-months-work-a-year womb."

"You'd be a superb teacher."

"The hell I would. I was lousy, always trying to go my own route. Screw the forms, the system. Maybe I was never academic enough. Never the intellectual. That's my trouble I suppose. I don't know enough, not smart enough to be a really good writer."

"I think you're very good."

"I'm a hack. Always have been. At everything I've done. My last job, I was fired. Canned. Given the old heave-ho. I'd been fired from three jobs in a row and I was in a blue snit. A panic. I didn't have the guts to look for another job, to fail again. I was going nuts trying to figure out what to do, how to survive. I envisioned myself waking up in the gutter, starving to death and alone."

"Not you, Mike. Never you."

"That's when I got the idea about writing. It was always in my mind, of course. A lingering fantasy that showed no signs of becoming real. But then I was desperate. It seemed that just about everybody I knew talked about writing. And a number of guys *said* they were writing. Novels, play, articles. Why not me, I asked myself. I'd done some writing as a press agent and I did know how to make the language work for me."

"So you sat down and wrote a book."

"A mystery. Nothing. You invent a plot and that's it."

"You do it very well. Your characters are real, you have a clean prose style, and you know how to tell a story."

"You begin with a crime and the motivation. Leave a trail of clues, then work your hero back over the trail. It's a snap."

"I doubt that."

He shook his head worriedly. "My new book doesn't make it. Weak. All words and no action. A bust. A great big zero."

She moved over to him, sat in his lap. The soft warmth of her round bottom went through the robes they wore, spread across his loins. He stroked her hip.

"You feel so good to me," he husked, kissing her neck.

"Mike," she said tentatively. "May I read your new book, tell you what I think? I'm not a writer, but if you can use a lay opinion."

"I think I've run dry," he said, against her skin.

"I'm serious."

"Maybe I've come to the end of it. It was a good run and——"

"You don't believe that."

"Maybe I do."

"Let me read the manuscript."

"All right. Take it with you when you leave in the morning."

"Am I staying here all night?"

"Yes."

She disengaged herself, rose and walked away. "I'm not sleepy," she said seriously. "Could I begin to read. I always read before I go to sleep."

"I had other plans for you."

"Please, Mike . . ."

He brought the manuscript to her. Without a word, she curled up in one corner of the couch and began to read.

He went into the bedroom and lay down. Seconds later he was asleep.

Chapter II

Neil

Tooling through the dingy East Village streets in the Mercedes provided Neil Morgan with a sense of importance, of being something special. The sleek gray sedan didn't belong here. It spoke of another world, one where objects were well regarded, sought after, a world where people had goals and accomplished their ends. Here the stench of poverty and failure was everywhere. This was the turf for those who would never make it.

He glanced at Marybeth. She had withdrawn into the corner of the front seat, small and pale, very still. Her hands were folded in her lap and she stared sightlessly ahead. Strange how much she reminded him of Susan. Yet they were in no way similar.

"Are you all right?" he said heartily. She gave no answer. "I'll have you home in a few minutes."

He drew up in front of her building and turned off the motor. There was an envelope in his pocket. He extended it. When she made no move to accept it, he placed it in her lap.

"You're going to need some money."

Her eyes met his. "I never asked you for money."

"Everyone needs money."

"Not all of us. Not the same way."

"Take it. You have to eat."

"All right." Her eyes stared straight ahead.

"There's five hundred dollars there," he reminded her. She had no sense of the value of things, he had long ago decided. A distorted view of life.

Without looking at him, she spoke. "I never asked you for money," she repeated. "I never asked you for anything. All I wanted was for it to be nice between us. And it was, most of the time."

"Listen to me," he said imploringly. "You're very young. You don't understand about so much. Later you'll thank me."

"You shouldn't have done this to me. I would never have done it to you."

"Dammit!" he shouted, anger flaring wildly. "This wasn't easy for me. It wasn't." He struggled to harness the fury, the desire to strike out, to hurt, to destroy. "Listen," he managed finally, in a thick, tight voice. "Try and understand that it wasn't easy for me. Sometimes a man must do what he thinks is best. What's right."

"It was wrong. We wouldn't have bothered you, my baby and me."

It was easy for her to say. But he wouldn't have been sure. Not ever. At best, she was unreliable, an unstable child. Living the way she did. Getting into this kind of trouble. Who could anticipate what she might do? She was capable of appearing one day, without warning, making all kinds of demands. She wouldn't have a legal leg to stand on, of course, but it could get sticky. A man in his position had to be careful. He had a wife, a son, a life of his own to consider. And with the TV scandal already on his record, he could afford no additional stain. There had been no other way to handle the situation.

"Marybeth," he began again, "I realize you're unhappy at the moment. You have a right to be. But in time the hurt will go away. You'll begin to see that there was no other choice open to us, to either of us. Nothing else would have been fair, and I include the child. Now I think you should go in, get some rest. I'll help you upstairs."

"No," she said. "I'll go alone."

"Are you sure you're strong enough?"

She almost smiled. "I know we're not going to see each other again. I don't want to see you. You wouldn't be comfortable with me, and I'm going to hate you for a long time." She got out of the car and made her way slowly around the front of it to the sidewalk. She stopped on the stoop and looked back at him. "I never wanted to hate you."

She disappeared into the dark hallway of the old building and he went back to where he belonged.

Roy

Roy was convinced. He knew Harry Nevin as well as the bookie knew himself. Maybe better. During the last three weeks he had spent almost all his time watching Harry, following him as he made his professional rounds from bar to laundromat, from restaurant to candy store, from the lobbies of lush apartment buildings to back alleyways. And always Harry carried that inoffensive attaché case.

Harry's schedule was precise. An hour here. Thirty minutes there. Taking phone calls. Collecting bets. Paying off winners. Seeing that all gears in his covert world meshed smoothly, were kept well-greased. Roy noted the frequent handshakes between the bookie and the beat cops, the clumsy exchanges.

Nor did Harry's routine vary at night. Dinner alone in a cheap fish joint in the West Forties near Times Square. Then the subway out to Brooklyn Heights. Never in three weeks did Harry visit a bank. Or any other institution where impressive amounts of cash might be safely stored.

It was not until the Friday of the fourth week that a change occurred. On his way in from Brooklyn, Harry got off the subway in lower Manhattan, went to a bank in the Wall Street area. There he pushed the attaché case at the teller who counted out its contents and subsequently presented Harry with two certified checks in the full amount.

Harry put the checks into separate air mail envelopes and posted them. Where, Roy asked himself. Some place secure from the probing of federal tax agents, he supposed. Perhaps numbered accounts in Swiss banks. Or a mail drop in Argentina. Or a trusted associate in Spain.

It had to be done on a Thursday. That much was clear. But Roy had to be certain. He kept the bookie under surveillance, pleased with how proficient he had become at it. And on the next fourth Friday, Harry again went to a bank. This time on Lexington Avenue, not far from Bloomingdale's. Again he received two checks for his cash, dispatched them by air mail. Roy was satisfied; the pattern was established.

He played it smart. Patient. Cool. On the third Saturday after the second fourth Friday, he called Harry, saying he expected to begin paying off his gambling debts that coming week. The bookie remained skeptical.

"Who died and made you rich?"

Roy summoned up one of his raucous laughs. "Harry, I'm a hotshot seller of things and stuff. I move the product. Believe, oh, ye of little faith."

"Bullcrap. I put you down as a fourflusher. And I've had it with you. Two weeks more. From today. Two weeks is all. Then my patience runs out."

"Tuesday Harry. Wednesday or Thursday the latest."

"You said it. Disappoint me this time and you have had it."

Roy blew a kiss at the phone. Everything was right. One hundred and ten per cent right. He went over to the modern oiled walnut bureau and opened the top drawer. The Luger lay in its wrappings. He stripped away the oilskin and hefted the pistol. A souvenir of his days in the Eighth Air Force, it still had a nice feel. Solid. Powerful. All these years, he had cleaned and oiled it every month.

Now he broke the weapon down, went through the process once again. Very carefully, he reassembled the pistol. Cocked it, squeezed the trigger.

Click.

More thunk than click. A reassuring sound. Heavy. Masculine. He cocked it again. Squeezed again. *Thunk.* He laughed briefly. Poor Harry would cream his pants when he saw the Luger. Absolutely cream. Roy returned the Luger to the drawer, next to the carton of bullets. A few more days and he'd have it made. Have the world in his hands. By the balls, baby.

Eddie

When Mike woke the following morning, Elizabeth was gone. And so was the manuscript. A note left on the coffee table explained:

> I'm halfway through the book and will finish it tonight after work. I have an idea, but I'm not sure yet. Your couch is very nice to sleep on. You are very nice. Thank you for being you and letting me be me. Thank you. May I come again? Please.

He went out and bought *The Times*, came back, drank coffee and read. He was on his second cup when the phone rang. It was Eddie Stander.

They said all the right things, about how long it had been, asked what was new and how things were. Your wife? Your writing? The baby?

"That was a nice girl," Eddie recalled. "What was her name, the one you brought to dinner?"

"Elizabeth Jordan," he said formally.

"Good looking. Smart."

"Thank you."

"You're wondering why I called. I would be, too. Mike, I want to talk to you. To let our friendship fall apart after so many years, it isn't right. I've been thinking on it since we met this summer. Let's have lunch, Mike. Okay?"

Mike was unable to refuse. They agreed to meet at Charlie Brown's, in the Pan Am Building.

"I'll reserve a table," Eddie said. "They know me."

He was there when Mike arrived. A few minutes later they were seated. They ordered martinis.

"You look terrific," Eddie said. "Not a day older." He passed his hand over his shaved head. "What do you think? Too much? Shaving it clean, I mean. Hell, I don't have enough to cover the bald spots. That's why the Yul Brynner bit."

"It looks fine."

" 'Dramatic', Edith says. Personally, I like it."

"It's fine." Mike noticed that deep ruts sliced into the pebbled cheeks, that there was a grayish pallor to Eddie's skin, that the fiery eyes seemed to have receded deeper into the round skull. "Just fine," he ended.

Eddie milked his fingers. "Marriage does it. A good woman. Greatest thing. Wife and kids. I look at those kids and I feel just . . . *immortal*. It's so great."

Eddie had always craved a family, Mike remembered. And now he had it. But Edith was hardly the wife he had envisioned years before. Eddie had yearned for a woman who was chic and cultivated, a woman delicate and slender, the kind of woman one saw shopping along Madison Avenue, the kind of woman who wore cashmere sweaters and straight skirts. It was not a description that fit Edith, he thought wryly. Not in any of its particulars.

"You should get married again," Eddie was saying. "Change your ways. Stop running around. Where does it get you?" he ended on a plaintive note.

"I may be less the lecher than I used to be."

"You always were too caught up with girls. Like anybody else, I have to have a woman now and then. But if I had to, I could live without them entirely."

"Not me."

"That's because you have some wild idea that you can seduce everyone you meet."

"Not so. A female presence is an added fillip to my life, a kind of excitement, a qualitative change for the better."

Eddie scowled, his brow rutted and creased. "That is something I don't understand. Give me my books and an occasional visit to a museum and I'm happy. I don't need anyone."

Mike raised his brows and looked into his drink.

"Don't get me wrong," Eddie said hurriedly. "I'm not anti-social. We entertain, have friends over, visit them." A quick grin split his mouth. "And three times a week I go over to the Y and play basketball. With kids sixteen, seventeen, Mike. Not bad for a middle-aged family man."

"Not bad," Mike agreed.

"I do all right, too."

"I'm sure you do."

"You work out, Mike? You're in pretty good shape."

"I keep meaning to."

"You should." Eddie flexed his right arm. "Keeps the

old body in shape. Adds years to your life." Again the grin. "You always did take your workouts in bed."

They had a second martini and ordered lunch.

"How's the writing coming?" Eddie asked. "Interesting, you becoming a writer. You were one of the few guys who didn't run off at the mouth about writing. Yet here you are doing it. Ironic, isn't it?"

Mike reflected on his conversation with Elizabeth, his inability to solve the problems of the new book, his doubts and fears.

"Of course," Eddie continued somberly, "mysteries are not precisely at the literary apex. Not that I put them down, you understand."

"I understand."

"But you aren't Count Tolstoy."

Mike looked at the other man without expression. "Not Tolstoy. Nor Chekhov nor Ibsen nor Arthur Miller. For that matter, I'm not even Dashiell Hammett."

"Hey, Mike," Eddie protested. "I didn't mean anything."

The waiter brought their food. Roast beef and salad. They ate slowly, speaking occasionally.

By the time they were finished, Eddie had grown expansive. "That was first-rate. I come here often for lunch. You know, Mike, we should do this more often. It isn't right for good friends not to see each other more than just once in a while."

"That's why you phoned me," Mike said deliberately.

"I wanted to see you, find out how things were, and all that." He passed his hand across his scalp. "Maybe there was another reason, too."

"I thought there might be."

An uncertain chuckle expired on Eddie's lips. "Well, it has to do with writing. Seeing you on the beach reminded me. I've never given up the idea of writing myself. Seriously, I mean."

"I see."

Eddie shifted closer, spoke in a confidential way. "Remember that play I was working on years ago. I re-read it recently, and it isn't half bad. I mean, it has a style, a texture that's well-married to content. A fairly artistic gloss, you might say."

"Have you submitted to producers?"

"Those profit-mongers! Not a chance. Not till I'm ready

and can dictate my own terms. Here's the deal. Indulge my frankness, Mike, but you aren't exactly rich and famous."

Mike grinned wryly. "So you noticed. . . ."

"Well, all right. Say someone presented you with the opportunity to become both? Wouldn't you snap it up? Of course you would. Anybody would. Now I give you the formula for success—a great idea, the market for a great idea, and someone who can execute it."

"*Your* play and a writer to work on it. Me, for example."

"It makes *sense*, Mike. You're on your own. No job. No responsibilities. Plenty of time to devote to the project. I'd do it myself, but there's my job."

"And we'd share any profits?"

"Fairly, Mike," Eddie said, fixing him with a steady, level glance. "I wouldn't cheat you."

"I'm sure of that, Eddie."

Eddie placed a large brown envelope on the table. "It's all in here, the material. Half of the first act, just as I wrote it sixteen years ago. Not one word changed. And my notes. All very explicit so you'll have no trouble getting the drift. Just follow my outline and you'll be able to knock it off in no time at all. All I want is fifty per cent for myself, which you have to admit is reasonable. Fifty per cent and equal billing. All you have to do is fill in the skeleton, so to speak."

Mike stared off into space, trying to collect his thoughts, to isolate his emotions. There was resentment, impatience and disappointment. Mostly disappointment. For all these years he had carried around the memory of a friendship between himself and Eddie and felt regrets for its demise. But it had been a lie. No friendship had ever existed, only a relationship of convenience, to be picked up and disposed of when suitable.

"Say the word, Mike."

The word is presumptuous, Mike said silently. And arrogance. And fantasy. Tell him, he ordered silently. Make him see the deception in all its nakedness, the illusion, the wastefulness. A placebo. Instead, Mike reached for the brown envelope.

"No promises, Eddie."

"Just read it, that'll convince you. You won't be able to put it down."

"We'll see."

Eddie laughed behind his teeth. "Won't this be terrific, after so many years, working together at last. . . ."

Chapter III

Neil

The secretary placed the bright red binders in a neat stack on Neil Morgan's desk. "One dozen copies," she announced. "And there are two more copies in the file."

"You proofread them? No mistakes?"

"They're letter-perfect."

He dismissed her with a nod and contemplated the binders. Each contained a copy of the complete presentation. And a very professional presentation it was, he assured himself. Once free of Marybeth, he had been able to function on all cylinders again. Able to fully apply himself, to rethink his idea. To gain a fresh perspective, make radical alterations in the presentation, in the script outlines.

In its present form, the show offered six spectaculars, each ninety minutes long, loaded with saleable action. He had been thorough in his research, exploring six crimes of the last century, altering the facts for dramatic impact. And the title: *World True Crime Theater*. A much more important sound.

He was ready. Beginning today, there would be interviews with the program directors at each of the networks, at all of the major advertising agencies, with the TV representatives of certain national firms. All companies that spent millions on the medium. This time he would make the sale. There was no reason not to; he had done everything the way it should be done—smooth, sleek, with all the professional polish he had taught himself over the years.

The idea was good. The script outlines complete. The budgets sensible. An ideal presentation. They would have to buy. His past bad luck would not stop him this time. He'd come a long way since his days as a press agent. He intended to go much further.

He placed two copies of the presentation into the thin brown-leather Mark Cross attaché case, made sure his fingernails were clean, and left.

Mike

Milton Vaccaro was a man of immense proportions with a graying lionesque mane. Slow to speak, he moved with equal caution, picking his way around stationary objects as if afraid of shattering them. He held his massive hands in a prayerful attitude and surveyed Mike Birns across the width of his big desk.

"You are my favorite client, Mike," he said in that measured way of his.

"And you're my favorite agent," Mike returned.

"I mean it, Mike. The way you're going, you won't ever make a fortune for me, but I love you."

"Sure, baby," Mike said lightly. He enjoyed kidding the agent, was genuinely fond of him. Vaccaro had a sincere interest in writing and writers, and he was a man to be trusted with money, with a manuscript, with a confidence. He had sought Mike out following publication of the first mystery, and they had been together since, without benefit of contract.

"For a smart fellow," Vaccaro said, "you are awfully dumb."

"Thanks, pal."

"You're my only mystery writer. Have you ever wondered why I represent you?"

"You about to dump me, Milton?"

The big features softened and the turned-down mouth

straightened out in what passed for a smile. "I believe in you, as a talent."

"I wish I did."

"You have more going than you know. One day you'll do something worthwhile. I'm sure of that. You've got a feeling for people beyond most writers of the genre. You make it with your people, understand them emotionally."

Mike exhaled heavily. "That's the new book, all character and no plot."

"Think about trying something outside the mystery field, Mike. A straight novel. Contemporary."

Mike shook his head. "I'm a writer by accident, Milton. You know that. No incessant muse plagues me, drives me. Luck got me this far."

"Nonsense. Talent did it. And hard work. But you've turned a corner, both personally and professionally, I think. You simply haven't realized it yet. Even as a mystery writer there is room for growth, for expansion. Think about it."

"I will."

"Good." Vaccaro leaned back, placed one big hand on the brown envelope containing Eddie Stander's writings. "How well do you know this guy, Mike?"

"We used to be friends."

"Have you read his stuff?"

"Yes."

"What did you think?"

"I didn't trust my judgment. Eddie's a smart guy. A walking encyclopedia. Maybe out of my league."

Vaccaro snorted disparagingly. "You can say that again. But he's in the low minors and you're swinging against big-time pitchers. This so-called play of his. It's nothing. Pedantic crap. Sophomoric posturing. Trying to show how smart he is. He has no sense of construction, of character, of drama. Nor of economy. Never uses one word where he can use ten. In other words, he can't write."

Mike grimaced and slumped deeper into the chair. He had hoped for better, for Eddie's sake. "I was afraid of that."

"You disagree?"

"Not really. But how do I tell him?"

"He's your friend. Do him a favor. Tell him to forget about writing. He's got nothing going for him."

Mike knew he could never be that blunt, that he couldn't shatter Eddie's dream. Instead, he wrote Eddie a careful note explaining that it was impossible for him to collaborate at this time, adding that he felt the demands of the material were beyond his talent. On his way to meet Elizabeth, he stopped at the post office, had the envelope weighed and stamped. At the last moment he changed his mind and didn't mail it. He couldn't.

Susan

Judd Martin propped himself up with a pillow and lit a cigarette. Light, filtered by Venetian blinds, modified the harsh sparseness of his room, camouflaging the cheapness of the furniture, the peeling paint on the walls and ceiling.

It was that way with Susan, he admitted to himself, watching her get into her brassiere. The tiny breasts sagged and were flabby to his touch. Her thighs bulged suspiciously and a platoon of dimples marched across her buttocks.

She drew on her stockings, attached the garters, and stepped into her panties. Better now. Clothed she was sensational.

She shrugged into her dress and ran a comb through the monk's cap of hair. "You were superb today, darling," she said over her shoulder.

He nodded agreeably. He had been good. There were days like that, everything falling into place. The kind of day athletes had when they put it all together and so starred for their teams.

She looked at him. "You're a magnificient animal."

His eyes traveled down his torso to where his penis, slack and faintly pink, rested easily, tinted with the mixed residue of her insides and his own semen. The scent of sex filled his nostrils, vaguely disturbing. As soon as she was gone, a shower. Then a leisurely bath, hot, soaking all suggestion of her away.

"Glad you approve."

"I never thought I'd pay for it."

"You're not paying for it," he said automatically. "Lending me some dough, that's not paying for it." They all needed that reassurance and he provided it willingly. It was worth it, the words said without strain. "You know I like you," he added, beginning to set her up.

"I wish I believed that."

He reached down and held the thick, now flaccid, tool of his trade in his hand, directed at her. "*This* likes you."

"You'd fuck a duck," she said, but not too harshly. She could take no chances with him. Not with *him*. God he was marvelous! Right from the start, that slow, practiced roll of his, the almost casual yet angry pounding. The way that oversized machine of his ripped into her. The way he used his hands, a fierce rough beast. His fingers on her clitoris, or the heel of his hand. And the times she rode his thigh, forgetting who she was or where she was, screaming out her joy and her need.

They saw each other four straight days in that first week. Then came the weekend, the time that belonged to Neil. That had been their agreement for years. Saturdays and Sundays, in New York or on the island, were family days. On weekends they maintained a proper facade, showing the world what appeared to be a proper marriage.

Being away from Judd was difficult. She kept remembering the lean hardness of him, the young passion, the pleasure he had given her. And soon she realized that there wasn't anything she wouldn't do to keep him.

"I'm a little short," he had told her during their third week. And she understood what was expected, had given him all the cash she had with her. Fifty dollars. Soon it went up to one hundered a week. Every week. The money presented no particular problem. She had savings of her own, investments of her own, property Neil had purchased for her when all that game-show money was coming in. Still, she had to be careful. Neil would not have approved.

But it was important to keep Judd happy.

"I don't like ducks," he said slowly, giving her that lidded smile of his, the smile that made her know he'd put it into any hole that came his way.

"The envelope's on the dresser," she said. She sat on the edge of the bed, dropping her hand onto his hairy thigh.

He handed her the cigarette he was smoking and lit another. "How's your husband doing?"

She spoke warily. "Why do you ask?"

"Just curious. I spotted his name in *Variety*, something about a new TV series."

"He hasn't sold it yet but there's some interest, I understand. He'll make a deal. He always does. Neil never gives up."

"He sounds like quite a guy," he said, giving her his most direct look. "I'd like to meet him."

"Don't be silly."

"I mean it. He's the sort of man I could like. You're a fortunate woman."

She searched his face for some hidden meaning and found nothing. "We've learned to live together, Neil and I. We make do. There were hard times but we worked out our problems."

"A truce."

"Better than that. A fair and equitable treaty that benefits both of us. He's got his faults but he does his best for me and my son."

"Does he know about me?"

"Of course not."

"What about the others?"

She stiffened up. "What do you mean?"

"I'm not the first lover you've had."

"You are a bastard. Isn't it enough that I come here, give you money?"

"Take your money," he said, with no special emphasis. "I don't give a damn. But get out, and don't come back."

She jerked around, face melting. She put her face in his lap. "Please, Judd. Don't be mean to me. You know I can't give you up, that I want to be with you all the time."

"Then no hard times."

"I'm sorry."

"That's better," he said, working his fingers through her hair, pushing her face into his crotch. A faint sound drifted up to him and he felt her mouth working. He laughed harshly, pulled her head up. "Better not start, or you'll never get home."

She rose and straightened her dress. A thought was born

in her mind, surfaced slowly. "Would you really like to meet Neil?"

"Yes."

"How do I know I can trust you? That you wouldn't say something to make him suspicious."

"Don't be dumb." He came off the bed and put his hands on her shoulders. "Your husband is a producer, I'm an actor, a writer. I need to meet men like him."

"I'd like to help you. . . ."

"Then arrange it. Soon. Like Thursday."

"How did you know about Thursday?"

"I read the society pages, baby. You're entertaining Mr. and Mrs. Irwin S. Davidson, vice-president in charge of Davidson Studios. The number one producer of television shows in the world."

"Mr. Davidson is interested in Neil's series."

"*I'm* interested in Neil's series. In Neil. In Mr. Davidson."

She hesitated, wet her mouth.

"How many people are you expecting?" he said.

"Twenty-one."

"Who is the odd person?"

"A woman friend . . ."

"I could be her escort," he said evenly. "I would be properly attentive, polite, but not in the least bit personal."

"No . . ."

His hands fell away. "This could be my big chance and you won't give it to me. Yet you insist you care for me."

"I do," she burst out, mind racing. She didn't want to open any avenues to other plateaus for him. She enjoyed the present situation, didn't want him to succeed as an actor or as a writer. She preferred him poor and dependent.

He smiled down at her, easy, reassuring. "That friend of yours, Maggie," he said conversationally. "You could introduce me as a friend of hers, that you wanted an extra man to round out your guest list."

She spoke guardedly. "I'd have to be very sure that you . . ."

"Depend on it. I'd be discreet, darling."

"Maggie has a husband so . . ."

"I'd present no threat to any husband. I'll be circumspect. No flirting, courteous toward my elders and betters. Give me this chance, Susan. I can go all the way."

"All right," she breathed. "I'll think of some way to handle it."

"I knew you'd come through for me, baby." He kissed her on the mouth. "You won't regret it, I promise you."

But she knew she would.

BB

The fuzz took Mother. And BB watched.

They were to meet at The Oral Satisfaction, a hamburger joint on Jefferson Boulevard, only one block off campus. A good place because it was always crowded with students and faculty and no one paid attention to anybody else. You could walk around the block or use the john to make the buy itself.

BB arrived early. Anxious. Nerves drawn and jangling. He carried money enough for two shots. The price of his habit was high, four smacks a week, and he was always on the prowl for bread.

A freshman coed had agreed to whore for him but before she could turn a trick she slugged another girl, sending her to the hospital. The result, expulsion. BB was sore as hell but there was nothing he could do. He rolled drunks twice outside bars on Sherman Place and purse-snatched a few times. But that netted him very small amounts of cash. For the last week he'd been hustling fags around Cooper Square. Just another way to make some bread. He knew he wasn't a queer. To prove it, whenever he let a fag go down on him, he thought about girls.

Though winter was in its terminal stages, the cold lingered on, and he felt chilled as he hurried toward The Oral Satisfaction. He strode past the Elwin Haywood Foundation for Psychic Research, the collar of his sheepskin jacket high around his ears, hands deep in the pockets. It had been Neil's Christmas gift to him and he had considered hocking it once or twice.

He increased his pace. Soon the buy, then back to his

room, shoot the stuff. He could almost taste the sense of well-being, of comfort, that would soon wrap itself around him.

The red flasher caught his eye. He stopped in his tracks, eyes frozen on the police cruiser up ahead. There were three of them.

"Mother . . ." he moaned aloud.

A crowd had collected in front of The Oral Satisfaction. He pushed closer. Two uniformed patrolmen stood outside the entrance, their broad blue-eyed faces flat and ominous. Some students jeered them but the officers made no response.

The double doors swung open and two more officers appeared. Mother was between them. He was a slender man, bony and pale, with limp yellow hair. He shuffled between the two policemen, each grasping one of his arms, a vague grin spreading under the dark green shades.

BB began to tremble. He was afraid he was going to be sick. He closed his eyes and fought for control. When he looked again, Mother was gone, the patrol cars speeding off. BB turned away, jostling his way through the crowd.

"Oh, Jesus," he muttered. "Oh, sweet Jesus. Oh, Mother, what have you done to me?"

"Hello, Boyd."

He stopped, head swiveling, eyes struggling to focus. A round-faced man with soft features and a voice to match stood in front of him. It was Professor Hailey. BB had taken his one-semester course in Christian Ethics the previous year.

"Seems we're having some excitement," Professor Hailey said. There was a sibilant, whispering quality to his voice, the words being manufactured along the roof of his mouth. "Does one good to set the adrenelin to running, don't you think?"

"I suppose so."

"I don't imagine you knew the man they arrested," Hailey went on. "He was a pusher."

"A pusher. . . ?"

"Drugs, Boyd. Heroin, marijuana. What do you students call it? Grass. Pot. Maryjane. Hash."

"Oh, yes."

BB resumed walking. Professor Hailey fell in beside him. He was about the same height as the younger man, but with no muscular delineation or strength to his body. He had once been described to BB as a man who had been molded out of gray clay, with the job ending short of completion.

"Mind some company, Boyd? We seem to be going in the same direction."

"I don't mind."

BB plumbed his brain. Mother had been his only contact. With him out of circulation, what would he do for a source? He knew no one else who was smacking H. A cry of desperation lodged in his throat. Soon the craving would intensify. There would be pain, chills, an agonizing need. Where would he get a fix? There was moisture in his eyes and he snuffled, scratched at his neck.

Professor Hailey was speaking, the soft, soothing tones seeping through to BB. He forced himself to listen.

"I must confess to something of an ethical dilemma, Boyd."

"What?"

"I am privy to certain pieces and bits of gossip. I hear about some of the small indiscretions of some of our students. Boys will be boys and that sort of thing. Not that I've told anyone. But sometimes I am troubled. Should I tell, I ask myself. Am I doing right by these fine young men who are given into our care by their trusting parents?"

It was colder now and BB walked faster.

"One would think, in a small school such as ours, that life would be tranquil and ordinary. Mundane. Yet even here it is possible to swim in a variety of waters, if one chooses to do so. For example, if one wants something badly enough, it may be obtained right on campus. Money is the key, of course. That hard green opens many doors, I'm afraid. What materialists we all are!"

BB stole a sidelong glance at the other man. The bland face told him nothing.

"This is where I turn off, Professor."

Hailey dropped a gloved hand on BB's arm. His grip was unobtrusively firm. "Must you run away, Boyd? I thought we might talk for a bit."

"I'm meeting a friend."

"I've been interested in you, Boyd, ever since you took

my class. You could be a fine student, if you applied your energies properly."

"I've got to go."

"To meet your friend?"

"That's right."

"But your only friend is in the pokey, Boyd." It was offered mildly, could be ignored or not, as one wished. Or was able. BB was unable to ignore it.

"I don't know what you're talking about, Professor."

The eyes in the round face retreated within folds of flesh, narrow slits of mystery. "Your mother, Boyd. Carl Avery, is his name, I believe. He was your mother."

BB shivered, eyes watering. He wiped at them with the back of his hand. "I don't know what you're talking about, Professor," he said again, desperately this time.

"I mean, it's very clear to me that you are hooked, Boyd. On hard stuff. Mainlining. I have my spies, you see, who tell me things. Not that I wouldn't know simply by looking at you. All the symptoms are present, Boyd. How big is your load?"

BB felt as if the top of his skull was going to blast off. He wanted to escape, to hide, but there was no sanctuary. Not anymore. "I was out walking, Professor. You see, I'd been cracking the books and I got uptight so I said, BB, let's air the body, then back to the grind."

That amused Hailey. "You were on your way to meet the man, Boyd. It's all there, the sniffing and scratching. A high degree of agitation. Poor boy. You've lost your supplier and you don't have another. Is that right, Boyd? That little bust left you out in the cold."

"Professor, you've got me all wrong. . . ."

"I've got you exactly right." The whisper was lined with steel now. "But fear not, Boyd. I shan't turn you over. We are brothers, Boyd, members of the same club. . . ."

BB held himself very still. He could hear Professor Hailey's watch ticking. He could feel the cold settling around his feet. Abruptly the other man's hand was on his arm, oppressively heavy.

As if to relieve him of that burden, the professor removed the hand, a Turk's moon smile on his plump mouth. "Trust me, Boyd. I would never cause harm to a pretty boy like you. Never." He looped his arm through BB's. "My flat is only a few steps from here. Join me and we'll talk some more. I have some excellent merchandise tucked safely away in the freezer of my fridge."

"You're a pusher?" BB said, not believing it.

"Nonsense, dear boy. And I never use horse or speed or anything else that might endanger one."

"Then—?"

"Acid, dear boy. Lysergic acid diethylamide. LSD. All ready to go in sweet cubes for a sweet trip. You won't need the hard stuff. This is so much better, full of amazing adventures and rewards. You'll love me for turning you on to it. Shall we go. My place is cozy and warm and private. We can get to know each other well. How fortunate that we met tonight, that I understand you, that I'm as friendly as I am. I'm so happy for us both. . . ."

BB wished he could walk faster.

Chapter IV

Mike

"Oh, *boy!*"

There was disbelief in the words, disappointment, a caustic criticism, sharp, full of barely repressed anger. Eddie Stander glowered at Mike Birns across the small table in Moriarty's. He lifted the brown envelope containing his writing and shook it fiercely in Mike's direction.

"Boy, you've really done it this time, Mike. Really broke it off."

The tone was abrasive, and Mike made an effort to control himself, to show no reaction. Eddie's feelings were damaged, his ego scored. Face it, Mike reminded himself, nobody enjoyed rejection of himself or his work.

"Try and understand my position," Mike said, choosing his words with care, remembering Eddie's temper, anxious to avoid a scene. "I earn my living as a writer. For whatever it's worth, I get paid for what I write."

"Important man," Eddie said tautly.

"That's not what I'm saying and you know it."

"What are you saying?"

"That I simply haven't got the time to work with you, to collaborate. That's no reason for you to lose your cool."

Eddie's head nodded almost amiably. "I never would have believed it, Mike. Never. If someone had told me, I'd've said they were wrong, that you'd never become a shit. But you have, Mike. A first-class shit."

Mike flushed and the muscles across his middle grew hard and ridged.

"Eddie," he said, issuing the words separately, "I am a professional writer. Today happens to be publication day for my new book. . . ."

"Crap on that! I'm not impressed. You were a chintzy press agent when we met. I remember, you were making under a hundred bucks a week while I was pulling down three times as much." He jabbed a stiff forefinger in Mike's direction. "We had a pretty good friendship going, but you just put an end to that."

Mike fought to keep his voice down. "Friendship's a two-way street. We see each other by accident or when you need something from me."

"That's a laugh, me needing you. I never did and don't now. I know the value of this"—he placed a possessive hand on the brown envelope—"and no lousy hack is about to put me down. I know literature, fella, remember that. American, English, French. There isn't an important book I haven't studied. Or play. I know what's good and I know what I've done is good. More than that, it's meaningful, vital. It's got guts and it's got humor."

Mike made himself breathe deeply, regularly. He felt his heart beat slow down and the tension in his arms and legs diminish. It should have been funny, all of this, but he was unable to find it so.

"All I said was that I won't be able to work with you."

"That's for damned sure. You're not going to work with me. You couldn't work *for* me." Eddie hunched forward, shoulders high and tight, the thick brows plunging, the smooth round head glistening under the soft lights. "I wanted to give you a break, Mike, elevate you to another level, make you a part of a work that *mattered,* that would *survive.* But you're too little a man to understand that. Still the small-time press agent mentality. You've never changed." He shoved himself erect. "It's how you were out on the island. Sniffing after every cunt that came along. No selectivity. No taste. Compelled to prove your manhood. Well, let me tell you, it takes more than getting layed to prove you're a man and you haven't done it yet. A home. Family. These things tell the story. Show what you really are. Look at you, middle-aged and alone. Chasing girls still. A fifth-rate writer going nowhere. Grow up,

Mike. People see through you. Talk about you. They don't like you this way. Wise up before it's too late for you."

Mike watched him stride toward the door, head bobbing aggressively, legs pumping, arms jerking back and forth as if punching out at some unseen assailant.

Mike finished his drink, paid the check, and went back to his apartment. The phone rang just as he put the key in the lock. He hurried inside. It was Milton Vaccaro.

The agent sounded excited. "Where you been, Mike? I have been on the horn to you for hours."

"I had drinks with . . ." a friend, he had been about to say, checking himself ". . . with a guy I know. What's up?"

"I've got good news."

"You made a paperback sale."

"Not yet. But I will. Depend on it."

"You better be right, Milton. Things are pretty tight for me. From book to book, the money just about stretches."

"This time is going to be different."

"Why should it be?"

"Because I just got word from my contact at *The Times*. The new book gets a rave review this Sunday, and a lot of space. A picture of you with the copy. Let me read you a couple of lines. Quote, and this is *The Sunday Times* talking, my friend of little confidence. Quote: 'Mike Birns, one of our best professionals, shows why again. His characters are real people with real feelings. They think and act as we would hope to act in similar situations as they pursue their adventuresome goals. Here is a book that surpasses the usual mystery-suspense novel, is in fact much more than that.' How does that grab you?"

A depressing weight seemed to bear down on Mike. He made an effort to shrug it away and failed. "What good will it do? Nobody reads mystery reviews. I'll be lucky if the book sells five thousand copies."

"There'll be some foreign sales, the paperback . . ."

"Sure," Mike said. "And a few bucks more, enough to get me through to the next pub date, providing I am able to whip the new book into shape. Which I don't think I can do."

"Writers," Vaccaro growled in exaggerated disapproval. "I should have my head examined, dealing with them. My good mother was right. I should have become a priest.

I'd have heard fewer sad stories in the confessional." He laughed encouragingly. "Do me a favor. Go out and get drunk. Get a girl. Live. Some day you'll be rich and famous in spite of yourself."

It seemed like an excellent idea.

Elizabeth and Mike

He took her to the Philippine Gardens. The prospect of a new and different kind of food excited her. They ate steak prepared with an exotic brown gravy and incredibly large shrimp, stuffed and served with a pungent sauce. The coffee was virtually undrinkable and they made their way over to a coffee house on Fifty-sixth Street where they held hands and sipped espresso.

Elizabeth had wanted to discuss the manuscript, had brought it with her. But he had restrained her during dinner, almost afraid to hear what she had to say. Now she referred to it again.

"Shall I speak the truth?" she began hesitantly.

"Not necessarily. You can tell me it's superb, some of the best writing you've ever read."

Her hand went to her mouth. "Oh."

He touched her cheek reassuringly. "That was a joke. A small, very bad joke. I think I shall have an electric sign made that I can wear on my lapel so that whenever I tease you it will flash on and off saying 'Mike is joking, Mike is joking'."

Her mouth lifted in a brief acknowledging smile. Then, briskly, she spoke. "You're right about the story. It doesn't work, I think, as a mystery."

He kept his mouth shut and leaned back, trying not to react too emotionally. Only to hear and understand. To think, the way he would at an editorial conference. He had allowed her to read the manuscript and in so doing incurred a responsibility to entertain her opinion.

"Why doesn't it work?" he said very softly.

She measured him shortly, pale face serious, the green eyes steady and grave. "There is no suspense, no real mystery. It is clear from the start what happened and who did what to whom. What is *going* to happen is obvious, too. To make matters worse, the story is too thin, the complications too transparent and contrived. Almost as if you didn't care while you were writing it, as if you composed it with your thoughts elsewhere."

"I see," he said carefully.

"Don't be angry with me," she urged, touching his hand.

He withdrew his hand. "I'm not angry."

"You're working yourself up to being angry though and that intimidates me."

He made a conscious effort to shake off the growing tension. He exhaled and produced a quick, reassuring smile. "Okay. Tell me the worst."

She put her elbows on the table and began. "There is no balance."

"I don't understand. How do you mean balance?"

"The idea is good. The desire for money, big money, causes the couple to cast off all restraint, all social inhibition, all morality. But the way the book is written the emphasis is on your hero, that professor, and his search for them. We know what their crime is, right from the start, and we can see from their bumbling ways that it's only a matter of time until they're caught."

"It's supposed to be a detective story."

"There's no need to be sarcastic with me."

"Apology rendered," he said, with forced lightness.

"Accepted." She went on. "I guess that's it. I was more interested in the hunted than in the hunt. You do women marvelously well, you know. Freda is vibrant, alive, rounded, and full of wonderful human contradictions. You have a nice feeling about women, I think."

"And Alec?"

She drew her brows together in concentration. "Well . . . I think that under that tough veneer he is a very frightened man."

"I agree."

"A couple of times I wondered how he ever found the nerve to go through with the scheme, to murder, not once but three times, and then to steal all that money."

"That's why the tough suit."

That troubled her and she said so. "It isn't enough for me. What if he did it for Freda?"

"He did. He's wild about her."

"That should be clearer then. He should be under her control to a greater degree, subject to her manipulations. How does she feel about him?"

"She's crazy about him."

"I don't think so. Oh, perhaps he pleased her in some ways. But she is primarily concerned about using him for her own ends. She's a very shrewd woman. Cold. Hard. And for all Alec's apparent worldliness, there is a kind of naiveté about him. I think she sees him as her last chance. She's older, her beauty is fast fading. She's afraid of being poor and alone. This is her big opportunity to secure her future once and for all. She would do anything. . . ."

"True. But that is only the background for the suspense story, for the hero tracking them down. That final scene on the peninsula in Mexico . . ."

She took her lower lip between her teeth. "Mike, tell me if I'm wrong. Or stupid. I read the manuscript twice and gave it a lot of thought. And then I did some other reading. Did you ever read *Treasure of the Sierra Madre?*"

"Traven's story. A classic."

"I didn't think it was well-written but it was a very fine delineation of the corrupting influence of gold. Of how distrust and fear—"

She was *right*. It was all there in the characters of Alec and Freda, in what existed between them *because* of what they were and who they were. The whole damned story! And he had missed it, seeing it only in terms of the kind of thing he had done previously. Another thriller. A small, conventional book by a small, conventional writer.

"You're a much better writer than you know," Elizabeth was saying. "Much better. Your prose is clean and direct, colorful, evocative. You use strong verbs and waste nothing."

He made a gesture that silenced her. She waited patiently.

"Tell me if I understand you right," he said. "You're saying that the real story occurs off the pages, outside the book itself." She nodded in affirmation. "I think I agree. But I'm not sure I can write *that* story, that I have the talent, the insight necessary to really get at the relationship. . . ."

"But you *do!*" she burst out. "You have more in you than you know."

"More in you . . ." The words skittered around the interior arc of his skull. Vaccaro had used the same words. "You make it with your people," he had said, "understand them emotionally. . . ."

"You're suggesting that I write a serious novel," Mike said. He raised his eyes to hers. "That means time and thought, a deep commitment, with many risks, a kind of personal exposure. I'm already established. I've made a place for myself. Something like this, I'd probably fall on my face, fail . . ."

"Or succeed."

"An even bigger risk," he added grimly.

As if by common consent, neither of them spoke about it again that night. They went for a long, aimless walk, looking into the darkened windows of antique shops, browsing in a paperback book store on Third Avenue where Elizabeth found some of Mike's earlier works in the mystery section. She insisted on placing copies more prominently on the racks, convinced that the exposure was necessary. A disapproving clerk appeared and silently returned the books to their rightful position. They left laughing, too loudly, attracting attention. They moved up Third Avenue, arms entwined, stopping to kiss on impulse, quick, noisy kisses that drew interested glances.

"Please, Mike," she said abruptly. "Please take me home now. To your apartment, please."

They made it inside and he managed to lock the door before she was at him, body close, arms circling his waist, mouth reaching.

His tongue went across her upper lip, explored her teeth, found the smooth wetness of her inner cheek. She closed her lips, sucking gently, tasting him. A damp flush, a spreading urgency tightened his groin and he pulled her closer. Her belly was pliant, agile, and she came up on her toes, positioning herself so that his swollen crotch could slip between her thighs. She moaned into his mouth.

"Why," she managed, "have you got all these terrible clothes on?"

"I was about to ask the same question."

They went into the bedroom, undressed each other, fingers trembling, stopping to kiss each patch of flesh as it was revealed, swaying, clutching at each other for balance, for reassurance. His mouth came to rest on one tumescent nipple. She spoke his name and he went lower.

"Oh. Never. Never like that."

"No one?" he muttered, suddenly alert to her response, to the nuance of voice and word. "Not one man?"

"None," she muttered.

He made an effort to squeeze the doubts out of his brain and succeeded after a moment. They went to the bed, naked and anxious, tasting each other feverishly.

"Do you," he husked from afar, "want to do it this way?"

"Oh. Oh, not this time. This time in me, all of you, flooding me. In me, please. In me."

They turned and shifted, adjusted, reached, guided.

"Ah, Mike. So big. So hard. Beautiful."

"You approve?"

"So much! So much."

Her thighs spread and raised up, and then it was all plunging darkness, that initial microsecond of timelessness, of being total, one with the universe, with *her*, with *him*, full and giving. The long, slow strokes. The quick rough blows driving her into the deep softness, the pleasurable pain, the heightened anxiousness as they climbed the mountain together, the sweet drifting scent of their union.

"Ahh!" she gasped.

"You're all right?" he asked, though he knew she was.

"Oh, fine. Yes."

"You're pleased?"

"Like never before."

"Here."

"Oh, yes, give me."

"Here."

They rose and twisted, heaved impossibly with frenzied strength, lifting and descending in a stormy paroxysm. She teetered on the peak, all forces mingling under unbearable pressures until she exploded. Again and again. Again. Flesh jerking, body wracked, squirming to be free of the tortured joy and begging for its continuation, pinned under his thumping power, lanced by his tempered sword safe in his gentle arms.

"You," she begged. "You. I want you," she pleaded. "Give me, darling. Give me. Please . . ."

He rose up, frozen, hovering like some great hunting bird. Then with a swift violent gasp, he plunged downward, reaching into her with a primitive violence that set off fresh trembling in her flesh. They erupted in natural harmony. He was a torrential stream; she the riverbed. He was a volcano; she the receptive slope. He was a wild beast; she a taunting vixen. He went off; she vibrated. He flared; she simmered. He banged and brayed; she whimpered and cried. Life was a lingering spasm.

They rested finally. Smoked, dozed, and smoked again. She began to think.

"It's very interesting."

"What is?"

"How good we are together. Right from the start."

"Interesting," he agreed.

"Is it always like that for you?"

"Not always," he said carefully.

"I mean with other girls."

"I know what you mean."

"It has never been so good for me."

"Never?"

"Never." Then, after a moment, "It is never like this in the beginning, the first time."

"But it's not the first time for you. For either of us," he amended quickly.

"That troubles you, doesn't it?" she said quietly. "That I was not the pristine creature you thought I was."

"It doesn't trouble me at all," he lied. "A virgin isn't what I want. I'm no instructor."

She laughed quietly. "Myron Birns, Professor of Sexology one and two. A three-credit course. A prerequisite to a degree in liberal arts."

"I don't think I can teach you anything."

"Mike," she said after a moment. "You're taking cracks at me and I don't deserve it. I've never deceived you. I did what I've had to do, lived the way I had to. Just as you have. I can't change what I've done. But I won't let you make less of me for it. I told you how it was, and I didn't have to. You mustn't use it against me."

"I didn't mean——"

"Yes," she broke in, "you did mean. You want to hurt me, to punish me. Maybe for not being what you would like me to be. Maybe for saying the things I did about your manuscript." She overrode his protests. "It's true, Mike, and if you think about it you'll know it is. So, stop, please. Unless you want me to go. Unless you don't want to see me again."

A pulse leaped erratically in his temple and he put his hand on her thigh. "Be patient with me. I'm having a bad time. I'm worried about the book. And about you, about my feelings toward you. Frightened . . ."

"I know. But I'm not asking you for anything, darling. Just that you be yourself and let me be myself. Now, please, kiss me, please. . . ."

On Saturday night, they ate dinner together and went to a movie. Afterward they returned to Mike's apartment with a copy of *The Sunday Times*. He had refrained from mentioning the review of the new book to her and now he located it, handed the book section to her. She read intently. When she was finished she kissed him on the mouth.

"I'm so proud to know you."

"In a Biblical sense?"

"You know what I mean."

"Well, you make it sound almost impersonal."

"Anything but impersonal."

He held her face between his hands. "Are you my girl?"

"I would like to be."

"Then it's settled."

"If you say so."

He kissed her and felt her breasts against him and after a while they made love. They did it on the floor in front of the couch and afterward they went to bed. During the night he woke to hear her making small frightened sounds, sobbing. He embraced her and kissed the back of her neck. She woke only enough to say she was having a bad dream, to thank him. Then she was asleep again.

But he was unable to sleep, remembering his conversation with Eddie Stander, wishing he had hit him between the eyes.

Chapter V

BB

April was splendid that year. The days were bright and warm and the buds broke out on the trees along Harkenton Street and the nights were crisp and invigorating.

It was on that kind of a night that eight of Professor Hailey's friends assembled in his apartment. Beside Hailey, there were two other members of the faculty and six undergraduates. Including BB.

A simple buffet was served. An Irish stew. Salad. Hot rolls. Ice cream and coffee. Good solid fare. Afterward, they lounged around the comfortably appointed living room listening to Stravinsky, the Sergeant Pepper album, and Noel Coward. Hailey insisted that Coward had a genius beyond any acclaim yet received.

The sugar cubes were served during the playing of the Sarah Vaughan album. Hailey placed them in the crystal dish on the coffee table. He waited until the music stopped before speaking.

"Boyd here," he began, in that mild and melodic voice, resting his hand possessively on BB's thigh, "has only taken one trip before. He's been riding a different horse, you might say. Horse!" he laughed. "Oh, that is prime! But tonight he will have a really wondrous journey. That's why you've all been invited. To guide him along his lovely trip."

"It's always more glorious," an associate professor said, "to fly when all your friends are flying with you."

"Exactly," Hailey agreed.

"May we have some suitable background music?" a student asked.

"Indeed, we shall," Hailey said. "There's a John Gage album, if someone will put it on. Meanwhile, I'll distribute these goodies. . . ."

He offered the crystal dish to BB who anxiously grabbed only for a cube.

"Put it in your mouth, dear boy," Hailey urged. "Suck on it. Get all the sweet joy. . . ."

Chapter VI

Judd Martin

Harriet Davidson peered with grave concern at her reflection in Susan Morgan's bathroom mirror. It was a custom-built make-up mirror, similar to those used in theatrical dressing rooms and in its impersonal glare every cruel crease, every enlarged pore, every weary sag, could be seen. Harriet grimaced and set about repairing the damage. She worked swiftly, confidently. Finished, she leaned back to appraise her efforts.

She saw there a small woman, delicately boned, graceful, with tiny hands and feet. She had always been exceptionally pretty, even as an infant, and she grew into a cute sprightly girl. An even more lively woman. People had always been attracted to her, had always liked her. Men especially.

At eighteen, having given no indication to anyone at home, or in the small town in which she lived, that she had such ambitions, Harriet went to Hollywood, California, where she presented herself, sweetly, at the offices of practically every talent agent in the area. Cute, lively girls with round hips and medium-sized breasts were in vogue that year and Harriet soon got what she came for—a movie contract.

She was cast as a cute young girl in small roles in a number of films that brought her no professional attention at all. People viewed her as a child. A toy, almost. They enjoyed her coquettishness, the way her small face was made, the fluttery brown eyes, the upturned nose, the quick display of neat white teeth. They enjoyed too her brittle, rising laugh, the way she punctuated her gay remarks, delivered in a voice pitched a little too high. They enjoyed the way she dressed. Those lacy blouses and little-girl dresses, that never failed to reveal the tucked-in waist, the fine hips, the shapely bosom.

She pleased men. She made them laugh, made them feel protective. After all, she looked so young, so innocent, untouched by the tough sophistication of the movie scene. They were careful of their language when she was around and reserved their dirtiest jokes for other occasions. Many of them warned her about the lecherous men who peopled the studios and the casting offices, detailed the wiles that might be used to bring her to no good end, and most of them never imagined her in a carnal pose.

Most, but not all. A veteran director undressed her without objection in his office and enjoyed her in his desk chair while swiveling in complete circles; a Hungarian screenwriter took her behind some flats one afternoon, squeezed her left breast, and did it to her standing, holding her aloft until they were joined; she did it in the executive dining room with the brother-in-law of a production chief and eventually with the production chief himself in the back of his custom-built Rolls Royce.

Sad reality jolted Harriet when, at the termination of her six-month contract, the option was not exercised. She was without a job, without income, her career seemingly over too quickly. But cute girls still had a certain currency and Harriet accommodated a casting agent at one of the majors who introduced her to an assistant director who, when he was through with her, sent her to his boss, a married man with a jealous mistress. He put Harriet on his payroll as a script girl and used her during lunch breaks.

This fortunate arrangement continued for another six months, allowing Harriet a great deal of time to herself at night. She managed to get herself invited to a number of very chic parties attended by important movie people and it was there that she met Irwin S. Davidson. She recognized him immediately as a man destined to carve his name deep and permanently into the Hollywood firmament.

There was that look to him. He was one of those tight men, alert, darkly handsome, with a controlled intelligence, a man who never said a word or made a gesture without twice considering it. At thirty, he had produced three money-making, low-budget projects, and was now preparing a film which would star either Gable or Tracy. A man like Irwin S. Davidson should be able to do quite a bit for a cute girl just starting her film career, she decided.

So when he phoned the next night and invited her to dinner she accepted at once. He took her to the Brown Derby and afterward for a drive. She kept waiting for him to make a pass, had made up her mind that she would be so good for him that he would want to keep her on a very tight string—like a part in his next picture.

Davidson had other ideas. He was looking for a suitable helpmate, a wife, and he was convinced that an innocent young creature like Harriet Henley from Sioux Falls, Iowa, suited his needs.

Harriet had always been able to think on her feet. She did now. Stardom was very appealing but it was at best a tenuous ambition, even with Irwin S. Davidson at her back. Wifedom was an entirely different matter. A much more certain end with a raft of promising ramifications that she was able to envision at once. Davidson she decided, was a man who might end up owning a large segment of Hollywood. And she craved a piece of that action.

The next day she had her phone number changed. Unlisted, of course. And in the weeks that followed, she withdrew completely from her former social circles. No one missed her very much, not even the director, who had no trouble finding another script girl. Besides, cute girls were going out of style.

She dated only Irwin S. Davidson. Saw only Irwin S. Davidson. Spoke only to Irwin S. Davidson. Which made things difficult for Harriet since Davidson made no sexual overtures in her direction, limiting himself to a chaste goodnight kiss at the close of each evening. It seemed that Irwin S. Davidson was a self-professed old-fashioned man who expected his wife to be a virgin on their wedding night. That was when she realized for the first time that he intended to marry her, though he had never made a proposal, taking their eventual union for granted. Harriet made no objection to this oversight; she had a more important detail to concern herself with; trying to remember how she had felt and acted on the occasion of losing her virginity, a dim, distant experience.

Four months after their first meeting, Davidson presented her with a five-carat diamond ring to signify their engagement. And three months after that they were married in an elaborate ceremony in one of the sound stages at the studio, with a party afterward that lasted for two days.

For their honeymoon they made a trip around the world, which Davidson was able to write off as a tax deduction since he visited cities in various countries to consult with film executives and exhibitors. Years later, when he became embroiled in a proxy fight for control of the studio, these distant friends remembered him and voted in his favor.

Eight days after their return to Hollywood, Harriet enjoyed her first adulterous act. She performed fellatio on a clear-skinned Mexican boy who worked with the gardener on their Bel Air estate. It was the first time that had been done to the boy and he was startled but pleased. He came back for more without being invited and so was rather surprised when he lost his job a week later.

After that, Harriet made her selections more carefully. Assistant directors or actors. They were best. Such ambitious young men seldom caused trouble, took orders very well. They knew how much the wife of Irwin S. Davidson could do to help them.

So it surprised her not at all to see the tall young man hovering about when she came out of Susan Morgan's bathroom. He directed one of those frank, charming young-man-on-the-make smiles at her and inclined his head. She supposed he was an actor. There had been twenty years of men like him and still they came. More than ever now that Irwin headed his own studio.

"Judd, isn't it?" she said.

"Judd Martin."

"And you're an actor."

He ducked his head boyishly. She waited for him to kick at an invisible pebble. He restrained himself.

"Mostly a writer," he said. "But I've done some acting."

"A playwright and a good one, I suppose."

He gave her his level, confident expression. She was the big chance. *His* big chance. And he wasn't going to pass it by. Besides, she was interested. He could tell. "I was a better-than-good actor and I'm an even better writer."

She measured him briefly. Tall, wiry, intense. He was drawn tight, a little too tight. She put that down to nervousness. He was making a very important pitch right now, one that obviously meant a lot to him. Well, she mused with silent amusement, let him work for it.

"And now you want to go out to the Coast," she said. "To get into pictures. Television."

It was said simply, without expression, and sent a sharp concern stabbing along Judd's nervous system. He had viewed her as just another middle-aged woman, bored and vulnerable to his manipulations. At once he knew that he was wrong. She was not that simple, not that hungry.

"That's where the work is," he said carefully.

"And the gold."

"The gold too." There was no point in trying to deceive her. He dropped the boyishness. "Is there anything wrong with wanting some of it?"

"Nothing." Her laughter lacked humor. "The question is how you will get it. Do you believe that you can seduce me and thereby get me to influence my husband in your behalf?"

He held himself very still, considering. He made up his mind. "That's exactly what I had in mind."

"Past tense," she commented easily. "I see you know when to quit."

"I haven't quit. Just changed my tactics."

That amused her and it showed on her face. "I have the impression that you belong to Susan Morgan."

He shrugged. "I don't belong to anyone."

"If I were to take you on," she said, voice dropping an octave, "you'd belong to me. Totally."

"That would be interesting."

"Perhaps you'd be good for a few laughs."

"I guarantee more than that."

"Men. I've never met one who admitted he was less than a superb lover. Most fall short, you know."

"I don't."

She walked across the room to the door. "Perhaps not. We shall see."

"When?"

She paused, not looking back. "When I say so. *If* I say so."

"You'll be going back to the Coast soon," he complained.

She faced him. "If you want it badly enough, you'll have to come after it." He took a step toward her and she stopped him with an upraised hand. "Not now. I'm staying at the Regency. Call me, if you wish. Any time after eleven. Try to convince me. I can be had, but I don't come easy."

"And if I do convince you?"

She smiled over her shoulder, that cute smile that had always made people want to ruffle her hair, pinch her cheek, that made him want to hit her. "Wait and see . . . Now I must get back inside before my husband misses me. I don't want to give him cause for concern."

He trailed dutifully after her.

Neil

Irwin S. Davidson looked fifteen years younger than he was. In a suit of black silk, tailored for him in Rome, he was lean and hard. A man who exercised for ninety minutes a day in the studio gymnasium. The bony face was brown with deep, far-seeing eyes, and his wiry hair was still black and abundant. He was specially proud that he still had every one of his own teeth.

He made himself comfortable in the big brown leather wing chair in Neil Morgan's study and allowed Neil to light his Havana Corona. They came to Davidson from Cuba via Mexico City; there were some pleasures he refused to give up, politics or no. He sucked on the cigar and blew smoke.

"That was a superb dinner Susan served," he said. "A wonderful woman, Susan. Beautiful. She should've been in pictures."

That pleased Neil. It had always been a secret fantasy of his—Susan as a movie star. Here was professional confirmation at the highest level.

"I've always wanted a wife, Irwin," he said sincerely, "not a star."

"Right. That's the way I feel about Harriet. She was in pictures, you know."

Neil gave him an expansive smile. "I *remember*. The cute little secretary in *Treasure By Twilight*. The kid sister with Davis in *Watch Out Girls*. I remember Harriet Henley all right."

"Well," Davidson said. "Well, thank you." He hawked his throat clear. "I appreciate your entertaining Harriet and me this way, Morgan. After all, we haven't been close."

"The business, Irwin," Neil said reasonably. "You've been on the Coast. I'm here. Geography."

"Right. We've got a lot in common though. We could have been friends."

"I agree. And there's hard evidence to support that, Irwin. When I filmed my *Trouble Will Out* series at Davidson Studios, you were more help than I can say, Advisor, coach, friend."

"It's good business to treat a man right."

"You made me a good deal, too, Irwin."

"A good deal for one is a good deal for the other. Make someone happy and he tries to make you happy, is my attitude."

"If only everybody had your humanity, Irwin."

"I've always meant to say something to you, Morgan. About that game-show affair."

"A mistake."

"A bad thing. To let that happen. A smart operator like you."

"I admitted my error," Neil said, restraining his resentment. That was over. Why couldn't people forget? Forgive?

"To be caught that way. In public. Your dirty laundry showing. That's bad strategy."

"I'm through with game shows, Irwin. I learned my lesson. I'm working on something else these days, a really prestige concept that is going to be a critical achievement of the first rank. And make a great deal of money."

"Ah."

"Let me tell you about it, Irwin. I would appreciate the opinion of a man like yourself."

"I'm listening."

Neil outlined his vision of *World True Crime Theater*. "I intend to get the best directors, big names for star value, dress each production richly. We'll go on actual locations, the sites of each crime. Use real people where possible and provide an epilogue with the police officer or district attorney or maybe the criminal himself, if he's available. A sort of historical summation. As for budget considerations, I say this kind of thing must be done well, with nothing held back. I learned that from you, Irwin. So I am going first class all the way. I want money to be spent and every dollar reflected on the screen. . . ."

"That's good thinking."

"I knew you'd understand. See it, Irwin. A series of specials that reflect the kind of professionalism Davidson Studios is known for."

"We believe in quality at Davidson's."

"That's why I wanted to give you first chance at this project. I treasure our relationship, Irwin. I put a lofty premium on your professional opinion."

"You want my opinion?"

"Oh, yes."

"You'll get it. Let me first ask you a question. If you were Irwin S. Davidson, in the position fate cast him, in his boots, so to speak, in his chair, what would you be thinking right now?"

Neil hesitated.

"I'll tell you what you'd be thinking," Davidson went on. "You'd be thinking that Neil Morgan is trying to sell me a TV show, is what you'd be thinking."

Neil arranged a properly sheepish grin on his face. "Irwin, you are some kind of a genius."

"To think that you could hustle me?" Davidson chided.

"Convince not hustle. Sell you, maybe."

Davidson grunted cynically. "It lacks."

"I don't agree," Neil returned quickly. "Dress it with stars, an experienced director, the production values . . ."

"It still lacks. Is it any different than a dozen other series? *Dragnet, FBI, NYPD, Naked City*. Strip away the conversation and you got cops and robbers all over again." He rolled the Corona between his fingers. "In my position, a man hears things. You've been hustling this show around."

"Not precisely," Neil corrected carefully. "There are changes, a metamorphosis . . ."

Davidson shook his head with grim finality. "I could say yes to you, Morgan. Put up the production money. Arrange sponsorship even. But I won't. And this is why. The Davidson track record. That is championship stuff. Morgan. Gold medal stuff. Sponsors trust Davidson. They line up with him. And why? I'll tell you why. Because I have a debt to the businessmen who do business with me. When I say go they go, knowing they are getting a good ride for their dollars. This 'World True Crime Theater' of yours. It doesn't give me the feeling I want from a project. That's why I say it lacks."

"I think you're wrong," Neil said, unable to conceal his disappointment. "This is a winner."

"It's better to miss the boat than to sink and drown."

"There are other people interested, Irwin," Neil said. "I wanted you to have first crack. . . ."

Davidson pushed himself out of the big chair. "You know what I think? Let me tell you what I think. That you're working the wrong side of the street."

"I don't understand."

"My point is what you're making. You don't understand. You've missed the true value of the material you have. Your vision is too narrow, a horse wearing blinders. Forget about television. Reorient your thinking, your planning. Rewrite your script. Make a movie, Morgan. For theatrical release. Go big. Come to Davidson with something sensational, a great package. The right writer, the right property. Two big name stars who mean cash at the box office. A director. Convince me, and in seventy-two hours you will have your financing, distribution, everything. It will be like digging oil wells and finding oil. Anybody can do it, if they think right. And there's no worries about thirteen-week options."

"You are a genius, Irwin! I always said so."

"Not so much a genius," Davidson said modestly. "Just good hard work and right thinking."

"Irwin, all this time, while you've been advising me—and I want you to know how much I appreciate it—I've been thinking, Irwin. Thinking right. Your kind of thinking.

On the right track. And Irwin, I have got . . . an . . . idea."

"Say it to me."

"My pilot film. It would lend itself perfectly to expansion. Hear me out, Irwin. A jealous husband, an unhappy wife with a young lover. They plot to kill the husband even as he is hiring a gunman to rub out the lover. Visualize this, Irwin, as I do. Newman as the husband and —get this, Irwin—Faye Dunaway as the wife. Is that *casting?*"

"Twentieth has Newman tied up for a picture."

"Steve McQueen then. But listen to *this,* Irwin. Are you listening?"

"I'm listening."

"We make the lover, the *lover,* black. A Negro. It's right. Maybe Poitier or Jimmy Brown. Or Cosby. This is where it's at. Capitalize on all the racial unrest. The world is ready for this one, Irwin. *In the Heat of the Night. Guess Who's Coming For Dinner? For Love of Ivy.* Now *this.* A can't-miss project, Irwin."

"Believe me when I tell you, Morgan. It could miss." He went to the door. "But you're thinking and that's got to be good. Let me know when you come up with the right thing. Now, shall we go back to the ladies? They must be missing us."

Neil made himself smile. "Be along in a moment." He needed time to regain control of his emotions, to suppress the rage and frustration that surged through him. He had depended on Davidson, planned for this evening. And now *this.* It was as if every channel was closed off to him. Somehow he had to break through. Somehow . . .

Chapter VII

Mike and Elizabeth

He became aware of the tension as they walked through Central Park. It had been mounting for some time. A gathering of emotion, of confusion. When they were together, he couldn't seem to get enough of her—enough of her gaiety and zestful curiosity about life, of her deep passion. Yet at the same time there was something that disturbed him, made him wary, uncertain. She was too much—too much passion, too much life—and the ballooning excitement he felt was frightening. Transient. She made him feel younger than his years and he kept reminding himself of the difference in their ages. They were of different generations, living at different tempos, aiming at different ends.

There was something else. His failure to read her accurately from the start. To think she was innocent, untouched, when in fact she had been in more beds, accepted more men, than she could remember. Done it all. Said it all. Over and over with strangers. With men whose faces and names had long since disappeared from her memory. He shuddered and tried not to think about it. But it kept coming back.

It was a Sunday, fine and clear, the sun glowing warm. Central Park was crowded with strollers and bicycle riders. With families and with lovers. With children.

They wandered over to Sheep Meadow where an army of young people had gathered. Beards and flowered shirts, beads and painted faces numbered in the thousands. Some plucked at guitars and others sat in groups and talked and sang. Others flew kites in the same field where some long-haired boys were playing softball.

Mike and Elizabeth stopped to watch a group shuffling in a circle around a youth who was beating a drum and another blowing into a conch shell. A boy with a shaved head and wearing the saffron robe of a Buddhist monk carried a brass incense jar and led the chanting procession.

"Hari Krishna. Hari Krishna. Krishna Krishna. Hari . . ."

They watched until Mike grew irritated, annoyed at the dancers, at himself for wasting time on such nonsense. "Let's go," he muttered.

She held on to his arm, reluctant to leave, enjoying the experience, a sympathetic smile on her slender face, head rocking gently in time to the drum beats.

His irritation spread. "You want to stay, okay," he said, making his voice elaborately casual. "I'm heading back to the apartment."

He disengaged his arm and turned away. She trailed out of the crowd after him, catching up finally. "What's wrong, Mike?"

"Not a thing," he said shortly.

"Did I do something wrong?"

He stopped and faced her. "I said nothing was wrong. Okay."

She walked beside him, neither of them speaking. Back at his apartment, she dropped down on the deep soft couch and kicked off her shoes, swung her feet onto the coffee table.

"Wasn't that nice?" she said lightly.

"Those kids try too hard."

"I thought they were cute. They like each other so much, enjoy each other."

"They bore me," he shot back. "All that talk of love, of doing their thing. Why is it they always do their thing in crowds? These love-ins, be-ins, all the rest. Everything organized. I don't like it. Also, I get the feeling that they think their thing is the only thing."

"I don't think so," she offered mildly.

"I suspect anybody who tells me he knows *the* road to Rome. I suspect ritualists with their own gods and heroes. I suspect their motives and their methods."

"Oh, Mike. Don't be pompous. They're all so young and innocent." She laughed easily. "I'm beginning to think there is something to that talk about a generation gap."

"What is that supposed to mean? That I'm too old to understand? Maybe I'm too old for you, too."

"Did I say that?"

"You meant it."

"I'm here, Mike, because I want to be."

"I think you'd rather be out there barefoot in that circle of screwballs."

"I'd rather be just where I am. With you."

He couldn't accept it. It was a lark for her, an affair with an older man, a writer. But time had run out on them. She had milked the experience for all it could give and now she wanted to move on. The generation gap. He supposed the years did make a difference. He recalled fights he'd had with his father years before. Mike had been ready to blame his father, his father's generation, for the ills of the world. For the Depression. For Hitler. For World War II.

"I suppose you believe in universal guilt," he challenged.

"What do you mean?"

"You think Viet Nam is the fault of my generation?"

"That's not what I think."

He ignored her answer. "If you're going to blame people collectively for what's gone wrong then why not credit them for what's gone right. This world is not entirely bad. Those kids in the park. They couldn't go that route if this wasn't an affluent and permissive society, willing to tolerate them. When I was their age, young people had to worry about making a living, trying to carve out a career. . . ."

"Mike, people have to live in their own time. They have no other. We all have to do our thing. Maybe those kids are saying something worthwhile to us—"

He stared at her. He wanted to let go of the passion that drove him but he couldn't. "You belong out there with them. You're one of them."

"No, I'm not."

"It's true. And we both know it. This business between

us. It was just an experience for you and it's over. You don't need me anymore."

"That's not so!"

A serrated laugh broke out of him. "I think it is. What you need is someone your own age, someone who understands the aims and aspirations of your generation. You do the shingaling and enjoy Godard and The Beatles. The lindy and John Huston and Frank Sinatra belong to me."

She laughed with relief. "If that's all that's——"

"That's not all," he snapped. You keep pushing me about my work. You expect me to write some earth-shaking book, to make some statement from on high. Well, forget it. I write mysteries and that's all. *War and Peace* is not in me."

"Why not *Crime and Punishment?*"

"I'm serious."

"So am I."

She chewed her lower lip. "I won't say anything about your work again. I promise."

She understood nothing, he reflected bitterly. She viewed him as some sort of special human being when in fact he was ordinary. Common. He was Myron Birns, a kid from the Bronx who had had pathetic, pimply dreams of authorship. In some strange way, it had come to pass but part of him refused to accept it yet.

Why? Why not accept the reality of his life, the rewards along with the obligations of success? Perhaps the obligations scared him even as his earlier ambitions had terrified him for so long. Obligations to whom? No one had ever given him a thing. No one had ever offered a helping hand. His mind reached back to his childhood. He could remember no one ever embracing him affectionately, remember no one offering encouragement or praise. Screw them all. He owed nothing to anyone. Nothing to Elizabeth Jordan. He had given full value for services rendered.

Even more, by what right did she push him and crowd him, direct him onto rough roads? He had served his apprenticeship in living and he wanted, deserved, to travel the easy path from now on.

"You and your damned optimism," he told her. "I can live without your idealism. I made my peace with reality. I know my limitations."

"What about your possibilities? There isn't anything you couldn't do."

"Drop it. There's no point in going on with this. It isn't only the writing. You want to get married."

"I haven't said——"

"You want a family and you're entitled to have what you want. I've been married. I'll probably stay single for the rest of my life."

"Do you have another girl?" she asked in a small voice.

"Of course not."

"I love you, Mike."

"Don't say that. We came together and it was fun. Now it's over."

"It doesn't have to be. If you're bored with me—in bed, I mean—I understand that. If you need other women. All right. I'll understand. As long as you don't tell me about it. But don't send me away, Mike."

The thickening filled his throat and he knew that if she went on he would give in, never be rid of her. No matter what she agreed to, no matter what arrangement they made, it would all come back eventually. It was inevitable. She would crowd him into a corner with her demands, spoken and silent, demands he wouldn't or couldn't fulfill. Do it now, he ordered himself. Break it clean and fast.

"I want you to go. There's no point in going on with it."

"Oh, please, no. What did I *do?*"

"Dammit! Don't you know when something's finished? When you're not wanted anymore? Get out, dammit . . ."

She stood slowly and walked unsteadily to the door. She turned awkwardly. "Mike, if you want to call me . . . To make love or anything. I'll come to you right away."

He gave no indication that he had heard and she left quietly.

Chapter VIII

Roy

On the first Thursday in May, Neil Morgan sat behind his desk studying the daily newspapers, searching for a contemporary crime that would suit his purpose. He read all the mystery and adventure magazines, too, but remained convinced that it would be the daily press that would provide the solution to his problem. After all, it had been a small newspaper item that had inspired Truman Capote to write *In Cold Blood*.

The phone interrupted. It was Susan. "I'm busy, darling," he said automatically.

"The forecast is good for the weekend. Let's go out to the island, open the house."

He agreed readily though it meant canceling his tennis games. He would work out on the beach, do some running. Wind sprints. He hung up and went back to the paper.

A few minutes after, Susan called Maggie, told her of their plans. Maggie agreed that it was time to begin preparations for the summer.

"I'll tell Bob that we're going out. Saturday morning is best for us."

That afternoon, Eddie Stander informed his group chief that he had a dentist's appointment, would be away from his desk for the remainder of the day. Twenty minutes later, Edith picked him up on the corner of Third Avenue and Fiftieth Street. They headed out to Great Neck to look at the house she had discovered. A bargain, she insisted, at any price. And they should grab it. Eddie said he didn't know. It was a little steep for them and besides he had something else in mind, something less suburban than Great Neck. Less bourgeoise.

At about the same time, Mike Birns bought a drink for a young blonde girl at a bar on East End Avenue. Three drinks later they went to her apartment and got into bed. But he was unable to perform despite her energetic and imaginative efforts. He left with her shrill denunciations echoing in his ears.

And on that same Thursday, Roy Ashe made a point of doing exactly what he did on every other Thursday. Careful to draw no unwanted attention to himself. He called on customers, as usual. Told jokes, as usual. Took the secretary at Fisher-Vahan-Cohen to lunch, and propositioned her.

He continued the routine until precisely four-thirty. That's when he walked down to Grand Central Terminal, went into the large men's room. There was an empty booth against the wall and he went inside, locked the door, sat down on the toilet, briefcase in his lap. He opened it.

His hands were sure and swift. Using a small lady's make-up mirror, he arranged a thick, drooping Pancho Villa moustache on his upper lip. When it was in place, he tested the spirit gum; it was secure enough.

He removed his shoes and put on others. Quickly he changed his shirt and tie, adjusted a soft cloth hat on his head. He stuffed everything into the briefcase and stood up, left the cubicle. He studied himself in the wall mirror. The lifts in the shoes made him a full two inches taller, seemed to slim him down, and the hat and the moustache altered the entire cast of his face, providing him with a slightly Latin look. Pleased, he left the men's room.

In the waiting room, he opened locker number 35479, removing an 8 × 10 manila envelope, replacing it with the briefcase. He put another quarter in the coin slot and shut the door.

He entered a phone booth, turned toward the wall. From the envelope he took out the Luger, jamming it under his belt; and a pair of soft black leather gloves, which he placed in his jacket pocket; and sunglasses. He put them on and left the phone booth.

He bought a copy of *The Post* at a newsstand and made his way to the downtown platform of the IRT subway. It was already crowded with the first waves of rush-hour workers. Roy checked his watch. Ten after five. Perfect. His train came along and he allowed himself to be carried on by the flow of the crowd. He opened the newspaper and began to read.

No one paid any attention to him, which was according to plan.

It was cooler in Brooklyn Heights. He walked briskly. To any casual observer, he was just another homecoming worker from the canyons of Manhattan. It was a lovely spring, Roy noted with a great deal of satisfaction. He hoped that presaged a good summer. Last summer had been an abomination, every weekend wet and chilly.

That set him to thinking about the future. He was going to have to be cautious. No dramatic show of affluence. Nothing that might attract attention. Or cause unwanted speculation. He would continue his normal way of life for a few months. At least until the end of the year. Perhaps he would take a house at Fire Island for the summer. That would be in character and in order. A warm sense of nostalgia took hold of him. There had been so many good days, and nights, on the island.

He issued a silent warning. Join a house with other people, Groupers. Share expenses. Be concerned about money. The idea pleased him and he established it in his mind. He might just run out to Ocean Beach on Saturday, see what he could line up.

He marched through the courtyard of the building and rode up to the top floor. He went directly to the stairway leading to the roof. A soft breeze came off New York harbor. A lovely view, he thought. He turned his attention to the street below. People hurried along, diminutive, unimportant, returning to their bland little wives and bland little lives without hope for the next day. The living dead.

Not Roy Ashe. He was a man who did things. Moved ahead. *Lived.* After today, he would be set. He would have all the money he needed, his debts wiped out. He would make a down payment on the film library. A judicious payment. Enough, but not too much. The good life would be his, beginning at once. And forever.

He drew on the leather gloves. It was cooler now, the air soft and pleasant against his face. He touched the Luger in his belt; it was reassuringly solid. He considered men who lived with guns. Criminals, soldiers, revolutionaries. Names flashed to mind: Dillinger, Sergeant York, Che Guevara . . .

He drew himself erect, narrowed his eyes. When his time came, he would go with good form, make a splendid corpse. He thought about Bogart in the High Sierra, holding off the cops. And the way the bastards did in Marlon in *Viva Zapata;* and Cagney getting it in the rain and Muni and Eddie Robinson . . . He stiffened, leaned further over the parapet. There was Harry Nevin, shuffling along in that distinctively flabby manner of his, the attaché case hanging heavily in his hand. When the bookie turned into the courtyard, Roy left the roof.

He took the stairs to Harry's floor, waiting in the stairwell until the elevator stopped. He listened to the door creak open and close. He stepped into the corridor.

Harry Nevin, back toward Roy, moved with no urgency in the direction of his apartment. Roy went after him, closing the distance between them.

The bookie had already opened one of the Segal locks when he sensed another presence. He looked back with mild curiosity but no alarm. Seeing Roy, he frowned, more in annoyance than anything else.

"What are you doing here?" he said mildly. "You ready to pay off?"

Roy took the Luger out of his belt and pointed it at Harry.

"Open the door, Harry."

"You sonofabitch. Put that thing away."

"Open the door, Harry."

"You must be crazy, to think you can pull off something like this."

Roy drove the muzzle of the Luger into Harry's middle. Breath whooshed out of him. After a while, he straightened up.

"Open the door, Harry."

Harry nodded. They went into his office.

"Put the case on the desk," Roy said. "Now open it."

Roy smiled at the neat stacks of old bills that were revealed. "How much is in there, Harry?"

"Forty thousand. Maybe fifty. But—" Harry shook his heavy head, jowls trembling. "You don't believe a man like me operates alone in this town? It can't be done. I got partners. Big, tough partners. This is not all my dough. You understand that? I have backers. Everything is part of the syndicate, even me. Don't be dumb. Go away and I'll forget the whole thing. Go away and nobody'll ever know what you tried to pull off. But take this dough, Ashe, and they're going to come after you. A couple of their contract men. They're very efficient people. You know that."

Roy was pleased by his coolness and amused at the same time by Harry's earnest logic. Had they been thinking along the same lines, it would have made sense. But of course they hadn't been.

"Funny," Roy said. "I go to all this trouble, the moustache, the glasses, the hat. The lifts in my shoes. And you recognized me right away."

The bookie snatched at that. "You see! You're not cut out for this kind of action. Forget it. Leave. That'll be the end of it."

Roy gave that dirty old man laugh of his. "But the disguise wasn't intended to fool you, Harry. Just strangers. On the subway. So they wouldn't be able to identify me."

"But I know who you are!"

"Close the case, Harry, and lock it. Give it here."

"They're going to find you, Ashe. No matter where you go. They have men all over the world. I'm going to have to turn you over."

Roy felt sorry for the bookie. "You pathetic jerk. Do you think I didn't figure that? Did you expect that I was going to come here this way and let you turn some syndicate killers loose after me? Come on, Harry. Think a little."

"But how—" The blood drained out of his fleshy face. "Ah, no. No, Ashe. You're not that way, Ashe. You're not going to do a terrible thing like that. Not for money. Not you . . ."

Roy pulled the trigger twice. Harry bent double clutching his belly, protesting wetly. He fell to the floor, his breathing harsh. Roy placed the muzzle of the Luger against the mastoid bone behind Harry's right ear and squeezed the trigger again. This done, he left, the attaché case in hand. Very tall, very strong, very rich.

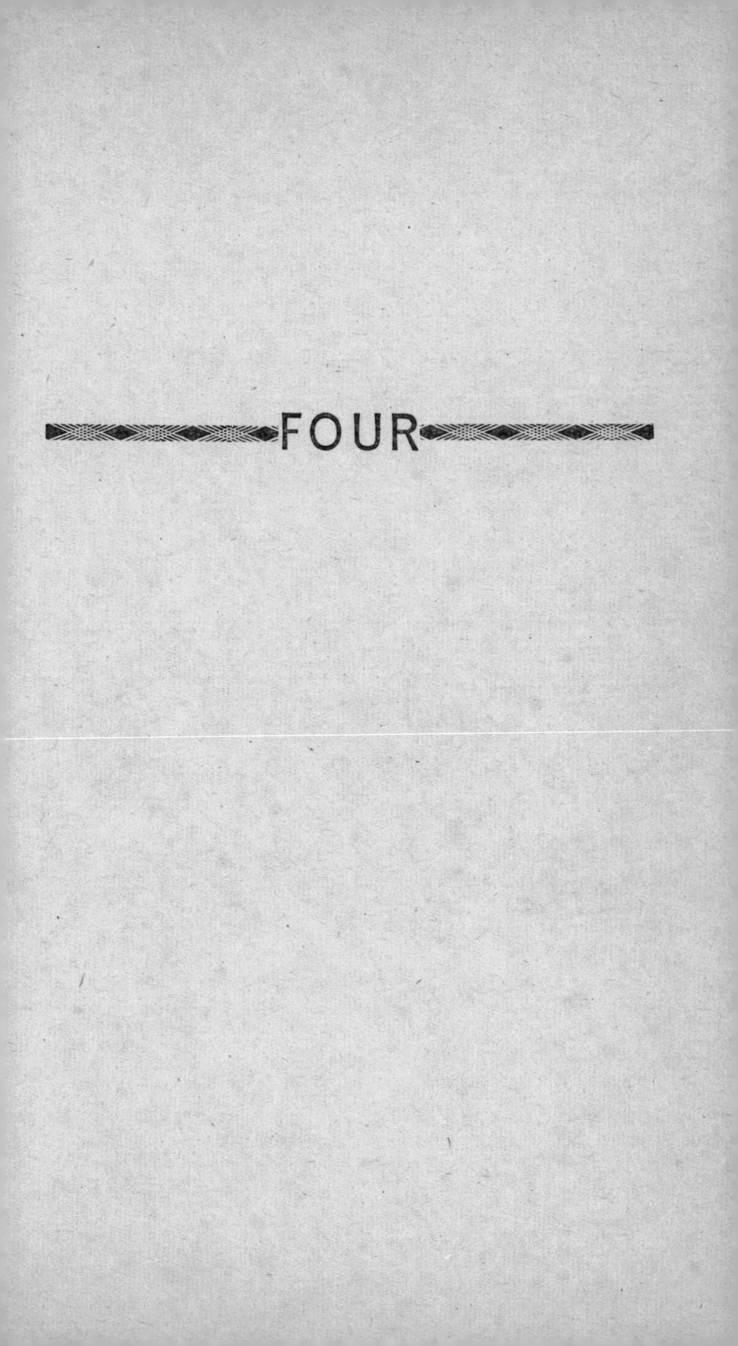

FOUR

THE SECOND SUMMER

That next summer, the wildest party ever took place at Cherry Grove. Drag, of course. Sooo campy! Two Lesbians fought with their fists over a graceful Hunter College freshman, new to the scene. And while they battled, she made it with the fag bartender on the marble-topped coffee table to the plaudits of the other guests.

That summer a lady psychologist invited her therapeutic group out for a weekend and led them into a forty-eight-hour orgy; her husband filmed the action. And more than two hundred thousand dollars changed hands in a four-day poker game. And a movie actor showed up at Leo's Place wearing only a jockstrap. And three people were felled by sunstroke on the Fourth of July. And seven express wagons were stolen. The police recovered three.

That summer people began to worry about erosion. And three girls showed up on the beach in bikinis. A Swedish girl lost her top and came out of the ocean, her huge breasts gleaming and jiggling in the hot sun. That summer the white wife of a brilliant surgeon went into the bushes with a black handyman. The next day her bottom was decorated with poison ivy. The surgeon bloodied her nose.

That summer a Youth Group was formed. The police force was increased. More prohibitions were promulgated. That year many of the summer people came out of the garment district. And there were more secretaries. And dentists. And shipping clerks. And shoe salesmen. And opticians. The girls wore make-up on the beach. And frizzed their hair up into odd shapes. And cloaked themselves in extravagant fashions and hues. High heels and incredibly tightassed toreador pants with sequins. And loud, shrill voices sliced through the soft sea air.

"You should have been here last season," people were saying. "It isn't the same anymore."

And it wasn't . . .

Chapter I

Eddie and Mike

The time between summers went swiftly for some of them. Too slowly for others. They came together during that time for dinners and at parties that were not much different from the parties on the island. The Ashes and the Morgans went to the theater together three or four times and once they went to the ballet; Neil said the ballet offended him. Eddie Stander had dinner at the Ashes at least once every week; and once Mike was invited for dinner.

Eddie and Mike saw each other with increasing frequency. At first, it was the dinners and parties bringing them together, forcing them to spend time in each other's company, to know each other better. Then they began going to hockey games at the Garden and they saw the Giants play football a few times. Sunday nights, after the game, they would go to Clarke's for drinks, dinner. See a movie sometimes. Mike suggested that they double-date and Eddie agreed. Those dates never materialized.

"You really do enjoy women, don't you?" Eddie asked one evening. They had gorged themselves on the veal parmigiana at Original Joe's, had gone to a movie and were now sitting over coffee. The remark came as Mike looked after the retreating form of the waitress.

He turned his attention back to Eddie, laughing. "Enjoy hell. I love them."

"You don't really mean it."

"Yes, I do. All of them, simply because they are female. And some of them, those I particularly like, those who move me in one way or another—well, they stand me on my ear."

Eddie puzzled over it. "Why?" he said finally.

Mike's impulse was to laugh but Eddie's earnestness was a deterrent. He arranged his features solemnly and considered the question.

"I told you, because they are female."

"Physically, you mean?"

"And more. Girls don't act or think the way men do."

"How can you believe that!"

"It's true."

"Crap. There's no real difference at all. Sure, the physical thing. That's obvious. But the rest is strictly conditioning, social and cultural influences. Pressures. Role-playing."

"It's a mistake to low-rate the physical. That's the crux of it, the root of all the differences. Anatomy is destiny. Freud said it, I think."

Eddie grunted heavily and passed his hand through his hair. He was combing it from side-to-side now, trying to cover the places where it had grown so alarmingly thin. "Granted the physical differences, what do you think the results are?"

"The nesting thing for one. Women want . . ."

"I want that too," Eddie said hurriedly. "A family, children. An Eames chair," he ended, making himself laugh.

The urgency still remained and a plaintive undertone.

"A woman is a nest, Eddie. And she knows it."

"Some of the reading I've done—. There are people who insist there is no such thing as instinct, not even to be a mother. Only socially imposed desires."

Mike considered that. "Maybe so. But put your shaft into a girl and she'll become pregnant, instinct or not. She knows it and so do you. Also, after sex, men get up and go home. It's over and often forgotten. Few girls want a man to leave."

Eddie scowled. "If that's what you believe, I don't see how you can go around with your pants open all the time. You do nothing but screw."

"It's not that bad," Mike said, laughing easily. He

hunched forward, spoke gravely. "I'm not making a moral issue here, Eddie. I'm not talking right and wrong. Just that this is how matters stand. Simply that, no more." He leaned back and grinned. "I got off to a late start with women. Maybe I'm trying to make up for lost time. Maybe I'm oversexed."

"Maybe you have to prove something," Eddie said flatly.

"Maybe. Or maybe I just enjoy being with a girl. Let me tell you something, I'm not as confident with women as I may appear. When I was in my teens, I always felt ugly and unattractive. Dumb and so damned inarticulate. Okay. So now I can talk and women seem to like me, want me. But I still feel the old way at times and I can't figure out what they see in me."

"Neither can I," Eddie agreed, looking into his coffee cup.

An uncertain laugh issued from Mike's mouth. "There are so many things to like about a woman," he said, to bridge the uncomfortable silence that had settled between them.

"Screwing, you mean!" Eddie challenged.

"More. The time before and after, the way they talk and sound, the way they do things. . . ."

"That's what I can't understand. There is so much that puts me off. They prattle about such crap and demand so much attention. The way they hang onto a man. Their *periods*—"

"You're *kidding*."

"It ruins me, Mike. Makes me lose all interest. Just to think about it. And women with hair on their breasts. And the way they hold on. Legs wrapped around you, trapping you, helpless . . .

Mike made no comment. At that same moment when Eddie felt trapped and helpless a warm gratitude and peace took hold of Mike. There was no way to explain that to his friend.

"I envy Roy," Eddie was saying. "To have a wife like Maggie. There's something so clean about her and she's so undemanding. She reminds me of those ads in the *New Yorker*, the models are . . . so perfect."

Mike spoke without emphasis. "Those girls don't exist."

Eddie's brows came together, bunched and rutted. "What is that supposed to mean?"

"The models don't have much relationship to the images printed. The models are skinny and get pimples and in the mornings their breath smells. They do go to the john, you know."

"That's pretty anal, to think that way."

Mike grinned. "Okay, I'm an ass-man, but I recognize facts." He took a deep breath. "A couple of months ago, I made it with one of the starlets in on a publicity tour."

"So you're a lover," Eddie said caustically.

"Let me make my point. I'd seen the publicity shots of her. Fantastic. Great boobs and a wild shape. Beautiful. She came into town and I spent a great deal of time with her. One night, after a few drinks, she invited me into her suite. The pictures hadn't lied. She had great boobs and a wild body—the first actress I ever made it with. There was just one thing wrong. It was a washout. She insisted that I tell her I loved her, though of course it wasn't true, and after it was over she cried like a baby. It seems she had an incipient ulcer and she never had an orgasm. She was a sad, frightened girl and no matter how good she looked in pictures her problems were real and continuing. *She* was real, not the girl on the big screen."

Eddie growled. "I still think there must be a perfect girl somewhere, a girl who would make everything all right. A girl I could believe is perfect," he ended.

"To hear Neil talk, Susan is *it*."

Eddie snorted. "She's got to be the world's dumbest broad."

"Why dumb?"

"She married Neil. That sanctimonious ass is living proof of her dumbness."

Mike laughed despite the feeling that he shouldn't. "Don't underestimate Neil. He's shrewd and determined. He'll make it big one day."

"Not a chance. There's no depth to the man, no class." Then, with a finality that marked an end to the topic, "He'll lose Susan one day. . . ."

That had been early in February. A week afterward, they all assembled at the Ashe's apartment for dinner. Maggie served a superb paella, along with a salad and a dry Spanish white wine. For Neil, she had broiled two lambchops and baked a potato.

By the end of the evening, it was decided. They would rent Neurotics Anonymous for the upcoming season. It was agreed that Fire Island, because of its proximity to the city, allowing the men to commute, was the best place for them to summer. Neil said it was a great place for kids, recalling how tan BB had gotten, how handsome.

"Is that okay with you boys?" Maggie asked Eddie and Mike.

"If you'd rather not go back . . ." Susan added.

"Hah!" Roy cackled, "why shouldn't they go back! They had a ball. And cheap, too. Made out like mad, the two of them. . . ."

It was settled. Neil got a letter off to the renting agent along with a deposit, and confirmation came by return mail. They began transporting personal effects at the beginning of May and two weeks later took their first weekend.

For Mike, it had been an unusually active, full winter. He had come away from the previous summer with a catalogue of telephone numbers, girls who were more than anxious to show how much they desired his company. For the first time in his life, he knew what it was to be popular. A kind of Hollywood, Andy Hary popularity to be sure, but no less pleasing for being so. He went from bed to bed with a facility that surprised and pleased him. If there were dark and empty interludes, they were quickly erased by the titillation of each new adventure, in the sensual enjoyment of a heretofore unknown body.

The island, during those early May weekends, was refreshingly different. Few single people were there and most of Mike's time was spent with his housemates or alone. He did a great deal of reading in the evenings. And the days were spent dozing on the sand, enjoying the contrast of the cool ocean breeze and the warming sun. Occasionally he played with BB and Cindy, allowing them to crawl over his prostrate body, swinging them, happy with their laughter.

As May came to a close, Mike concluded there was an indefinable difference about the island, despite the familiarity of the surroundings. The houses were the same, the red-winged blackbirds, even the beach grass rustling atop the dunes. Yet the sea was somehow more alien and the sky more remote. Even his friends seemed to have changed. Matters were clearly out of keeping with his notion of fitness and order. Unable to isolate and name what he felt, he finally put it all down to unknown alterations in his own being.

Chapter II

Maggie

Eddie had been without a job since Leona Tate's show had gone off the air. When asked about his prospects for a new assignment, he would say only that he had a number of irons in the fire. Then one weekend he appeared at Neurotics Anonymous with a brand new portable typewriter, announcing his intention to remain on the island on a full-time basis, to write television scripts for the prime-time dramatic programs.

Mike envied Eddie's courage, the commitment to his talent, the gamble with his time and his future. And told Eddie so.

Eddie accepted the compliment. "This is the right time for me. I know I can write as well as those guys getting produced now. Chayevsky, Miller, Serling. I can do at least as well as they can. Oscar Morrison may be doing a new show. I'm sure of a top spot there, if I want it."

So it was that every Friday evening as the *Fire Island Queen* eased into the ferry slip, Eddie stood with Maggie and Susan and the children on the dock, waving at the Daddy boat. Once, Eddie brought along a thermos of chilled martinis and stemmed glasses and they began partying as soon as Roy, Neil, and Mike set foot ashore.

"How's the writing coming?" Mike asked Eddie one Friday, as they headed back to the house.

"Okay."

"Finished a script yet? I'd love to read something you've written, Eddie."

"I don't let people read my work," was the brusque reply. He made the same answer when Maggie put the question to him in the middle of the following week, but his manner was much milder, the words less curt.

"I understand," she said, turning back to her book.

It was late at night and the house was quiet. Eddie had built a fire, which gave off a pungent aroma. The sound of the crackling flames provided him with a feeling of permanence, of proprietorship. He measured Maggie across the space that separated them. After a while, she frowned, the smooth brow wrinkling. She changed her position and looked up.

"You're staring."

"I was thinking. With the children asleep and us alone. It's as if we are married."

She looked at him steadily. "We're not married. Roy is my husband."

He folded his fingers into a fist and stared at it. "I wish I was your husband."

"You're not," she said quietly.

He placed the fist carefully into the palm of his other hand, and began to press. "If you were my wife—"

"Eddie, don't say anything to me."

"Do you know what I'd like to do?"

"I know what you should do. You should work on your script. It's been almost a month and you spend very little time at the typewriter."

"It's hard, Maggie."

"Everything is hard."

"Maggie," he said, after a while, "Susan should be back soon. Will you go for a walk with me then?"

"No."

"Just a walk."

She closed the book and put it aside. The neatly structured face was bland, the large eyes without expression. "Roy asked me the same way," she said absently. "Just a walk. We were at a fraternity party and everyone was drinking beer. Just a walk, he said. I went with him and he took me down to the lake behind the campus. It was a favorite necking spot. You could hear the lovers, all the words, the heavy breathing, the wet body sounds. It was very exciting for me. In my world, nothing of a private nature is done in public. I saw Roy as a tremendously different kind of man, the kind I had never known, and the difference was very stimulating to me. I was appreciative of his energy, his zest for life, the way he got along with people, made them laugh."

Eddie wet his lips. "That night at the lake. Did you let him make love to you?"

Her gaze was level and her voice controlled. "Of course. It was very exciting, almost like being involved in an orgy."

"I see."

"Do you?"

"I understand something else, too. About our beautiful Susan. You know she's playing around." When Maggie made no answer, he went on. "Don't you think it's funny? You remember what Neil said. That he'd kill any man who made love to his wife. That is a joke."

"You're cruel, Eddie."

"It's easy where Neil's concerned. He's such a pompous ass. And a hypocrite."

"I suppose you're right. But he's got a lot of company."

"I say exactly what's on my mind. I deceive no one."

"Good for you."

He searched her face, found no criticism.

"Would you be hapiper if I went back to town, didn't spend so much time out here?"

"Make your own decisions."

"If it bothers you . . ."

"If it bothers me, I'll tell you."

"That sounds encouraging," he offered hopefully.

She stood up. "Don't expect me to show you the way, Eddie. I don't know how to do that for myself. Nor for my husband."

He started out of the chair, but she waved him back. "You know what I think about you," he said.

"You're my husband's best friend. Beyond that, I don't know anything."

"I don't believe that."

"You'll believe what you want and you'll do what you must. Now I'm going to bed. Good night, Eddie."

He watched her climb the stairs and it was a struggle

not to follow. What if he did? Had she ever considered him as a man? As a lover? Probably not. She seemed never to speculate on the future, seldom planning, reacting to events only as they occurred. That, he told himself, was a good way to be.

He went into his room and got into bed. After a while, he began to tremble and his eyes overflowed; he was careful not to make any noise.

Neil

Earlier that same day, Neil Morgan sat behind the desk in the cubby-hole office provided by Sy Melman and made one phone call after another. He contacted everyone who might be able to help, but drew a blank for all his effort. Finally, only Roy Ashe remained. He hadn't wanted to bring Roy into this, had hoped to keep it removed and secret from his personal life. But in the end, he had no choice. Now he waited for Roy to call him back and waiting he was frightened and excited.

Norman Wallace came into the forefront of his mind. The stocky movie star had not been out of his thoughts all day. Sy Melman's most important and profitable client, Wallace was known around the world. His income was immense and he paid impressive commissions to the agency for representation. Norman Wallace was a valuable property, a man to be courted and catered to.

Ordinarily Neil would never have worked with Wallace, might never have even met him. Though he had been working for Melman for nearly a year, he remained an unimportant gear in the office, an agent of no stature. He handled clients whose place in the show-business firmament matched his own; they were still the unknowns.

Norman Wallace was an actor of a different breed.

Sy Melman was away from the office. Word had it he would be gone for two or three days. And the two ranking agents were absent, too. One in Boston with a touring musical, the other in Hollywood for a week of studio conferences. Only the secretaries remained in the Times

Square office. And Neil Morgan. Summer was a slow period and nothing serious ever occurred.

Neil had just failed to place the new ingenue on "Studio One" when Sy Melman's secretary called him on the intercom.

"It's Norman Wallace. He just got into town and he wants some company. He hates to be alone. And Sy never leaves him alone. I told him you'd call him back."

Neil called and arranged to meet the actor for lunch at Sardi's. Afterward, they went shopping at Saks and Dunhills and later had drinks at the Drake. Wallace, a square man with quick gestures and strong, veined hands, was an incessant talker, who boasted of his exploits and complained about his enemies with equal facility.

"Can't blame Sy for not being around to meet me," he said. "Didn't know I was going to show. Hell, I pop up here and there without notice. That's my style. Impromptu. Ad lib. I was in Europe. Fourteenth trip. Ever been? Go. The dames are wild. Sardinia, this time, and the Greek islands. Did a picture there. Whole thing in a bathing suit showing off my muscles. A rotten piece of dung but it'll make a fortune. Me and that big-titted Italian broad. Made it with her on a rocky beach the second day. She looks great but forget it. Lays there like a lump of liver. Ugh. Italian dames are nowhere. And Greeks. English girls are terrific and Americans. When they go, that is. I think it's because they're more athletic. French woman always smell a little. You noticed that? It's all the garlic in their diet."

"Had enough of Europe, though. Flew back post haste and am here. Slept for two days straight and am primed for some action. That Sy Melman, that's a stiff cock, that one. Screw a dead sheep, if it was still warm. We've had some high old times, him and me. Has he told you about me? Go all night, go all day. Sy's good, as a cocksman, but not up to Norman Wallace, pal. So let's have us a brawl. It'll clear the pipes."

"A brawl?"

"A party, boy. Booze and broads. In large amounts. You supply both. That is, the agency does. Hell, I pay Melman enough for a couple of dozen parties and he'd still be rich. My suite at the hotel. About nine tonight. And, say, pal, only good-looking dames. No creeps. I can't stand ugliness. . . ."

Neil stared at the phone on his desk and willed it to ring. A random thought drifted to mind. Pimp was the name for men who supplied girls for other men. He wouldn't accept that. He was arranging a party, a social gathering, a perfectly legitimate activity. People did it all the time. Entertained each other for their mutual benefit.

Besides, he couldn't let this pass. A second chance might never come his way. Norman Wallace might easily become the single most rewarding factor in his life. The phone rang, startled him. He snatched it up. It was Roy Ashe.

"You're all set," Roy laughed raucously.

"How many?"

"Five all together. Oscar Morrison's coming and Hal Woodward."

Neil didn't like it, involving so many people who knew Susan. But he had no choice. "What about costs?"

Roy's laughter this time was harsher, biting. "Consider it a bargain. Fifty bucks a head. Half-price. They tell me this is the slow season. You take care of the liquor, right?"

"Right," Neil said. "Nine o'clock."

He hung up, both relieved and worried. He'd have to cash a check to pay for it all, but the agency would reimburse him.

A low laugh sounded back in his throat. What irony, if Sy Melman had to pay for his own losses.

Susan

"I'm for a drink. How about you?"

"Yes."

Sy Melman swung his long legs out of bed. He disappeared into the living room, coming back with two gins and tonic. He handed one to Susan. She sat up in the bed, leaning against the headboard. Sy lit two cigarettes, gave her one.

"I like the way you make a drink," she said. It was cool against the tissue of her throat, it's bite mild but distinct.

He reached for her thigh, squeezed gently. "Is that all I do well?"

She dragged on the cigarette and directed the smoke toward him. "You make good drinks, you make good love."

"Was it better this time?" he said, not looking at her.

"Better."

She wondered about that. Did all men have to be reassured? Was I good, they wanted to know. Was I marvelous? Great? Better than anyone else? Neil put the question to her nearly every time.

"I want to please you," he said in a soft voice. There was that about him, a gentleness so in contrast to his driving public personality. He was affectionate and soft when they were alone. It pleased her and confused her at the same time. She had come to believe that all men were like Neil.

"You do please me," she replied.

He cupped one breast, kissed the nipple. She shivered. "I love your breasts."

"My husband prefers women with big boobs."

"Your husband is a fool."

She felt traitorous, forced to defend Neil. "He's really very clever."

"Not as clever as I am."

"That's true, I suppose."

He straightened up. "Better believe it," he said. He sucked an ice cube, let it fall back in his drink. "Neil is ambitious and therefore valuable to me. He minds the store pretty good."

"While you sleep with his wife."

His laugh was deep, chesty. "Exactly. If you were my wife, I'd make love to you so much that you wouldn't ever think about another man."

"Why don't you get married, Sy?"

"Ah, I'm an old bachelor, confirmed and dedicated. I'm almost fifty years old."

"You're in marvelous condition."

"And I never exercise. Maybe I should find a wife, a good-looking young woman like you."

"I have a husband."

"You could leave him."

"Divorce Neil!"

"Why not?"

Her mind turned back to an icy day when she was eight years old. Winters in Thomas Crossing, Minnesota, were long and cruel. But Susan had never been able to enjoy the cold the way some did, never got accustomed to it. On this day, she came back to the house on the edge of town, anxious to get inside, to warm up next to the big black kitchen stove. Hungry for some of her mother's preserves spread across thick slices of home-baked bread. But her mother wasn't there. Instead, her father was home —an unusual occurrence in the middle of the day—and Susan's five sisters and brothers, and her grandparents.

"Where's Momma?" she had asked.

"Gone," her father said. "Gone."

For good. She had run off with another man, never to be seen again. Or heard from. Susan remembered easily how it had been, the aching anguish in her bony chest, the sleepless nights full of longing and emptiness and tears. And over and over she vowed that she would never do what her mother had done. Would never desert her family, her husband, her children.

"Well?" Sy Melman said. "Will you divorce your husband and marry me?"

She took a long, slow swallow of the drink. "You might be wrong about me and Neil. Perhaps I love him more than you know."

"I doubt it. You never loved him. He filled some kind of need for you. Smooth, big-city guy, sophisticated. You'd never met anybody like him in that place. That Thomas Crossing. What you didn't know was that Neil is just a minor leaguer. He should have kept you locked in a back room. He didn't and now you're out where the big boys play. . . ."

"Boys like you, Sy?"

"And others." He shrugged. "Some better, and there'll be more. You're a beautiful woman, Susan, in ways that you can't even imagine. I think you're on the verge of finding out what you're really like, about to understand how much value you have for a man, beginning to realize what the world can give to you."

She thought about Arthur Rand. The two that had come after him. And now Sy. "I feel soiled. Used."

"Because of me? Of bed?"

"I never wanted to betray Neil."

"That sounds like a nineteen-thirties movie. If there's any betrayal it's on his part, not providing you with the kind of life you deserve."

She shook her head to silence him. Sy talked swiftly and well, too well, the words flowing, the ideas confusing. Disturbing. With Neil, all questions were simple. All answers easy. With Neil, she knew exactly what was expected of her, the limits of her freedom, the limits of her possibilities. She had only to perform as Neil wanted her to.

There was the still vivid memory of that first night they had slept together. He had made all the arrangements, reserved a room at a motel. She had prepared carefully for the occasion, showering, shaving her legs, anxious to be perfect for him. And once in the room, she had disappeared into the bathroom, showered again, perfumed herself. Only then did she present herself for his approval.

They held each other and kissed and each time she reached for him he altered his position so that she was unable to find his crotch with her hand. "I'm not going to put it into you," he announced at last. She was confused and said so. He explained in a precise and ordered way, certain of what he was doing, of the rightness of his position. "You are going to be my wife and I want us to begin in a proper manner. On our wedding night, we'll make love. Not before. My wife is not some tramp to be treated cheaply and without respect."

Respect. Of course, she had assured herself. He had too much respect for her to make her do anything that wasn't proper. Respect was what he had for her and she for him. She told herself so.

"I've been giving it a great deal of thought," he had gone on. "With the war over, I'll be getting out of uniform soon. I've written to my parents, told them all about you, that I intend to marry you. They agreed with my plans, naturally. What we'll do is this. You'll quit your job at the insurance office and I'll send you to New York. You'll live with my parents, of course. My mother will take you around, buy a new wardrobe for you, teach you how we live. You'll have a chance to learn your way around. When I get back, once I'm settled in my job, then we'll be married."

She was unable to speak. There had been no mention of marriage before. Not even a hint that it was in his mind. Yet here it was, all settled, her future carved out.

"I've already arranged for a job," he continued, lying on his back, looking up at the ceiling. "Bonten and Crenshaw. Public relations. Crenshaw was my commanding officer for a while and I made a point of maintaining the relationship when he was transferred. He's promised me a spot with his organization. A few years and I'll have it made and that means you, as my wife, will too. Susan," he said, coming up on one elbow, assessing her somberly, "I intend to become very successful. I think you should understand that."

A flood of softness broke over her. She extended a tentative hand. "Neil, please. Please. Do you love me . . . ?"

He blinked three times. "What kind of a question is that? Of course, I love you." He kissed her hard on the mouth. "There." He lay back down. "It's late and we should get to sleep. I believe in eight hours sleep each night. . . ."

Susan slid out of the bed and began to dress.

"Do you have to go?" Sy Melman asked. "Stay with me. I want us to *sleep* together."

She shook her head. "I'm a married lady and I have to protect my reputation. My family."

"There are times when I feel you don't really care about me, that you're just using me."

She gazed at him with surprise. "I think you're very . . . sweet."

He made a face and she laughed. He went over to her and held her by the shoulders. "It would be nice if it could be this way always. The two of us. And you didn't have to run away. We've been together six times now and it's always good for me. There's no rush for you to decide anything, Susan. Just consider it. I mean it, about leaving Neil, about marrying me. Think about it and I will, too. All right?"

"I'll think about it," she said very softly.

He reached for his clothes. "I'll take you back to the house."

"No. Maggie and Eddie are there. I don't want them to know about us."

He put on his robe and when she was ready, walked to the front door with her. "There's something I want to know. The first time, Susan, why did you agree to let me make love to you?"

The corners of her mouth twitched. "Because you're sweet."

"I want an answer from you."

She sighed. For a moment, she thought it was Neil's voice she heard. "Because you seemed to want me so much." She saw the disappointment on his face. "And because I wanted you," she added.

She walked back along the beach, in no hurry, mind wandering back over the evening, over all her evenings with him. She had gone with Sy for only one reason, to confirm once again that Neil Morgan was not the ultimate man she had supposed him to be. And now there was no doubt—he wasn't.

Neil

Neil gazed around the suite. The living room was spacious, with a high ceiling and a false fireplace, imitation Louis XIV furniture. Norman Wallace was sprawled comfortably on the couch opposite the fireplace, with a pretty girl on either side of him. He raised his glass in Neil's direction, a happy grin splitting the square face.

"Hey, pal," he shouted. "How you like harem living? Pick yourself a houri and make like a sheik."

A spectacular blonde in a crimson sheath headed for the bedroom, Roy Ashe close behind. He reached for her bottom. She squealed as she disappeared into the other room. Roy went after her, slamming the door.

A small girl came over to where Neil stood at the portable bar. She was precisely tooled, features delicate, her figure a succession of flaring bends and curves. Her skin was creamy, her eyes immense and round. She spoke in a slow drawl.

"Ah have been lookin at you and ah reckon you are kinda ka-yute."

She kept talking, words flowing in a slow, steady stream, an aimless, faintly amusing verbal onslaught. She drew Neil into the vortex of obvious jokes and raucous laughter and though he never felt at ease, neither was he stiff or withdrawn. Soon his own voice added to the clamor, his own laughter echoing. And when Roy appeared out of the bedroom with the bosomy blonde, it was Neil who led a chorus of pointed barbs.

The cocky man showed his teeth in a broad, smug grin. "Would you believe I'm ten feet tall?"

After that, time lost all meaning. There was the hum of air conditioning, locked in a losing cause with the hot, static air. The dulling verbal uproar. The constant outpourings of the little girl with the slow drawl. All served to make Neil light-headed, fuzzy, his reactions slowed.

"Having a great old time, bay-bee?"

Neil squinted through the smoky air into those wide black eyes. "Bet on it," he thought he said.

"Ah am so glayud for you." She was very close suddenly, hands sliding around his waist, perky breasts flattening against his middle. Such a small girl, the scent of her thick and heady, the nearness of her triggering a growing desire in him. A faint trembling began in his knees.

"Ah have been studying you, honey. And ah have discovered somethin'. You are very, very flat. Yoah belly, that is. Ah am simply mayud about men who are flat." Her hand went to his stomach, decended below his belt, rubbing gently, insistently.

This girl, a puzzle. His brows knit and he worried his brain for a suitable answer. None came.

"Hey, Neil, pal!" It was Norman Wallace, calling from the couch. "How can you tell the best French whore houses?"

"How?"

"All the truck-drivers eat there!"

The pace quickened. Each word signaled fresh laughter, joyous whoops and hollers, the clapping of hands, the stamping of feet. People came closer to each other, breathed into each other's faces, spoke into each other's mouths. There was an excess of touching. Body to body. Hands here and there. Time went on.

Abruptly a new element. At once novel, yet somehow a continuation of what had gone before. A girl, with narrow, anxious eyes and full hips, went down on the floor, legs in the air, skirt settling around her hips. She peddled with furious concentration until the skirt came to rest on her belly.

"The trouble with this party," she complained, "is there aren't enough men. We're short of johns."

Norman Wallace stroked the white flesh between her stockings and panties. "Anybody here is short, lady, it ain't Norman Wallace, Esquire."

A redhead took center stage, stretching languidly. "No need to fret. Numbers don't count. Learn how to use what talent there is."

The little dark-eyed girl gave a rebel yell.

"Go, team, go!" Oscar Morrison crowed.

The redhead began to sway with a serpentine grace. Her eyes fluttered and closed, her arms came up to shoulder height, limp and flowing. A hush descended on the room and the air moved sluggishly.

Softly, almost to herself, a melody dribbled out of the redhead's mouth, a crooning, wordless strain. Now louder, it took on a primitive beat, insistent, and all at once her body was in fierce and total motion. Her hips responded to the twists and turns of her knees, her belly jerked and thrust after her hips. Her breasts bobbled in mad syncopation. Her shoulders rocked and rolled. She was all fluidity and her head swung loose in a wild frenzy.

An infinity of movement, a smooth flow. Her voice grew louder, the beat seeping into dark areas. Neil stood frozen, tuned in to every nuance of the flesh, to every subtlety of bone and muscle, of emotion and desire. He watched with absorption as the redhead stripped off her dress with practiced ease, stepped out of her slip, kicked her shoes away. It was right, he thought clumsily. Inevitable. A natural beginning. A strange and compelling elation reached out, embraced him, a dim knowledge of achievement.

Soon naked, the redhead generated a fresh energy, danced with increased freedom. Great leaps took her through the air and she twisted into provocative and enticing poses. Golden flesh swelled steeply, and rippling female muscles played teasingly beneath her skin.

The girl with the black eyes raked her sharp nails down Neil's chest. "Let's all of us get naked."

Moments later, wearing nothing, she was dancing beside the redhead.

Neil's eyes darted everywhere. The trembling moved up his legs, settled in a tight, nauseating concentration in his gut. Fear gripped him and a thick craving. Clothes littered the room and others were naked now, dancing. Norman Wallace, wearing only his shirt and socks, grabbed for the redhead, bore her to the floor. Hal Woodward was undressing with frantic haste. Across the room, the girl with the big hips, the bicycle rider, was helping another girl undress. Neil, throat swollen and fast closing, brain a roiling sump, fought to see it all. To *understand*.

At once someone was at him, the dark-eyed girl, mouthing alien endearments, all slowness gone, hands tearing at the fastenings of his trousers. Neil saw it happening with a kind of detached interest, knowing he would soon command her to put an end to the foolishness. Soon he would turn away from this debauchery. Soon he would proudly take himself away. Untouched, unscarred.

He stayed. And through the detached interest, through the swirling mist, through the throbbing in his temple, an awareness of himself, of his flesh, of his parts, swept along the complex of nerves and arteries, of gushing blood, skittering under his tight skin.

Everything fell away. Everything. But not his maleness. It rose to the challenge. A throbbing lance, filled with fiery blood, a swelling creature with its own needs, its own existence. Angry, seeking inexorably. A divining rod that would not be denied. All processes were quickened and there was a honing of sense.

This maleness.

Aching with it. Pendulous, launched into being from before the last time with Susan, coming from a place and a time without recall, having nothing to do with before, with an occasional coupling. The present soared and surrounded him. A narrow vision was upon him, a shortened focus, a contempt for past and future both.

Now.

Now mattered.

Now. Erratic pulsations thumped at the bounds of his brain. All was swelling and rock-hardness. A near bursting, twitching, winking with wetness, crying out. A spasmodic urgency stretched across prior limits and a blooded mist descended across his eyes.

Hands tore at him until he was naked. More hands than there should have been. Another female was at him, frantically struggling to accommodate him.

A tuneless cry seeped out of him and he went down with the faceless stranger, her softness rising up around him. A fierce challenge echoed in his ear and the other girl went at him, making a place for herself.

Neil was drawn into a pit of melting flesh. Now liquefied, he floated deep in a black, sentient pool. He fought to breathe. To surface again and breathe. To survive. A futile effort. He sank deep into bubbling depths and was lost forever.

And was free.

Chapter III

Neil

A week later Sy Melman left for Europe. An agency client making a film in Rome had become embroiled in a dispute over script changes; and Melman intended to establish an office in London.

"Two weeks should take care of everything," he declared.

That Tuesday morning, Neil accompanied him out to Idlewild in a rented Carey Cadillac. Neil checked him in and waited until the plane was airborne before leaving. On the return drive into Manhattan the idea came flickering alive and he toyed with it all the way back.

In his office he phoned Norman Wallace, invited the actor to be his guest for the weekend at Fire Island. Wallace could use the childrens' room; they would spend the two days sleeping with their parents. He was sure Roy and Maggie would offer no objection. Not when they knew who it was he'd invited.

Wallace didn't accept at once. "What about dames?" he inquired directly.

"The place is loaded. *You* won't have any trouble."

Wallace snorted cynically. "That's your story. You'd be surprised how it is for a guy in my spot. I got to be careful, number one. Number two: there's always people hanging around me, which keeps me from getting a snatch alone."

Neil grew fearful that the actor was about to refuse the invitation. He wanted very much to use the weekend to solidify their relationship, bring him closer, perhaps even pin him down. "I'm sure that I can——"

Wallace broke in. "Never mind. I'll bring my own."

Neil didn't want a strange girl in the house, was concerned about the kind of girl Wallace would bring, afraid that an incriminating remark might be passed. But he hesitated not at all before answering.

"Terrific, Norman. I'll pick you and your friend up. We'll drive out together. We're going to have a real ball. . . ."

Wallace brought the redhead who had danced naked at the party. A tall girl, her physical endowments seemed even more spectacular in clothes. She had a slow, enigmatic smile and was given to gazing lengthily at people before speaking, as if deciding if they were worth the effort. Her name was Roberta.

As soon as they reached the house, Neil got Roy alone, explained what he had done, explained that he wanted to use the childrens' room for his guests. Roy produced a harsh laugh.

"Why're you sucking around Wallace, buddy-boy?" The weathered face grew thoughtful. "Hey! You're trying to cut him out for yourself." His voice dropped confidentially. "You plan on opening your own setup?"

Neil flushed. "He's just a weekend guest." A skeptical look appeared on Roy's face. "Norman brought a woman with him," Neil continued. "Remember the redhead? From the party."

Roy's dark eyes glittered with anticipation. "The one who danced! Oh, crazy. What a weekend this is going to be!"

"Be careful, Roy. Neither one of us can afford any slips."

"You can depend on me," Roy said in a deceptively mild voice. "You know that."

Neil's fear of trouble diminished as the evening wore on. Norman dominated all conversation, somehow managing to turn everything said to himself and his career. He told jokes, remembered incidents that had occurred during filming at sites all over the world, recounted his courage in doing his own stunts. But he avoided all mention of the party in his suite. As for Roberta, she was quiet, attentive, with the unobtrusive manners of a finishing-school graduate. Best of all, Maggie and Susan seemed to like her; and when it came time to clean up, do the dishes, Roberta insisted on helping. Neil began to relax. But not completely.

Neil wanted to spend the evening in the house, to keep Norman Wallace isolated. But Roy shattered that hope, suggesting they make the rounds of the bars.

"I thought Norman might like a quiet evening," Neil said tentatively.

"Hell, no!" the actor burst out, rubbing his palms together. "I'm here. Let's do it up brown." He slapped Roberta familiarly on the belly. She made no response. "What say, baby, fun and games?"

They all went. First, MacCurdy's, where they danced and Mike and Eddie played three games on the bowling machine. Next Leo's. The bar was jammed, the crowd overflowing into the dining area. It took nearly fifteen minutes for Mike and Eddie to get drinks and they remained standing against the bar, listening to Leo at the piano. He was playing the score of *Guys and Dolls.*

"Greatest musical ever produced," Eddie said.

Mike hesitated. It occurred to him that he had begun censoring what he said to Eddie. Was he doing so for Eddie's benefit or his own? And was it fair to either of them? No satisfactory answer came. Why was he doing it, he asked silently, and a reply came quickly. He had frequently witnessed Eddie come close to rage over a seemingly innocuous remark. It was as if any comment that failed to mirror exactly his own views was in fact an attack.

The previous weekend a group of people had been discussing Picasso's work, then on exhibition in a Madison Avenue gallery. A plump, inoffensive lady allowed as how she didn't really understand or care for the artist's painting.

"Who the hell are you not to like what Picasso does!" Eddie had demanded, with grating intensity. He milked his stubby fingers as if to stretch the joints. "The man is an absolute genius and it isn't for ordinary people to question or understand. . . ."

He went on, anger mounting, spitting out harsher insults, eyes rolling.

It was Mike who had finally calmed him. "Come on, Eddie," he had drawled, making himself laugh in a quiet, reassuring way. "You don't mean that. We all respect Picasso as an artist. But it isn't required to like everything the man does. Even Pablo probably doesn't go that far. Right, Eddie. . . ?" He had directed himself to the others then, talking rapidly. "The dominating factor about Picasso's work, it seems to me, is his incredible inventiveness and productivity over an extended period of time. I know Eddie agrees with me on that. Here is a man who began painting in one style and . . ."

There had been other such sudden flareups. An exchange with a draftsman in a Second Avenue bar about the relative genius of Frank Lloyd Wright versus Le Corbusier; a near fist fight over the merits of Joe Lewis and Jack Dempsey. Mike came to understand that Eddie's heroes were complete, infallible, untouched by the failings of ordinary human beings, and so not to be questioned without swift and sometimes vicious retaliation.

"Do you prefer *Guys and Dolls* to *South Pacific?*" Mike replied with mild, conversational interest.

"You're kidding. Rodgers and Hammerstein are cheaply sentimental. Corny. Too commecially slick."

"A little romantic for my taste but *Pacific* has a lovely score. 'Bali Hai' is excellent and 'You've Got to Be Taught' and——"

"You sound like Neil. He goes for that junk, along with Irving Berlin. Can you see any of them composing 'Fugue For Tinhorns'? Or 'Sit Down You're Rocking the Boat'? Not a chance. Hacks, the bunch."

Before Mike could reply, Roberta came swaying up to them. She presented a lush, attention-getting figure in tight saffron slacks and a silk blouse to match. There was a quizzical expression on her triangular face as she swayed up to them, apparently oblivious to the collective masculine interest directed at her.

"Now," she began, her mouth slowly transforming itself into a wide smile. "Which is Eddie and which is Mike? Don't say, let me guess." She chewed on the lip of her glass and eyed them speculatively.

Mike couldn't restrain his appreciation of what he judged to be a practiced and skillful performance by a woman who knew how to focus attention on herself without giving offense.

"You're laughing at me," she murmured to him. Then, to Eddie, but without looking at him: "Why is your friend laughing at me?"

"He has peculiar habits with women," Eddie said heavily.

"What does that mean?" she asked Mike.

"Perhaps I like men only," Mike offered.

She shook her head. "I think not. The reverse more likely. That women are your real pleasure and that's too rare."

"Women are always complaining about men making passes at them," Eddie said. "How do you reconcile that with. . . ?"

She measured him thoughtfully. "Men need to sleep with women. But few of them genuinely enjoy them." Her eyes drifted back to Mike. "I think this one does."

"I would like to think you're right," Mike said.

She appraised him. "How did you grow so tall?"

"Practice."

She laughed shortly. "Has practice made you good at everything?"

"I don't think I'm good at everything."

"The important things. You're good at those. I can tell."

"How?" Eddie put in. "How can you tell?" His brows were bunched and he spoke in a low, intense voice.

"Practice," Roberta said lightly.

"I'm smarter than he is," Eddie said. "I know more. I'm stronger and a better ballplayer. I make more money."

She turned back to Mike, surveying the length of him with patient interest. "It must be very nice for a girl to have a big man put his arms around her."

Eddie spoke in a tight, thin voice. "Too bad you didn't pick a bigger man than Wallace."

She placed her hand flat on Mike's chest. "I pick you."

"You *really* go for him?" Eddie said. He scowled as if in pain. *"Why?* I mean, women go for him. But *why?"*

"Knock it off, Eddie," Mike said mildly.

Roberta's fingers danced lightly against Mike. She removed her hand.

"People give off what they are," she offered. "This one, he makes a woman know what she is. It's something you can tell right away. He'd never bore me."

"*I* bore me a lot," Mike said, trying to end it. She was a beautiful woman, almost too beautiful to be real, and she belonged to Norman Wallace. All that put her beyond him, despite her flirtatiousness. It meant nothing, would go nowhere.

"All of us bore ourselves once in a while," she said.

"I don't bore myself," Eddie said. "My thoughts are . . ."

Roberta handed Mike her empty glass. "I have to get back to Norman now." She pursed her lips in a silent kiss in Mike's direction, then left.

"Don't let it go to your head," Eddie warned.

Mike grinned. "What a beauty she is! That Wallace is a lucky bastard to have her."

Eddie swore. "Try not to be a jerk. She's a whore."

"That isn't fair, Eddie."

"She is."

"Have it your way."

"Roy told me, dammit. There was a party. An orgy. Roy, Wallace. Oscar Morrison was there, Hal Woodward. Roberta was one of the girls, hired for the night. Roy said she was wild, went in every direction." His angry eyes glittered. "Besides, she's too rich for your pocketbook."

Mike searched through the crowd to where Roberta stood with Norman Wallace. His arm was around her waist, hand idly stroking her hip. She was, Mike knew, *knew*, too rich for him in any number of ways.

Susan

A fine mist began to fall during breakfast the next morning and a damp chill filled the big house. Neil built a fire which helped a little.

"I wish I'd known we were going to have skiing weather," Roberta said to Mike. "I'd have brought proper clothes."

He looked away.

Susan came into the living room. "The shopping list is complete and I'm going. I could use a masculine back to pull the wagon."

"I'll go," Mike said, anxious suddenly to be away from the house, away from the others. He went into his room and put on the tennis shoes he had bought at Abercrombie's. They had finally become soiled, achieved that coveted, properly worn look. Mike wondered if he would ever get to play tennis. In his neighborhood tennis and golf were games for other people; he had been raised on team sports, contact games, and there was nothing polite or social about how they were played.

They left the wagon outside the market and Mike trailed Susan through the aisles as she filled the list. She glanced back occasionally.

"You do this very well," she said. "You'll make some girl a fine husband."

"I doubt it."

"Don't you want to get married?"

"I've never thought about it, seriously, that is."

"I better buy a couple of extra milks," she murmured. "Neil was furious when we ran out last Sunday." He offered no comment and she went on without looking back at him. "Living with people like us probably sours you on the institution, I suppose."

"I think you wouldn't have been capable of making that kind of remark last summer."

"That was a year ago and I'm ten years older now." Her laughter was brief and edged. "Live and learn."

He was tempted to ask what she had learned but thought better of it.

"I see things realistically these days." She swung around, the Tartar face solemn, the eyes veiled, steady. "You know what's going on, I suppose?"

"I don't know anything."

"Then you should. Maggie says that Roberta is a call girl. That Roy and Neil have been living it up in town with Norman Wallace. You knew that, surely?"

"I don't believe any of it."

"Masculine loyalty," she broke off bitterly, turning away.

Oh, *God,* he said to himself, I hope it doesn't rain all weekend.

Mike

The rain fell harder and they began drinking after lunch. Maggie brought out the Monopoly board and she and Neil played with Norman and Roberta. Roberta won most of the property.

Eddie, sprawled on his belly on the floor in front of the fireplace, reading a book. The Monopoly game over, Roberta came up behind him.

"What are you reading?"

"*Art and Life in America,*" he said, not looking up.

She tried again. "What's it about?"

The heavy features were transformed into an expression of annoyance. "It's about art and life in America. A history by O. W. Larkin. It won a Pulitzer Prize last year. That's an award bestowed by Columbia University for excellence."

"I *know* what the Pulitzer Prize is," she said quietly. "And I also know what's wrong with you."

She went over to where Mike sat on the window seat, looking at the rain. "Your friend is a grouch."

"He has moods."

"And they're all bad." She settled down opposite him. "Don't you play Monopoly?"

"I'm not very good at games."

"I know a lovely game for rainy days," she giggled.

Before he could reply, BB came trundling into the living room, leading Cindy by the hand. A delighted squeal came out of Roberta and she went dashing over to them. On her knees, she began to talk to BB. He made some reply that pleased her and she embraced him, lifted him off his feet. Cindy, laughing silently, watched.

"Be careful, Roberta," Neil offered, unable to entirely conceal the disapproval he felt. "Don't teach my son bad habits."

Mike suppressed an angry retort. He announced that he was going for a walk.

"It's pouring," Neil reminded him.

"Got something good on the string, Mike?" Roy laughed.

"How about you, Eddie?" Mike said.

Eddie didn't look up from the book. "No."

"May I come?" Roberta said. "I love to walk in the rain."

"You heard Roy, honey," Norman Wallace said flatly. "Maybe Mike wants to be alone."

"Oh," she said. "Sure."

Mike put on his parka and left.

Eddie

At four o'clock, Bette Miller and Peggy Woodward materialized out of the rain. Peggy held a pickle jar filled with gin and tonic from which she took long, deep swallows.

"What a day!" she began cheerfully. "Fantastic! Great! Let's live it up!"

"Oh, shut up," Eddie growled. He heaved himself erect and marched out of the living room.

"What a darling-tempered man," Bette Miller cooed.

"We're having a party," Peggy said happily. "Everybody's invited."

"Thank God," Maggie said.

"When?" Roberta asked.

"At our house," Bette Miller said. She lowered her voice insinuatingly. "We're living together this summer," she told Roberta. "*All* of us, that is."

"Everybody come," Peggy exclaimed. "Right now. It's party time!"

"Let's go," Roy said.

"We can't leave the children," Neil pointed out. "We have no sitter."

Eddie came back into the room. "You all go on. I'll take care of the kids."

"Are you sure?" Maggie said.

"Yes."

When they were gone, Eddie sat down on the floor, began to play with the children as if they were his own. Almost.

Mike

"Eddie's giving them dinner," Mike repeated.

"It isn't right," Neil said angrily to Susan. "We should have gone back before this. I wanted us to."

"You heard Mike," Susan said diffidently. "Eddie's feeding them."

"That's a mother's job. To take care of her son. I don't like BB being left alone."

"He's not alone."

"Neither of his parents is with him."

"Stop it, Neil," Susan said. She finished her drink. "I don't neglect BB. Not ever." She looked at her glass. "I'm going to get another drink."

"You're becoming an alcoholic. It's time we went back. I want my dinner." He took hold of her wrist.

She wrenched free. "All *right!*"

Mike watched them leave. These barbed exchanges between them came with increasing frequency, reminded him of the way his parents had battled throughout the years. It upset him to witness it and he turned it out of his mind, went after a drink.

Mike looked for a friendly face. Oscar Morrison loomed up alongside. "You a poker player?" he began.

"How big is the game?"

"Dollar ante. Five dollar limit."

"No thanks. Too rich for my blood."

Roy joined them. "What's the holdup? Let's get the show on the road." He issued a throaty laugh. "The winning player is ready."

Mike found a place for himself against the wall and surveyed the room. People clustered close together, faces animated, flushed, eyes glassy. They were a handsome group, he thought, and for the most part, young and terribly successful. The men were account executives, television directors, photographers, lawyers. He recognized two successful theatrical producers and besides Normal Wallace, there were three or four well-known actors. The women were younger, dramatically lovely to look at, models and production assistants, actresses, designers. People of accomplishment. People who did things and did them well.

People who had carved out places for themselves very early, were still marching ahead.

Yet there was something wrong. A depressing cloud that drifted over them made Mike anticipate some kind of disaster. He felt uneasy and wished he were somewhere else.

That's when he saw the girl with the bangs across the room. Four men were vying for her attention and Mike watched with interest as she dealt with each in turn. Now she was laughing and her alert face exhibited no tension. It was a fine face, he decided, sensual, with the promise of something more than just prettiness. A restlessness settled behind his navel and he tried to formulate a plan that would spirit her away from the quartet.

Finished with his drink, he went after another, returned to take up his vigil against the wall. He was determined to be with her and no one else would do. How much time passed he never knew; how many people spoke to him, he never knew; how many drinks he downed, he never knew. All his attention was focused on the girl with the bangs, waiting for the opportunity that he was sure would eventually present itself.

At last it came. She detached herself from the men. Mike went after her. Through the living room, along a short corridor, into the kitchen and beyond to the enclosed sun porch. Six people were waiting to use the toilet. She took a place on line. Mike stood behind her.

"Nothing is easy in this world," he said quietly.

She glanced back at him, allowed herself a small smile.

He tried again. "I have a confession to make," he said.

She turned partially. "To me? And I'm not even Catholic."

He grinned. That was better. "I really don't have to use the john."

Her eyes were large, soft brown, with an amused glint in them. "It isn't fair, then, for you to take up someone else's place."

He leaned toward her. "I am following someone."

"A crime has been committed and you are Sam Slade, hot on the trail."

"Hot on the trail, yes. And the name, young woman, is Sam *Spade*."

She laughed and faced the front.

"Are you out just for the weekend? Too bad it had to rain."

"Too bad," she agreed absently.

He had been closed out. A flood of ancient sensations ebbed and flowed, an awareness of his clumsiness, his inability to woo and win a girl, to speak easily and well. He was too big, too dull, too homely.

She turned around. "I'm a Grouper," she told him. "An alternate."

That was better. "All girls in the house?" He had to keep her talking, involved.

"Coed." She laughed, a deep rich sound that made him conscious of her voice. It matched the look of her, darkly provocative. "At first it was uncomfortable. Now I'm used to it. Sort of a family arrangement."

"How did you get into it?"

Again that fine laugh. "An advertisement in *The New York Times.*"

"You're not a New Yorker," he said.

"How can you tell?"

"The accent."

She frowned. "I'm not supposed to have an accent."

"Oh, you don't," he said hurriedly. "I mean, the absence of any sectionalism in your speech."

Her manner lightened. "I'm from Texas. But I've been here for a few years."

"You're an actress. . . ."

Her brows rose. "You're very good, you know. How could you tell?"

"The way you speak. I used to be an English teacher. I guess I'm aware. . . ."

"Do you still teach?"

"No."

It was her turn at the toilet and she disappeared inside. He waited for her return. He took her elbow and guided her to one side.

"I should go back," she said. "I was with some people. . . ."

"Stay with me."

"I said I'd come back."

He shook his head. "There were four of them. I am more valuable to you than all of them."

"Really!"

"Come away with me. I'll buy you drinks and tell you all about myself. A fascinating tale, I promise."

"I'm not sure I want to be fascinated," she returned, repressing a smile.

But she made no objection as he steered her out the back door. A wooden walk led them around to the front of the house. The rain had stopped, the air was fresh and brisk, and he was very pleased with himself.

Her name was Jean Harvey and she had been born in Austin, raised in Dallas. She had decided to become an actress when she was eleven and nothing had ever occurred to change her mind. She had lived in Hollywood for three years, doing small roles in pictures, acting with a little theater group.

"But New York is the place to be," she explained. "Television is coming on strong and it's all here."

They were seated at a table in MacCurdy's. Billie Holiday was singing something sultry on the juke box. He asked her to dance. She followed easily, her body pliant and receptive. Her breasts touched his chest and once her belly brushed against his middle. Sweat broke on his palms.

"That house we were in, the party," she said, laughing easily.

"What about it?"

"You know those people? The Woodwards and the Millers."

"Yes."

Someone told me the story. They met last summer, you know. Now they're spending this summer together, sharing a house, and each other. They've switched partners, you see."

He wouldn't allow his surprise to show. "What about you," he said, keeping his manner light. "Do you think you could do it?"

She shrugged. "I wouldn't want to swear for myself, one way or another. When I was married, I played it straight." She raised her eyes to his. "You've never been married." It was not a question.

"No."

She nodded and lowered her forehead to his shoulder. He eased her closer and there was no resistance. The craving returned, thicker now, deeper. A faint stirring in his crotch.

"Let's go for a walk," he said quietly.

Her gaze was penetrating and he was sure she knew exactly what he was thinking. He felt guilty.

"I don't think so," she said.

Neil

Neil sat at the kitchen table drinking his before-bed glass of milk. He sloshed it around in his mouth to warm it before allowing the liquid to seep into his throat. It was vital not to chill one's digestive tract, he believed. Also to chew food thoroughly, to ease the demands made on the stomach. A man took care of his body and his body would take care of him.

Opposite him Norman Wallace clutched a glass of straight vodka. "You've a very careful guy," he noted.

"About certain things, I suppose I am."

"I'm a lot more casual. I'll probably have a coronary before I'm fifty. Hope it happens while I'm in the saddle. That's the way to go, humping away."

"You should exercise more. I'll be running in the morning. Want to join me?"

"Run! Me?"

"It's about a half-mile across the island at this point. I run it several times each day. I can break three minutes now."

"But why?"

"To keep in condition, Norman. That's very important in a lot of ways. General good health, of course. Keeps the digestive system in order, the bowels open. . . ."

"Terrific."

"And a man in shape can make love more. Did you know that?"

"That part appeals to me."

"Then you'll run with me? I'm working toward two and a half minutes."

"I'll pass." He drank some vodka, put the glass down. "About what you said, Neil."

Anticipatory tension came to life along Neil's nerves. "It could be a good thing. For us both."

"I wouldn't be expected to put up any money?"

"Not a penny, Norman. It's just as I told you. With you at the top of my client list I'd be able to sign up other good people. And I can promise you that I'll give you a better shake than Sy Melman Associates, work harder in your behalf."

"Sy's done okay for me."

"I won't argue. I won't say anything against him. He's been good for me, too. But times change and so do people. Sy's been around for a long time. Too long, perhaps. He's got it made. He's comfortable, smug, runs a comfortable office. Let's say he fails to sell a client to a film producer. Sy Melman doesn't have to worry. He isn't concerned about a few dollars more, about another sale. He isn't in there pushing the way I'd push. He isn't hungry, Norman. He wouldn't service you the same way I would."

Wallace eyed the other man speculatively. "I admit you're a pusher, all right."

"Then come along, Norman. It would be good for Norman Wallace and good for the Neil Morgan Talent Agency. . . ."

"Which doesn't exist without *me*."

"That's true," Neil said in a level voice, waiting.

"I might be interested, at half commission."

"Five per cent."

"Five per cent."

Neil considered swiftly. The income received from Wallace was less important than having his name on a contract. Had the actor insisted on it, Neil would have represented him without a commission.

"It'll be tight," he said sincerely. "But I want to be Norman Wallace's agent. Five per cent." He held out his hand.

Wallace took it. "There's one more thing," he said casually. "I promised Roberta I'd do something for her. I want you to take her on as a client, help her get started. Get her some work acting."

Neil agreed without hesitation.

Later he took Roberta aside. "What's this about you becoming an actress?"

"I think it's a swell idea. I want to turn square, Neil. Why not? I can shake my fanny and show my boobs as well as most of the girlies in Hollywood. Norman said you would help me."

He scowled and blinked three times. "There are risks. If anybody finds out about—"

She shrugged. "To hell with that. I'll quit the trade right away. As of this minute, if you tell me to. I've got enough cash to ride it out until I begin making money acting. In a couple of years nobody's going to remember me. And if they do, so what? There's always gossip about people in show business. Sometimes I think it does more good than harm. Of course, if you don't want to help I'll have Norman find someone who will."

He arranged a pleasant smile on his face. "I'll do my best for you," he said.

"I was sure you would," she said sweetly.

He wanted to hit her, to destroy her. Instead he continued to smile. After all, an agent couldn't go around slugging fifty per cent of his client list.

Maggie and Eddie

Neurotics Anonymous was quiet. Maggie sat on the floor, her back against the couch, staring into the smoldering fire. She didn't look up when Eddie appeared.

"You're supposed to be asleep," he began in a husky whisper.

She gave no sign that she had heard.

"I couldn't sleep either." He indicated his jeans, the sweater he wore. "I was going for a walk." He slid down next to her. "Mike's still out. Probably found another girl. To him women are some disposable item to be cast aside when he's finished using them."

"He's single and free. He can do what he wants. The girls know what's going on."

"I don't think so. They think he intends to marry them."

She looked at him. "That's nonsense. Men want to get

layed and women know it. They may be hoping to snare a husband, but they *know*."

He grunted his assent. "Maybe I should be more like Mike."

"Yes, you should."

"I can't."

She said nothing.

After a while, he spoke again. "Is Roy asleep?"

"He's playing poker with Oscar Morrison."

How had she failed Roy, she asked herself, without self-pity. How had she failed herself? She remembered how it had been before they were married. For almost a year and a half neither of them dated anyone else. It had been a wonderful time. All fun, gay, with the promise of great things to come. Roy was bright, curious about life, with the kind of drive the men she usually met didn't possess. He excited her and made her want to be with him always. Now all that was gone. The gaiety had evaporated, to be replaced by a craving for kicks, for new thrills. And a desperate, brutal lusting was all that remained of their love.

She turned so that Eddie could see her clearly. She lifted the bottom of the Shetland sweater she wore, Roy's sweater, exposing her torso. Purple bruises were splotched across her rib cage.

"What happened to you?"

"Roy beat me," she said simply.

"The bastard!"

"He came out here during the week. He'd been drinking and drank more. But he wasn't drunk. Roy never gets drunk. He wanted to make love and I didn't. I haven't wanted to for a long time now. He hit me and kept hitting me until I let him."

"The rotten bastard!"

"It's his legal right, I guess."

"I'm going to kill him."

Her laugh was brief and bitter. "No you won't, Eddie. You won't do a thing."

He reached out and touched the bruises, fingers slack and gentle. He knelt and kissed each one in turn, then buried his head in her lap. He sobbed out her name and she took his head in her hands. He was going to be bald soon, she noted idly. Fortunately his head was round, well-shaped. It might be an improvement.

"Sit up," she commanded.

He obeyed. In that moment, he reminded her of Roy, the boyish yearning on his face, the wary set of his eyes. The way he cocked his head.

"You once invited me to go for a walk on the beach," she said. "Is the invitation still open?"

"Of course."

"It might be a good idea, Eddie, if you brought a blanket. . . ."

Roy

Oscar Morrison issued a coarse, satisfied laugh. He raked in the pot. "Never bluff a bluffer, Roy baby. It don't pay."

The table in front of Roy was clear of chips. He reached into his pocket, knowing what he would find. Nothing. "People," he announced, with mock helplessness. "I am flatter'n my wife's chest. Lend me fifty, Oscar."

Morrison considered it. "Sure, Roy." The round face was somber, the tiny eyes hard. "I know you're good for it." He arranged the chips in front of him, counted off fifty dollars worth. "I'm a serious poker player, Roy. I do it for money, not fun."

Roy thanked him and took the chips, divided them into stacks according to denomination. Cards were dealt and he studied his hand. Three, four, six, seven, king. He swore silently and showed his grin around the table.

The man on Roy's right opened for five dollars and he called. His eyes followed the betting. All the players came along for five dollars.

"That's it, suckers," Roy gloated. "Bring money to the middle. Build up my pot."

Opener drew three cards.

Roy asked for one.

The next draw was three. And the next.

Oscar Morrison studied Roy from across the table. "Two cards for me. A triple beats two pair, Roy."

"Keep thinking that. You're my meat, Oscar."

The dealer folded. Five players left.

"Openers bet five dollars," the dealer droned.

Roy squeezed out his draw. A five of spades. The straight was fleshed out. He kept his features unchanged. "Call the five and bump it ten."

The man on his left turned over his cards and the next player called, but with no enthusiasm. Thanks for the fifteen, Roy said to himself.

Oscar Morrison flicked a finger at his hand. "I hate to do this to you, Roy." He let the words out singly, giving each an importance it would not ordinarily possess.

"Make your bet, Oscar."

"Call the raise and raise twenty more."

Roy kept his face expressionless, waiting for the next man to make up his mind. He folded. Without looking, Roy knew that he had only thirty-four dollars remaining. He looked at Oscar. Nothing showed on that round face. Roy refused to believe that he had bettered his three-of-a kind. "Call the twenty and I'll kick it fourteen more. My all, Oscar."

The remaining player dropped out.

Oscar squinted across at Roy. He spoke from between lips that barely moved. "Bet whatever you want, Roy. I trust you for the money."

Roy was sure now. Oscar was running a bluff. Well, screw him. He deserved to get taken. "Thanks for the ride, Oscar. I'll go for a hundred more, in that case."

"Poker going up," the dealer said.

Somebody clucked.

Oscar arranged his cards in a neat pile on the table, removed his hands. "You sure, baby? That's a lot of cash."

"A hundred and fourteen to see."

Morrison nodded once. "I call. Show cards, Roy."

An icy finger touched Roy at the base of the spine. He had guessed wrong. Oscar had it, had beaten him. He was through. "Straight," he said harshly. "To the eight."

Oscar turned up his cards, fanned them out. Four tens and the king of hearts. "Matched up the triple. Pretty, isn't it?" He chuckled smugly.

Roy leaned back. "Well, hell. It's only money. Back me for another fifty, Oscar?"

"Sure, pal. Why not? You're good for it."

Roy continued to play, continued to lose.

Chapter IV

Mike

July arrived and the days were long, all sunshine and heat. In Manhattan, there was no relief. The air was thickly oppressive and still and the weekends on the island grew more and more appealing.

For Mike Birns life had taken an abrupt turn. He had been seeing Jean Harvey two or three times a week since they met, thinking about her constantly when they were apart. They dined together and went to the movies, and occasionally to the theater. Afterward, a bar for a nightcap. Or coffee somewhere. They found a lot to talk about and seemed to come close to agreement in most matters.

There was one problem, however. She shared an apartment with another girl, which meant that Mike was never able to be alone with her. They would stand in the hallway outside the apartment door and neck but whenever he became too amorous she would stop him.

"I'm not ready for that," she would say.

One night they had dinner in a French restaurant on West 46th Street. On her recommendation, Mike ordered a baked salmon, only to find it too rich for his taste. He nibbled without enthusiasm. He looked up to find her staring at him.

"What?" he said.

"I'm sorry about the salmon," she offered, fingering the bangs. The soft brown eyes were hooded and secretive.

He shook his head. "Is that why you're looking at me that way?" A distant warning sounded back in his brain. Leave it alone. Don't press her. "Is something wrong?" he heard himself saying.

"I think you know. At this minute, you know."

"Tell me. Say it."

"Yes. I want you, Mike. So very much. And right now. Please take me to bed. . . ."

He touched her hand. "Your roommate?"

Jean shook her head. "No good. She's there. We'll have to go somewhere else."

A helplessness enveloped him. "Where?"

"A hotel."

He withdrew his hand. A hotel meant registering as man and wife, meant exposing what they were going to do to strangers, it meant brazening past the desk clerk without luggage. He had never taken a woman to a hotel and the prospect frightened him; surely he was the only twenty-eight-year-old man in New York who had never taken a woman to a hotel. A shudder passed down his spine. He felt weak. Helpless.

"We'd better wait. . . ."

"I don't want to wait anymore. I'm sure now. There's no need to wait."

"I want it to be right for us, the first time."

An insinuating smile lifted the corners of her sensuous mouth. "It will be, darling. I promise."

He rocked his head from side to side. "Not in a hotel. There's something"—he searched desperately for a convincing word—"something soiled, osbcene, about it. Sneaking around."

"Deliciously forbidden," she giggled.

"I won't do it!" He announced stiffly.

The softness went out of her face and an impenetrable mask settled over her features. The brown eyes became opaque and when she spoke it was with a conscious formality.

"I made a mistake. I apologize for embarrassing you."

"What are you talking about!" he said desperately.

"I thought you wanted me. I was wrong."

"Try to understand—"

"I think I do. I want to go home now. Will you take me or must I go alone?"

He tried to explain, to reach through the barricade she had erected. It was too high, too strong. Resigned, he paid the bill and they left the restaurant. She set off at a brisk pace along Central Park South and he hurried to catch up. Neither of them spoke until they stopped at Sixth Avenue, waiting for the traffic signal to change.

"Can't we talk about it?" he pleaded in an urgent whisper.

"You've said it all. You rejected me."

"Oh, God, no."

"It is self-evident."

"I want you so much."

"What an odd way you have of displaying desire."

"I told you . . ."

"I heard what you said. I know what you mean."

"Please, please. Don't do this to me. To us. Please, let's talk."

She measured him. Abruptly she swung away and started across the street toward the park. She looked back. "Well," she said briskly. "Are you coming or not?"

They found an empty bench just inside the park, facing a small lake. "Listen," he began, his guts so twisted he was afraid he might break down or become ill. "Listen to me."

"You're not saying anything." Her voice came down to him from lofty heights.

"I lied," he confessed in a small voice, misery etched on his face. "I'm a coward."

She looked at him, then touched the back of his hand lightly, her expression changing. "What is it?" she said gently.

"I've never gone to a hotel with a girl. I'm afraid. Embarrassed . . ."

"Ah."

He averted his eyes and for a lengthy interval they sat that way. Another couple, arms entwined, crossed on the walk in front of them and sat down on the next bench. The sound of their kisses and their breathing reached them. "Ah, Mike," Jean said in a low voice. She placed her head against the curve of his neck. "I was afraid you didn't want me."

"I think about it and sometimes I'm almost sick with wanting you. The bottom seems to drop out of my stomach."

"I know." She nuzzled against him. "We can't continue this way. . . ."

He bent over her and she accepted his mouth. He pushed his tongue between her teeth and she admitted him. He cupped her breast and she made tiny noises back in her throat. Her hand found his belt, the fingers hooked, pulling urgently. She reached lower, caressed him.

"You must," she husked. "You should have your own place. Why haven't you got an apartment?" she said heatedly. "A man your age, you must have a place to take girls. . . ."

"To take *you,*" he heard himself say.

She giggled. "When we met, I thought you were such a lecher. Smooth, dangerous. You wanted to take me for a walk on the beach. You would've tried there."

"You excited me from the beginning."

"Do you think I would have let you? The first time."

"Would you?"

"Maybe. Maybe that's why I didn't go. Because I would have let you and I didn't want you to think I was that easy."

"I wouldn't have thought that."

"Yes, you would. But it doesn't matter now, does it?"

"No," he said, wondering if she was easy. If it was this way for her with every man. He reached under her dress, slid his hand under her brassiere. She moved to make it easier for him. Her breast was warm and round, the nipple erect. "You feel beautiful," he said. "This weekend, at the island. I'll arrange something, for us to be alone."

"It's not my weekend."

He swore.

She laughed and took his hand away. She adjusted her dress. "My roommate will be away this weekend. She's going off to Virginia to visit her parents."

He filled his lungs with air. "When is she leaving?"

"Friday afternoon."

"We'll have dinner Friday," he said.

Her smile was a mobile challenge. "Oh. But what about Fire Island? I know how much you enjoy it, how precious it is. Surely you wouldn't want to miss any time there."

"We'll spend the weekend together," he declared, loud enough so that only she could hear. "In bed, all the time. . . ."

"*All* the time! How boring that will be."

"The first thing I'm going to do to you——"

She put a finger across his lips. "Don't tell me," she murmured. "Not now. Friday . . ."

Chapter V

Neil and BB

On Saturday morning, Neil was up and dressed before Susan was out of bed. He glanced down at her, said her name, told her it was time to get up. She sounded a sleepy agreement and changed her position. But her eyes remained shut. It was the constant partying, he told himself. They stayed up too late, spent too much time in smoky rooms. And Susan drank too much. He was going to have to talk to her about it again.

He went downstairs to get BB. Both children were awake, playing in their cribs. Cindy watched as Neil dressed his son.

"Your mother should be doing this, son," he told the boy. He glanced up at Cindy. "And your mother should be here, too. I don't understand women who neglect their children for their own selfish pleasures. Well, son, your father will always be there when you need him. Depend on it. Now, how about some breakfast, BB?"

"Breakfast," the boy agreed cheerfully.

"Some nice boiled eggs would be a perfect way to start the day."

"Fried eggs," BB replied absently.

"Fried food isn't good for people. I'll boil eggs for us both, BB. You'll eat exactly what I eat. Won't that be fun? And we'll have some crisp toast, with margarine. But first, a big glass of freshly squeezed orange juice."

He got BB seated at the kitchen table and filled two glasses with orange juice. A quick count revealed that only five oranges remained and he made a mental note to have Susan buy more.

"Breakfast is the most important meal of the day, BB. Gets a man off to a flying start. You can understand that."

"Boiled eggs is goopy," the boy said.

"*Are* goopy," Neil corrected. "You see, a proper diet is mandatory to good health, son. You must get all the vitamins and other nutrients that will make you strong and healthy, give you good muscle development and solid bones. And to provide the energy for all the great things you're going to do in life."

"What things?"

"Boyd Benjamin Morgan can do anything he wants to, BB. Remember that. It's simply a question of setting your mind to it. And you have a very fine mind. Quick, intelligent, retentive. You are going places."

"What places?"

"Good things are happening to your father, son, and that means good things for you. You are going to be able to go to the best schools, the best college. Maybe Harvard or Princeton. You are going to make your mark. Politics, maybe. Governor or the Senate. The point is, I expect great accomplishments from my son and I know you'll never disappoint me."

"I want to be a lifeguard on Fire Island," BB said, playing with his spoon.

Neil laughed. "Why a lifeguard, son?"

"They wear pretty bathing suits and play on the sand all day."

"Well," Neil said thoughtfully, "you can always wear red bathing trunks but life is much more than cavorting around the beach. Living is serious and a boy with your background, your opportunities, simply has to produce more. Make a contribution to the society. Now drink the rest of your juice. The eggs are ready."

"Don't like boiled eggs."

"You'll eat them," Neil said. "They're good for you."

BB heaved the spoon against the far wall.

Mike and Eddie

Roy arrived that afternoon, explaining that he had attended a business conference, saying something about a big film sale pending with one of the networks. Minutes later he was out on the beach tossing Cindy in the air and catching her, making the child laugh.

Eddie watched with mounting envy. Cindy was a plump, pretty child, with a striking resemblance to her mother. Holding her filled Eddie with a deeper satisfaction than anything else had ever provided. But seeing Roy with Cindy, knowing that his spermatozoa had triggered the miraculous process that gave birth to her, knowing that Maggie had accepted Roy within herself, visualizing them coupling; it disturbed Eddie and a cloud of irritation began to build up in him.

Abruptly, Roy was finished with Cindy. He returned the child to the playpen under the striped sun umbrella, then went bouncing down the beach in that typically aggressive style of his. That bothered Eddie even more. Roy's casual disregard for his child. For his wife. While Eddie ached with wanting, with need. The appearance of Mike Birns with that new girl of his, Jean, offered some relief from the tension.

"We're going clamming," Jean announced, holding a child's pail aloft. "And there's no coming back until this is filled. Anybody want to join us?"

"I do," Eddie said, standing. "You'll have to show me how."

"It's simple," Susan said, from her place on the blanket. "May I come along?"

"Go if you like," Neil said. "But don't expect me to eat those things."

"They're very good," Jean offered. "Raw or steamed or breaded and fried."

"Fried food isn't good for people," BB put in seriously.

They all laughed at that. "You may be right," Jean said. "But we don't always do what's best for us. Sometimes the things that are the most fun aren't good for us, BB."

"I'll go," Susan said, with sudden conviction.

"Anybody else?" Mike said.

There were no more volunteers.

On the bay side of the island, at a spot west of Ocean Beach, they waded out into the still, warm water. More than one hundred yards from shore, the water was barely waist-high.

"This is where the clams are," Jean declared finally, clearing away the kelp. "Start digging."

"How?" Eddie said.

"Feel in the sand with your feet," Susan offered. "Your toes. If you touch a rock, well, it will be a clam. Just reach down and pull it out. They don't bite," she laughed.

"I've found one!" Jean cried, holding the small shell aloft. She let them all see it, then heaved it as far as she could. "An offering to King Neptune," she explained happily. "Must keep the gods happy. The rest belong to us."

"Let's make it a competition," Susan suggested.

"Only if I get to name my own prize," Mike said, leering broadly at Jean.

"Is he really as sexy as all that?" Susan asked.

Jean kept her face expressionless. "Rumors. Hearsay. No real evidence exists to support the theory."

"How sad!" Susan said.

"Listen," Mike shouted. "With a pound or two of these little devils inside me, I'll be a veritable Henry the Eighth. Not a woman on the beach will be safe from my lechery."

"You mean oysters," Eddie corrected gravely.

"Same thing," Mike said, coming up with a clam.

As if by accord, the two men drifted deeper into the bay, beyond the hearing of Susan and Jean. Eddie carried cigarettes tucked under the waistband of his trunks. He lit one, puffed anxiously.

"Can I talk to you about something?" he said, running his hand over his balding scalp. "Christ, it's hot."

"You should wear a hat." Mike dug around in the sand. He suspected he already knew what Eddie wanted to speak about and he wanted no part of it. Still, he felt obliged to listen. "What's on your mind?"

"You know about Maggie and me," Eddie began, avoiding Mike's eyes.

Mike reached for another clam. It was a rock. "What about Maggie and you?"

"I love her."

Mike tossed the rock away. The sun was very hot and he splashed water over his head. "Love is beautiful," he said tonelessly.

"I mean it. I really love her."

"She's married, in case you've forgotten. To Roy Ashe. That pale and pathetic man who laughs at his own jokes. You remember Roy Ashe? He's your friend."

"That's what makes it so rough." Eddie moved nearer to Mike, voice larded with urgency. "You can't know what a rotten sonofabitch he is. The way he treats her."

"Don't tell me anything."

"You know he screws around. With other women, I mean. And he gambles. They're in debt."

"What else is new?"

"He beats her. Did you know that? He actually hits her. And whenever he wants to, he uses her."

"That's called marital prerogative."

"You can't justify such behavior. He practically rapes her."

"Practically. That is the operative word."

"Dammit, man! Can't you see that this is serious!"

"I was beginning to think you didn't understand that."

Eddie appraised him at length. "You knew, didn't you, about us?"

Mike nodded.

"Since when?"

"A while. One day, I just knew."

Eddie grimaced. "It's not like you think, the way it would be with you."

"What is that supposed to mean?"

"Well, we only began to—" He broke off, started again. "It's not only sex, you understand. I mean, I'm different than you are. I don't require a lot of different women. One is all I want. The right one." He squeezed his eyes shut as if in pain. They fluttered open. "How did you know?"

Mike shrugged and dug up another clam. "Sometimes I see things and know what they mean. In my gut, I mean."

"You've got more perception than I gave you credit for."

Mike decided that Eddie had a rare skill for turning a compliment into an insult. He said nothing.

"It's a bad marriage," Eddie pointed out.

"It was a bad marriage last summer. You're not helping it to get better."

"I love Maggie." He waited but Mike made no reply. "What do you think I should do?"

Surprise showed on Mike's face. "You're asking for my advice?"

"Yes."

"Okay. Here it is. Get off the island. Today. Go back to the house. Pack your clothes and leave. Go away. Don't come back."

"I can't do that."

"You wanted my advice, I gave it."

"I can't do it."

"It's bound to explode."

"I love Maggie. I want to marry her."

"She's still got a husband."

"She's going to divorce him."

"What about Cindy?"

"She's a marvelous child. I want her, too."

Mike exhaled audibly. "You've made up your mind," he said. "Let's talk about something else. That kid the Giants brought up, Willie Mays. He's a winner, I think. But I don't think the Giants have it. The Dodgers look awfully good to me. . . ."

"To hell with that!"

"Right. How's the writing coming along?"

"Nobody can write under these conditions! I can hardly think properly, let alone create. You don't know how it is, doing original work. The demands. The need for internal stability, for total concentration . . ."

Mike restrained the angry retort that came to his tongue. Again Eddie was making less of him, to his own credit. Always it was Eddie Stander who was the sensitive man, the creator, the one who understood the nuances. Had Eddie applied some ordinary discipline to his life, his work, some old-fashioned character, Mike would have been more tolerant of his lack of progress with the writing.

"One day, Eddie," he said conversationally, "let's have a little contest. We'll dream up an idea for a story, the same story, and each of us will write his own version. It might be interesting to see what comes out." And which of us finishes what he began, he amended silently.

"What the hell are you babbling about? I have a serious problem and you talk to me about some stupid contest. Can't you see, I don't know what I'm going to do."

Mike dug up another clam. "I wish I could help," he said, meaning it.

Susan

"Two consecutive weeks!"

Neil issued the words with more than his usual precision, displaying his disapproval.

"It isn't my fault," Susan said.

"I think it is. The same situation existed last Saturday when I made breakfast for our son. I squeezed each of us a tumbler of orange juice. And do you know how many oranges remained afterward? Five. Only five."

"I buy a fresh bag every Friday, before you come out."

"Let's be logical Susan. Are you saying that you and Maggie and the children use more than half a bag of oranges overnight?"

"No . . ."

"I'm glad you admit that. Consider the facts. If the oranges aren't used, and they aren't in the refrigerator, then perhaps they never existed. That is, were never purchased."

"But I told you—"

"Please, Susan." He stared at her with patient disapproval. "Very well. Let's go step by step. How many oranges come in a bag?"

"I don't know."

"You should take the trouble to find out. I did. I went down to the market and made a count. Thirty-six to a bag. That's three dozen. I counted six bags at random. A fair sampling, I would say."

"I suppose it is."

"You know it is. If you think otherwise, tell me. I don't want you saying that I'm being unfair."

"You're very fair, Neil."

"I'm pleased to hear you say that, Susan. Now. Thirty-six oranges to the bag. BB and I used ten between us. Five per glass. That means twenty-six oranges should have been left. But by my count there were only five remaining. What happened to the others, if you bought a new bag?"

"I don't know." There was an unrestrained shrillness in her voice.

"I think you should know. We are discussing the health of your family. Of your son. Your husband. Facts are what we're concerned with here. Fact one: I'm a young man, Susan, not yet thirty. My future lies to the front, my entire life. But what if my health should break down. Which brings us to fact two: You and BB would be deprived of my full energies and talents. My full span of productivness. Perhaps of my life itself. Now that could happen, Susan. Oh, yes, there is insurance to take care of you and BB and there's going to be more, because I care about my family. But insurance is hardly the answer to life. Is it? *Is it?*" he persisted.

"No," she said thickly.

He arranged a pleased expression on his face. "All I ask of you is a reasonable degree of attention to these matters. If someone else wants to use the oranges, that is all right with me. They are members of this summer household and therefore hold equal claim on every item in the pantry, so to speak. But I insist that you provide enough oranges every weekend. Consider the problem and all the possibilities. If you must purchase an extra bag, then by all means do so."

"I will, Neil."

He took her face between his hands. "That's my girl. Beautiful, that face. I want it to remain that way. Young and beautiful. Untouched." He smiled down at her. "I'm going out to the beach now. We're having a big volleyball game today, weekenders against the lifeguards. I want to loosen up, protect against muscle strain. I feel very strong, agile. I expect to play exceptionally well today. Come and cheer for me."

"I will," she lied.

Five minutes after he left, Susan took BB to the beach and left him with Maggie. This done, she went looking for Sy Melman.

Mike

Jean Harvey didn't tell Mike about the part until after the contract was signed. Three weeks in stock in western Pennsylvania.

"A week's rehearsal and a week of playing time. The second play will be rehearsed while we're doing the first one."

"I'm going to miss you," he told her, wondering if he would. "Maybe I'll visit."

"There's no point in it. I'll be too tied up, too busy. We'd never have any time alone."

"Except at night."

She shook her head grimly. "Not even then. In stock, the nighttime is for memorizing the new play. And for grabbing a few hours of rest. It's only three weeks."

He experienced a sense of relief that she was going. They saw each other frequently, almost every evening. Instead of growing closer, however, a spreading unease came into being, seemed to move them farther apart. They argued often, attacking each other obliquely, each criticizing the other's behavior, lack of selflessness. Yet afterward, when he tried, Mike could seldom remember what it was they had fought about. He was left with an insistent gnawing with no relief in view. To be with her meant unrest, frustration, anger; yet away from her, she was on his mind always, his desire vibrant, increasing. This separation would be good for them both. It would give him a chance to clear his mind, to understand what was happening between them, to decide what he wanted to do.

"Besides," she was saying. "You'll have fun with me not around."

"You think so," he said cautiously.

She nodded. "All those pretty girls at the island. You'll have your pick."

"Maybe I don't want any of them."

She laughed without humor, a short, biting sound. "Obviously you don't want me very much, either."

"Now what the hell does that mean?"

"You don't appear to have much interest in making love to me."

"That's not true and you know it."

"I don't know anything of the sort. For all the time we spend together, we seldom get into bed. We neck like kids but that doesn't do it at all."

"If I could find an apartment."

"Have you been looking?"

"Of course I have. I told you—"

"Three times, Mike. Three times in all these weeks. Is there something wrong with me?"

"Oh, God, *no*. You're exciting . . ."

"Prove it. Find a place for us to be together. But if you don't want me enough, say so. I'll go my way and you go yours."

He shivered. "By the time you get back, I'll have a place. I promise."

"If you don't . . ."

"I said I would."

Her eyes glittered and her mouth flexed tauntingly. "I don't suppose you want to be with me tonight, to make love to me."

"Of course I do. But—"

"I arranged things for us. This afternoon. I reserved a room, checked in. Luggage and all. Very proper. All we have to do is go." She brought a key out of her purse. "See!"

"I'll call my folks," he said, grinning. "To tell them I won't be coming home tonight."

They came together shyly, as if for the first time. Soon she grew more aggressive, exploring, experimenting, caressing with her fingers, her lips. He swelled at her touch, the flow of energy darting along his limbs, gathering strength in his viscera, concentrating with quivering power in his erect desire. Under her, his skin grew taut, the nerve endings vibrating in a sensory migration toward the center of things.

In the yellow glow of the nightlamp, he tasted the pliant roundness of her fine buttocks, the deep shadow of the calipygian cleft, the hang of her heavy breasts. The insistent lips.

He felt himself draw tight, an acute focus, cocked ready to explode. Then, the eruption. A driving outburst that arced his body high into the air, rocking him, twisting and distorting him, emitting powerful spurts of his manhood. She rode him skillfully, guided him back to the damp sheets, urging him to a final, fulfilling spasm. Easing him back to quiet and contentment.

"I'm sorry," he said, when she returned from the bathroom. A warm lassitude gripped him and he wanted very much to sleep. He watched her put on her brassiere.

"What are you doing?"

"I'm going home."

He sat up. "Why?"

"It's a mistake."

Panic came alive deep in his bowels and a nerve began to leap erratically in his thigh. "I'm sorry. I was so excited. You made me so excited."

"I won't accept that. You owe me something. You owe *us*. If you truly cared about me . . ."

"I care. I love you," he heard himself say, for the first time. "I do. I love you." And saying it he knew that it was true and he was surprised and pleased. "I've never loved anyone before. . . ."

She faced him squarely. "I want you to love me, Mike. I want to be able to love you. But you must let me love you."

"Come here," he said.

"You're spoiled. A spoiled man. Too many women have been too good to you, made things too easy. Including me."

"You're beautiful."

"Women react to you. I've seen them. On the beach. You know so many of them. But I won't let you treat me casually, for your own pleasure only."

"It isn't that way."

"You're going to have to prove it."

"Come back to bed and let me."

A challenging glitter lit her eyes. "Are you man enough . . . so soon?"

"Take off that brassiere." He felt himself stir. "See. And that's just the start of things."

She stretched out alongside him on her back. "This time," she said breathily, "you are going to have to do it all. I think I shall just lie here and let you. . . ."

He gazed down at her, breasts sagging to the sides, belly

rising and falling in gentle rhythm, legs spread enticingly. He touched the warm flesh. "Yes," he muttered, bending over her. "You hold still. As long as you can. And I'll take care of everything. Everything. Everywhere. Enjoy me, darling, the way I enjoyed . . ."

"Ah," she said, after some time had passed. "Ah. That is . . . perfect. Softer . . . yes . . . soft and sweet. So good . . . Oh, oh, yes . . . I will be . . . so much . . . better for you . . . for you . . ."

And she was. Later.

Eddie and Maggie and Roy

Earlier that same night, Eddie and Maggie decided to go to Cherry Grove for dinner. He arranged for a taxi—one of the jeeps that went from community to community along the beach at night—to transport them.

He faced this first visit to the predominantly homosexual community with a rising anxiety, though he showed none of it to Maggie. He had always felt a certain antipathy toward homosexuals, a simmering hostility. He resented their flipness and their superficiality. He resented, too, the queens who had carved out important positions for themselves in the theater, in advertising and television—and only because they were charter members of this tightly knit subgroup.

Darkness had not yet descended when they arrived at Cherry Grove and Maggie suggested they stroll through the community. They picked their way along narrow, white-edged catwalks. The houses, on locust posts for the most part, were painted a variety of pastel colors and were decorated with signs and banners. Pink and powder blue, bright yellow and chartreuse dominated the scene.

"What fun! The boys have done a lovely job with their houses. It's really quite pretty, the manicured shrubbery, the decoration. I like it."

"They're so damned *au courant*. You'd think they were so in tune and the rest of us out."

"Maybe they are," Maggie said wistfully.

"That isn't funny," he shot back. "Come on. Let's eat." They made their way to the Sea Shack. They ordered shrimp cocktails and barbecued steaks with French fries and salad. They ate with enthusiasm—the food as good as any to be had on the island—observing the flow of svelte and delicate youths drifting in and out of the restaurant, each one more handsome than the others. Some wore make-up and others had tinted their hair, and all of them were carefully garbed so as to display their bodies to advantage.

"They're like a pack of bitches in mating season," Eddie complained. "They wear their sexuality like a signal flag."

"Don't take them seriously."

He grunted and said nothing. After an interval, he spoke again. "I know one agent, a flaming fag, who won't represent any actor who isn't queer too. "That's a hell of a thing. And it's ruining the theater. I suppose if I was gay I'd have more success with my writing."

"Have you been doing much writing lately?" she asked mildly.

"I'd rather be with you."

"I don't want to take you away from your work."

"I've been considering a new idea. I'm working it out now."

She turned back to her food, vaguely troubled. This was familiar; she had heard it all before, and she tried to recall where it had been, who had said the words. It came slowly, an image of her husband explaining why he had been unable to accomplish the many things he had planned to do since leaving college. She stole a glance at Eddie. He was larger than Roy, more impressive to look at, different in form and feature. Yet he reminded her of Roy; in some strange and undefinable way, they managed to look alike. It was a disturbing concept and she thrust it out of her mind.

They ordered coffee and brandy and while waiting Eddie excused himself to go to the men's room, which turned out to be a small cubicle with a door that had no lock. He addressed himself to his reason for coming. Seconds later the door opened and a slender youth in tight white trousers and a turquoise shirt, open to the waist, slipped into the room.

"Busy," Eddie rasped.

The young man pursed his mouth thoughtfully, smiled an ingratiating smile. "So I see, love, but I simply cannot postpone the inevitable. The floodwaters are rising and about to overflow." He unzipped and stepped forward, reaching for himself. "You won't mind if I join you at the bowl. This is an *emergency*. . . ."

Eddie shifted to make room, tried not to notice that their streams joined in midair, splashed as one, the water foaming. The young man laughed gaily.

"Aren't we the pair, love! Pissing up a veritable storm."

Eddie directed his stream to another section of the bowl. The boy sent his arc in pursuit. He laughed again.

"*Allons, mes enfants!* Ze duel. We cross water at three paces!" Again that laugh, softer now, more insinuating. "Have you ever had a peeing contest? When I was a boy we had them all the time. For distance and for accuracy."

Eddie grunted, considered stopping, leaving. But the pressure remained and the ride back would be rough. Bumpy. He tried unsuccessfully to keep his eyes away from the other's member.

The slender man noticed. "Do you approve? I must say that's a fantastically strong stream you have. Much better than my own, sad to say. I suppose it's because of that marvelous dark prick of yours. A magnificent tool."

A glob of emotion lodged in Eddie's throat. He tried to hawk it clear.

"Do you know the derivation of the word, dearie? Prick, that is. Sailors used to be issued tobacco wrapped in canvas and tied into a cylinder and tapered suitably. It was called a *perique*. *Perique*. Prick. You see."

Eddie stepped back and adjusted his clothes.

"Oh, must you go so soon? Perhaps we could have a drink together. That woman you're with, she's just a beard, isn't she? A cover? Of course she is. I knew you were one of us the minute I layed eyes on you. My name is Adrian, love, and there isn't anything I wouldn't do to make you happy."

Eddie turned to the door.

Adrian dropped a limp hand on his arm. "See, sweet, what you are doing to me, making Adrian all hard and full of love for you. We will have an incredible time together and you will make me oh, so happy. Let me give you just a taste now. . . ."

A deep tremor rode down the length of Eddie's torso, the play of opposing forces tearing at him. A low moan tore out of his mouth and he stumbled past Adrian and out of the men's room, back to Maggie.

"Come on," he muttered. "We're leaving."

"The coffee—" She broke off when she saw the expression on his face. "What is it, Eddie?"

"I want to go. Right now."

They went out on the beach and waited until the beach taxi came along. Aware of the seething emotion in him, she asked no questions. And he said nothing, offered no explanation.

The ride back was eerie, neither of them speaking as the taxi swerved and jolted along the sand. The beach was deserted and black beyond the searching cones of the headlights. The ocean was a dark heaving stain under a low gray sky and the crump of the waves a rising threat from which there seemed no escape, not even when they returned to the ancient shingled confines of Neurotics Anonymous.

"Would you like a drink?" she asked.

He stared at her as if he hadn't heard. His eyes squeezed shut and when he allowed them to roll open there was an anxious, frightened expression in them.

"I want to make love to you," he said thickly.

"Let me make sure Cindy is all right."

She came to his room wearing only a robe. She allowed it to fall to the floor, slid into bed next to him. His arms went around her and his mouth, hard and demanding, found hers.

"Eddie," she gasped finally. "You're hurting me."

"I want you."

"Darling, you have me."

His knee went between her legs, forced them apart, and he thrust himself at her in a series of short intense probes.

"Wait," she said. "I'll help you. . . ."

At her touch, the blood drained away and with it all strength, all manhood. His loins pounded at her in furious futility.

"Rest, darling," she murmured, trying to sooth him.

"I want you," he moaned. "I want you now."

"It's late and you're tired. You try so hard. We don't have to do it all the time."

"I want to," he pleaded. He tucked his head against her throat, began to breathe heavily. His middle rolled against her, his slack member flattened against the feathery wedge. She responded, moving under him, stroking the hollow of his back, determined to accommodate him. But nothing happened.

He began to sob. His body grew tense and his legs jerked spasmodically. Hot tears wet her flesh. She cradled his head and made soothing sounds.

"It's all right, darling. These things happen. It doesn't mean anything. Even Roy . . ." She broke off.

"I love you," he said against her throat. "I want you so much. I want to please you, be good for you. I have to . . ."

After a while, he ceased crying and they lay in each other's arms dozing. Neither of them heard the door open or noticed when he came into the room. It was Maggie who sensed the intrusion first, head swiveling.

"Very nice," Roy said mildly. "A pretty scene. Like something out of a bad play. Best friend making it with best friend's wife. Gives a man something to think about."

For a long time, neither one of them moved. It was Maggie who recovered first. She slid out of bed and reached for the robe. Roy picked it up and handed it to her.

"Thanks," she said automatically. "When did you get here?" she added conversationally.

"I took a water taxi." He grinned triumphantly at her.

"Very nice," she said. "You deliberately waited until after the last ferry to come over. Until I was sure you wouldn't be coming."

"Do you think I'd do that to you, Maggie?"

"That's dirty pool."

"I thought somebody was getting into you, Maggie. Mike, I figured, not Eddie. I'm a little surprised."

"Let's go up to the room, Roy," she said. "We'll talk about it privately."

"You are my friend, Eddie," Roy said. "And you fuck my wife. I wouldn't have done that to you, Eddie," he added plaintively.

"Oh, God," Eddie muttered.

"Stop it, Roy," Maggie commanded easily. "All of us

talking this way, it's ridiculous. I'm going upstairs." She left.

Roy watched her go. "Great girl," he commented. "Terrific lay." He looked back at Eddie, a quizzical expression on the weathered face. "Two, three times a week, Eddie, you ate at my table. I can understand Maggie making it with someone, Eddie, but it shouldn't have been you. That wasn't right."

"Oh, *God.*"

"I guess I should be getting upstairs. Maggie's waiting for me."

Eddie wanted to cry when he was alone. He wished Roy had hit him, hurt him. He deserved at least that.

The next morning, after breakfast, he left the island, vowing never to return.

Mike

The apartment was on the top floor of a four-story building on Lexington Avenue. Two rooms overlooking the street. But no kitchen. Mike wondered how he would tell his parents that he was leaving home. His mother would throw a large fit, he was sure.

"I'll think about it," he told the landlord.

"Do that. If you decide yes, phone me. But if somebody else comes along I'll rent it. That's my business."

Mike went back to the Civic Theaters offices and thought about it. The rent was seventy-five dollars a month, plus telephone and utilities. That wouldn't leave much out of his salary. There were other problems, too. The idea of being alone was frightening; he considered the details of living, all of which his mother took care of for him. There were meals to be cooked, cleaning, laundry. And at home, he never had to be concerned with being lonely.

Against this, there was Jean, and the time he would be able to spend with her. The time in bed. His mouth went dry at the memory. What the hell was she doing in Pennsylvania when she should be with him? He visualized her, the faintly mocking cast of her features, the scent of her, the way she felt. And the way her fingers felt on his flesh. His skin wrinkled and desire expanded.

A hot plate could be put in, he told himself. And a second-hand refrigerator shouldn't cost too much. As for the rent, the other expenses, he had no choice. He would have to earn more money. He took a deep breath and rang Teddy Turner on the intercom.

"Mike, Teddy. Can I come in?"

"Make it quick."

Teddy Turner was vice-president in charge of advertising, publicity, and exploitation for Civic Theaters. Though the same age as Mike Birns, he looked twenty years older. It was less a matter of physical deterioration than manner and life style. He had always thought and acted with the dark conservatism of an older man, considering, analyzing, acting only when certain of success. Craggy and pale, his brooding eyes observed a world to be measured only in terms of personal gain.

"What's hot, Mike?" He spoke crisply, a man who had no time to waste.

"Teddy, I've been with Civic for almost four years. . . ."

Turner leaned back and folded his fleshy hands across a pudgy middle. He appraised Mike Birns with the confidence of one able to forecast the outcome of this discussion even before it fully unfolded. He interrupted finally.

"You want a raise."

"I have to have one, Teddy."

"The question is whether or not I have to give you one," Turner corrected. "What do you make now?"

"Eighty-seven fifty."

Turner tapped the side of his nose. He had been paid more than that before he reached his majority, had doubled his income the following year, currently drew thirty-five thousand a year, plus unlimited expenses. Birns would never make it into his league. Nor would any of the others under him. A reassuring thought.

"Money's a little tight right now," he said to Mike. He considered departmental salaries; the budget was below estimates for the year, had been since he took over. He had doubled up on assignments and hired no new people. Perhaps there was an extra something available for Birns.

He wasn't a bad press agent and might be thinking about leaving. Teddy hated to lose any of his people.

"Let me tell you how it is, Mike," Turner said. "You write a pretty fair story. Especially your features. But in other areas you fall short."

Mike felt a stab of fear. He'd made a mistake, brought himself to Teddy's attention. He wasn't going to get the raise, might in fact be fired. He braced himself. "Tell me what you want, Teddy, and I can give it to you."

"What I'm giving you is constructive criticism."

"I understand, Teddy."

"Ideas are what count most in this business. Exploitable concepts. I demand the extras from my people. I know you have more in you and it's simply a question of getting it out. This is no nine-to-five job."

"I understand that and I'll do better, Teddy."

"Right. And I'm going to take a chance you'll come through for me, Mike. Starting next week, you're up to one hundred bucks even. How's that sound?"

Relief made Mike weak. He managed a smile. "Thanks, Teddy. I really appreciate it."

Teddy could see that. It made him feel good, expansive. "Tell you what, Mike, from now on you put in an unitemized expense voucher every week. Keep it between ten and twenty dollars above actual expenses. That ought to make you happy for a while."

Back at his own desk, a pulse leaped erratically in Mike's temple and the palms of his hands were moist. There was a sick, empty sensation in his stomach. The way it had always been when he played football. Before the start of the game.

He waited for the excitement to diminish, for the nervousness to evaporate. He realized for the first time just how much this raise had meant to him. More than being able to rent the apartment. More than the time with Jean. More than being on his own at last, which suddenly seemed very desirable. The raise signified Teddy Turner's approval of his work, of *him,* and it boded well for the future.

Calmer now, he picked up the phone and dialed the landlord of the building on Lexington Avenue. And that evening, after work, he paid a visit to Brooks Brothers for the first time, bought two suits and a sports coat. And a dozen button-down shirts. All blue.

Neil

On that same day, Neil Morgan met with Norman Wallace and Roberta Davis. Contracts were signed, making them the first clients of the Neil Morgan Talent Agency. Soon there would be others, Neil vowed silently. Many others.

Norman Wallace and Roberta toasted their collective futures in champagne. Neil raised a glass of ginger ale.

Susan

BB scampered ahead. Susan watched him plunge down the sloping beach toward the surf, then retreat screaming in mock terror at the attack of the waves. Face the threat, Neil would have said to the boy. Conquer your fears. Learn to control yourself in the water.

She repeated the phrases aloud, imitating the flat authoritative tones of her husband. Neil always spoke to their son as if they were equals, his language and manner intimidating. He demanded too much of BB, she had long ago concluded. There was that about Neil; he had established a body of rules to which they were all expected to conform—BB, herself, Neil, too. Especially Neil. One had to measure up. To test oneself. Triumph. Another Neilism Aphorisms that summed up life in simple terms. Pithy. With only one flaw. They frequently failed to work.

Susan no longer wanted to measure up. At least, not to Neil's standards. It was perfectly all right with her if he chose constantly to pit himself against certain barriers, measuring and weighing. But he had no right to demand that others do likewise.

BB came running toward her, hand outstretched, offering half of a mussel shell. She admired and named it for him, watched him scamper back to the ocean, searching for the missing portion of the mussel. She lowered herself to the sand, damp and rough against the underside of her thighs, and leaned back on her elbows. She stared past BB out to the sea. A fishing boat moved slowly across the horizon.

She wished Neil would change, become less rigid, less demanding, more accepting of human shortcomings. But there was no reason for him to change. He was certain of who he was, and enjoyed that fact, knew where he was going, and enjoyed that. A hard man.

An image of Neil's father floated to mind. Stocky, muscular, his pink face haloed by hair that refused to turn gray, he had the kind of wintry eyes that peered under your skin, past all defenses. She shivered and hugged her knees. A projection of Neil in twenty-five years.

Richard Morgan had been a successful businessman, starting out in plumbing supplies, eventually becoming involved in land development, construction. In three years time, he went from building individual homes on order to putting up an entire township, including roads, sewage systems, schools, shopping centers. As soon as half the units had been sold, he disposed of the remaining properties to a real-estate management concern at a profit to himself of one million dollars. He repeated the procedure during the next decade, establishing himself as one of the northeast's foremost builders.

Rich and getting richer, Richard Morgan hadn't been content. He opened a chain of inexpensive burger joints across Long Island that catered to motorists. Cheap meat, highly seasoned and quickly served. After one year's successful operation, including a high pressure advertising campaign, he began to sell franchises. Within the next three years, he tripled his wealth, extending the chain into upstate New York and New England. The burger joints led inevitably to a trucking concern and from there it was one more easy step to the purchase of a meat-distribution company, a packing house, and subsequently retail sales to food markets across the country.

By the time he was forty, Richard Morgan was a millionaire many times over, a man with influence and a growing power—a power that eventually brought him into local and national politics. He never stood for office himself, never wanted to, cautious about exposing himself to criticism, to the public eye. But his money and his influence put a number of men into office, men who were anxious to call Richard Morgan a friend, anxious to please him, to help protect his interests.

Along the way, Richard Morgan had supported positions and candidates favorable to the Police Department and had been rewarded with an honorary membership, and a miniature captain's badge that would get him past police lines at fires, draw a respectful salute at major public events, put an end to the ticket-writing propensities of traffic officers. Richard Morgan was prouder of that badge than of all his other honors, all his other accomplishments.

"Backbone of our civilization," he liked to say about the police. "Finest bunch of men ever assembled. Dedicated to the public good, to improving the national morals."

And when an outcry was raised concerning the fervor with which the police applied their nightsticks to the heads of high-school students during a melee at a football game one fall, Richard Morgan made clear to his family where he stood.

"Too damned easy," he had sputtered angrily, pounding a fist into his palm. "Too damned easy. That's what's wrong with these punk kids. They have it too damned easy. Life owes them everything, they think. Well, I've got a message for them. Life owes nothing to nobody. You got to go out there and whip life, make it conform, sit up and cry uncle. You remember that, Neil, when your time comes to take over from me and my generation. Get out there and hustle, son, compete and win. Make your mark. Don't let the other guy pass you by. Play by the rules and remember the rules are there to protect men like us, to help us. There are always legitimate ways to work around them.

"But these punk kids causing trouble. They're going nowhere. They have no respect, and they have to be taught respect. A nightstick over the head and a swift kick in the ass. That's what gets them back in line."

Susan had always been fascinated by Neil's reactions to his father. He was inexorably drawn to the older man, becoming quite agitated whenever a visit was in order. They spent a great deal of time together talking. After a while Susan came to realize that what transpired between father and son could hardly be characterized as conversation. Instead, it seemed as if Neil was submitting himself, his ideas, for approval. He would air his views on a subject and this would serve as a stimulant for his father, who would embark on a long monologue criticizing, destroying, mocking. Neil would never rebut his father's arguments, withdrawing instead into an almost servile silence, listening with concentrated anguish.

Thinking about Richard Morgan, Susan remembered the awe he had inspired in her when she had first met him. She had never known a man so confident and obviously strong, a man so in control of his destiny. And the destinies of those around him. She had mentioned this to Neil following one of their regular Friday night dinners at his parents' home.

"There aren't many like him," Neil had boasted. "He's taken the world by the tail and made it cry uncle."

"Sometimes I wonder if it's good to be that sure of yourself, that sure you're right about everything."

Neil had blinked and grimaced and produced a humorless laugh. "Men like my father, they make things happen. They are the producers, the men who made this country what it is, will keep it strong and vital. Men like my father are perfectionists. My father isn't an ordinary man. He won't allow ordinary obstacles to stop him from getting what he wants, from going where he wants to go."

"Not everybody can do everything."

"True. And that's one of the advantages to be profited from. When I was a kid I played baseball. I wasn't very good in the beginning and I wanted to quit. My father wouldn't allow me to. He insisted that I had to play, even more, that I become a regular."

"But if you weren't good enough. . . ."

"My father wouldn't accept that. He took me to a doctor for a complete physical examination. It took three whole days. It was finally determined that I had poor depth perception. When the doctor told my father that, I figured it would be the end of my baseball-playing days. I underestimated my father. He took me aside, told me I'd just have to try more, work harder."

"If you couldn't see."

"That's just it, he was *right*. He had me fitted with special glasses which helped some. And I concentrated on judging distances, practicing almost all the time. I used to go out to the ballfield early, pace off the distances from third base, where I played, to second and to first. I got to know every angle until I could make the throws blindfolded. And I cheated on fielding batted balls. I played up close, taking risks other players wouldn't take. I'd throw myself in front of a ball, knock it down with my chest. Anything to stop it." A tight, reminiscent smile turned his mouth. "I was a real, gutsy player." He became grave. "I've learned a lot from my father and some day I intend to show him how much he's taught me. You'll see, Susan, one day I'll be a bigger man than he is and I'll do it on my own. One way or another."

Susan had believed him. She believed him now. Neil would find the way to the end of his rainbow. One day he would own the world. Or at least a substantial portion of it. A disturbing thought caused her to sit up. Would any success satisfy Neil? She doubted it; instead he would continue on toward some vague and pristine summit.

She brought her eyes to where BB played in the surf. He would grow up to be just like Neil. Just like his grandfather.

"Courage and determination," she had heard Neil say many times to their son. "These are the qualities that make a man into a man. Decide what you want to do and do it. Life is there to be had, to be conquered. . . ."

Susan imagined BB growing up to become a stiff-spined general, his chest laden with medals; or an evangelical preacher, the kind she had often listened to as a child, bellowing out God's Law and damning forever those who failed to heed him; or Chairman of the Board of United Fruit, ordering peasants whipped because they couldn't load bananas quickly enough.

Such thoughts circled around her brain with greater frequency in recent days. How much of that was due to Sy Melman? A guilty shiver contorted her body.

She had to reach a decision. What choices were open? It was useless to expect Neil to change; he wasn't capable of that.

Divorce. The word scurried along her nervous system like a living creature gone beserk. A weakness trickled into her stomach. She was no different than her mother, quitting her responsibilities in selfish flight, deserting her family. No. She was not like her mother. She could never desert BB. She would take him along, lavish love upon him.

A terrifying thought. Neil would never permit that. BB the sole product of his loins. *His* son. She had always been aware of that sense of ownership, as if Neil alone had conceived the boy, as if her womb had not nurtured and sheltered him until he was ready to be born. As if she had been an incidental carrier.

She would fight for BB. But fighting did not mean winning. And Neil was undeniably a better fighter than she could ever hope to be. He would find out about Sy Melman, use that against her. But Sy had asked her to leave Neil, to get a divorce and marry him, promising to care for BB as if he were his own son.

Early on the prospect of marriage to Sy appealed to Susan. There was a glamor to it all; a divorce, marriage to her husband's employer. But the appeal soon diminished. More and more he reminded her of Neil. Oh, yes, a softer man, gentler, and in bed more concerned about her pleasure. But otherwise not much different. Like Neil, Sy seldom *listened* to her, seldom made an effort to understand her thoughts or her feelings. Both of them were concerned with how she looked, how she made *them* feel.

"I'd be so proud to take you places," Sy often said. Neil might have said the same thing. A sigh expired on her lips and she heaved herself erect. She knew what she had to do.

"BB," she called. "We're going back."

Chapter VI

Mike and Jean

Mike Birns was at his desk studying the tearsheets of the Sunday papers. He had broken *The Times* theatrical section for the first time with a feature story. The editor hadn't given him byline credit, but he was happy nevertheless. It was becoming increasingly difficult to get into *The Times,* and it signified professional acceptance at the highest level. He was on his way to deliver a copy of the story to Teddy Turner himself, to enjoy that pleasure in person, when the telephone rang. It was Jean Harvey.

She had returned to the city late the previous night, she told him, voice husky and full of sleep, and had just awakened.

Excitement inhibited his brain, making speech difficult. He stuttered and muttered and hawked his throat clear and repeated himself.

"I want to see you," he said at last.

"I'm still in bed," she protested, laughing back in her throat, a crotch-swelling sound.

"I'll be right over."

Again that laugh, fuller, content. "Let me wake up."

"How soon?" he said, thinking that he could not wait until evening to see her, ordering himself to curb his impatience.

"I'm anxious to see the apartment," she said evenly.

"You made it sound lovely in your letters. It'll be fun helping you furnish . . . have you bought many things already?"

"Just the bed."

"Oh . . ." Her voice trailed off.

"It's foam rubber," he said, suddenly nervous, compelled to fill in the silence. "They told me at Macy's that it would last for twenty years."

"A very impressive bed. You must show it to me sometime. . . ."

"When?"

"What time do you go to lunch? I could meet you at the apartment."

She was waiting when he got there. They hugged, talked in short bursts, visually exploring each other as if for reassurance. Halfway up the first flight of stairs, he kissed her. Their bodies came together tightly and he backed her against the bannister.

"Are you going to throw me down?" she murmured at last.

"God, you feel good to me." His hands went down to the swell of her buttocks and he pushed against her.

"You too," she said softly.

"I am going to—"

She laughed. "Not here. Not on the steps."

They ran up the rest of the way, fighting for breath.

Once inside she examined the two rooms.

"The refrigerator is mine and the burner," he explained.

"It's lovely."

He reached for her but she avoided him, looked out the window. "The view is not much."

He went after her, hands going to her waist. "I don't intend to spend much time admiring it. Not when you're here. I missed you very much, Jean," he said, into her hair.

"It was hard to tell. Your letters didn't say much."

"I'm not much of a writer."

"For a man who earns his living with a typewriter, who is as verbal as you are . . . I think you're afraid to say anything in a letter. Too cautious, afraid to commit yourself on paper. In a personal way, I mean."

"I think you talk too much." He kissed her neck and cupped her breasts. "I missed this."

"Is that all?"

One hand rode across her belly, lower. She sighed and pushed back against him. "Ah, that's nice." Then, after a long interval. "If you go on this way, you won't have time to eat."

"I'm going to have a non-caloric lunch. You."

She twisted around to face him. "Come on," she said gravely. "Come on. Let's inaugurate that twenty-year bed of yours. . . ."

They had dinner together that evening and hurried back to the apartment and made love again. They dozed and later showered together. She insisted on soaping his body, laughing as he came erect under her hands, helping him to rinse off, drawing him down on top of her in the tub with the warm shower splashing them, wet skin sliding and sloshing noisily as they struggled to remain locked long after both of them were drained and full of each other.

They went back to bed and slept and when they woke she made each of them a Scotch and water. They lay side-by-side drinking and smoking. She told him about the tour and he told her what had happened at Fire Island. About Eddie Stander and Maggie.

"I thought there was something wrong between the Ashes last summer," he recalled. "I wasn't able to pin it down, but it was there, something I sensed. Then I changed my mind, decided I was wrong."

"But you were right."

"Apparently. But how could I know?"

She nibbled on the swell of his pectoral muscle. "Because you are a genius." Her voice was tinged with gentle mockery.

"Be nice or I'll cut off your source of pleasure."

"Oh, sir! Not *that*. To deprive me of that precious gift would be unusual punishment and unfairly cruel." Her laughter died away and she spoke soberly. "You are very clever, you know. No, not clever. That too, of course, but much more. Oh, damn, I don't have the words. Mike, you see things other people don't, recognize what's going on and understand. It's an instinct, I suppose."

He puzzled over what she had said. "I'd like to believe that. But I haven't learned to trust my instincts. For example, why should my perception be sharper than Eddie Stander's? When you compare us, I come out second best. He began making important money right out of college. For me it's been a struggle. He's well-read and serious. I imagine he'll end up becoming a famous television writer or doing a play on Broadway. Or take Roy Ashe. He's so quick. Shrewd."

"Cunning, I would say."

"Maybe. What about Neil Morgan? There's a man who is sure of himself, who he is and where he's going. I can't say the same."

She thought about it. "People don't move at the same pace," she offered after a silent period. "They mature at different rates, the way some children are far out in front of their peers at certain stages, only to fall back later on. The race is not always to the quick."

"I'm a tortoise?"

"I mean that you are just starting to find yourself, to know what Mike Birns is all about. You are much better than you realize, in any number of ways."

"Exactly what I was thinking," he said, laughing so that she would know he wasn't boasting.

"Don't let it go to your head," she returned easily. "You're not all *that* good."

He allowed his eyes to drift over her body. In the soft light, her taut breasts gleamed and the round belly looked promising.

"My," she said, with slow admiration. "What is happening?"

"You approve?"

In answer, her head came forward. Her lips were cool from the Scotch but her tongue was warm, electric. He took the glass out of her hand and placed it on the floor with his own.

They rode out to Fire Island on the train together on Friday afternoon. That evening, they walked to Ocean Bay Park and ate broiled fluke and French fries at Flynn's. Afterward, they strolled back along the beach, exclaiming over the phosphorescence that had washed up on the sand. Neurotics Anonymous was still when they got back and they went to his room and made love. With Eddie gone, she could stay all night. And she did.

The others were awake when they rose in the morning, and there was no way to get her out of the house unseen. But the confrontation seemed to cause Jean no embarrassment. Her greeting to the Ashes and the Morgans was light, entirely natural, Mike thought with satisfaction as he walked her to her own place. When he got back to his house, the others were in the living room.

"Mike," Neil began. "I want to talk to you."

"Oh, Neil," Susan said.

Roy laughed.

Mike looked from face to face. "I want to get some coffee."

"This will only take a minute," Neil said. "Mike, I wouldn't want you to think of me as some kind of a Victorian prude."

Mike felt the muscles of his face grow taut, tug downward. "What is it?"

"You understand that I have a duty as a parent," Neil declared solemnly. "To my son."

A caustic burst of laughter broke out of Roy and he headed for the door. "I'm beaching it. Anybody want to come along?"

Maggie followed him silently.

Mike stared at Neil.

"Roy believes I'm wrong about this. And so, I might add, does my wife. But that doesn't deter me from doing what I know to be right. Children are impressionable. Those early years, especially before the age of six, they are vital to the formation of character. I know you understand that. . . ."

"Get to it," Mike said.

Neil jerked his head downward in assent, blinking rapidly. "It simply isn't proper for you to have a girl stay overnight in the house. Fortunately, I was able to get BB out of here before you and that girl—"

"Her name is Jean," Mike put in quickly.

"I am determined that my son not be exposed to that kind of thing, Mike. You see my position?"

Mike held himself very still. "Is there anything else you want to say?"

"I intend for my son to grow up with a proper moral

point of view, Mike. It's important. I'm sure Jean is a very nice girl and all that, but you aren't married to her. I don't feel I can ask you not to bring a girl into your room, but I do think you have to consider the rest of us and get her out of the house before breakfast. My position——"

"Your position," Mike broke in, "is clear. It ends here, Neil. We are not going to discuss Jean. Nor anything else concerning my personal life. You can be sure of one thing, Jean will never stay here again."

After Mike left, Neil looked over at Susan. "That kind of emotionalism is unnecessary. I made a reasonable request. I'm surprised that Mike refused to understand."

She looked away. "He understood everything."

Susan and Maggie

Maggie left the island the next morning, taking Cindy with her. Susan learned about it at breakfast, when Maggie came down with a swollen mouth, her eyes streaked.

"He hit me," she explained, "when I refused to make love. He hit me and made me do it. But no more. I thought that we could at least separate and get a divorce in a civilized fashion. I was wrong. I won't come back to the island again."

"I'll help you pack," Susan offered. "And Neil will drive you into the city."

"Of course," Neil said forthrightly. "Any help I can provide. . . ."

"Roy is letting me take the car," Maggie said, a wry smile turning her mouth. "He's very generous about such things. He'll go back by train."

"Why is he leaving?" Neil asked.

"I don't know," Maggie said. "He should stay. He had fun here. There's always a poker game and available girls. . . ."

Susan accompanied Maggie to the ferry, waited alone until it disappeared in the mist of Great South Bay. She continued to sit there, staring sightlessly at the distant

Long Island shoreline. It seemed to her that her world was crumbling, that life held no meaning, no permanence, that only anguish and destruction were constant. At once, Fire Island was a bad place to be, ugly and barren. Evil and loathsome. When she got back to Neurotics Anonymous, she began to drink. . . .

Chapter VII

Mike and Eddie

Mike's vacation fell during the second and third weeks of August and Jean arranged to be out at the island at the same time. They spent nearly all their time together, day and night. With Neil absent, Susan made it clear that Jean was always welcome.

The days went by unmarked and suddenly the holiday was over. It was time for Mike to return to his job. He soon discovered an unexpected bonus in being back in the city, in his apartment. There was furniture to shop for, kitchen equipment, pictures. With Jean, he made the rounds of the department stores, studying the model rooms, transcribing what they saw into terms that would work for him. On Saturday mornings, they wandered the streets, exploring antique shops, finding stores that sold a variety of inexpensive items, buying frugally but always with Mike's taste and comfort in mind.

"It's beginning to look like a home," he said, grateful for her help.

"It's time you gave a house-warming," she replied. "Made a party."

It was an idea he had never considered. But the more he thought about it, the more it appealed to him. He compiled a guest list and began phoning people the following Monday. He called Eddie Stander that afternoon. A sad, depleted voice answered. Eddie's mother.

"My son isn't living here anymore," she informed Mike. "He moved away."

Mike concealed his surprise and restrained an impulse to salve her hurt. "Is there any place I can reach him?"

She provided a phone number. He dialed. A soft, sexless voice came on the wire. "YMCA."

Mike checked the number. He had dialed correctly. He asked for Eddie. Seconds later the connection was made and the familiar dark voice came on.

"Yeah . . ."

"Eddie?"

"Who's this?"

"Mike. Mike Birns."

"Oh. Yeah."

"How are you, Eddie? It's almost two months since I saw you. I called your home and your mother told me . . ."

"What do you want, Mike?"

"I called to invite you to a party."

"I won't be able to come."

"You don't know when it is. How——"

"Look. I'm not going to parties. You understand? I'm busy. I've got things to do. Work. Important work. Now, is there anything else?"

"I don't get you," Mike burst out. "I thought we were friends. I call to—"

The phone went dead.

On Thursday of that same week, Eddie called back. Mike's initial impulse was to slam the phone down in return, but he didn't.

"I was wondering," Eddie said, in a voice heavy with desperation, "if you would have dinner with me tonight. . . ?"

Mike hesitated. He had hoped to meet Jean for dinner. He could call her, explain. She would understand. "All right, Eddie. Where and when?"

They met at Goldie's. Eddie was at the bar when Mike arrived. The glowering visage was drawn and unhappy, with swollen pouches under his eyes and deep gashes etched in the corners of his mouth.

Mike ordered a drink. "You look terrible," he said, his manner easy.

Eddie grunted. "I feel worse. That dirty rotten bastard. I'd like to kill him." The fingers of his right hand doubled into a fist. He knuckled the bar. "He beat her up again."

"I didn't know that."

"Hitting his own wife, the bastard. What kind of a man hits a woman, forces her to live in a hotel with an infant daughter? He thinks he can make her come back to him. He's crazy. You know that, crazy."

In profile, Eddie looked older than his years, features turned down, heavy, words coming slowly from between trembling lips.

"What about you, Eddie? What have you been doing?"

Eddie rocked his head from side to side in an uneven motion. "That sonofabitch. He's having her followed. Trailed around by some cruddy little private detective, as if she's some kind of a slut. To do that to a girl like Maggie. He knows she sees me."

"Then why?"

"To build a case. To go into court and make a case for adultery. So he can embarrass her. So he won't have to pay alimony."

"Are you sure about the detective?"

Eddie glared at him, lips working. "What the hell kind of a dumbass question is that? Sure I'm sure. Maggie told me. And I've spotted the crumb a couple of times. A ratty-looking guy, trying to appear casual, disinterested. But there's no doubt what he's up to. Once on Third Avenue and another time along the river. Doing that to Maggie, to a great girl like Maggie. He ought to be ashamed." He shifted closer to Mike, voice lowered, eyes wider. "It isn't as if we're sleeping together, you see. We're not. It would be stupid to risk anything. Give Roy a chance to build a case. We go for walks and have a drink or see a movie. That's *all*. The bastard. He ought to let her go."

"Do you intend to marry her?"

"As soon as she's free. I love her, Mike. I really love her. Let's face it, hoping from bed to bed, that's not for me. It's Maggie I want. I think about how it would be, to be married to her, to be with her all the time, to have more children. . . ."

Mike finished his drink. "How about some spaghetti for dinner?"

"Whatever you want."

"Original Joe's okay?"

There were two restaurants in the same block on Third Avenue, each laying claim to the name Original Joe's. They went to the one nearest Sixtieth Street and found a table along the mirrored wall.

They ordered spaghetti and salad and some Chianti and Eddie explained how he came to be living at the Y. "I couldn't stand it at home anymore. My mother is a killer. I mean literally. What she does to my father, the way she treats him. She rips him, tears him to pieces, dismembers the poor bastard. How can a man let a woman do that to him? I couldn't live with it anymore. And it's destroying my kid sister. She's seventeen. A good kid, gentle, and confused. She needs something to hold onto. Someone to look up to, to believe in. I can't do it anymore. But I want to help her. I'm looking for a psychiatrist. She needs help."

"Is that what she wants?"

Eddie stared into his wine glass. "Sure, that's what she wants. I talked to her, convinced her."

"Have you found a doctor?"

"I will."

Mike decided to change the subject. He produced an encouraging smile. "How's the writing coming? Living alone gives you a great opportunity——"

Eddie broke in. "My writing, that's a private area. For me alone. I don't talk about it."

Mike nodded and sipped some wine. The Chianti had an acceptable bite to it. He smeared butter on a chunk of bread. Chewing absently, he allowed his eyes to work around the room. A pretty blonde girl caught his attention. She looked up and moistened her mouth. He thought about Jean and turned away.

Eddie milked the fingers of one hand, then the other. The wary eyes swam into focus. His voice, when he spoke, was gravelly, almost inaudible. "I'm in trouble, Mike. Bad trouble. I don't know what to do."

"If it's money," Mike said. "I've got a few dollars. . . ."

Eddie shoved out his right arm, yanked at the sleeve of his jacket. The thick white wrist was crisscrossed with crimson welts. "I tried to kill myself." He cleared his throat and now the words came out clearly, almost good-naturedly. "As you can see, I used a razor and botched the job. Dependency and hopelessness, Freud says, are the motivating factors in a potential suicide. He claims that no one kills himself who doesn't wish to kill someone else. I can't argue with Freud. But I really don't want to harm anyone." A vagrant smile came and went. "Do you know that men commit suicide three times as often as women in this country? I've been reading up on it ever since . . ." He broke off and pulled at his sleeve. His brow bunched and his eyes went glassy again. "Jesus, I couldn't even finish myself off."

"What can I do?" Mike said quietly, after a lengthy interval.

Eddie made an effort to concentrate. "All I ever really wanted was to play shortstop for the Giants."

"That damned curveball. Too tough to hit."

"The bastards are curving me to death." Eddie jammed his knuckles against his teeth. Mike waited patiently. "When I write, nothing comes. Nothing that matters. Stiff sentences. Clumsy similes. Hollow phrases. I'm so fucking A-one smart, why don't I have something to say?"

"There are all kinds of writing."

"Don't patronize me. I've got it, something in me that's worthwhile. Important. Something meaningful. Why won't it come out?" He leaned forward, gripping tightly at Mike's forearm. "Can you imagine what it must be like to be a Hemingway or Jackson Pollack? To have all that genius seething around in your guts." He measured Mike narrowly, released his arm. "You don't know. You're interested only in getting your gun off. You can't imagine greatness. A lousy press agent."

"Ease off, Eddie."

"Shit. The worm of discontent is eating away at my insides. I can't work. I can't be with the woman I love. I can't even kill myself. Don't tell me to ease off, you smug bastard. How could you know what a man like me feels?"

In that instant, all compassion for Eddie drained away. Mike refused to act as a whipping post for the other man. He stared into Eddie's eyes. "I imagine you could really pull it off, if you wanted to die."

Eddie showed his surprise. Shock, almost. "That's a rotten thing to say. You know how that makes me feel, like smashing your face, really smashing it."

Mike grinned mirthlessly. "I may be the nearest thing to a friend you've got. Can you afford to dump me?"

"Ah," Eddie said presently, "I'm not going to hit you."

"Why don't you get a square job?" Mike said. "Keep occupied. This way is no good."

Eddie sat hunched, head low, as if too heavy for his neck. "I tried. I sent out résumés. I phoned people. I made appointments for interviews. When the time comes, I shave and dress and go to whatever agency it is. I get to the front door and put my hand on the knob and you know what, Mike, I can't turn the knob. Isn't that a pisser! I can't turn the knob, can't open the door, can't go inside. So I go back to the Y and stay in my room."

Mike let his breath out slowly, silently.

Eddie was talking again. "It's true about finding a psychiatrist for my sister. The poor kid. I spoke to a doctor yesterday. Someone sound. A Freudian, of course, with all the proper credentials. Not one of those quacks. A real analyst. Four, five times a week. I went to the library afterward, took out some of Freud's writing. I want to know what I'm doing."

"I don't know what you mean."

"I talked to the doctor about Sheila. For almost the entire hour. When I was finished, the doctor looked at me for a long time and then he said, 'What about you?' Isn't that a joke? What about *me?* He thinks I should come to him as a patient. He said never mind about Sheila, that I needed help."

"What are you going to do?"

"Twenty-five bucks a session. Four times a week. Where am I going to find that kind of money? I've got a few thousand and when that's gone . . ."

"Then you're not going?"

Eddie pushed his plate aside. He had eaten none of the spaghetti. His eyes fluttered and his hand came up to his mouth. "Dammit," he said, from behind his palm. "Dammit, yes, I'm going. I'm so goddamned scared. So goddamned scared . . ."

Chapter VIII

Neil and Susan

It was Sunday, the Labor Day weekend. A volleyball tournament was scheduled, a case of beer to the winning team. Neil's team was eliminated when it lost the second game played. Afterward Neil railed at his teammates over their failure to take the game seriously enough. They walked off and left him standing alone.

He went back to the house and put on sweat socks and sneakers for a final sprint across the island. From seaside to the bay, he made it in 3:10. His worst effort since the beginning of August. He rested for five minutes before running back, determined to improve on his record. He checked his stopwatch. 3:17. Breathing hard and furious with himself, he strode into the house and dropped a couple of ice cubes into a tall glass, filled it with orange juice, and went into the living room.

Susan sat in the big wicker chair, a glass in one hand. Her tight burnished face was withdrawn, almost sullen as she stared up at him.

"What are you drinking?" he said.

"Vodka," she said deliberately. "With tonic. But not much tonic." She lit a cigarette, inhaling deeply.

"Smart," he said, sitting on the couch. "Kill yourself."

She grinned thinly. "You lost the tournament."

"It doesn't matter."

"I'm glad you lost."

He stared at her without comprehension. "That's a stupid thing for you to say."

"Everybody isn't like you. Everybody isn't trying to become perfect, to win all the time. Most of us lose more than we win."

"I suppose there's a point to all this."

"Why does it all have to go your way, Neil? Why must you manage everything and everyone?"

"You must be drunk."

"Why can't you permit other people to go their own way? If they don't want to play to win, they don't have to. Let people make their own mistakes, suffer or not, as they please."

"You don't talk this way sober."

She heaved the glass at him. It missed, smashed against the wall behind the couch. He stared at her with no change of expression. "Did that make you feel better?"

She heaved herself erect, ran up the stairs to their bedroom. He finished the orange juice and went after her. She was shoving clothes into a valise.

"What do you think you're doing?" he demanded.

She answered in a tight voice, without turning. "I'm leaving."

"What is that supposed to mean?"

She jerked around. The sun-tanned skin of her face was blotched, the dark eyes glittering. Her ordinarily shrill voice climbed even higher. "I am leaving, Neil. Leaving this place. Leaving you."

"You are drunk," he said, after a moment. "You must be, to say such a wild thing."

"I mean it. I want a divorce."

He stared at her. After a long interval, his lips tightened and he began to blink. "There will be . . . no . . . divorce. For better or worse. Till death do us part."

She shook her head. "I'm going away and taking BB with me."

"Just like your whorish friend, Maggie. Who have you been screwing on the side?"

The words sobered her. He sounded remarkably like her own father, on that long ago night, spitting out denunciations of her mother.

"I used to think that you were the best man in the

world, Neil. The only man. I was wrong. And it hasn't to do with bed. But even there, you are not the beginning and the end for me."

"You admit it! You've been unfaithful to me! Who is he? I'll kill him."

It was difficult for her not to laugh. "I don't think you're prepared to discuss fidelity with me, Neil. You might have to explain Roberta Davis, explain about too many girls like her."

That frightened him. For the first time he realized that she was worldly and perceptive enough to comprehend the life he had led away from her. He took a step forward. She retreated.

"We can talk about this," he said.

"There's nothing to talk about."

"Do you intend to marry this man?"

"I want to be free, Neil. Free of you, to be able to think for myself. To act for myself."

"You can't leave me," he said speaking rapidly. "I won't let you."

"You can't stop me." She turned back to her packing.

His mind reached out to his father. What would *he* say? He would never let a woman get away with such a thing. "You mustn't do this, Susan," he muttered. "You really mustn't."

She glanced up at him. His face was bloated and his eyes moist.

"I'll do anything you want, Susan. Live any way you want. But you mustn't go away. I couldn't live without you. I'd be lost. Empty." He took a single step forward and improbably, incredibly, unnervingly, sank to his knees in front of her, clutching at her, face raised beseechingly. "Do you hate me so much? To treat me this way. I'll do whatever you want. If he's important to you, this man, see him. Keep seeing him. Anything, as long as you stay with me. Anything you want . . ."

She tried to move away, but his grip tightened and she was immobilized. Her hands went to his head as if to balance herself. He buried his face between her thighs. The smell of her, strongly female and almost overwhelming, made him light-headed, giddy. And through the giddiness, through the thick muskiness, through the tears and the torment, his brain pitched and tipped in a triumphant jig.

For he knew that he had won, that she would remain with him, that he would be safe.

He made a silent vow to be more careful in the future. To invent a thousand small ways to tie her closer to him, until she was completely dependent, to erode all desire to rid herself of him. She had become a plus factor in his existence, her dramatic beauty a visible merit badge to his taste, to his own attractiveness, his ability to travel first class. And in the future he envisioned, she would prove to be an even more valuable asset.

"Oh, no, Neil," she murmured weakly. "If I stay with you, you'll have to allow me more room to be myself, to find my own place. . . ."

"Anything."

She quivered under his mouth and he wondered what it would be like to do it to her that way. It was an act he had always reserved for other women, an act performed outside the sanctity of marriage. But now . . . it might bind her more tightly.

"I want to make you happy," he said, tugging at her bathing suit.

She stopped him, stepped toward the door.

"Where are you going?" he said, the fear flooding back over him.

"To get another drink. Then I'll come back and you can do whatever you want."

He slumped down on the floor, gloating in his victory. A terrific victory! On the edge of disaster, he had kept hustling, charging, going after what he wanted, utilizing every weapon he had, breaking through finally. A *winner*. A fantastic victory. He strained to hear her footsteps on the stairs, anxious for her to come back, wishing he could put an end to the flow of tears and the blinking.

Chapter IX

Mike

Hurricane warnings were posted the following Wednesday and by the next morning the reports became increasingly pessimistic. Neil Morgan made his decision. He drove out to the island that afternoon, brought his wife and son back to the safety of the city.

By Friday, the storm grew hesitant, standing off the coast of North Carolina, measuring the bulge of the continent with a jaundiced eye.

"Shall we chance it?" Mike asked Jean that afternoon.

"Let's."

The ferry ride from Bayshore was across a choppy bay and it began to rain by the time they made it to the house. A sense of impending danger heightened the experience for them both and they drank hot toddies and broiled steaks over the open fire, listening to the wind and the rain on the shingles.

After dinner they put on rain gear and went out on the dunes to watch the ocean. The gray hillocks were foam-topped and flicked spray high into the air. Waves rolled up the beach, almost to the dunes themselves.

"Is it going to be dangerous?" Jean wanted to know.

He made himself appear nonchalant. "We'll listen to the radio reports. If it gets too bad, we can always leave."

They went back to the house and drank some more and

made love on the floor in front of the fireplace. Afterward Mike laughed.

"Imagine if Neil walked in, found us this way. He'd have a fit."

They fell asleep in place, covered only with a patchwork quilt. Mike woke once and listened to the sea; the waves sounded closer now, more threatening, and the house creaked and groaned under the buffeting wind. When next he woke, Jean was sitting up, shaking him, a startled expression on her face.

"What is it?" he said.

"Do you hear a knocking?"

He listened. Someone was pounding on the door. He found his robe and answered. A Coast Guardsman in oilskins stood there. "Hurricane due by morning," he shouted, over the din of the storm. "The cutter's at the ferry slip. Be there in twenty minutes."

Mike went back inside and told Jean to get dressed. She stood up, naked and pale, obviously very frightened. "It's all right," he assured her. "They're going to take us off the island. Get dressed."

She obeyed wordlessly and he appreciated her calm efficiency. He finished first, began stuffing some of his belongings into a bag. When she was ready, they put on their ponchos and, bending against the wind, headed into Ocean Beach.

The Coast Guard had provided a forty-one-foot diesel-powered cruiser. But on the angry waters of Great South Bay it was heaved about like a rudderless skiff. Mike and Jean huddled together on the open deck, backs against the storm.

"Are you all right?" he asked.

She looked up. Her face was glistening and she laughed. "My first adventure!" she cried.

"You're insane," he cried over the wind.

She shouted back. "Mike, I love you."

He kissed her. Her mouth tasted of salt water. "I love you."

She pressed closer and put her mouth to his ear. "Isn't it time you asked me to marry you?"

He was aware of his heart thumping and the thickness in his throat. Did he want to get married to anyone? If he told her he didn't, would she leave him? It was a risk he didn't dare take.

"I am asking you," he heard himself say.

"I'll make you a very good wife, darling."

She raised her mouth and he kissed her. "I love you," he said, afraid of what he was doing. And glad.

At four-thirty-two the next morning, they were asleep in Mike's bed in the apartment on Lexington Avenue. At that precise moment, the high seas sent sideswiping waves along the beach, undercutting the pilings that supported Neurotics Anonymous, hooking the house off its foundation, sweeping it out to sea. Only the black pilings were left behind to mark its former place.

The second summer was over.

FIVE

THE LAST SUMMER

From the first weekend, the weather was superb. And got better. After a hot and humid week in July, the days were bright and clear, the sky high, the horizon floating at infinity.

That was the summer they murdered Martin Luther King. And Bobby Kennedy. And cops and blacks shot it out. The summer of the political conventions, of Nixon and Humphrey, of the Soviet invasion of Czechoslovakia.

That summer parties were given to raise funds for Paul O'Dwyer and Eugene McCarthy. And people argued over William Styron's Nat Turner *and the reaction of the black critics. That was also the summer many people said they would not come back to the island, that they would leave New York, leave America.*

That summer Frank and June Liebman gave a costume party for two hundred and fifty people. Uniformed guards kept out the uninvited while inside the house June did her belly dance on the bar, stripping off her clothes, as usual, while her husband accompanied her on the recorder.

That summer a deck collapsed at Bayberry Dunes during a cocktail party, breaking three arms and two legs. That summer three tough youths from Bayshore mugged a middle-aged homosexual at Cherry Grove and later raped two girls at Davis Park. It was the summer the shoreline at Ocean Beach was deeply cut by the sea and a policeman was assigned to keep day visitors from eating on the sand.

That summer a wasp bit the Michelson's youngest son in the eye. And a harlequin Great Dane sent his stream into the face of a man sleeping on the beach. And the beach taxis were allowed no farther west than Point o' Woods, until after six. Four marriages broke up and two others were made, and a number of young wives committed their first indiscretions. All of it happened during that last summer. . . .

Chapter I

Eddie

They would buy the house. Oh, yes, it would require a lot of work, most of which would fall into her lap, and it came up short of what she really wanted, but it would do. All things considered. Her eyes worked around the huge corner room. The high ceiling, the French doors opening onto the expanse of lawn to the rear, the huge working fireplace, the delicate parquet floor. The master bedroom, the agent had informed them. Edith Stander grinned at the description. Master, *hell*. She would rule in this room, just as she would command in all the others.

Footsteps sounded above her. Eddie and the agent. They crossed to the staircase, began the descent. Three floors, eighteen rooms. Plus a three-car garage. Wasted space, so much of it. But something to mention, a badge of honor—in a manner of speaking—of accomplishment.

She had made up her mind to close off the top floor, use only the other two. That was enough to keep her busy. Eddie would have to pay for a maid, at least twice a week. She wasn't about to break her back. A real house in Westport, Connecticut. Wow! Wait until her mother heard the news.

She had experienced a brief moment of indecision. Westport was frightening, the distance from Flatbush measured in more than miles. But no more frightening or different than Eddie Stander had been when they met. From the first she had figured him only as a short-term fling. A few laughs. A change of pace from the sort of man she was used to.

She had never known anyone like Eddie. And she was sure he was out of her league in his J. Press sports coats and Lloyd & Haig shoes. That other world she had never known about, the so very chic and expensive shops on Madison Avenue. Press, Chipp's, Arthur Rosenberg, the others. Small, most of them, the salespeople quiet and low-pressure, establishing *relationships* with their customers. Eddie sometimes received phone calls from a salesman named Jack. "Some exquisite shirting materials came in this morning, Mr. Stander, and I was sure you'd want to see them first chance." "A shipment of silk and wool cravats from England, Mr. Stander. Superb colorings and fabrics. You'll want some, I know." Worse than women, the men who patronized those shops, seriously discussing the placement of a button, considering the fall of a trouser leg. They were discreet and discriminating, understating everything, giving the impression of not caring how they looked, as if they were above and beyond such superficial matters. They weren't, she knew. That stylish carelessness was a carefully contrived and arrived-at end, the result of much planning and considerable expenditure. Hypocritical bastards.

Eddie and the agent appeared and she turned her round face to them, a pleasant smile on the plump mouth. "Have you reached a decision, darling?" she said, with a helpless dependence.

Eddie passed his hand across his round bald head in what had become a characteristic gesture. "It's a little large for our use," he replied carefully. "And a bit overpriced, I'd say."

The agent smiled a mirthless smile, tiny eyes behind rimless glasses cool and appraising. He'd played this scene before. Many times. "There are other folks interested . . ." He let it hang there.

Edith gave him the full benefit of her capped teeth. "There would have to be, Mr. Chandler, it's such a lovely house. But it is old and requires a great deal of money to make it livable, I'm sure you agree."

"Eighteen rooms, Mrs. Stander," Chandler cooed. "Plus

the garage and two and a half acres. A considerable purchase."

"What do you think?" Eddie said, trying not to sound anxious, and failing. He drew his brow together worriedly.

Chandler addressed him with manly intimacy. "Consider the deal, Mr. Stander. You won't do better anywhere. But don't take too long. If someone else says yes, I'll have to close the deal. Give me a ring on Monday."

"Yes, do that, darling," Edith said coolly. The house would be unsold in a day or so. She intended to extract a firm commitment from Eddie before closing the deal. She had no intention of tolerating recriminations later on. After all, she reasoned, this was going to place them in economic hock for a long time. It meant he'd have to keep that lazy nose of his to the grindstone, meant he'd have to hustle, a commuter for the next twenty years or so. She looped her arm in his and gazed up into his face.

"We'll discuss it, Eddie, and you phone Mr. Chandler when you've reached a decision, darling."

Eddie nodded quickly. There was very little that had to be said because he'd already made up his mind. Westport, by Christ! Wait'll the word got around. Wait'll some of those snotty bastards along the Avenue heard about this move. Those cocksuckers who'd laughed behind his back during his troubles, all the way back to the Leona Tate days. Eighteen rooms in Westport. They'd choke laughing over *that*.

It was going to be worth the effort, the money, the travel. He visualized himself riding the New Haven into the city every morning, reading *The Times*, getting friendly with the other men on the train, establishing friendships, new business contacts. And during the day, while he was involved in the limitless details of his work, Edith would be back in Westport taking care of his house. Raising his children. *Children.* Two were not nearly enough; he wanted a large family. He could see himself old, but vigorous still, surrounded by his sons and daughters, his grandchildren. Perhaps great grandchildren. Why not? He was strong and healthy.

"Yes," he agreed. "We'll discuss it and reach a decision."

Chapter II

Mike

Milton Vaccaro spread his hands helplessly, but the swarthy hawkface remained impassive. There was a crisp professionalism to his voice.

"I say it to you the way it is."

Mike Birns made a face. "But I don't have to like it."

"Maybe you think it's my fault," Vaccaro said slowly. "Maybe you'd rather split, find another agent."

"Milton, you want to dump me, say so. Otherwise, knock it off."

"I do my best for you, Mike. I want you to understand. Sometimes writers get hung up. A change can do them good, any change. Even an agent as good as I am can only do so much," he ended, grinning.

Mike grunted and slid lower on his spine. The reviews of the book had been uniformly good, some raves, all promising much for its success. Four film producers had asked for copies and additional submissions had been made. The result—a blank. Not a nibble. No talk of even an option. A groan of despair died in Mike's throat. This book was the one that was going to do it for him, take him around that corner where the Golden Lady stood waiting with open arms. And only now did he realize just how much he wanted to make it with her. Perhaps if the new book were going better he would not have been so disappointed. But a new element had been introduced. Or rather an old one—fear. Fear of failure. More, he was too old to be marking time, drifting aimlessly.

"Tell me what you want me to do," Vaccaro said, pulling him back.

Tell 'em to shove it, Mike ordered himself with silent courage. He didn't need their crumbs. Didn't want it. A swirling uneasiness lodged in his belly and he straightened up. "Five thousand is the best they'll do?"

"That's it. If I thought there was more to be had, I'd go after it. It's a one-shot and TV is not springing for the big money."

"I hoped this book was going to do it."

"You listen to your Uncle Milton," Vaccaro said, leaning across the desk. "I say you're going to make it to the big leagues. Just a question of time. You're better than you know, better than what you've been."

There was the irony, Mike reflected. Who could say how good a man he was, how good a writer, until he proved out. Produced the best that was in him. Wrote the best book.

"The new book stinks, Milton." He waited but Vaccaro said nothing. "I mean, it just doesn't work. It's as if I can't make up my mind whether to write another mystery or a straight novel." He looked at a point on the wall behind the agent. "That talk about me doing something better, Milton. You really think I've got it in me?"

"Y'know, Robert Louis Stevenson considered himself as nothing but a writer of thrillers. He wrote Jekyll and Hyde as a thriller. Later he destroyed the manuscript and rewrote it entirely as a serious work. I think mysteries have been a prelude for you, Mike. An apprenticeship. I've seen you grow, watched your skills develop, seen your thinking become freer, take on new depths. It's in your work, Mike. You should read your own books, see how they've changed for the better." He folded his hands in his lap. "Of course, no amount of talk will convince you. This is something you've got to find out about yourself, for yourself."

"When is this miracle of internal revelation going to take place?" He stood up, sat down again. "A mystery, that's a tight form. A plot. Action to carry the reader along. You don't have to fret about characters too much, about the overall environment, about *meaning*."

"Yet all of those things exist in your work. More so now than ever. When you're able to see it, you will. When you're no longer afraid to see it."

"Well, thank you, Dr. Freud. When I'm not afraid! Dammit, you know better than that. I'll always be afraid. That's the constant in writing, the fear. The fear that it will simply stop working for you, that magic power that makes you write, that dark and mysterious piece of yourself that functions in its own time and its own way."

"I think there's a better Mike Birns in you than you dare admit."

"Sure," Mike said with mild bitterness. "You know it and I know it. Try to get elected on that backing." He stood up and went to the door, swung back. "Call the man at the network. Take the money."

The next morning Cindy Ashe thrust herself into his life.

He was in no mood to work when he woke, no mood for much of anything. He went to the corner and bought the *Times* and came back to the apartment. He drank orange juice while waiting for the coffee. When it was ready, he carried a mugful into the living room and sprawled out, reading the sports pages first.

The phone rang and he debated whether or not to answer. Curiosity won out.

"Is this Mike Birns, the famous and handsome writer?" a female voice began.

"Who is this?"

"Guess."

He hung up. Seconds later, the phone rang again. He picked it up.

"Don't hang up, Mike. Please."

"Who is it?"

"Cindy Ashe, you terrible man."

It took a long moment before he made the connection.

"Are you always so rude to women who call?" There was a flirtatious note in her voice.

"Okay, Cindy, what's the occasion for this call?" he said, with mock severity.

"It's like I said, you're a famous and handsome writer." A tentative laugh came over the wire.

"Knock it off, kid," he said, doing his imitation of Bogart.

She laughed again. "You are a writer," she said. "And I thought you might want to help me. I'm having some kind of trouble with a paper I'm supposed to do. For English Lit. Analysis of the contemporary novel. I've done the research but the writing is simply blah, Mike."

"Well . . ."

"I know I'm imposing, but if you'd just read the paper, criticize. Honestly, I mean. I wouldn't want to put you to any trouble so I'd come over there. . . ."

"All right," he said slowly. "When do you want to come?"

"Now."

"Oh. All right."

Forty minutes later, he admitted her to the apartment. In a loose-fitting miniskirt and a yellow sleeveless sweater she looked like the college freshman that she was.

"I'd forgotten how pretty you are," he told her.

She curtsied and grinned up at him. "Thank you, kind sir."

There was a faint resemblance to Maggie, but her features were softer, and there was a more sensual cast to her mouth. Her hair was darker than he remembered, pulled back off her forehead, gathered at the nape of her neck. Her eyes were large and steady. Unlike Maggie, she was full-busted with round hips and her legs were strong and shapely.

"Well," he said, the amenities out of the way, "let me read your paper and see if I can help."

She handed it to him. Five typewritten pages in which she discussed the work and relative literary merits of Norman Mailer, John Barth, John Updike, and Bernard Malamud. It was a thoughtful essay, tightly structured, the prose concise and clear. It required no help from him. He looked up to tell her so.

She sat opposite him, uncrossing and crossing her legs. There was a flash of the pale underside of her thighs. A thick glob of emotion lodged in his chest. He forced himself to look directly into her eyes.

He said, "You write very well."

"You're kind to say so."

"I'm telling you what I believe," he said carefully. There was something about her, a taunting glitter in the wide eyes, a sense of her own physical place in space. It troubled him. He stood up. "I'm going to have another cup of coffee. Would you like some?"

"I'd like a drink."

He turned away. "You're seventeen years old. Too young to drink."

Her laughter trailed him into the kitchen. "Are you afraid of corrupting a minor?" she called gaily.

He offered no response.

"Did you hear what I said?" Her voice was quiet, controlled, from a place close behind him. He spoke without turning. "Go back inside. Sit down. I'll be there in a couple of minutes."

Her laugh was thick this time, a short, chesty sound. Full of mockery and promise.

"Are you afraid of me, Mike?"

He turned to face her. He'd forgotten how tall she was. Or had he ever noticed? She stood an arm's length away and the scent of her drifted into his nostrils—warm and provocative.

"I think you'd better go, Cindy."

"I haven't gotten what I came for."

"I read your paper."

"That was only an excuse." She threw back her head, thrust out her chest. "Look at me, Mike. Don't you think I'm good-looking? Most men do. They think I'm a real groovy chick. I have to fight them off, those I want to fight off."

"Out," he ordered.

She didn't move. "What are you worried about?" Her brow furrowed, then smoothed out. "You don't think you'd be the first! Oh, man, I lost it when I was thirteen. It happened on Fire Island," she went on conversationally. "Do you know Tim Craig? His wife and Maggie are good friends. He initiated me one night. I had been baby sitting, and on my way back home I met him coming out of Leo's. He'd been drinking and was flying low. He started kissing me and feeling me. I was a little scared, I guess, but it felt pretty good too. He took me out on the beach and laid me on the dunes."

"I don't believe you."

"It's true. Since that first time there have been forty-one different men. Including a couple of gang-bangs when I hustled."

He took a deep breath, remembering all the women he had known. All the faceless women. "I want you to go now. Take your paper and go."

"I don't want to," she murmured. "You see, I picked up one of your books in a paperback bookstore. And that turned me on. It made me realize that I'd never made it with a writer. Judy Brookeman made it with a writer. Two of them, she says. And she claims they were the best she ever had. Why don't I get undressed?" She unhooked the miniskirt and it fluttered to the floor. She stepped out of it. Very quickly, she took off the black lace panties she wore.

"There," she said, smiling at him. "Now the sweater."

There was a kind of detachment about it, as if he stood outside himself watching, as if he was in fact no part of this moment. Only an observer. The psychologists had a name for it—ego-splitting. He viewed her naked, her breasts heavy round globes with soft brown centers. She drifted closer, hands reaching for his belt.

"Now," she murmured through the shimmering veil. "Now I'll do you. . . ."

The word broke out of him with explosive force. *"No!"* He brushed past her into the living room. He spun around. She was following, thighs rubbing sensuously against each other, breasts taut and gleaming, a hooded, knowing expression on that unlined face.

"Get dressed!" he managed, voice cracking. "I want you out of here."

She stared at him in disbelief. "You're putting me on."

"Right now, Cindy."

Her face clouded over. "Oh, man, what a bust you are."

She disappeared into the kitchen and when she came out she was dressed again. She gathered up her belongings and walked, without urgency, to the door. "What a shame," she said, looking back at him. "All that fancy advertising and no goods in the shop."

Chapter III

Roy

Roy Ashe took pride in his office. Situated on the nineteenth floor of a new building in East Fifty-fourth Street, it looked down on Madison Avenue. Roy's private office was a large room with paneled walls and expensive modern furniture. A color television set occupied the space opposite the deep corduroy-covered couch. Another set, a small-screen portable, perched on the rosewood and stainless-steel desk. A bar and a club chair completed the decor.

Attaché case in hand, Roy went into the reception room. Helene glanced up from the magazine she was reading. A tall girl with bony features and a beehive of glittering gold hair, she was addicted to tight sweaters and short skirts. Roy hadn't decided whether or not to make it with her. There was so much gash, he reflected. Single-o, that was the way to go.

"I'm on my way to ABC, Helene."

"Yes, Mr. Ashe."

He looked past the edge of the desk at her legs. Long, curved gracefully heavy in the thigh.

"Nice view," Roy said, grinning.

She crossed her legs but made no attempt to adjust the skirt. "Thank you, Mr. Ashe. Will you be back today?"

"Make it worth my while and I will, Helene."

She pursed her lips. "You're teasing me, Mr. Ashe."

He pointed to her bulging breasts. "Are those real, Helene?"

"Mr. Ashe," she remonstrated gently.

"I may just arrange for you to work late some night."

"You're the boss, Mr. Ashe."

"Why not tonight?"

"Oh, I can't tonight. Tonight I have a date."

He went to the door. "Don't use it all up in one place, Helene. I'll call in later."

"I'm leaving at five o'clock, Mr. Ashe. On the dot."

"Call me Roy."

"Roy," she said.

Murray Baumgarten, being a vice-president, rated a corner office with carpeting and a desk of real walnut veneer. He invited Roy to sit, offered him a drink. Roy declined. He placed the attaché case on his lap and opened it, withdrew a manila folder, handed it to the other man.

"This is your library?" Baumgarten said. He was about forty but looked ten years older, his skin stamped with creases and furrows, his eyes almost invisible under sagging lids.

"Only the features," Roy answered. "Title, studio, producer, director, stars. Also running time uncut."

"Let's talk price."

Roy closed the attaché case. "That depends. What kind of a deal are you interested in?"

"A straight buy would be——"

"Not a chance," Roy put in. He grinned tightly. "I rent, Murray. That's all. All rights stay in my pocket, no matter what deal we make. Costs vary according to what the play is. Network or local. One shot or multiple play. There are some special cases in the list. Big pictures with big names. Built-in audience appeal that means massive ratings. For them, the ante goes up. Let me give you an example. . . ."

"Relax, Roy. I'll check the catalogue and make a decision. If the list is good, we'll do some business. Otherwise not." Baumgarten dropped the manila folder on his desk and leaned back in his chair. "You've done okay, Ashe. Your own library. I knew McNally wanted to sell but I never figured to you. Frankly, I wouldn't have believed you had that much bread."

Roy laughed too loudly. "A man works hard all his life, Murray, he accumulates a little loot. Right?"

"How'd you do it? For twenty years I've been pulling down good dough and I wouldn't be able to make the scene. Not with my responsibilities. You got a head for a buck, boy."

Roy decided it was time to change the subject. "When can I look for an answer, Murray?"

"Three days. Ring me then. I imagine I'll take some of your stuff."

Roy stood up. "Good deal. Three days. I'll need a decision because I'm going to swing around the East, peddling the library to local stations. I'll want to know where I stand with the network here. . . ."

Chapter IV

Judd Martin

An incredible gaffe. Judd Martin knew it and blamed only himself for the mistake. Turning his back on a sure thing for a longshot. He should've known it wasn't going to come off. She was too shrewd, a tough broad. Experienced. And she'd read him from the start.

To drop Susan Morgan for Harriet Davidson. Where were his brains, to go that route. Sure, Harriet had looked like a ticket to the pot of gold; wife of Irwin S. Davidson and clearly turned on to Judd's version of fun and games. He'd worked on her, figured she'd get him out to the Coast, talk her husband into signing him to write for one of those TV series of his. What a gravy train that would be!

But he'd struck out. Oh, he'd serviced Harriet almost every day while she was in New York. And she had promised to intercede with her husband. Judd had made her out to be a woman who got exactly what she wanted. But she'd been unable to swing it. *If* she had even tried, he amended bitterly. He swallowed an angry oath. Of course she hadn't tried. To her he was just another stud. A few laughs, a couple of bangs. Back on the Coast, she probably had a select stable of cats just like himself, happy to respond to her calls in return for an occasional job in television or films.

"Don't think I've quit on this, honey," were her final

words to him. "I'm going to keep working on Irwin. But he can be sutbborn sometimes and I have to be careful. I'll keep in touch, sweetie. . . ."

Cunt.

That had been Saturday morning in his room while she dressed. She'd hustled over for one last sampling of his kind of jazzing, making some excuse about last minute shopping. And that afternoon she and Irwin had flown back to Los Angeles, to Hollywood, to their mansion on top of a hill, complete with pool and tennis court.

Oh, *Jesus*. What did it take?

Now it was Tuesday and Judd was due at the unemployment office to sign for his check. That used up twenty minutes of his time and afterward he stopped off for some coffee, then strolled over to the playground in Central Park. He struck up a conversation with a pretty young mother and suggested that she accompany him back to his apartment. She laughed good-naturedly and said she wasn't at all interested.

He left her abruptly. Once back in his apartment, he soaked in a hot tub, smoking cigarettes, and letting his mind roam listlessly over the past weeks. He seldom goofed this way and be brooded over it. Susan Morgan had been real gold and he'd allowed himself to be diverted by a piece of glitter like some rank amateur. Weeks had passed since he had last seen Susan or spoken to her; he should have kept his hand in there somehow. An occasional visit or at least a phone call. The damage was done and there was no way of repairing it.

Or was there? He heaved himself erect and turned on the cold shower. The icy spray was almost painful, but he forced himself to suffer its sting. The warm lassitude drained away and his mind began to turn over. This was Tuesday and that meant Susan and her friend—Maggie was the name—would make the rounds of gallery openings tonight. That and Fire Island, he snickered. Toys in the same bag.

He got out of the tub and rubbed himself dry. Naked, he found the art section of the Sunday *Times*, tore out the list of openings. A couple of dozen. Too many to cover effectively. He picked up the phone and dialed. A disgruntled male voice came on.

"Shit man, you are bugging me."

That was Marc Levine. "Hey, baby, Judd Martin here."

"You interrupted my work."

"The word is you're making it, Marc. That you have cracked the Establishment."

"Shit, man," Levine said hotly. "You want small talk go somewhere else. I'm dropping the horn."

"Slow down, baby. Just want some advice. I'm hitting the galleries later on. Where's the action, I want to know."

"Oh, you are a sweet turd, Martin. You'd hustle your own mother for a free drink and some canapés."

Judd kept his voice light and cheerful. "I dig the art you cats produce."

The painter mentioned the names of four galleries. "In that order," he added. "Avant-garde, all of it. Some computer garbage and a sampling of plastic shapes and colored water. Bring a straight pin and puncture the bullcrap. The phonies will all be there. You'll love it."

"I am in your debt, baby."

"Shit, man."

Mike

At about that same time, a rising irritation gripped Mike Birns. A restless seething skimmed through his mind and body, a tide of mingled emotions, of desire and rage, of unclear thought and surging response. He struggled to pick apart the elements, to isolate and comprehend. Nothing happened.

Since eight that morning he had been tied to that diabolical machine. He attacked the typewriter and beat hasty retreats for six hours and came up with two and a half pages of ink marks for his effort. He snatched up the pages and stood in the light of the window and read what he had put down.

Nothing. Zero. A cipher.

Not one idea worthy of the name.

Not one character that interested him.

Not one well-designed phrase.

Garbage.

He read the pages again. There was no novel here, serious or otherwise. Not even the germ of one. Just pretentious prattling.

A cruel joke. Played by Elizabeth Jordan—stay dormant crotch; she is of the past—and Milton Vaccaro, oh, agent mine. Twin assaults on his ego, stimulating fantasies of a literary glory far beyond him, exciting him to believe he was more than he appeared to be. A man was only what he had done. The issue of his brain and of his body. Not more and likely less.

Mike Birns, mystery writer of no particular importance, was simply a collector of middleground rewards. That said it. He folded the pages into a ship, launched it in his kitchen sink, set it afire. A proper Viking funeral.

He would think of it no more. He put on jeans and a sweat shirt and went for a walk. It was a fine day, the sun bright and warm, the air clear. He wandered east, appraising the contents of shop windows, enjoying the great old apartment buildings with their trimwork of gargoyles and concrete scrolls.

He looked at girls.

May was an excellent month to look at girls. With warmer weather, they had shed their coats, moved at a brisk pace, breasts and bottoms cheerfully jiggling. Mike kept pace with a large brown-haired girl, admiring her immense round behind as it heaved and humped and swayed. After three blocks, he transferred his attention to a leggy model with shapeless limbs and a fine, free stride. He lost her at Bloomingdale's, switched over to a pair of young matrons strolling leisurely along Fifty-ninth Street. They minced ahead with little steps as if afraid of dropping something from between their inviolable thighs. A swift-walking black girl caught his eye and he followed her for a while, staying three appreciative strides to the rear. At Third Avenue, he split.

After a hot sausage and a Coke at Goldfinger's, he opted for a movie. Coronet, Baronet, Cinema I, Cinema II. All in one block. How to choose? He dug out two coins and flipped. Cinema I and Baronet made it to the finals. He flipped again. Baronet.

A lousy picture. He knew it was bad after five minutes. There was the usual tortured young man who found it difficult to talk to girls and impossible to talk to his parents. But he did like to play pinball machines, to watch the lights go on and off. Quick cut followed huge closeup followed tilted camera. Art, Mike noted. To hell with Art and Tortured Youth, too. He was riding tortured middle age.

Why didn't they make flicks about Mike Birns, ignoble loner in a world of abrasive couplings, a medium talent with nothing to say. If only he had dedicated himself to some Great Truth, to some Higher Cause, to some Literary Eternals. Then. *Then.* Then, he thought happily, he would be able to sell out. He was ready. If only someone would make him an offer. Peddle his artistic soul to the devil? Hell, yes. In return for one best-selling novel. One substantial movie sale. One book-club choice.

Selling out was no easy endeavor. That too took special talent, a gift nurtured and polished, carefully applied; he would gladly join the ranks. But to whom did one sell out? And how?

He went home and considered the problem. Perhaps he should write a novel about tortured youth. The conflict between generations and the strivings of the enlightened young to survive even as they maintained their purity of purpose. Or the tentative sexual strivings of a sensitive and innocent teenager. Why should the French maintain a monopoly over all the sensitive and innocent teenagers? It would make a marvelous film, he decided. Elizabeth Taylor could play the older, worldly wise woman who contributes her body to the education (and pleasure; forget not pleasure) of the gentle young man. He, naturally, would be portrayed by Dustin Hoffman.

Youth, he decided, tortured or otherwise, was a pain in the butt. Take Elizabeth Jordan. There was a prime example of tortured youth. Dumb dame. Marching through the jungle, naked and inviting attack. Another victim in search of an oppressor.

He would not think about her. He turned his attention to his friends, his family, to people he had met over the years, people who had drifted into his orbit and then drifted out again. All the girls, for example. And Harvey Futterman, an accountant who had embarked on a round-the-world journey by kayak. Harvey had made it as far as Atlantic City before the kayak capsized. And Frances Wallace, a political activist who had gone to Cuba when

Castro was fighting up in the Sierra Maestra, never to be heard of again. There was Tommy Bonds, who had been writing a novel that would contain everything Bonds had known or done. He had lived off malted milks and raw eggs and squirrels, which he killed in Central Park with a bow and arrows. The list was long: the Millers and the Woodwards, with their interesting sex habits, Roy and Maggie Ashe, *Cindy Ashe,* Eddie Stander, the Morgans. Jean, his former wife. There had been so many, people with aspirations and hopes, with needs and fears, a weird and wonderful bunch in many ways. Perhaps he should enshrine them in words. It was a distrubing idea, conjuring up a kind of self-probing that chilled him.

To hell with it.

Mysteries were his bag. And an honorable bag it was. Poe, Hammett, John Dickson Carr, Rex Stout, John Creasey. Solid writers all. First-rate performers. Professionals. Knowing who they were and what they were doing. As for the new book, he'd discover what mistakes he'd made, correct them, turn it into a typically well-crafted Mike Birns product.

Mike Birns wasn't Hemingway or Thomas Wolfe or Faulkner. No heavy muse motivated him; he had no pretensions to literary greatness. He was a mystery writer privately conceived and made, a role contrived carefully for himself by himself in order to create the kind of life he wanted.

Wanted!

Yes, that's what he wanted—to produce an exciting and entertaining dish. To mix the right ingredients, add the perfect seasoning, cook properly, and allow to simmer until the plot boiled over. Indeed, an exciting and entertaining dish.

Up yours, Milton Vaccaro.

And yours, Elizabeth Jordan.

Bug me no more.

He undressed and got into bed, tried to sleep. Couldn't. He changed positions, lay on his stomach. The pressure against his loins caused a physical pain. He needed a woman. He rolled onto his back and considered the problem. Who to call?

He phoned that big redhead at her office. "She's not

here anymore," a shrill female voice informed him. "Moved to Denver about six months ago."

He tried the one with the agile hips. Her voice was edged and defensive. "It's been nearly a year since we spoke. No, I won't have dinner with you."

Next, the oral Arab belly dancer. "Mike Birns? Fuck you, Mike Birns."

More calls. More rejections.

Married. Engaged. Seeing someone. Not interested. Resentful. Busy. Gone.

Finished. He was finished. Cut off from his past and without a future. No girl would have him. He would drift through the rest of his days celibate and miserable. Never again would he bathe in the liquid warmth of a woman's passion and love. Elizabeth was the cause of this calamity. She had exercised some subtle brand of witchcraft, suckered him into turning his back on all the others, isolated him, occupying his time so that he would not find replacements for those sweet ladies who went away.

What a cunning and delightful creature she was! A wild and imaginative bed partner, with that unique, athletic and soft, gentle and demanding body of hers. Experienced, with an overlay of naïveté. It amused him to remember his own naïveté in viewing her as an innocent. A virgin. He wondered how many men she had lain with. There was nothing she hadn't done, a girl with her appetites. He grew annoyed with himself. He should have kept her around, used her as she had used him.

He closed his eyes and visualized her undressing in front of him, slowly, letting him enjoy the progressive delights of her flesh. Now she was advancing on him in that deliberate way she had, legs reaching, thighs rubbing against each other, chin tucked down, peering at him from under her brows, a faint and promising smile bending that lush mouth. She was reaching, bending over him, uttering soft, sensual sounds back in her throat. Then she pleased him.

Eddie

The antique shop was on lower Second Avenue. A dim and musty place. Edith Stander, eyes glowing acquisitively, was waiting when her husband got there.

"You're going to love it," she greeted him, leading him toward the rear of the store. "I wanted your approval before I bought it."

He wet his mouth. "Bought what?"

"An authentic early American hutch. It dates back to seventeen sixty-three. Isn't that fantastic?"

A familiar sense of strain surged under Eddie's skin. "Edith, I don't have much time. I'm meeting some guys and this could be important to me. To *us*. Very important."

"Of course, dear. We'll look at the hutch right away."

A bony man with an olive complexion appeared and stood silently by, an encouraging half-smile on his thin mouth.

"This is my husband," Edith said. "Meet Mr. Michaels, dear."

Eddie grunted.

Mr. Michaels nodded.

"And here is the hutch," Edith said.

It stood against the side wall, a full seventy-two inches wide and equally as high, the wood richly burnished and obviously old, scarred here and there, with the square corners and scalloped wood skirts so typical of the period.

"It's just what we want," Edith enthused. "Don't you agree, honey?"

"How much?" Eddie said.

"It isn't cheap," she warned, squeezing his hand. "But such a beautiful piece."

"How much?"

Michaels answered, his voice whispery and distant. "Eighteen hundred and seventy-five dollars."

Eddie suppressed a groan.

"Why don't we discuss it, sweetheart?" Edith said. "We'll be back in a few minutes, Mr. Michaels. . . ."

Once in the street, Eddie turned to her, a worried frown

corrugating his naked pate. "Nineteen hundred bucks for a lousy hutch, Edith. Are you out of your mind?"

She maintained her calm. "It's a terrific buy. An investment. People seeing it, people coming to our home, Eddie, are going to know what kind of taste we have, what kind of a man my husband is."

"Don't do that, Edith."

"I mean it, Eddie. I want to be proud of my home. . . ." She went on, talking swiftly, manipulating, developing her case. He knew what she was doing yet couldn't help responding as she wanted him to. Damn, it *was* a great-looking hutch.

"That kind of money, Edith. My income is . . ."

"You make thirty-five thousand dollars a year, darling. That's seven hundred dollars each and every week."

"Not quite," he pointed out peevishly.

"My father never made seven hundred dollars in any single month of his life, darling."

"He didn't have a house in Westport with a mortgage. And he didn't have a wife who insisted on buying antiques."

She produced the frozen mask expression, stared up at him. "Very well. You've made your point. Let's go back. I'll tell Mr. Michaels we aren't taking the hutch, that we can't afford it."

"That's not fair, Edith."

"It's what you want, Eddie."

"I just want us to consider our expenses a little more carefully. We've already put out more than eight thousand for furniture, and a desk, a love seat, and a dining-room table is all we've got to show for it."

"The desk is for your study," she reminded him.

Neither of them spoke again until they were at the door of Mr. Michaels' shop. "Edith," he began, "you must remember that we've got less than five thousand left in savings. The money goes so damned fast. And expenses keep mounting. The children. Two cars. Plus Dr. Shanker and Miss Lockhart . . ."

"Miss Lockhart was your idea," she said stiffly. "A marriage counselor . . ."

"She's helped. We don't have those raging battles anymore.

She put her hand on his arm. "That's because we love

each other. Oh, darling, we can do without Miss Lockhart. I know I love you and want to make you happy."

"I want to make you happy, too."

"Then it's settled," she said happily. "No more Miss Lockhart. And while we're getting rid of expenses, why not Dr. Shanker, too? You don't have to have your head shrunk anymore."

"No," he said quickly. "Forget about Shanker. He's part of my life and when I'm prepared to terminate, I'll know it." He ducked his head, and she could see a layer of perspiration on the taut rough skin. "All right," he said. "Buy the hutch, if you want. But from now on, you'll have to be a little more conservative about money. Okay?"

She stretched up and kissed his cheek. "Of course, sweetheart. You run along to your meeting. I'll tell Mr. Michaels what we've decided before he sells it to someone else. . . ."

Susan

The Granger Gallery was one flight above Madison Avenue, its huge windows overlooking the street. Most people had already departed when Judd Martin got there and red-jacketed waiters were busy collecting empty champagne glasses. Judd went to the bar and when he had a drink in his hand looked for Susan Morgan. She wasn't there. He swore to himself. Things just weren't going his way. He decided to wait.

He drifted across the room to where a length of transparent plastic tubing coiled like a pink snake at rest.

"It could be used," a bosomy middle-aged blonde informed her skeptical companion. "Use your imagination, darling. See it as a flexible couch, curl it any way you like, *lay* all over it."

The man laughed. "Wouldn't you adhere to the plastic?"

"Darling, you have such a *practical* nature."

Judd moved on, studied the hangings. Within an ornate gilt frame, he discovered ordinary butter knives, crossed. Further on, an electric bulb painted sea-green. Next, a telephone, candy-striped, jutting straight out, with a pair of ping-pong balls dangling from its base.

"Is that supposed to be what I think it is?" a woman cooed.

"What else?"

"What a penetrating comment on our times!"

A waiter offered Judd another drink. He took it, then wandered behind a dividing panel at the rear of the gallery. There was Susan Morgan amidst a group of people, listening to a plump gray man who was delivering a short course on the purposes of modern art. He took a deep breath and moved toward her.

He took her to a dimly lit bar a few steps below street level and ordered martinis for them both. She reached for a cigarette and he lit it.

"Well," she said, without a smile. "You're trying, aren't you?"

"I don't know what you mean."

"I agreed to have a drink with you, Judd, because I was curious to see what technique you would use."

"Technique?" he asked cautiously.

She dragged on the cigarette. "You are going to try to get me back, aren't you?"

"I didn't know I'd lost you."

She laughed briefly. "What a bastard you are! You've been getting it from Harriet Davidson. You thought that would help with her husband. But it got you nowhere."

"I suppose I deserved that. Even if it isn't true. I haven't seen you for a couple of weeks . . ."

"Six weeks, to be exact."

"I got involved."

"With Harriet."

"With my work. I've been writing a new play."

Her laughter was edged with disbelief.

He stared at her with no change of expression. He couldn't indulge the anger he felt. Not now. Now he needed her. A story in *Variety* had announced that her husband was forming a new production company. He craved to be part of that.

"Sitting here and looking at you, Susan, I can almost taste you, the way you smell, the way you move under me. . . ."

"Stop it," she said quietly.

"You felt the same about me."

She swallowed half of her martini. "You're a walking hard-on, Judd, for any woman who might do you some good. I know that." A harsh sound trickled out of her. "Why don't you go into the business, Judd? Sell it outright. So much a hump."

He stared at her. "Maybe I should. You could be my first customer."

"Touché! How much will you charge me?" She cocked her head and eyed him speculatively. "How much would I pay? I confess you're good at your job."

"I'll make you a bargain price. Fifty bucks a throw." He pushed himself erect. "Thanks for nothing, Susan . . ."

"Where are you going?" she said.

He jerked around. "Back to my apartment."

"Without me?"

A slow grin of triumph slanted across his mouth. "For fifty a throw. . . ?"

She shrugged. "Why not?"

They sat facing each other on the floor, staring at the red light of the tape between them as it gave forth with Ravel's *Bolero*. Susan squinted at the furry crimson glow, trying to understand it. Somewhere locked in that core of light lay a precious secret that could reveal all truth to her.

Absently she placed the joint between her lips and sucked hard, swallowed the smoke. She sucked again and again. Beautiful . . .

"Last summer," she giggled.

"What happened last summer?"

"The police raided the Gilbert's house on the island and found some of this stuff. . . ."

"Marijuana."

". . . Arrested the Gilberts. We were having a party that night and someone came around trying to raise bail money. My husband was furious, claimed it was an intrusion on his privacy to come around that way, to inflict other people's troubles on us. He said if the Gilberts wanted to break the law they had to suffer the consequences. He would have a fit if he knew I was smoking marijuana."

"Aren't you glad I turned you on?"

"The music . . . so pretty . . . like nothing I ever heard . . . so pure . . ."

A random thought rose up in his brain. "Under mary-jane making it is like nothing in this world."

"Different?"

"Better. Goes on like forever. A come that won't quit."

"From a little cigarette?" she marveled.

He crawled toward her, the journey taking forever. At last he arrived, pushing her backward onto the floor, lifting her skirt, dragging at her panties. Sound leaked into all the spaces of her skull and reverberated like holy bells.

"Oh furry grail!"

He fell forward, plunging into her in a single motion and she sensed a new freedom, an openness. She received him with a crazily tilting joy.

"Ah . . ."

"Jesus . . ."

"Great, huh?"

"Best ever . . ."

"Go forever."

After an eternity it ended and her insides were empty, aching. A chilling terror spread. . . .

"Forever, right."

"Forever . . ."

"A dozen times."

"More . . ."

"Flooded with protein."

"Fantastic," she sobbed.

"You're crying," he said with clinical concern after a while.

She hid her face in her hands and he lost interest.

Chapter V

Mike

Maureen Sawyer was her name but everyone called her Tom. The rooming house she ran on the last street in Ocean Beach was called Tom Sawyer's Inn. No matter how popular and crowded Fire Island became, Mike had always been able to rent a room from Tom Sawyer at the last moment.

Memorial Day fell on a Thursday that year which meant a long weekend; the island would be flooded with people. But Mike's luck held.

"Won't be able to give you one of the grander rooms," Tom Sawyer said when Mike phoned on Tuesday. "Can't let you have Tom's Suite or Huck's Place. But Jim's Room is available. . . ."

It rained Tuesday and Wednesday, almost five inches falling in the city, and he thought about canceling the reservation. There was nothing worse than spending a weekend in a rooming house. But when he woke Thursday morning the sun was shining and he took the early train.

On the ride out he allowed his mind to reach back over the years. So much had happened since those first summers. So much was different.

He thought about Jean, of the disintegration of their marriage. It had ended abruptly, all the soft, diseased places exposed in an epidemic of frustration and disappointment. The failure had been his, he still believed, the result of a flawed character.

How long since he had really thought about Jean? How long since he last saw her? There had been an attempted reconciliation after the divorce, a three-month affair, the time spent mostly in bed. The sex had been more intense than ever, more obsessive. Yet nothing had really changed.

Away from bed they still fought, argued over the most trivial things, hitting out at each other over his failure to shave before making love, over the worsening quality of life in New York, over which restaurant served the best *antipasto*. Had they really battled over such trivial matters? It was difficult to recall with certainty.

Children was what they were. Overgrown and playing at adulthood. How much, he wondered, had he grown in the years since? No satisfactory answer came.

The ferry was new. Sleek, swift, newly painted. It crossed Great South Bay in only twenty-five minutes. The wind was penetrating, the spray chilling. Mike went below decks, blaming the desire for comfort on his age. He was forty-five but appeared younger, despite the complex of tiny lines around his milk-colored eyes. The auburn hair, still thick and long over his ears, showed a considerable amount of gray. And though he had not put on any appreciable weight, a girdle of flab circled his waist.

He was a mature man in his middle years, he reminded himself. Grooved if not groovy. A visitor to many of the places and experiences a girl like Elizabeth Jordan had yet to know. She had been too young. Too demanding in ways both obvious and subtle. Ridding himself of her had been a good move.

That was one of the reasons he had come to the island. To exorcise Elizabeth from his mind. The beach would be crowded with women, all ages, all shapes. He would make a liberal sampling, keep those he found suitable, ignore those who in any way were wrong for him.

Add another reason for the weekend. He carried his portable typewriter and a ream of copy paper. The idea—still only that; he was far from certain about it—had a strong appeal, and he had already begun making notes, searching his memory for incident, for character, for color. He marked the weekend down as a professional interlude in concentrated research. A mental and physical exploration. Neither should be difficult and both might be fun.

He ate dinner alone that night at Leo's. Roast beef,

coffee, and some of that good pecan pie. He noted the physical changes in the place, that now a small space for dancing was provided and the dancers did the funky Broadway and the boogaloo. They were dressed differently, too. Men and women were more stylish than they had been years before.

He reached back in time and recalled a Broadway actor making a pass at one of Leo's waiters, receiving a broken nose for his ardor; a famous model leaping atop the long bar, auctioning herself off, leaving with a trio of men, each of whom refused to be outbid; a Manhattan congressman, falling down drunk, being sick; and more.

He left Leo's and went to Mom Stone's. It was called The Fireboat now; and had been changed into a discotheque with flashing lights, cinematic projections, incessant and overwhelmingly loud music. He stayed only for a short drink, recalling exact conversations, the structure of a face, the boy who had provided an imitation of Johnny Ray, ancient emotions. His drink finished, he went back to Tom Sawyer's Inn and got into bed. He read his notes over, made some corrections, some additions and, satisfied, went to sleep.

He woke early. The sky was low, overcast, but he put on his swimming trunks and went out to the beach, running along the shore. It felt good, his muscles straining, lungs beginning to burn. Out of breath he slowed to a walk, the damp air cooling his skin. At Robin's Rest, a tiny community about half-a-mile east of Ocean Beach, he turned and retraced his steps, running all the way back. He finished off with a quick dip. The ocean was cold, rough, and gray. Invigorated and gasping, he hurried back to his room.

After breakfast, he strolled around the village. Changes had been made: new shops and another bar, another restaurant, the marina greatly enlarged. Past the village green, he ducked into Kline's, the general store, purchased a khaki hat to wear in the sun and a pair of jeans. He found a paperback copy of *The Legacy Lenders,* Harold Q. Masur's new mystery and bought it. Masur was a competent pro whom he had met at the Mystery Writers' award dinner a few years before.

Outside, he turned back toward Tom Sawyer's Inn when he heard his name spoken. He looked around. A remarkably attractive woman confronted him, blue eyes wide and laughing, a gay set to her fine features.

"Mike Birns, isn't it?" There was a mocking lilt to her voice. "You don't remember me."

"I'm not sure . . ."

She laughed easily. "I wouldn't expect you to remember. It's been so long. I have this crazy memory for names and faces. Hetty Carpenter," she said. "Molinos," she corrected. "Hetty Molinos. Do you remember now?"

His mind turned over frantically.

"We met at a party, Mike. Here, on the island. Fifteen, sixteen years ago. We were younger, of course, and . . ."

It came flooding back. An aggressive little girl, pert, freckled, almost begging to be taken to bed. She had made love to him with her mouth; the first time it had happened that way for him.

"I remember," he said.

"We didn't see much of each other." Her cheeks pinked and her laughter this time was brief and nervous. "I was running then, away from something. Always searching . . ."

"Did you find whatever you were searching for?"

"I had it all the time," she said gravely. She tapped her stomach lightly. "Right here." She shook her head and smiled up at him. "What about you, Mike? I heard that you had gotten married."

"And divorced."

"Oh, I am sorry."

He shrugged. "That was a long time ago."

"Children?"

"No children."

"I have two sons," she said proudly. "Fine boys. I've been married for nearly twelve years."

Twelve years and two children. He explored her face, the lines tranquil and comfortable. A lovely woman. Beautiful. At once, something came crashing back. "Tell me you think I'm pretty," she had pleaded then, desperate for reassurance. And he had said, "Yes, you are pretty," though he hadn't really thought so. She *had* been plain then. Not bad to look at, but plain. All the girls he had dated in those days were plain, he recalled, none pretty.

But *no*, that wasn't true. None of it. Hetty Molinos had been pretty, always. But she hadn't known it and he had been incapable of seeing it. All his girls had been attractive, bright, charming. His blurred vision alone had made less of them.

"I read one of your books, Mike," Hetty was saying. "I enjoyed it very much."

"Thank you."

"Our house is on Bungalow Walk, a pink house with flowers out front. Come and see us, Mike. Eric will be glad to meet you, and I know you'll like him. Everyone does."

When he got back to his room, he typed out everything he could remember about Hetty Molinos. About all the Hettys he'd known. About himself in relation to them. It took time.

That afternoon, Mike walked along the beach. It was cool and he wore a sweat shirt and the khaki sun hat. The volleyball net was up and a game was in progress. He spied a familiar figure, arms folded across the barrel chest, legs planted solidly apart, watching the play.

Mike came up alongside. "Hello, Neil."

Neil Morgan turned from the game with apparent reluctance. He manufactured a smile. "Mike Birns. I didn't know you were on the island. How are you? It's been a long time. Susan's on the beach somewhere with some of her friends. She'll be glad to see you, Mike. You've always been one of her favorites."

"I'll look for her."

"Do that." Again he produced that smile. "Why don't we ever hear from you, Mike?"

"I never figured you wanted to."

"Of course we do. You should give us a call."

Mike spoke deliberately. "Why don't you call me?"

"Mike," Neil said, spreading his hands helplessly, "you know how busy I am."

Mike swallowed an angry answer. He knew Neil was oblivious to the implied insult.

"I'm producing," Neil offered. "Got a project going now. So big it frightens me." He laughed to show he was only joking. "Theatrical film. Lots of money. A very complicated affair."

"Good luck."

"I make my own luck. Simply a matter of doing it, pushing the right buttons, so to speak."

Mike asked about BB and Neil said nice things about

his son. Mike asked where they were living these days, and Neil talked about a cooperative apartment on Fifth Avenue.

"Things like that keep a man on his toes," Neil pointed out. "The upkeep on the apartment, BB's college. A very chic wife. It costs a lot just to keep up. Expenses go on. A man does what he has to. . . ."

Chapter VI

Roy

At midnight Leo's was crowded. The dancers swayed in a collective rhythm that made them appear to be separate units of some great heaving beast, invisibly linked. The music ceased and Roy guided Helene back to their place at the bar. He looked down the front of her green silk blouse.

"You really throw it around out there," he told her.

"I'm glad you approve. After all, you are my employer and it's important that you approve of me."

He laughed raucously and stroked her arm. "Come on back to the room and I'll give you some of my approval."

She arranged an exaggerated pout on her mouth. "But I want another drink."

"There's a bottle back at the room."

"Here," she simpered, "I'm having so much fun. Besides, it's too early to go to sleep."

"Did I say anything about sleep?" His hand went to her hip, caressed the curve of her bottom.

"Mr. Ashe, you mustn't."

"I must," he said, leering. He looked down the front of her blouse again.

"Mr. Ashe . . ."

"You'll never guess what I would like to do right now."

"Buy me a drink," she said, with feigned innocence.
"Just one more," he said, signaling the barman.

Susan and Neil

Ten of them huddled around the table in the far corner of Leo's beyond the dancers, near the windows. Neil and Susan Morgan, Maggie and her second husband, Bob Marshall, a brooding, silent man, three other couples.

"You can't ever tell who may show up on a holiday weekend," Neil said.

Maggie located Roy at the bar, squinting through the drifting haze of cigarette smoke. "I suppose it would be polite to go over, say hello."

"I met Mike Birns on the beach," Neil said.

"It's all right with me," Bob Marshall said to Maggie. "I don't care."

"Why didn't you bring him to see me?" Susan said, an annoyed ring in her voice. "You know I like Mike."

"I know you don't care," Maggie said, rising. "Want to come along, meet Roy?"

"He'll probably show up here," Neil said.

Bob Marshall shrugged. "Why should I?"

"How is he?" Susan said.

"Because you two have a lot in common," Maggie replied very softly.

"You?" Bob said.

Maggie smiled enigmatically. "More than that."

Neil watched her pick her way toward the bar. "Fantastic ass on your wife," he said to Bob.

"I'm not an ass man, myself."

Neil assessed him. "You surely didn't marry Maggie for her bazzooms. She doesn't have any."

"That's true. It must've been something else. I forget what."

"Bastards, the both of you," Susan bit off. She lit a cigarette.

"My wife is determined to give herself lung cancer," Neil said.

Susan blew smoke in his direction and smiled sweetly.

"I smoke myself," Bob Marshall said to no one in particular.

"Where's Mike? Susan said abruptly. "You said he would be here," she accused Neil.

"I said he'd *probably* show up."

"It's the same thing," she said.

"Not really," Bob Marshall pointed out.

"If I know Mike, he's out hunting gash," Neil said.

"And getting it," Susan added sharply. "That's one very sexy man."

"Aren't we all?" Bob said cheerfully.

Susan made a disparaging sound.

Neil decided it was time to change the subject. "Mike's still turning out those little mysteries of his," he commented blandly.

Susan fixed him with a steady stare. "Read them. His last book received a rave in *The Times* and it's going to be a TV special. He's a good writer."

Neil studied her. That Tartar face. A little blurred perhaps, a few more lines visible. But no less sensational. She was still a wife a man could be proud of, take anywhere, show off. "I didn't know you'd read any of his books."

"All of them."

"Oh."

"I bought each of them when it was published. They're on our bookshelves. You ought to look sometime."

"A mystery writer. A category writer. Not important. Nobody ever discusses Mike Birns or his work seriously."

She started to reply, thought better of it. She looked around for the waiter, spied him serving a party a few tables away. He was a tall youth, dramatic looking, with a faint resemblance to Judd Martin. *That* prick. He'd run a true course, done precisely what she'd expected, gone off to Hollywood the first chance he had. As soon as Harriet Davidson crooked her little finger at him. A short phone call was his way of telling her.

"I've got to go, you understand. I've signed a contract to write six episodes on *The Law and Henry Smith*. Cops and robbers stuff. Right up my alley. You wouldn't expect me to pass up my big chance."

She had wanted to scream at him, to gouge out his eyes, to scar that devilish face of his, to slice off his balls. Instead, she had said, "Drop me a line and good luck, Judd." To hell with the sonofabitch! What he had to give was readily available. She beckoned to the tall waiter. Up close, he looked even younger. She smiled up into his face.

"Do you have a name, lover?" she murmured.

"Steve."

"How sweet. Be a darling, Steve, and bring me another gin and tonic. Heavy on the gin."

"Yes ma'am."

"Susan," she corrected.

He went after the drink and she admired his small hard behind.

"That's the fourth drink tonight," Neil said. "You will ruin your figure."

She looked at him without speaking until he started blinking rapidly and turned away.

Mike

Mike leaned against the bar in The Fireboat, nursing a Scotch and water and listening absently to Serena, who had picked him up five minutes after he arrived. She was a tall, dramatic woman in her early thirties. She wore two sets of false eyelashes and her lids were painted purple and rings glittered on every finger of both hands. A hard cast detracted from her finely featured face and her lush body was enclosed in a striped cotton blouse and bell bottoms. She was intently cataloguing the faults of her second husband.

"You should have stayed with the first husband," Mike put in.

"Are you kidding! What a lemon *he* was! A ruin. Sidney didn't have a gut in his whole miserable body. At least Jerry got it up once in a while, knew where to put it." Her eyes drifted down the length of his body with leisurely interest. "I'll bet you know where to put it. Every single place." She waited but he said nothing. "What I can't figure is why some smart bird hasn't hooked you yet.

Good-looking, big, a writer. You got all the qualifications. You must be something in the saddle." He stirred the drink with his forefinger. "You're too nice," she went on. "I mean, I really like you and that scares me, see. The thing is, what's wrong with a guy like you, I keep asking myself. There's got to be, with you running around loose. . . ."

"Maybe I'm a fag."

"Oh, no." She eyed him warily. "You're not, are you?" He grinned and she grinned back. "I knew you weren't. Listen," she said, inching closer, "I know where there's going to be a little bash later. These friends of mine, Charlie and Miriam. They're swingers. We could go over there. Suck a couple of sticks, ball it up. That Miriam is wild. There isn't anything she wouldn't do. One look at you, and she'd have your pants off. That would be a kick, seeing you ball with Miriam. . . ."

Mike straightened up and finished his drink. Without a word, he left the tall woman and her grotesque concept of a good time. Outside, the street vibrated with movement. Groups of people, mostly young, huddled together, as if sharing a common secret. Couples licking the chocolate sprinkles off ice-cream cones strolled aimlessly. A team of uniformed policemen watched the parade. Three men, tanned, with long sideburns and white turtleneck jerseys, beads and medallions dangling from around their throats, prowled past.

Mike considered bed and sleep, rejeced the idea. Restlessness, a vague craving, stirred him. Go back to Serena? The party she had mentioned. An orgy. A new experience. Impersonal, lost in a mist of sensuality, of lust. An orgasm, cold and clean, objective. It had a sharp appeal and at the same time he turned away from it. He closed his mind to the idea and went for a nightcap to MacCurdy's.

The girls were very young here, very attractive, with that bold, receptive look. Almost challenging a man to avail himself of their bodies. Well, hell, that was why you came. To find women. To line up a new team, to organize your social life, sexual life, to arrange something to fulfill your needs, to gain the pleasure you want. To get laid, now and in the future. Then why *not* Serena? Why not her friends? No, no. Not his route. Community activities had never turned him on. One girl was all he wanted. One girl to please him in and out bed. One girl for him to please. One girl . . . Almost a brand new thought.

He became aware of a presence at his shoulder, wanted to see who it was, was unable to turn. He gathered his resources and forced his head around.

"Hello, Mike . . ."

A hot flood sloshed around in his stomach and his throat went dry. Sweat broke on his palms.

"I never expected to see you here."

Elizabeth smiled wistfully. "It's permitted, isn't it? Fire Island is a place for single women, too."

He struggled against the confusion that filtered through his brain. He produced a smile and kept his voice conversational.

"You're looking well," he said.

"So are you."

"Thank you," he said. "Are you alone?" he said. "Let me buy you a drink."

"I'm sorry," she said in that curiously serious manner that was so much a part of her. "I can't. I saw you while I was dancing and I wanted to say hello. I must get back."

"Of course, you're with someone."

She nodded and started away. He said her name and she hesitated. The music suddenly closed in on him and a flock of random images circled wildly in his brain. To pierce the closing haze, to make sense, demanded a mighty effort.

"Where—where are you staying?"

"I have a share in a house. Right on the bay, at Robin's Rest." That mysterious suggestion of a smile. "I answered an advertisement again. And you?"

He shook his head. "I'm out for the weekend. A place called Tom Sawyer's Inn. The other side of Ocean Beach."

"Well," she said, "enjoy your weekend."

"You, too."

She looked back. "Mike, is it all right with you?"

"Couldn't be better," he heard himself say. "I'm at the top of my game. The top . . ."

He watched her take a seat at a table across the room, next to a black-haired man with the profile of a movie star. He looped an arm across her shoulder with an easy familiarity, said something that made her laugh.

Mike left.

Sleep refused to come easily. A damp yearning seeped through his bowels and reminiscent passions clogged the passages of his skull. When finally he did sleep, he dreamed badly, making small sounds, legs leaping reflexively. He woke startled and afraid in the dark loneliness, his brain a sump of despair.

Damn. Where was she now? This minute. With the movie profile, accepting him inside her, doing what she had done with him, saying what she had said with him, feeling—? A soft moan dribbled across his lips. Anger flared, was swiftly transfigured to depression. To self-pity.

He willed himself back to the protective oblivion of sleep. Deep blackness wrapped itself around him and he drifted, fighting to give himself to the drift. Something called him back, a sibilant intrusion, a soft voice, a gentle plea.

"Mike . . ."

He sat up and listened. An amalgam of night sounds filled his ears. Crickets and the crumping of waves. Creaking floorboards, a distant gush of laughter, a love song.

"Mike . . ."

He went to the door and opened it. Elizabeth stood there, a tentative expression on her delicate face. He stood aside and she walked into the room.

"I'm sorry I woke you," she said absently.

"I was awake. I'll turn on a light."

"No. Please, no."

"What happened?" he said harshly. "Wasn't that guy enough for you?"

He heard her breath quicken. "Why do you want to hurt me, Mike?"

He swore and sat on the edge of the bed. "How did you find me?"

"I asked people. And I said your name outside another room." She giggled. "I woke someone and he was furious with me. But he told me where you were." She grew solemn again. "I was afraid you wouldn't be alone. That there would be a girl with you."

"I'm alone."

"Mike," she said, after a short silence, "I can hardly see you in the dark. Are you wearing anything?"

"No."

"Then why am I completely dressed? Don't you think I should be naked, too?"

"You're a fool. An absolute fool. To come here this way, like a beggar. . . ."

"Oh, no," she said quickly. "I'm no beggar, Mike. I love you, Mike. Really. And when I saw you, it all came back. I went back to my room, tried to sleep. But I couldn't. I kept thinking about you and I had to come."

"I'll use you. I use people like you. It's what I'm all about."

There was movement in the darkness, the rustle of garments against smooth flesh. Out of the black she came, a pale blur.

"If you were smart . . ." he offered tightly.

"I think it's stupid for us both to be undressed and for you to keep talking. I think you should make love to me now. Please, Mike, it's why I came. . . ."

She took his head between her hands and directed his face against her belly. "No promises," he muttered, hands reaching for her buttocks. "You're going to get hurt."

"Don't threaten," she said from a great distance.

His mouth traveled across her belly and down her left side, then made the return journey, finding the feathery forest, breathing in the faint scent of passion. His tongue embarked on a tantalizing trip. . . .

She came down on him and they accommodated themselves to each other, spreading and thrusting, lunging, swelling to dangerous heights, goading and pleading, choking with each other, accepting with gratitude, coming off in a riotous detonation that contorted their limbs and constricted their flesh, harmonious end that drifted to slow last gasps. . . .

It was a long time before either of them spoke. "Oh, you. *You.* You man. *Man.* Oh, Mike. So nice . . . beautiful. Most beautiful." She swallowed a giggle and licked his earlobe. "In the morning, will you love me again?"

"A kid like you, you'll kill me. I'm an old man."

"You'll never be old. The youngest man I've ever known. So much life."

"Go to sleep."

"I love you, Mike."

He took a long, deep breath. "I love you, Elizabeth."

She put her head on his chest and arranged her leg across his thighs. She sighed and kissed his chest. Moments later, they were both asleep.

Chapter VII

Roy

Roy rolled off Helene and reached for a cigarette.

"You could offer me one," she said caustically.

He handed her the pack and the matches. They lay side by side smoking.

"Look," she said after a while, "I don't want you to think that I'm putting you down or anything."

"Don't put me down and I won't think you're doing it."

"It's just that . . . is it always that way? I mean, three times we made it and you go off before I even get started. You gotta get some control."

"Don't tell me what I got to do. I'm paying the freight and I don't want to hear any complaints. If the action's not your bag, you know what to do."

"And what then? Am I fired?"

"You know the name of the game—when I want you, you're there."

"What makes you think the job is that important to me? If I have to put out I can get better wages than you pay."

"Take off, anytime you like."

"I'll think about that." She crushed out the cigarette. "I'm hungry. Will you buy me some breakfast?"

"Get dressed."

"I want to shower first."

He watched her walk to the bathroom. Great shape. Big round fanny and boobs to match. But just a fair lay. On Monday, he'd begin looking for another girl. He wasn't taking crap from anyone. He went to the window and looked out. The sun was shining. That pleased him. He wanted to work up a little tan. It contrasted neatly with the gray of his temples, gave him a smooth, worldly appearance. A knock at the door interrupted.

"What is it?" he called.

"Mr. Ashe," came a tremulous female voice, "it's Mrs. Gorgan, the landlady."

"What, Mrs. Gorgan?"

"May I talk to you for a minute . . . see you for a minute?"

His mind raced. What did she want? He had registered as man and wife, was paying for a double occupancy, so there could be no difficulty from that direction. And Helene was clearly past twenty-one. "Be right there," he said. He stepped into a pair of Bermudas and opened the door. Three men confronted him. One of them was a local policeman, in uniform. The other two wore sports jackets and had square faces and crew cuts. Mrs. Gorgan stood behind them.

"What is this all about, Mrs. Gorgan?" Roy snapped, letting his anger show itself.

"We're police officers," one of the sports-jacketed men said. He displayed his shield. "I'm Challenger and this is my partner, Miller. We work out of Bayshore, Mr. Ashe. We got a call from New York City, Mr. Ashe. There's a warrant out on you."

Roy was afraid he was going to faint. He made an effort to maintain his composure. He produced a derisive laugh. "Is this some kind of a practical joke?"

"No joke, Mr. Ashe," Challenger said. "You are Roy Ashe."

"Sure, but——"

"You're under arrest, Mr. Ashe," Miller said.

"What for?"

"Homicide, Mr. Ashe," Challenger said blandly. "You'll have to come along with us."

"You're entitled to the services of an attorney, Mr. Ashe," Miller intoned. "And you aren't required to make any statement without your lawyer present. And you are warned that anything you say may be used in evidence against you."

Jesus, Roy thought. How did they ever find out? He'd been so careful, so goddamned careful. . . .

Charlotte McManus—whose husband was in Atlanta on business—was on her way out of the rooming house opposite the police station where she had spent the night with a mutual-fund salesman she had met in Leo's. She was the first one to find out. She asked one of the officers on duty why they were taking Roy Ashe away on the police launch and he told her. Charlotte repeated the story to Amy Wenders, on her way to shop at the market. Amy told the girl at the checkout counter and she promptly phoned her boyfriend who informed his mother. She called Leah Ben-Ezra. Leah had already gone out to the beach so she told Leah's husband Wilbur. He went across the street to Sid Mack's house and they both went to see Jay Richards, a poker buddy of Roy Ashe. Jay rang up Tommy Amato, a long-time house owner, and a summer friend of the Morgans. He paid them a visit.

"I don't believe it," was Susan's immediate reaction.

"It's true," Amato said happily. "The cops took Roy off the island. Imagine that little guy a killer."

"It's impossible," Susan said.

"The story was in the papers," Neil commented authoritatively. "A bookie."

"I didn't know Roy went that big," Amato said.

"A man's got to be responsible for his actions," Neil said.

"That Roy," Amato said admiringly. "He must be something. The papers said it was a real top hit. A couple of slugs in the gut and one in the old head. Zap! Just like that. What a gutty little character!"

"Poor Maggie," Susan said.

"Why poor Maggie?" Neil said. "He's not her husband, which is a break for her. Feel sorry for Cindy, if you want to feel sorry for anyone. The kid's future is ruined, her father a murderer. A man should consider his family first."

"I'll buy that," Amato said soberly.

"I'm going over to Maggie's house," Susan said.

"Why?" Neil said. "There's nothing you can do."

"She's my friend," she answered and left.

"Women," Amato growled.

"Sentiment's all right in its place."

"Right." Amato laughed. "Isn't this a blast? Most excitement we've had around here since that narcotics raid last season. It's right up your alley, Neil."

"How do you mean?"

"Make a great movie."

Neil shrugged. "It's been done," he said firmly.

"Yeah."

BB

Beautiful, baby.

All spinning light and undulating forms, vivid colors and total sound. Intensified. *Pro*-found. He peered inside himself and what he saw was a figure all curled up and growing rapidly, taking shape, heart large and dominating, gaining strength along with size. Abruptly wings appeared and the foetus had become a startlingly handsome golden eagle.

Fly, baby. High and fast. Great wings lifted him above a diminishing planet, green and insignificant. Up here, *fantastic,* only the glory of sky and clean cool air, a bright sun.

He surveyed the receding earth with eyes that could see forever, spotting a doe and her fawn peacefully grazing, a scampering jackrabbit, a rancher bouncing along a fenceline in a dusty jeep. All of it was one with nature and full of rare beauty. He viewed the universe with fantastic clarity of vision, understanding *everything.*

Now he soared higher on a thermal current, hanging on the draft, allowing himself to be carried. Below, peaks and valleys, hillocks and bald patches of wasteland, sparkling streams, forests, green meadows. Life was simple and innocent.

"Oh, man . . ."

"A fine trip."

"That BB, he is in never-never land."

Professor Hailey was content in his comfortable red leather chair. Turning BB on to acid had been a good thing. An act of mercy, of kindness, of Christian charity. The boy was sweet, loving, too beautiful to be permitted to waste himself on hard stuff. The professor allowed his soft eyes to circle the room. The usual Friday night group. BB and himself, Milko Fredericks, of the sociology department, and his townie girl friend, those two coeds who were always with each other, a few other people. All turned on, full of love, expanding their experiences. Tonight Hailey was overseeing the others, staying cool and clear in case of any freakouts. But it was a great night. All trips good. Perfect.

He never heard the front door of the house open. Never heard the advancing footsteps until the intruders were in the living room. Five of them. Clicking on the harsh overhead lights.

Hailey blinked. He recognized Dr. Kamins, president of the college, and Jeanette Seaver, Dean of Women, and Louis Perietta, head of the campus security force. Two of his uniformed men brought up the rear. Hailey squinted against the unexpected glare and arranged a halfmoon smile on his placid features.

"Dr. Kamins," he began, in that so reasonable classroom manner. "I hope you're going to understand . . ."

"I'm going to try, Professor Hailey," came the icy response. "I expect you'll provide an explanation that may help me to do that. Meanwhile, Mr. Perietta, I want the names of each of these students and the faculty members. The young man in the corner, he's a teaching assistant in biology research."

"You must understand, Dr. Kamins," Professor Hailey offered, "this is by way of being an experiment. Somewhat unorthodox, I admit. But its possible value is limitless. Here we reach across heretofore uncrossed frontiers that have walled off the inner reaches of the mind. I hope to demonstrate . . ."

One of the girls began to tremble. A thin rising wail came out of her, and she began to slam her head against the floor with terrifying force.

"My God!" Dr. Kamins cried. "Stop her, Perietta."

The security chief did so, placing the girl carefully on

the couch, holding her firmly immobilized. She whimpered and called for her mother.

"What's wrong with her?" Dr. Kamins asked.

"A bad trip," Hailey said. "But it will pass. She's perfectly all right."

"That isn't my opinion at all, Hailey." Dr. Kamins swung toward Perietta. "I'll interview Professor Hailey and each of these people in my office tomorrow at eleven. See that they are present, please."

"Yes, sir, doctor," Perietta said.

"And I want them all given medical examinations tonight. I want to know exactly what caused them to be in this condition. Can you see to all that, Perietta?"

"I'm sure I can."

"Good. Then I'll leave you in charge."

Hailey wanted to call out to Dr. Kamins, to ask his indulgence, to explain, to make him comprehend the purpose of evenings such as this. Instead, he sank silently back into the leather chair, eyes darting about, coming to rest on BB squatting on the far side of the room. The handsome youth was oblivious to what was happening. His head rolled loosely on his shoulders, his mouth slack, his eyes opaque. Happy boy, Hailey thought. Suddenly a chilling numbness advanced along his limbs. He felt very old. Very much alone.

Chapter VIII

Maggie and Eddie

Maggie went back to Manhattan on Sunday night and tried to visit Roy in prison the next morning. But it wasn't until Tuesday that she was able to see him. By then he had been arraigned, formally charged. The court had appointed a lawyer to represent him.

"Isn't that a big yock?" he snapped curtly across the separating partition in the visitors' room. "They accuse me of killing the guy for his money and I wind up without a cent, not enough for a decent lawyer."

Concern was etched into her face. "Did you do it, Roy?"

"Come on," he said. He checked the uniformed guard observing them with bland interest. "You know me better'n that. Do you think I could murder a guy?"

"I want to help, Roy."

"You can," he replied intensely. "Get your husband to advance me some dough, enough for a first-rate lawyer. I need a Lee Bailey or a Louis Nizer. Someone who can get me off the hook. You know me, kiddo, I never did a wrong thing in my life, except some traffic violations."

He had acquired eighty-seven tickets for illegal parking, speeding, reckless driving, and had neglected to respond to any of them, she remembered. Until he was hauled before a judge, fined, and threatened with a jail term.

"I'll speak to Bob," Maggie said. "But it won't do any good. He doesn't like you."

"He doesn't even know me. Not really."

"He knows you," she said thoughtfully. "The way he knows himself."

"What's that supposed to mean? Hell, did you come here to help or to give me a hard time?"

"I'll talk to Bob."

He grunted. "How's Cindy taking it?"

"I don't know. We don't talk to each other very much." She rose, put on short white gloves. "I'll do whatever I can for you. What about your friends, can't they help?"

He snorted cynically. "There are no friends. Not one. Some joke. Roy Ashe, always a smile and a quip, a million laughs. Not one friend. Well, screw it! I've had one sweet ride, as far as it's gone."

"I'll do what I can."

Riding uptown on the subway, Maggie picked up a discarded copy of the *Daily News*. Roy's arrest rated nearly three full columns, plus a photograph on page four. The story claimed that his apprehension was the result of expert police work. Persistent questioning of people living in Harry Nevin's neighborhood had spotlighted a man with a red moustache. A man unfamiliar to anyone. Descriptions were provided and from them a composite photo-drawing was constructed and circulated. The rendering was compared against a list of Harry Nevin's customers, friends, known enemies, and debtors. Files were checked and photographs of the most likely suspects were collected and submitted to taxi drivers, to the subway change clerks at the station in Brooklyn Heights, to residents of the area.

But it wasn't until Detective Seigal cut and shaped some moustaches out of red paper and arranged them on each of the suspects photographs that real progress was made. Closer identifications were made, corroborated, until the investigation narrowed and intensified.

In the East Side precinct where he had done business, Harry Nevin's activities were no secret. His collection habits were relayed to Detective Seigal through certain unnamed police sources. Now the photographs of the suspects—at this stage there were three—were shown to barmen, a grocery clerk, a cigar-store operator, the patrolman on the beat, others. Roy Ashe was the one man that each of them knew, had seen with Nevin over the years.

Detective Seigal became a specialist in Roy Ashe. His activities, business and personal. His finances. His acquaintances. His sex habits. His tastes. He was, it was noted with growing interest, a man who enjoyed the good things in life, the expensive things. But he was also a man who seldom held onto money for very long, a man with an uneven employment record, a man who had never achieved economic luxury or even security. Nevertheless, he had been able to purchase a film library, to make a rather substantial down payment. Yet that sum, Detective Seigal had noted when interviewed, was considerably less than the amount of Harry Nevin's estimated Thursday take. Detective Seigal, by nature and training a curious man, had inquired about the discrepancy, supposing Roy Ashe to be the bookie's killer.

"I'd like to check the guy's apartment," Seigal told his assistant.

"I'll get a warrant."

"Do that. And when our man on Ashe's tail calls in, I want to talk to him."

That had been Thursday, the day Roy had gone to Fire Island with Helene. Detective Seigal and his men appreciated his absence. It made their work easier and they searched the apartment with neat efficiency. They found nothing and were about to leave when Seigal suggested the refrigerator. His partner made a face that indicated his opinion of the idea. He opened the white door.

"Nothing but canned fruit, a couple of apples, and two bottles of champagne. Imported. Any more ideas, Seigal?"

"Yeh. Check the freezer compartment."

There, behind a pair of finely marbled steaks, in plastic-wrapped packages, was the remainder of Harry Nevin's money.

Poor Roy, Maggie thought, coming into the sunlight at Grand Central. She walked over to Brooks Brothers and bought some shirts for Bob. Three blues, two whites. Button-down, of course. She went out into Forty-fourth Street, heading for the Chock Full O'Nuts on Fifth Avenue. Poor Roy, always so hungry to become a big man. Poor Roy, all appetite and no jungle skills. Poor Roy.

"Maggie!"

She turned and saw a familiar figure in a tan gabardine suit, the wary eyes glowing, the sleekly shaved head brown and smooth. It was Eddie Stander.

She stopped. "Hello, Eddie. How nice meeting you this way." She glanced at the package he carried under his arm. "Been shopping?"

"At J. Press. Some new bathing shorts and a couple of ties, a summer belt. You're looking wonderful, Maggie. Prettier than ever. Have you had lunch? Be my guest."

She protested and he insisted and in the end she agreed, curious, wanting to know about him after so many years. They went to the Algonquin and when they were seated and martinis brought, she tried to analyze her feelings. She tried to recall how close they had once been, how intimate. At the same time, being with him was like being with the most casual of acquaintances.

The solemn expression on the battered face was no different than it had been years earlier. The eyes still darting, unable to rest. The same gravelly voice, almost angry, almost pleading. He milked the fingers of his left hand.

"You, Maggie. Still the greatest-looking girl on the beach."

"You haven't been on the beach lately."

"I know what I'm saying."

"I'm a middle-aged lady with lines in my face and a thicker waistline. I drink too much and there have been too many long nights. Once I was pretty and fresh. I can remember that."

He took her hand. She removed it at once.

"I don't want to hold hands with you, Eddie." She sipped her martini. "You know about Roy?" He nodded. "That jail, a horrible place. I had to visit him."

"I thought about going. But he wouldn't want to see me."

She almost asked how he knew that, decided against it.

"Tell me things, Maggie," he said presently.

"What things?"

"About yourself. The kind of life you live."

"There's nothing to tell. I get up some mornings and manage to make it through the day without being ill. Those are the good days."

"Are you sick?"

"Not in the way you mean."

"How is Cindy? What a terrific kid she was. First-rate."

"Cindy is going to Europe next week."

"Europe? She can't be more than eighteen. Isn't that a bit much for a girl her age?"

A wistful smile lifted the corners of Maggie's mouth. "She announced to me that she was going. She didn't ask. Insisted that it was right for her to go. Bob and I both objected. She said if we didn't send her, she would refuse to return to college in the fall. It's a different generation, these children. I don't understand them."

"Still, eighteen. Aren't you worried?"

Her brows drew down. "I'm glad she's going," she said quietly. "I don't like Cindy, what she's become. I don't like the way she behaves. I don't like her friends and I'd rather not have her around. Does it sound terrible? But it's so. Without her my life will be much more quiet. I require a great deal of quiet these days."

"If she were my daughter—"

Maggie laughed briefly. "Don't say anything you'll regret when your children are older, Eddie. They go their own way, do their own things."

"I guess you're right. I have to admit, I was a bit of a rebel myself."

"I never thought of you as rebellious."

"Well," he said, "what was between us."

"That wasn't very daring or different, I think. Rather pathetic, in retrospect."

He studied his drink.

"Are you still in television, Eddie?" she asked.

"I'm thinking about changing my job as a matter of fact. A couple of men I know, an artist and a production man, they want us to open our own shop. I'd handle copy, you see."

"It sounds exciting."

"We'd only have a few accounts to start and the money might be a little tight. Later, it's reasonable to anticipate pulling in some of the big boys. We've got experience, intelligence, talent—"

"Yes."

"The risks are great, of course. Agencies do fail."

"That's true."

"It's important to consider all the angles." He paused. You can see that, I'm sure."

"I think so."

"A man has to consider his future, but also his family, the personal responsibilities. I'm not afraid to gamble but I want to know what the odds are. The risks and the rewards. It would be a kick to have my own place, be my own boss. I would like that very much. . . ."

"Then do it."

He swallowed the last of his drink. "I have to tell Edith about it, get her opinion. She has an investment in this, in me."

"I understand."

Later, on the street, before parting, he suggested that they meet again, for dinner some evening.

She looked up into his face. "I don't think there's any point to that, Eddie."

"Why not?" he argued plaintively. "We like each other. We get along. . . ."

She extended her hand. "It was good to see you. Good luck with your new venture."

"Think about it," he insisted. "Having dinner, I mean." He gave her his business card. "You can phone me."

"I'll think about it," she said. The doorman had a cab waiting and she climbed in. As they drove away, she shredded the card without looking at it.

Chapter IX

Neil and BB

Neil refused to believe it.

There was BB sitting on the bench across from him and Susan in Dr. Kamins' outer office, looking the way every young man ought to look. Handsome and cleancut, the eyes level and steady, the fine wide mouth, the intelligent brow, and a jaw that indicated strength and resolution. These absurd charges, they couldn't be true. Not about his son.

"Susan," he said from between clenched teeth, "I don't mind telling you that I am sore as hell about this and I intend to tell Kamins exactly how I feel."

"That should be interesting, considering the circumstances."

"What is that supposed to mean?"

"It means that Dr. Kamins is not the person for you to be angry with."

"Who then?" He twisted around to face her, keeping his expression unchanged, his voice low, so the secretaries would be unable to hear. "I can't make you out, after all these years. Your son is accused of using narcotics, of breaking the rules of his college as well as the law of the land. Don't you recognize the seriousness of the charges?"

An angry glow, materialized in the soft brown eyes, quickly disappeared. "I know what BB's done."

"He's done nothing," Neil retorted hotly.

She glanced around, bewildered. "There doesn't seem to be much doubt."

"There's a hell of a lot of doubt in my mind. I know BB. He's my son."

One of the secretaries interrupted, indicating the heavy oak door with the brass nameplate on it. "Dr. Kamins will see you now." Neil opened the door, allowed Susan and BB to precede him.

Dr. Kamins was a pudgy man who, even on the warmest of days, wore a vest. A Phi Beta Kappa key dangled from a gold chain across his protruding middle. Behind metal-rimmed glasses, he appeared solemn, owlish.

"Mr. and Mrs. Morgan," he pronounced, as if rehearsing for some later presentation. "How good of you to come to see me. Please, sit down. You too, Boyd."

Neil crossed his legs and arranged his trouser legs so as not to ruin the creases. He tugged his jacket lower on his neck and shot his cuffs. This done, he settled back in the chair and assessed Dr. Kamins, seated behind his big desk.

"It's unfortunate," Dr. Kamins began, "that you had to interrupt the normal course of your lives for this visit."

"Our son's welfare takes precedence over all other matters," Neil said flatly.

"Of course," Dr. Kamins said. "I wish all our parents had the same interest in their children."

Neil hawked his throat clear and began to smile. He willed the action to cease and finally it did. "Let me begin by stating unequivocally that my wife and I have complete faith in BB, in his judgment, in his word."

"Such sentiments are laudable in parents. However, there are times when our children do not justify such confidence."

"You're implying BB does not warrant my confidence?"

Dr. Kamins lowered his eyes and made a steeple with his fingers. "I am implying nothing, Mr. Morgan. I am telling you that your son was caught in the act."

"I won't believe that!"

Dr. Kamins glanced sidelong at BB, sitting stiff and still, staring straight ahead. "Have you told your parents the facts of the matter, Boyd?"

When BB said nothing, Neil spoke hurriedly. "BB was visiting this Professor Hailey, an informal discussion group.

It was no secret around the campus. There was nothing to hide. There was nothing wrong going on. A weekly gathering, there's no crime in that."

Dr. Kamins gazed at the high carved ceiling of his office. "Drugs were being used. LSD."

"No!"

"I'm afraid it's true, Mr. Morgan. The evidence is quite clear."

"Nonsense! My son has no need for narcotics. He knows how he's expected to perform and he does so. Look at that boy, Dr. Kamins, at that face. Is that the face of an addict?"

"Oh, my God," Susan said softly. "Please, keep quiet."

He jerked around. "My son is accused of a terrible thing and you expect me to keep quiet. I will not permit his name to be blemished. My name."

"Mr. Morgan . . ."

"Father, listen to *me!*"

"This matter must be cleared up right away," Neil said forcefully. "Remember, Dr Kamins, you are dealing with a man who knows how to get things done. I get what I want. I have power, influence, and money. Unless these ridiculous and insulting charges against my son are dropped immediately, I am going to turn this matter over to my lawyers. I shall instruct them to institute proceedings against Robert Bradford College and against you personally, in a large amount, for defamation of character, libel, and whatever else is legally feasible. I will make you regret doing this to Neil Morgan's son."

"Father," BB said quietly, "I did it."

"I'll show you how Neil Morgan fights. And when he fights he wins."

"I did it," BB said again, louder this time. "I was on a trip when they came in."

"A trip. . . ?"

"LSD. I've been on it for a long time. And before that I was stretched out on hard stuff. Heroin. If you want to do anything to Professor Hailey, you ought to thank him for getting me off H."

Neil squeezed his eyes shut. When he opened them he shuddered. "Who are you protecting, BB? Accepting unwarranted blame is very noble but purposeless at this time.

It's Hailey, isn't it? Why, boy? Tell the truth. Trust me to fix this mess."

"No," Susan said, "you aren't going to fix this one, Neil."

He ignored her, displaying a smile of encouragement to BB. "Level with me, son. You'll see how your father can fight for you."

"That's just it. I don't want you to fight for me. I was there," he went on in a tight, desperate voice. "I was on acid. *I was on it.*"

"You're lying."

"No."

Neil seemed to grow taller in the chair, drawn taut as if about to spring, then he slumped back, head sinking between the high shoulders, eyes watery and unfocused. His mouth opened and closed and opened again. "Why? What did I do to deserve this, BB? Tell me."

"Mr. Morgan," Dr. Kamins put in, with academic efficiency. "The question that truly concerns us all is what can be done to help Boyd."

It was Susan who responded. "I kept reading articles about young people taking dope but I never believed BB would be one of them."

"It's not your fault, Mother," BB said.

"Then whose fault?" Neil sputtered, coming to his feet, body bent as if in pain, face contorted. "You're his *mother*. You should've been taking care of your son while I was earning a living. You should've been at home being a proper mother, a proper wife—"

"Recriminations will achieve nothing," Dr. Kamins offered, hands raised placatingly. "This matter can be settled."

"I'll take whatever's coming to me," BB muttered.

Neil jabbed a finger at his son. "Right now no one is interested in your opinion. Your judgement leaves a lot to be desired. You have an awful lot to learn and I hold myself responsible for that. Well, from now on I'm going to teach you right and wrong and——"

"Shit!" BB burst out, striding toward the door. "You taught me a whole fucking lot, enough to get us all here." He slammed out of Dr. Kamins' office.

Susan began to sob.

Neil stared at the closed door. "I don't understand," he muttered. "Is he blaming me for this? I never used narcotics. I don't drink or smoke. Of course, my wife does. An occasional cocktail. A cigarette after dinner. Social amenities, Doctor. You understand." He sank back into his chair. "That boy had everything he wanted, his future all decided. All he had to do was stay on the track, keep out of trouble. Why couldn't he have done that?

"I suppose I should've seen it coming. The way he kept things to himself, excluded me from his life. Secrets, always. And that rudeness. He never learned *that* from me. Manners are important, all that keep us from tearing each other apart like beasts in the jungle. I taught him honesty. Honesty and courage. Directness. The rewards of industriousness, hard work, how to run the race and win it.

"I didn't just mouth empty platitudes at him. I provided a living example of what I meant. My wife will vouch for that. I made it, better than my own father did. I told BB how I had used my father as a target, something to shoot at, to surpass. A standard of accomplishment.

"And I beat him. And when I did, I knew I had really accomplished something worthwhile. I've made a lot of money, Dr. Kamins. A great deal. But it isn't all money. Oh, no, don't think that. There's the game. The business of achievement. That's what keeps me going. I could retire now, if I chose to. Go off and sit in the sun and let the world pass by without a care. But I don't. I'm not that kind of a man. Neil Morgan is a worker. He keeps moving ahead."

"Please, Neil," Susan said.

"Keep out of this," he shot back quickly. "We both recognize your contribution to this affair, your failures. People must live according to the rules. Be a proper husband, a proper father. A proper wife and mother. To fail in these roles is unforgivable. I put it to *you,* Dr. Kamins. You know my history: Where did I go wrong? Nowhere is the answer. From start to finish, Neil Morgan is a straight line. Oh, I admit to an occasional error. But what I did was accepted behavior. *Accepted.* The kind of thing everyone was doing. It was *in order.* And I never made the same mistake twice. But this—this drug thing . . ."

"There's more you should know," Dr. Kamins said.

"Yes," Susan said.

"I've heard enough," Neil muttered. "I want this settled quietly and at once. I want to sweep this affair under the carpet, so to speak, and——"

"What is it, Dr. Kamins?" Susan said, sitting erect.

Dr. Kamins produced a grateful little smile. "Professor Hailey is an excellent teacher, let me say at once. He's had an impeccable academic record. He's taught at Chicago, Ohio, Wesleyan, Princeton. Obtaining his services was a great prize for Robert Bradford. . . ."

"He's an addict." Neil snarled.

"We make it a practice not to pry into the personal lives of our faculty, to allow them the dignity of privacy."

"So they can corrupt the students!"

Dr. Kamins compressed his pudgy lips. "Certain information has come to my attention that I feel you should be aware of. Professor Hailey is a homosexual."

Neil's eyes glazed over. His brain revolved in an uncontrollable blur. Through the swirl of changing images, one recollection began to emerge gradually from the moving mass; it took shape, repeated itself, became increasingly clearer.

Another office, all walnut and black leather. Susan was there, pristine and beautiful in a white dress; and himself; and another man. An expert on conception, an authority on the making of human babies. A fucking know-it-all, was Neil's private nickname for the doctor.

"I won't burden you with the Latin," Dr. Fucking Knowitall had said. "It's simply a matter of weak sperm. A layman's term, if you'll excuse a bad joke."

A comedian, Neil had thought bitterly. Making jokes at *his* expense. Well, Dr. Knowitall wasn't so smart at that. Neil Morgan's sperm were as vital and determined as any man's. *Here, baby. Here. Here it comes. Right up into your belly, all that baby-making juice. Millions of little Neil Morgan's anxious to be born. Here, baby. Fuck you, baby.*

"But we had BB," Susan had replied.

"Ah, yes," Dr. Knowitall said smugly. "There's every reason to believe that your son was conceived on the very first night of your marriage. The pitch of excitement, a heightened passion. A very normal occurrence. But it is to be doubted that you will have another child. I would suggest you adopt . . ."

"Neil. Neil, what are we going to do?"

Susan's voice drew Neil back to Dr. Kamins' office. His brain slowed, steadied, came to a full stop. "Are you suggesting, Dr. Kamins, that BB allowed that pervert to touch him? If you are, I'll——"

"Oh, God, Neil!" Susan spoke with unaccustomed fervor. She turned back to the school president. "What's going to happen?"

"To begin, Professor Hailey has taken sick leave. He will not return to Robert Bradford College. That is also true of the other faculty members involved in this matter."

"And BB?" Susan said.

"It would be best," Dr. Kamins suggested kindly, "if he dropped out of school at once. Health reasons are acceptable."

"No," Neil said.

"Whatever you think best," Susan said.

"No!" Neil insisted. He leaned across the desk, face mottled, the lid of his right eye leaping erratically. "I won't let you do this to my son. He must continue here, get his degree."

"I'm sorry, Mr. Morgan. It simply isn't possible."

"Crap, Kamins. Anything is possible. If the price is right. Okay, what's your price? How much to keep this thing quiet, to keep BB in school? You can have a contribution to the school or a little under-the-table payoff to you personally. Name it."

"Mr. Morgan," Dr. Kamins said, the round face flushed. "You don't understand."

"Neil," Susan put in with no particular force, "BB has to be punished finally. We've always made it easy, bought his way out."

"Go to hell!" Neil cried. "He's my *son!* I won't let this phony intellectual ruin his life. Now I'm going to tell you how it will be, Kamins, and you listen and remember."

Dr. Kamins rose deliberately. The pudge around his mouth firmed up, the eyes gleamed, the soft brows came together. "You had better leave now, Mr. Morgan. I will not tolerate your attitude. Boyd will withdraw from school quietly *today,* or he will be expelled. And we know what kind of furor *that* my create. You would be wise to take the first course. Next fall you may be able to enter him in another college. There will be no blemish on his record here. It is not our purpose to do injury to young men. Now you must excuse me. I have appointments. . . ."

Chapter X

Mike and Neil

It was one of those white-hot days that sometimes comes in June, the sky high and cloudless, the sun merciless. The ocean lay flat and lifeless, small waves lapping at the shore as if pleading for succor.

Mike sat up and looked down at Elizabeth. They had been soaking up the sun for a couple of hours and he felt dehydrated, irritable, his skin stretched too tight. A pulse throbbed in his temple.

He said her name and she made a small, sleepy sound. "Let's take a walk."

"You go."

Damn. How long could she lie there without moving, without conversation. Sleep was a form of death, he reminded himself. A waste of living-time. He stood up, anxious to be away from this place, from *her*. He needed to clear his mind, to think, to comprehend what was happening.

"I'm going for a walk."

She made a weak sound of assent.

Some men were playing rugby on the hardpack. Members of an athletic club, who spent weekends at Robin's Rest. This was their bag. Rugby and beer and discussing girls with a crude sexuality. Mike wasn't sure whether they turned him off because of what they were or because so much of what they were still remained in him. He went past them into the ocean. He dived and swam out, stroked a course parallel to the beach. When he came out of the water he was near Ocean Beach.

His mind was functioning more competently now. He thought about Elizabeth and himself. What was happening between them? To him? Since that night at Tom Sawyer's they had been together almost constantly. Day and night. In Manhattan and on Fire Island.

He was frightened.

He loved her. These were more than just an assemblage of words. He meant it, felt it, wanted to look at her, to talk to her and listen to her, to be with her always. There it was. Always. That required a commitment he wasn't at all certain he wanted to make.

Marriage?

Sweet Jesus. He had gone that route! Jean drifted to mind and a weakness came into his middle. They should've made it together. Each of them had brought so much to the other that was agreeable and right. He had loved *her*. And the time in bed had been incredibly exciting, always good and frequently fantastic. Yet their marriage had failed—suffered from a slow disintegration until abruptly it wasn't worth having or trying to save. At least, neither of them had been up to making the attempt. The desire to be rid of her, free, had become almost overwhelming. There was an almost physical relief when the divorce was granted, legal and binding.

Those first months afterward. One long bash. Girl after girl. Bed after bed. Sliding easily from one to another. A lot of laughs, some quick loving without love, without entanglements. Six months of it and suddenly everything had changed. A deep depression, a sense of loss, of failure. Of guilt. Looking back, he believed he could now read and understand those earlier inadequacies and he had no intention of making the same mistakes again. Before committing himself to another woman he would want to be very sure of what he was doing.

Elizabeth Jordan.

Could he ever be sure of her? He knew what she was, what she had been. There were no secrets remaining between them. She'd been to the same places, along the same road, living it up. Taking it where she could. He imagined her doing with other men what they did, saying to a succession of them what she said to him. It made him ill, and he braced himself against the swift nausea. Even now, with him absent only a short time, there was no way to be sure about her. He had no trust.

He cursed himself. Crud, he named himself. An immature, bourgeois, sanctimonious double-standardized Puritanical sonofabitch with hypcritical blood running in thin veins. He forced the image out of his mind. It was time to decide about Elizabeth, about himself. Would he ever remarry? Or would he live his years out alone, drifting, without responsibility?

Responsibility. Emotional. Sexual. Economic. Money had always played an important role in his life. First by its absence and then by a growing talent for making it in larger amounts. Money, Depression, Relief—those were the facts around which his childhood had turned. He remembered his father finding a job with WPA, his mother working in an office for eleven dollars a week. They moved often in those days, skipping out on the last month's rent, taking advantage of the concessions given to attract new tenants.

Money had to do with everything about his life. Once he had wanted to buy a copy of the old *New York Journal,* to read the comics. His mother couldn't give him the necessary three cents. And to see a movie on Saturday morning took the deposit money from five empty milk bottles.

All that was long gone. Money was no longer a problem. As a press agent he'd been paid well. And the earnings from his writing had stabilized at about thirteen thousand dollars a year. He had nearly ten thousand in savings and another eight thousand in mutual funds. He wasn't rich and would never become so, but he lived well enough and was able to support a wife.

What about children? Elizabeth was a young woman and would want to have a child. Was entitled to that.

Children changed everything. A house, probably, furnishings, doctor bills, clothes, their education. Once there were children, Mike Birns would forever be hung up, emotionally and financially. Forced to earn more money. One mystery a year would no longer pay his way, not even when there were subsidiary profits. He had avoided the trap successfully up to now and wondered if he wasn't too old, too set in his groove, to change. A decision was in order. And soon.

"Mike. Mike Birns!"

The sound of his name being called wrenched him back to the present. BB was hurrying toward him, a pleased smile on his handsome young face. Behind him, moving almost reluctantly, Neil Morgan. Greetings were exchanged and comments made about looking good and not aging, and BB went on enthusiastically about Mike's latest book, about how much he enjoyed it, about admiring Mike's ability to come up with such exciting stories.

"Did you hear about Cindy's father?" he ended brightly. "Boy, he really got himself into the wrong bag. Murder one, right, Mike?"

"I guess so."

"Wow. He's lucky they knocked out the death penalty in this state."

Neil grunted. "Roy's a fool. He's going to have to pay the price."

"It's hard to believe," Mike said. "Roy killing anyone."

"As a mystery writer," BB said, "isn't there a murder in every one of us?"

Mike grinned at the boy. "If so, it's pretty well contained in most people. Conditioning, I suppose. But Roy Ashe. He was always happy, enjoying life, taking nothing seriously."

"If he'd been more serious," Neil said grimly, "this would never have happened. He's ruined his life. Destroyed his marriage, his career. The result of a lifetime of not caring. . . ."

"That's a story," BB said. "A real psychological thriller. You should write it."

"Maybe someone will."

"You could do it the way Capote did *In Cold Blood,*" BB continued. "You could interview everybody who knew Roy. Including *me.* How about that! And Cindy, too. She's in Europe now but she'll be back. I bet she could give you some really blue material." He laughed with pleasure.

Mike thought about Cindy's visit to his apartment. He wondered how well BB knew Cindy, *what* he knew about her.

"It's an interesting idea," Neil commented, without emphasis.

Mike nodded agreeably. "Ideas are not the problem. You have to find one that fits you as a writer and vice versa. Execution is finally the crux of the matter."

"How would you handle Roy's situation?" Neil asked. "As a writer, is there enough story material there? I mean, a man needs money and commits murder to get it. Nothing new there."

"I suppose that's true. You could tell it as a straight mystery, from the police point of view."

A short, deprecatory laugh issued from Neil's flat mouth. "That's just another big cliché."

"What about a documentary?" BB broke in.

"Why not?" Mike said. "Make it more of a character study of a man's downfall. A man with a limitless potential, with all the opportunities, a man who somehow doesn't make it."

"I like that," BB said.

"Tell the story chronologically," Mike went on, enjoying the game. "From the moment he decides on murder as the solution to his problems. We follow his activities as he plots and schemes and finally commits the deed. All this interspersed with flashbacks showing the external and internal forces that shaped and drove him to this final act that seems so logical to his disordered mind. . . ."

"Are you saying Roy's insane?" Neil asked thoughtfully.

"No. But murder is an irrational act for such a man. He must be brought to the point where no other course remains."

"Sounds terrific," BB enthused.

"It might work," Neil added.

Mike looked at him curiously. "As a television show, you mean?"

Neil gazed out at the ocean. "Not unless you could bend it to fiit the format of the shows on the air. Perry Mason or one of those."

"A lot depends on the outcome of the trial," Mike offered. "Whether or not he's convicted."

"Could Roy get off?" BB asked.

Mike shrugged. "With a good lawyer, maybe. There have been a few cases in recent years where the defendants were clearly guilty and a conviction still couldn't be obtained. Legal guilt is not always so easy to prove."

Neil's mind floated back to the scene in the visiting

room. He had felt obliged to see Roy, to cheer him up, had spent nearly five minutes with him.

"Is there anything you need?" he had asked.

That made Roy laugh, that same mocking laugh, that too-loud laugh. "You name it, I need it. I need to get out of here. I need a good lawyer who can work a jury and get me off. An Edward Bennett Williams. Maybe Belli. I need the dough to buy that kind of representation and I'm stretched out flat."

"How can you be broke? The papers said——"

"All legal stuff. This bookie Nevin had a family and they claim that his dough paid for my film library. They've put some kind of a hold on it, on everything I've got, which isn't so much. I can't use a dime of my own money. That's why I wanted to see you, Neilie. I need dough bad, to hire a lawyer. You've got it. I want you to lend me——"

Neil didn't buy any of it. He knew Roy too well. In jail or out. Advancing him that knd of money—perhaps twenty-five thousand to start—would mean throwing it away. So he told Roy how he felt. Exactly. Told him in that straight-from-the-shoulder way of his. Direct. Honest . . .

"Ironic," Neil said to Mike, "the way lives unfold. You, me, Roy Ashe. We go back a long time together."

Hardly together, Mike reflected. Though they had walked the same strand of sand, vastly different avenues had brought them here.

As if in recognition of that, Neil went on. "In a way, I envy you, Mike. You seem to enjoy what you're doing."

"Why shouldn't he!" BB burst out. "He's a free man."

"Well, not entirely," Mike said wryly.

"Sometimes I wish I had done something else," Neil said. "Not that I have any complaints," he added quickly. "I made it pretty damned big and that's hard to do. Still, sometimes I wish I'd taken a real stab at writing songs. You know, I had a knack for composing."

"I remember."

"Or I could've been an actor. I always loved to perform. For a while, when BB was very young, I belonged to an amateur group. I could have been a professional and a good one. But no regrets. Not one."

Mike made no answer.

"Well," Neil said briskly, "guess I'll head back now. Got a tennis game scheduled. Mike, drop over to the house whenever you want. You're always welcome, you know. Susan enjoys seeing you. Anytime at all. Don't wait for an invitation. Come by and have a drink. Susan keeps a well-stocked bar. Coming, BB?"

Mike watched them head up the beach. Neil was still the same aggressive, confident man he'd always been, certain of where he was going. Mike wished he were that sure of himself.

Chapter XI

Eddie

Eddie Stander let his eyes drift around the living room of the big house. On the wall facing him was the fireplace, framed in old tile, now faded red and yellowing white. Next to it the poker and tongs, the firescreen; equally ancient. And expensive, he added silently. Against the far wall, a credenza that had cost nearly two thousand dollars; and flanking it, cane-backed chairs. Two of them had cost five hunderd dollars. A small hooked rug with an eagle embroidered in blue covered a patch of floor in front of the fireplace. Otherwise the room was empty and would remain so for a long time, he assured himself. But it was worth the money, he was convinced. Everything was authentic. The real thing. And people visiting them would know it.

He walked through the connecting corridor to the kitchen and out back to where Edith was sunning herself. He lowered himself into the captain's chair alongside her and gazed out at the expanse of land that reached to the stand of trees beyond a small stream. All his. It gave him a good feeling.

"This is another advantage," Edith said.

"What's that?"

"We don't have to worry about a summer place. You can get your tan right here."

"I suppose." He considered for a minute. "I enjoy the sound of the waves. There's something about being near the sea that I like."

"You're too romantic," she said.

He closed his eyes and allowed his head to hang back. The sun drenched his cheeks in warmth and he made an effort to enjoy it, to close off the worries that kept invading his brain. It was a futile effort.

He'd met with Bill Levinson and Albert Hurd on Monday. Hurd was the production man, Levinson the artist. They wanted a decision, and rightly so. He'd stalled long enough. Office space had been located and the clients were waiting for an answer also. Nothing was easy, Eddie reflected unhappily. He straightened up.

"Edith," he began tentatively.

She rolled over on her stomach. "Oil my back, darling."

He spread the amber liquid evenly. "What would you say if I went into business for myself?"

"Why would you do a thing like that? You have a perfectly lovely job. By the way, I've been meaning to talk to you. When the Whites were over the other night. You simply weren't doing your job as a host."

"Oh?"

"You should pay more attention, see if they want anything. Another drink."

"I mixed the first drink for them. After that, let them take care of themselves. I don't see why people have to be waited on."

"Because it's a kindness, Eddie. And they were our guests."

"You enjoy waiting on them."

"Well, I wish you'd try. It's important that we make friends in the neighborhood. You will try, won't you?"

He said he'd try.

"I knew you would. Now my legs, darling."

He oiled her thighs. They were flabby, dimpling in back. A network of blue veins were visible under the skin behind her knees. He averted his eyes.

"Let me tell you about Bill Levinson and Al Hurd," he said. "We have a chance to open our own agency. A couple of good accounts to start—"

"Is that what you meant by your own business?"

"What do you think of the idea?"

"It isn't my place to inject myself into your professional life. It's enough to be a wife and a mother and a housekeeper."

"I see. But this affects you, too. All of us. It wouldn't be the same. No more coming home on the five-twelve. And the money would be less at the start."

"You know me and money, darling. You'll have to figure those things out for yourself. The mortgage, the insurance, how much it costs to run the house. All those other expenses."

"If this worked, Edith, it would be great. You can see that. No more working for some dumb bastard with half my talent and a quarter of my brains. No more fighting to get a piece of copy on the air, worrying about some young snot squeezing me out. You know, I'm not a kid anymore. There are no old copywriters on Madison Avenue. If you don't make it to a management level by the time you're forty—. Understand what this could mean to me. . . ."

"If this is what you want and it's right, you'll do it."

"It would add fifteen years to my life."

"That's a little dramatic, I'd say. In your own words, you'd be working harder for longer periods of time and getting less money in return. Still, if it's what you want—"

"Eventually those things would square off, get better."

"If the agency succeeded."

"Oh, we'd make it—Bill, Al, and me. We've got talent, experience, energy."

"Nobody appreciates your talent more than I do. Still, agencies do fail. You've told me about men who went into business for themselves and never made it. Men as talented as you and your friends."

"If you don't take a chance—"

"I won't argue, Eddie. If you feel such a gamble for a married man with a family is justified, then you must take it."

"You don't think I should?"

"I think you should do whatever you think is right. I wouldn't want you to feel imprisoned by me, by us. Whatever you decide, I'll go along. We can always sell this lovely old house."

"Come on, Edith. Nobody said anything about selling

the house." He milked his fingers. "It's just that I have to give them an answer by Monday."

"And you will. Make up your mind and tell them what you've decided to do. It's that simple."

"Do you want me to say yes or no?"

"I want you to do the best thing for us all, including yourself."

He looked down at her speculatively. He owed her a great deal. A whole life. Without her there would be no family. No house. He would be alone and frightened, the way it used to be.

She stood up. "It's awfully warm, darling." She patted his cheek affectionately. "Why don't you lie down while I get us both something cool to drink. Some of my homemade lemonade, all right?"

It seemed like a good idea and he told her so. He stretched out and closed his eyes, not thinking, waiting for her to come back. He could relax now that it was all settled.

Chapter XII

Neil and BB

Neil surveyed the new Pennslyvania Railroad terminal. Sleek, modern, clean, with the gloss of today.

"Terrific improvement," he said.

"I suppose," BB replied absently.

Neil looked at his watch. "It's getting on to that time."

"I guess I'll get on the train."

"You've got your luggage checks?" Susan asked for the third time.

"Yes, Mother."

"BB," Neil said, "you know what I expect from you, what both of us expect."

"I know, Father."

"Ridgeton Military Camp provides the training and discipline you require. I know you understand that."

"I understand."

"You're no longer a child, BB. You're expected to begin acting like a man, performing up to standard, assuming your manly responsibilities."

A mocking glint came into BB's eyes. "What are those, Father, those manly responsibilities?"

"I can do without sarcasm, BB," Neil said sharply. "That's one of the things I hope Ridgeton will do for you, knock that wiseguy out of you."

"I'm sure they'll try."

"The authorities at Ridgeton, Commandant Abernathy and Captain McCoy, they know about your difficulties at Bradford. They ask only that you abide by their rules. You will, of course, be under the care of a physician who is also aware of your case history."

BB grinned thinly. "Sounds like a nut farm to me."

"Nonsense! Nothing like that. Just a camp for young men like yourself who've had some difficulty adjusting."

"You know, Father," BB said mildly, "I'm not at all sure I want to adjust to the world, to your world. . . ."

"Please, BB," Susan husked. "Please try."

He nodded after a short interval. "I'll try, Mother."

He kissed Susan, offered his hand to Neil.

"I'll walk to the train with you, Son. I want to say one or two more things to you. In private."

They were on the station platform before Neil spoke, his manner uncertain. "BB, about you and that Professor Hailey, the things that Dr. Kamins implied. I mean, they weren't true. Were they?"

BB stared at his father. "I was an acid head, Father. And before that I was on heroin and pot."

"I didn't mean drugs."

"What then?"

"The reason I never raised the question before was that I didn't want to embarrass you."

"Not much embarrasses me anymore."

"About Hailey. He was a—a homosexual. A *pervert*. What I mean is . . . you didn't . . . *go* with him?"

BB raised his brows quizzically. "You want to know if I'm queer?"

"Of course you're not! No son of mine would do anything so disgusting and vile. . . ." Neil's face appeared to sag and age. His mouth worked reflexively and he scowled. "Tell me the truth, Boyd. You didn't do anything like that, did you?" A pleading note crept into his voice.

BB stared directly into his father's eyes. "Your son could never do that kind of thing, Father."

Neil straightened up and squeezed BB's arm. "I knew it all along. Just wanted to hear you say it."

"And now I have."

"Yes," Neil said, the old briskness back in his voice. "Do good, BB. Fly right and in the fall I'll have a little present for you. A new car, maybe. How's that grab you?

A Sting-Ray, maybe. Red. I bet that'll get you the girls. What do you boys call them? Pussywagons? You think about that, son. Keep that Sting-Ray in mind. Meanwhile I'm going to manipulate a little bit, pull a few strings. In September, you'll be registering at a college with a national reputation. I'll see to it. You'll run up a score to make us all proud before you're through. Right?"

"Right, Father."

They shook hands and Neil clapped BB on the back. Then Neil went upstairs to where he had left Susan. "Well," he said, "that's out of the way."

"I hope he'll be all right."

"He should be. This damned camp is costing enough. That's what he needs, a firm hand. All this other crap, the testing, interviews, that damned head-shrinker. I never bought all that Freudian doubletalk, all that sex business." He jerked his head affirmatively. "Ridgeton is going to make a man of BB."

Susan shifted around to face him. Her eyes were streaked and there was a faint starburst of blue veins in her cheek. He turned away.

"Maybe we should have kept him with us, at the island," she offered.

"You wouldn't like that. He'd be in the way of your good times."

"You," she said after a long silent beat, "can go straight to hell."

Neil

Hugo Morse towered over Neil Morgan. He was a lean man, six inches more than six feet tall with wide, bony shoulders, a flat chest and a long, thrusting neck. His rectangular skull was capped with an aureole of untamed black hair and the face beneath was a succession of shadowed hollows. His nose was a jut of gristle, his mouth a meaty red gash, and behind horn-rimmed glasses were swollen black orbs.

"Long time no see," Hugo Morse muttered, slumping

into his swivel chair, heaving his feet onto the desk, picking idly at a hangnail. "Last time was when I had one of my authors on that game show of yours."

"You've got a great memory, Hugo," Neil said, producing a pleasant laugh. "It was Christy Colvin."

"That crazy bastard," Hugo Morse rumbled.

"Remember, he said 'fuck the President' on the air."

"That crazy bastard. But his novels sell. You've got to adimt that. Still, you know you can't trust writers. They're all careless about the language, when they talk, anyway. On paper, each word is transformed into spun gold. Being a publisher has its headaches, Morgan, believe me." He gave up on the hangnail and lifted his head. "I should be in your business."

"I'm putting together a fantastic package, Hugo. For theatrical release."

"A movie! You want to buy one of our books? Which one?"

"I've got an idea that I know you're going to love."

The publisher eyed him suspiciously. "I'll listen."

"Is it possible to make a best seller? I mean, create one from scratch, force it onto the best-seller list."

Hugo Morse attacked the hangnail again. After a brief struggle, it succumbed. He spit it onto the floor. "Sure, but not absolutely."

"What would it take."

The big man shrugged. "A lot of work—and money."

"How much money?"

"There's no limit. I know a publisher who puts out one book every month, pours his entire effort into selling it. He emphasizes sex, violence, a kind of novelized gossip column, aiming at a particular market."

"Does it work?"

"Not always. There are intangibles. None of us is that sure of what the public will buy."

"What if a great deal of money were put behind a book. More than usual. Double, triple, four times the amount generally spent. Advertising money, column items, press stories, radio and television interviews, advance material in national magazines."

"My press department can't guarantee that kind of a campaign."

Neil nodded knowingly. "Perhaps I can. With the publicity department of a major motion picture studio behind me."

"How would you manage that?"

"If there was a book, the right book with all the salable elements, with the smell of truth to it, a sense of the immediate, of an inside story. And if I owned that property. I'm sure it could be sold to a film company. I know the film business. I could make a deal with one of the majors, raise the kind of money required."

"You'd go with the book?"

"As producer or executive producer. I would control the purse strings."

"And?"

"And I would purchase the film rights from the author, from the publisher."

"Suppose the author decided not to sell?"

Neil laughed without mirth. "Not a chance. Before anything was done, I'd have an option on the book, through my own production company. I'd control it from the start."

"Suppose you couldn't interest a major studio?"

"A cinch. I'd have the property, a best seller. I'd have the writer, whose value would increase in direct proportion to the success of the book. And I can get Norman Wallace to star in the picture. Maybe Roberta Davis. They both owe me favors."

"Sounds interesting. Let's get back to the book. Who wrote it?"

Neil grinned. "That's the kicker, Hugo. It isn't written yet. Shall I go on?"

"Please."

"Do you know Roy Ashe?"

"I don't think so."

"A man about my age, I've known him for a long time. Right now he's in jail on a murder charge. He killed his bookie."

"I read about it. He's the subject for your best seller?"

"Yes. I want a book that will trace his life, how he came to commit murder, follow the trial step by step. Here's a guy who had every advantage. Education, family, a beautiful, cultivated wife. Early success. An attractive man in every way, intelligent, popular. Yet he ends up on trial for murder. How come? I say there's an exciting story there."

"You may be right."

"I *am* right." Then, with less intensity. "Can it be done, Hugo?"

The publisher nodded thoughtfully. "First, assume the book is written, and that will be no easy task. You've already indicated some of the methods to be used in making a book a commercial success. We could do every one of them and still fail to put it across." Neil started to speak but Hugo Morse raised one huge hand. "But there is a way."

"Say how."

"A few years ago a novel was published, an incredibly bad book. No one ever accused the author of being able to write. But she had a rich father who happened also to be a skillful public relations guy. He maneuvered her brainchild onto the best-seller lists."

"He bought the newspaper people making up the lists!"

"No, most book editors are legitimate. To a fault, very often. Dealers are another matter. They can be reached directly and indirectly."

"Tell me."

"All publishers make arrangements with bookstores. A dealer takes ten copies of a book, he gets one free. That kind of thing. Under certain conditions, if I chose to push a particular book, I would make a better offer to dealers."

Neil hunched forward. "There's more . . ."

"Yes. And this is where money is so important, the vital ingredient. The kind of money a movie company could afford to put up. This bad novel I spoke about, the author's uncle hired people to go into key bookstores round the country, those shops that are usually checked by the top newspapers in compiling sales statistics for the best-seller lists. His people bought copies, some forty thousand dollars' worth. The result was that despite horrible reviews the title leaped onto every list and people were influenced, bought the book."

"Did it pay financially?"

"A week after publication, the uncle consummated a movie sale for better than half a million. There's your answer."

"Beautiful," Neil breathed. "We could do that. The

film distributors have field men around the country, exchanges. We could buy up every book put out, the entire first printing."

Hugo Morse considered. "I am intrigued by the proposition, Morgan. It has potential. To the right writer, I'm ready to offer a substantial advance and guarantee publication. What will you guarantee?"

"I will take an option on the *unwritten* work for all movie rights, all dramatic rights. I'll put up an amount of money to be decided upon. . . ."

"I want thirty per cent of all movie income, plus other subsidiary rights."

"Simple enough. After all, we're inviting a writer into a set deal, a *fait accompli.* He knows what he's getting. All he has to do is bang out the words."

The bony face tightened. "Let's talk about the writer. My first thought was Capote or Norman Mailer. But a big name won't do, won't split this the way it should be split. We need somebody hungry. But a pro. A real pro. Somebody good."

"I've got the man. Do you know Mike Birns?"

"The mystery writer. By reputation only. Can you deliver him?"

"He's in my pocket," Neil exulted.

The meaty mouth pursed reflectively. "Birns is good. He just made a television sale and——"

"He's got peanuts. Nothing to give him a big head."

"He won an award some years ago. The Mystery Writers of America, their Edgar, the highest prize . . ."

Neil concealed his surprise. He hadn't known that, had never heard Mike mention it. The sneaky bastard. Neil supposed it was something he used on broads, a lever to impress them, get into their pants.

"The Edgar," he said to Hugo Morse. "That's one reason why I chose Birns. A good craftsman, respected, honored. Something to sell to the studios later on."

"Birns is completely acceptable to me. One more thing. This can't be done without the full cooperation of Roy Ashe. What if he won't go along?"

Neil grinned. The question was expected. "Ashe and I had a talk recently. He's flat on his butt. No dough. He's running scared, believe me. If he's convicted, he faces a life term. But I don't want him to be convicted. I want a happy ending to our story and I intend to provide it. I'm going to hire the best available attorney to represent him. And in return, Roy talks to no one but Mike Birns. No press interviews. No radio or TV. Nothing. We'll wrap him up like a mummy. Anybody wants to know anything about the case is going to have to read the book. And see the picture," he ended laughing.

Hugo walked to the door with him, arm looped across his shoulders. "We are going to make a lot of money, Neil."

"I'm sure of it."

"But you'll end up making more than anyone else."

Neil grinned up at the tall man, his eyes glittering. "Yes, Hugo. More than anyone."

Chapter XIII

Mike

Mike spent three hours with Neil Morgan on Thursday afternoon and when they parted a rising exultation filled his chest. Here it was at last, the big prize, and all he had to do was what he did best. Did naturally. He walked all the way back to his apartment, reviewing everything that had passed between them, exploring and assessing, planning, pausing occasionally to make a note. Considering the rewards. This was no plaintive hope for success. No lonely foray into an artistic wilderness. No tenuous effort that offered only a minimal return on his investment of talent, time, and energy. Here was a guarantee of fame and riches, of status, of the kind of freedom he had always longed for.

Reservations? Some. But minor in nature. Nothing that would stand between himself and all that Neil Morgan offered. A full, rich laugh broke out of him.

At home, he went directly to his typewriter, began to list possible sources of information, all the people he knew who had known Roy Ashe. They would lead to still others. He would check the newspaper morgues, the police files, Harry Nevin's history. Again that triumphant laughter. This was going to be enjoyable in so many ways. He would do a fine job, eventually penetrate the facade behind which Roy Ashe existed, lift that laughing mask, locate the core of discontent that had brought Roy to where he had to kill. Mike made another note: interview psychiatrists, those experts in human behavior. He would build a mosaic that would finally cast light on the shadowed areas of Roy Ashe.

At eight o'clock he presented himself at Elizabeth's apartment for their dinner date, anxious to tell her about his good fortune. When she opened the door, he planted a long, noisy kiss on her mouth. She flung her arms around his neck.

"More," she said, eyes closed, mouth upraised. "More, more, more."

"Enough."

Her eyes rolled open. "I deserve more. I am the best thing that ever happened to you. Be grateful."

He laughed. "I'm too good for you. A very rich, very successful author like me."

"Oh, Mike," she said, suddenly serious and uncertain, "something nice has happened."

"Very nice. I'll tell you all about it over dinner."

He took her to an intimate bistro with marble tables and an elaborate menu. They drank chablis out of heavy goblets and ate oysters baked in pernod and fennel, a well-crisped duck, and black cherries. And he told her about his meeting with Neil Morgan. She listened intently, the sea-green eyes solemn, twice forgetting her food.

He told her what he hoped to do with the book, the depths to which he intended to probe, indicating his desire to slide back and forth in time illuminating contemporary portions with the past. Over dessert and coffee he spoke of the demands Neil had made, the controls both economic and artistic that he wished to exercise.

"If you must include certain elements to satisfy Neil—" she began.

He interrupted, smiling confidently. "How will I be able to write an honest book, you're going to ask."

She wet her lips and nodded.

"Maybe it won't be *the* book I'd prefer to write," he admitted grudgingly, "but it will be true."

He waited for some response. "Do you really want to do this book?" she said at last.

A wave of irritation broke over him. "That's an absurd question, Elizabeth. I'm going to do it." He took her hands. "Try to understand what this means. Between Neil and Hugo Morse, the advance money will be twenty-five thousand dollars. My share. I've never gotten that kind of money before."

"Do you need it?"

He released her hands. "Maybe I don't *need* it. But I want it. Can't you see this is my chance to hit it big. I will be guaranteed a fee on the final movie purchase in keeping with the production budget and the ultimate sale of hardcover copies. It might run as high as half a million. Maybe more. I also get to write the first and second drafts of the screenplay. Most important, it will establish me as a known quantity, a writer of some renown. For the rest of my life, I'll be home free."

"And that matters?"

"Hell, yes!" He lowered his voice. "I have been scratching dirt for a long time."

"You told me you do well financially."

He made a disparaging sound back in his throat. "One year I made sixteen thousand. But to make it I had to stay on top of that damned typewriter every day. I didn't tell you about all the junk I've had to write, the potboilers under pseudonyms. But here, this time, the payoff makes it worthwhile. Besides, I will do a good book."

She said she was sure he would do a good book, but her doubts, the distress she felt, were clear.

"What is it?" he asked. They had left the restaurant, were strolling along First Avenue, passing beneath the Fifty-ninth Street Bridge. "Here's an opportunity I've been after all my life, and you act as if it's a disaster."

"You spoke about a novel. Something you cared about, were close to."

A harsh sound died on his lips. "Let me tell you about that I gave it a lot of thought, even did some preliminary work. That was going to be the story of Neil Morgan and his wife, of Roy Ashe and Maggie. Of the kind of people I've known through the years. Myself included. People who began so young and beautiful and full of aspirations and never quite made it in any of the ways that people can make it. As husbands and wives, in their work, as fathers and mothers and lovers. Is this so different? I'll be telling the same story from another point of view."

"All right, Mike," she said softly.

He swore to himself. He wanted her to understand. To approve. But why should he care what she thought? It was his work they were discussing, his *life*. From what lofty moral plateau did she presume to pass judgment on him? What did she know of those dark cravings that constantly gnawed at him? What did she know of his fears? His needs?

"I'm tired," she said. "I think it might be better if I went back to my own apartment tonight."

He stared at her. "Sure," he said after a moment. "I'll get a cab."

In front of her door, she faced him with a wistful smile on her mouth. "Give me a little time, Mike, to get used to the idea."

"What are you talking about? This is no criminal act. I am going to make a lot of money, what every writer in his right mind longs for. This is my fuck-you money. My independence. I don't have to take anything anymore. Not from anybody."

"Is that so important?" She half turned. "A man like you, you're better than you know, Mike."

"You think I'm selling out," he accused.

"Not selling out. Quitting on yourself. Quitting before you've had a chance to fail."

"You don't understand."

"A man should do what he has to do, what he truly wants to do."

"And if it turns out worthless? A failure?"

"That's beside the point. It's time Mike Birns did something that was deeply and purely himself, for his own sake. Call it a catharsis, if you like. I'm sure it would be good for you, for both of us. I see so much in you, Mike."

"Maybe too much."

"Not nearly too much."

"But not enough to come back to my apartment with me. Not enough to make love to me tonight."

"It would be a fake, the way I feel."

"You've faked it a thousand other times," he snapped. "Why not with me?"

Her face hardened into place and the eyes grew veiled. "I wish you didn't have to ask. What happened is past, Mike. I thought you knew that about me. I lived a certain way and when I decided it wasn't for me, I changed. I discarded the worst of it and kept the best and tried to give it to you. What I feel for you is real, Mike. With you, there is no faking it."

"And if I write this book, you'll stop loving me."

"I don't think so. But I have to get used to the idea."

"What do you expect me to do?"

"Just to be the best Mike Birns you can."

The prospect terrified him.

Chapter XIV

Mike

Mike began drinking at noon on Saturday and by six o'clock he viewed the world through a shimmering pink haze. He found himself in Eleanor's, a dating bar on the Upper East Side. He bought a drink for a cool-mannered woman who talked in a measured style. He bought her three more drinks and wondered what she looked like naked. Soon he suggested they go to his apartment and she said hers was only a few blocks away. They walked.

Inside, she excused herself and disappeared into the bedroom, returning a few minutes later with a sleepy-eyed boy of six.

"This is Gordon," she said. "My son."

"Hello, Gordon."

Gordon hid his face.

"He's sleepy," Mike said.

"I wanted him to meet you. Say hello, Gordon."

"Put him back to bed."

"Oh, Gordon wants to stay up for a while, don't you, Gordon?" She giggled drunkenly.

"Put him to bed," Mike said.

"Oh. Yes. Say good night to the man, Gordon." She went back in the bedroom. When she returned she sat close to Mike on the couch, her hard breasts flattening against him, her lips reaching for his mouth.

He kissed her. Her tongue was hot and she began to squirm against him, desperate little noises sounding back in her throat. She put her hand between his legs, fingers stroking expertly.

He thought he heard something. "What if Gordon wakes up?"

"Don't worry." She worked the zipper down, reached inside his trousers. "Oh, sweet. I am going to be good for you. So good. Ah, how nice you are. Are you nervous, sweet? I'll work you all the way up."

He couldn't do it. He pushed her head aside and stood up, adjusted his clothes.

"What are you doing?" she whimpered. "Come back. We're just getting started."

"I'm sorry," he said, going to the door. "This was a mistake. It's not the way I am. Not anymore."

He took a cab to Pennsylvania Station and drank coffee until the next train to Bayshore. He arrived to discover the last ferry had long departed. A search turned up a teenager with a motor launch willing to take him across to Robin's Rest for fifteen dollars.

The small boat ran aground twenty yards from shore and Mike had to wade the rest of the way in. Head spinning, suddenly weary, shoes and socks in hand, pants rolled to the knee, he headed for Elizabeth's house. The sound of music and the babble of voices announced a party in progress. He braced himself and went inside. Elizabeth wasn't there. Someone suggested he look on the beach.

She was seated at the foot of the dunes with a man—one of the rugby players. He was square-jawed, lean and very muscular, with a dramatic resemblance to Rock Hudson. Mike wanted to drive his fist into that beautiful face.

"Mike," Elizabeth said, rising. "Where did you come from?"

"Boy," he muttered, wishing his brain would stop tilting. "You didn't waste much time making another connection."

"What's he mean?" the rugby player asked.

"He doesn't mean anything," she said.

"Stay out of this, jockstrap," Mike snarled.

The rugby player rose. "I think you're drunk, fella."

"Bet your sweet ass I'm drunk."

"No need to be vulgar in front of the lady."

"A boy scout," Mike snickered.

"How did you get here, Mike?" Elizabeth asked evenly.

"Screw the small talk. I come to visit the girl I love and find her laying on the sand with this dumb-ass cocksman. Gotten in yet? It shouldn't take long . . . she's easy."

"Knock it off, fella," the rugby player said, making it sound like Paul Newman. "We were talking."

"That's good. Talking. She can be talked into the sack. Believe me, I know."

Elizabeth stood up. "You two can discuss me. I'm leaving."

Mike reached out to stop her. The rugby player shoved his arm away. Mike swung a looping right fist. It landed against the other man's chest. He made a small expression of annoyance and hooked a short punch to Mike's middle. The breath whooshed out of him and he bent double, gasping.

"Oh, Mike . . ." Elizabeth said.

"I'm sorry, Liz," the rugby player lamented. "The jerk shouldn't've hit me."

"Go away, please. Leave me with him."

"Are you sure?"

"I'm sure."

After the other man had left, Elizabeth eased Mike back on the sand, began massaging his stomach in gentle, rotating strokes. "He's right, you know," she murmured. "You are a jerk."

An agonized moan trickled out of him; soon he began to breathe normally. He struggled to stand, ended up on his knees, great gasping heaves racking his body. He bent low, head almost resting on the sand. She held his brow until the spasms stopped.

"Can you get up?" she asked. The effort left him weak and trembling. "Oh, what a mess you are! You've been drinking," she accused quietly, leading him across the beach.

"Where are you taking me?"

"To the ocean."

"You're going to drown me," he lamented.

"What a marvelous idea." When they reached the water she wet his handkerchief, bathed his face. It felt good and he told her so. She repeated the process.

"Am I going to survive?" he said.

"Unfortunately, yes."

"You hate me."

She looked out to sea. The ocean was calm, streaked with silver. A fishing boat cruised the horizon. "I don't hate you."

"I've been miserable."

She sighed. "Me, too." She put her arms around his waist, her cheek against his chest. "Whatever you want . . . well, that's Mike Birns, and I love Mike Birns."

"I won't do the book for Neil."

"Why not?"

The familiar anger gathered in a knot in his chest. "Dammit," he broke off, "you gave me a hundred different reasons."

"Now you give me one."

The anger drained away. "Because it's not what I want. The man I am now doesn't want to do it. I'll try to write my own book, Elizabeth, my own way. I don't know how good or bad it's going to be, but it will be mine."

"Yes . . ."

"I've been thinking, all the way out here. Something happened tonight, something that made everything coalesce for me. I'd divided the world into heroes and villains. I no longer see it like that. No villains, only sad people." He drew her closer. "What's between us, that's precious to me. We fit together."

"Oh, yes. We fit very well."

"I'm going to have to tell Neil what I decided, so he can find another writer." He laughed with the pleasure of discovery. "This is what I want to write about, two people finding each other, how I came finally to this place with you. How I came to be able to say no to Neil Morgan . . ."

Chapter XV

Susan and Neil

The deal was closed the following Thursday before lunch. Contracts had to be drawn and signed, of course, contracts that would satisfy the lawyers. But that was merely a matter of legal detail. A rare awareness swelled and swung under Neil Morgan's skin, a sense of power and triumph, of ownership. This would put him over the top, into the big leagues. *He had done it.*

There had been a moment, the previous week, when Mike Birns had turned him down, that fear had taken over. He had spent an unhappy few hours until he realized how he could turn the setback into an advantage.

That's when he put in the first call to Irwin S. Davidson on the Coast. It had taken two more calls and an exchange of letters, a meeting with Davidson's New York representative. They discussed casting, the director, the budget. Davidson stressed the need for off-beat sex in the book, a hint of incest, perhaps, some sadism. He pointed out that a lot more could be done in films these days. Neil clinched the deal by conceding to Davidson the right to choose the writer of the book.

Davidson flew into New York Thursday morning for a meeting with Neil and Hugo Morse in the publisher's office. He brought his writer along.

With everything settled, Neil decided to head out to the

island a day early, to share his great moment with Susan. This was no cheap afternoon game show, no hustle for a one-shot, no thirteen week appetizer. Here was a project that would make the world his personal yo-yo, the string firmly attached to his middle finger. A gleeful laugh echoed in the cavities of his skull as he stepped off the ferry. He would really give the world the finger now. There would be parties all weekend and he would attend every one, bask in the acclaim that was bound to come his way.

The house was still when he arrived. Susan was probably still on the beach still, he supposed. With Maggie. He would join them, get in a little sun time. He loosened his tie and undid his collar and headed for the bedroom.

The curtains were drawn and in the faint light he barely noticed the figures on the bed until one of them sat up.

"Susan?" he said.

"Oh, shit," came a masculine voice.

Neil switched on the overhead light. In its harsh glare, he could see that they were both naked. Susan and a thick-necked muscular man with a hard, bulging body. Neil felt a choking grip his throat and his eyes began to water. A rising wail of despair formed in his mouth.

"I'm going to kill him," he gritted, making himself advance toward the bed.

The young man came to his feet, fists clenched.

"Don't hurt him, Timmy," Susan said. "He's my husband."

"Then keep him off me."

Neil paused. "I'm going to kill him," he repeated.

"Be still, Neil," Susan said, reaching for a robe. "Timmy is a policeman and I imagine if anyone gets killed it'll be you. Timmy, get dressed and get out of here."

Neither of them spoke again until they heard the front door slam shut behind Timmy. Neil lowered himself into a chair. He looked up at Susan with wet eyes.

"Don't you care anything about me?"

"We have an agreement," she said, not unkindly. "You are not to come out during the week without calling first."

A shudder wracked his body and she held his head against her belly swell. "Something happened," he muttered. "Something wonderful for me. Something I've always wanted."

"The movie deal?"

"I thought it was going to fall through when Mike turned me down. But I let Davidson choose his own writer. He picked some TV guy named Judd Martin, brought him to New York this morning. He starts work right away."

She began to laugh, a full-throated sound, and he was confused. Gradually he understood that she was genuinely glad for him, appreciated what he had managed, shared his victory. After a while she stopped laughing and reached for a cigarette. He lit it for her. "Tell me all about it," she said.

And he did, with a rising awareness that this was the greatest moment of his life. The very greatest.